Mayne Reid

The White Gauntlet

A Novel

Mayne Reid

The White Gauntlet
A Novel

ISBN/EAN: 9783337032807

Printed in Europe, USA, Canada, Australia, Japan

Cover: Foto ©Andreas Hilbeck / pixelio.de

More available books at **www.hansebooks.com**

𝔄 Novel.

By CAPTAIN MAYNE REID,

AUTHOR OF "THE SCALP HUNTERS,"—"THE RIFLE RANGERS,"—"THE
TIGER HUNTER,"—"THE WAR TRAIL,"—"THE WHITE CHIEF,"
—"THE HUNTER'S FEAST,"—"THE WILD HUNTRESS,"—"THE
WOOD RANGERS,"—"WILD LIFE,"—"THE MAROON,"—
"OSCEOLA THE SEMINOLE,"—"THE WHITE GAUNT-
LET,"—"THE HEADLESS HORSEMAN,"—
ETC., ETC., ETC.

NEW YORK:
COPYRIGHT, 1892, BY
G. W. Dillingham, Publisher,
SUCCESSOR TO G. W. CARLETON & Co
MDCCCXCII.

CONTENTS.

CONTENTS.

CHAPTER I

A woman in a wood—encountered accidentally, and alone! 'Tis
an encounter to challenge curiosity—even though she be but a gipsy,
or a peasant girl gathering sticks.

If a high-born dame, beautiful—and, above all, bright-haired—curiosity is no longer the word; but admiration, involuntary, unrestrain-
ed—bordering upon adoration. It is but the instinct of man's heart
to worship the fairest object upon which man's eye may rest; and
this is a beautiful woman, with bright hair, met in the middle of a
wood.

Marion Wade possessed all the conditions to merit such exalted
admiration. She was high-born, beautiful, and bright-haired. She
was alone in a wood.

It did not detract from the interest of the situation, that she was
mounted on a white horse, carried a hawk on her hand, and was followed by a hound.

She was unaccompanied by human creature—hawk, hound, and
horse being her only companions.

It must have been her choice to be thus unattended. Wishing it,
the daughter of Sir Marmaduke Wade might have had for escort a
score of retainers.

Autumn was in the sky; and along with it a noonday sun. The

golden light straggling through the leaves, was reflected upon a field
of blue; brilliant as the canopy whence it came. It was not the
blue of the hyacinth, gleaming in the forest glade; nor of the modest violet that empurples the path. In October it could not be either.
More attractive was that cerulean tint, seen in the iris of a woman's
eye—the eye of Marion Wade.

The sunbeams danced upon her yellow hair, with apparent delight,
kissing its tresses of kindred color—kissing her radiant cheek, that,
even under the shadow of the trees, looked luminous.

What does she in the wild wood unguarded—unattended? Is she
a-hawking?

The "kestrel" perched upon her gloved hand should say, yes.
But more than once, game has sprung up temptingly before her; and,
still the hood has been suffered to stay upon the hawk; and its jes-
ses are retained in leash.

Has she lost her way—is she wandering?

Equally unlikely. She is upon a path; a noble park is in sight,
with a road that runs parallel to its palings. Through the trees she
can obtain glimpses of a stately mansion standing within its enclosure. It is the famed park of Bulstrode—ancient as Alfred the
Great. As she is the mistress of its mansion, she cannot have lost
her way. She cannot be wandering.

And yet, why does she fret her palfrey in its paces—now checking, now urging it onward? If not wandering in her way, surely
she is astray in her thoughts?

She does not appear to be satisfied with the silent solitude of that
forest path; she stops at short intervals, and leans forward in her
saddle, as if listening for sounds.

Her behavior would lead to the belief that she is expecting some
one.

A hoofstroke is heard. There is a horseman coming through the
wood. He is not yet in sight; but the sound of his horse's hoot
striking the solid turf tells that he is riding upon the track, and towards her.

There is an opening in the forest glade, of some six roods in extent. It is cut in twain by a path, which parts from the high road
near one of the gates of Bulstrode Park; thence trending over the
hills in a northwesterly direction.

On this path rides Marion Wade, straying, or dallying, certainly
not traveling.

She has entered the aforementioned opening. Near its centre stands a tree—a beech of magnificent dimensions—whose wide spreading boughs seem determined to canopy the whole area of the opening. The road runs beneath its branches.

Under its shadow the fair equestrian checks her palfry to a stand, as if to shelter hawk, hound, and horse from the fervent rays of the noon-day sun.

But no; her object is different. She has halted there to wait the approach of the horseman; and at this moment, neither hawk, hound, nor horse claims the slightest share of her thoughts.

The horseman soon appears, cantering around a corner—a rustic in rude garb, astride of a common roadster !

Surely he is not the expected one of Marion Wade?

The question is answered by the scornful exclamation that escapes from her pouted lips.

" 'Sh ! I might have known by the clattering it wasn't the foot-fall of that noble steed. A peasant ! "

The despised rustic rides on, as he passes making awkward obeisance, by a spasmodic pluck at his forelock.

His salutation is scarcely returned; or only with a nod, apparently supercilious. He wonders at this; for he knows that the lady is the daughter of Sir Marmaduke Wade—Mistress Marion—usually so condescending to, and a favorite with all of his class. He cannot guess the chagrin he has given her.

He is soon out of her sight; and equally out of her thoughts; for it is not the sound of his departing hoofstrokes her ear is now requickened to catch; but others of bolder bound, and clearer resonance, awakening the echoes of the wood.

These are soon heard more distinctly; and presently a second horseman appears, advancing around an angle of the road.

A striking contrast does the new-comer present, to the rustic who has just ridden past. A cavalier of elegant carriage, spurred and plumed; mounted on a superb steed, of jet-black color, his counter clouted with flakes of snow-white froth, loosened from his chamfering lips.

A glance at the horse is sufficient to show that he is the "noble steed " mentioned in that muttered soliloquy; and half a glance at the rider proclaims him the individual for whom Marion Wade has been waiting.

As yet she has not given him half a glance. She has not ever turned her eyes in the direction whence he is approaching.

She sits silent in her saddle, and to all appearance calmly indifferent. But this air of *insouciance* is only assumed. The quivering of the kestrel, roosted upon her wrist, tells that she is trembling; while the high heaving of her bosom indicates the presence of some strong emotion.

Going at a gentle gallop, the horseman glides out into the opening. Perceiving the lady, he checks his steed to a slower pace, as if to pass more respectfully.

Marion continues to affect an air of non-observance, studied and severe; though the cavalier coming forward is at that moment the sole subject of her thoughts.

Her reflections will disclose the character of these thoughts, and enable us to obtain an insight into the relations existing between these two splendid equestrians; whom chance or design has brought together on the lonely forest road.

"If he should speak to me," soliloquizes the lady, "what shall I say to him? What can I? He must know that it is not accident that has brought me hither, and now so often. If I thought he knew the truth, I should die of shame!

"I wish him to speak, and yet I fear it. Ah! there need be no fear. He will not. How many times has he passed me without a word! And yet his glances, do they not tell me that he would—oh! —this etiquette of our high life, that without shame strangers may not be civil to one another!

"Would I were a peasant—and he the same—only handsome as he is now! 'Tis cruel to be thus constrained by silly social custom. My sex, too, against me. I dare not speak first. Even in his eyes it would undo me!

"He is going to pass me as before! Is there no way by which this painful reticence may be removed?"

The fair equestrian appeared to ponder on some plan—only half-formed and half-resolved as her muttered reflections indicated.

"Dare I do it? What would my proud father say if he were to know? Even gentle cousin Lora would chide me! A stranger whose name I only know, and that's all. Perhaps not a *gentleman!* Oh—yes—yes—yes! He cannot be other. He may not be a lord of the land—but he is *lord of my poor heart!* I cannot restrain myself from soliciting him—even if it bring shame and repentance. I shall do it—I shall do it!"

The speech betrayed a firm determination. To do what?

The act itself following close upon these words answered the question. With a quick jerk the lady dislodged the kestrel from its perch, tossing the bird to the neck of her palfrey—where it clung, clutching the snow-white mane. Then drawing off her glove, a *white gauntlet*, she dropped it negligently by her side—permitting it to slide down the skirt of her riding-dress. It fell into the middle of the road.

A short moment intervened. The lady, apparently unconscious of the loss she has sustained, tightened the rein upon her palfrey; and with a slight touch of the whip, moved out from under the branches of the beech—her horse's head turned in a direction opposite to that in which the cavalier was approaching.

At first she rode slowly apparently desirous of being overtaken. Presently she increased the pace; then faster and faster; until she went at a gallop—as though by a sudden change of thought she had determined to avoid an interview. The thick tresses of her golden hair escaping from the comb swept down upon the croup behind her. The natural red of her cheeks had become heightened to the hue of carmine. It was the suffusion of burning blushes. Her eyes were flashing with a strange excitement in an expression that spoke of something like shame. She had repented of what she had done; and dreaded to wait the consequence of the act!

For all that she was dying to look back, but dared not.

A turn in the road, at length, offered her the opportunity. As she reined her palfrey around the corner, she glanced towards the spot, where she had abandoned her glove.

The tableau that saluted her eye was not displeasing. The cavalier, bending down from his saddle, was just lifting the gauntlet upon the point of his glistening rapier.

What would he do with it?

She waited not to see. Her palfrey passed behind the trees; and the horseman was hidden from her sight.

On that splendid steed he might easily have overtaken her; but, although listening as she rode on, she heard no hoofstroke behind her.

She did not desire to be overtaken. For that day she had submitted herself to sufficient humiliation—self-administered—it is true; but she slackened not the pace, till she had passed through the gates of the park, and sighted the walls of the paternal mansion.

CHAPTER II.

BET DANCEY.

If tumultuous were the emotions of Marion Wade, as she let fall that significant token; not less so were those of *Henry Holtspur*, as he took it up.

Had the lady remained a moment longer looking back, she would have seen her glove taken gently from the point of the cavalier's sword, pressed with a wild fervor to his lips, and proudly placed alongside the plume in the frontlet of his beaver.

She only saw that her challenge had been accepted; and, with a thrill of sweet satisfaction, contending against a sense of shame, she had ridden rapidly away.

The cavalier, equally gratified, appeared also perplexed: as if hesitating whether he should follow. But the abrupt departure of the lady seemed to say that pursuit was prohibited; and checking his ardor, along with his steed, he remained by the tree, under the shadow of which he had halted.

For some minutes he sat in his saddle, apparently absorbed in reflections. That they were not all of one character, was evinced by the expression upon his countenance; which kept continually changing. Now it betokened triumph, with its concomitant pleasure; anon could be traced the lines that indicated doubt, accompanied by pain; and, once or twice, an expression that told of regret, or *remorse*, was visible. These facial changes will be better understood by giving in detail the thoughts that were causing them.

"Was it intended for a challenge? Can I doubt it? Had the incident been alone, I might have deemed it accidental. But the many times we have met—and upon this lone road! Why should she come this way, unless——? And her looks? On each occasion bolder and *lovelier!* Oh, how sweet to be thus favored? How different from that other love, that has had such unhappy ending! Then I was prized but for my position, my prospects, and my fortune. When these fell from me, only to be forsaken!

"If she loves me, her love cannot rest on circumstances like these. She knows me not—not even my name! That she may have heard, can suggest neither rank nor fortune. *If she love me, it must be for myself!* 'Tis a thrilling thought—thus to believe!"

The eye of the cavalier lighted up with an express.on of triumph; and he sat proudly erect in his saddle.

Only for a short time did he preserve this high attitude. Reflections of a far different character succeeded, dissipating the happiness he had for the moment experienced.

" She will know in time! She *must* know! Even I, myself, must tell her the terrible secret. And then what is to become of this sweet but transient dream? It will be all over; and, instead of her love, I shall become the object of her hatred—her scorn! Oh God! To think it must end thus! To think that I have won, and yet can never wear!"

The features of the speaker became overspread with a deep gloom. " Why did I enter upon this intrigue? Why have I permitted it to proceed? Why do I desire its continuance? To all these questions the answer is the same. Who could have resisted? Who could resist? It is not in man's nature to behold such beauty, without yearning to possess it. As Heaven is my witness, I have struggled to subdue this unholy passion—to destroy it—to pluck it forth from my bosom. I have tried to shun the presence of her who inspires it. Perhaps I might have succeeded; had not she——. Alas! I have no longer the power to retreat. That is gone; and the will as well. I must on—on—like the insect lured by some fatal light, to self-sought and certain destruction!"

It was then that remorse became plainly depicted upon the countenance of the cavalier. What could be causing it? That was a secret he scarcely dared declare to himself.

" After all," he continued, a new train of thought seeming to suggest itself; "what if it be an accident—this, that has made me at once so happy, and yet so wretched? Her looks too—those glances that have gladdened my heart, at the same time awaking within me a consciousness of wrong-doing, as, too ardently, I gave them back— may I not have misinterpreted them? If she intended that I should take up this glove—that I should restore it to her—why did she not stay to receive it? Perhaps I have been misconceiving her motives. After all, am I the victim of an illusion—following but an *ignis fatuus* kindled by my own vanity? "

At the moment the look of remorse gave place to one of chagrin. The cavalier apppeared no longer to regret being too much loved; but rather that he might not be loved at all— a reflection far more painful.

"Surely I cannot be mistaken. I saw it on her hand but an instant before—with the hawk perched upon it. I saw her suddenly fling the bird to the neck of the horse, and draw off the gauntlet, which the next moment fell from her fingers. Surely it was design."

He raised his hand to his hat, took the glove from its place, and once more pressed it to his lips.

"Oh, that her hand were in it!" he enthusiastically exclaimed, yielding to a sweet fancy. "If it were her fingers I held thus to my lips—thus unresisting—then might I believe there was bliss upon earth!"

A footstep, falling upon his ear, interrupted the enraptured speech. It was light, betokening the proximity of a woman, or rather the presence of one; for, on turning, his eye rested upon a female figure, standing by the side of his horse.

The cavalier saw before him a comely face—and something more, He might have deemed it beautiful; but for that other, still present to his intellectual eye, and altogether engrossing his thoughts.

It was a young girl who had thus silently intruded; and one worthy of a gracious reception, despite the peasant garb in which she had presented herself.

Both face and figure were such as could not be regarded with indifference, nor dismissed without reflection. Neither owed aught to the adornment of art; but to both had nature been liberal; even to profuseness.

A girl, closely approximating to womanhood; largely framed, and finely developed—in arms, limbs, bust, and body, exhibiting those oval outlines that indicate the possession of strong passions and powers.

Such was the creature who stood by the horse of Henry Holtspur.

But for their blackness, her eyes might have been likened to those of an eagle; but for its softness, her hair resembled the tail of his own steed—equally long and luxuriant; and her teeth—there could have been nothing whiter, even among the chalk of the Chilterns—her native hills.

Robed in silk, satin, or velvet; it was a form that would have done no discredit to a queen. Encircled with pearls, or precious diamonds; it was a face of which a princess might be proud. Even in the ordinary homespun of a rustic gown, that form looked queenly—beneath those glossy plaits of crow-black hair—bedecked with some freshly plucked flowers—that face might have inspired envy in a princess.

In the glance bestowed upon her by the cavalier there was no sign —either of surprise, or admiration. It was simply a look of recognition; accompanied by a nod, acknowledging her presence.

In the eye of the maiden, there was no such indifference. The most careless observer could have told, that she was in love with the man upon whom she was now gazing.

The horseman took no heed of her admiring glances. Perhaps he noticed them not. His attention was altogether given to an object, which the girl held in her outstretched hand; and which was instantly transferred to his. It was a letter, sealed, and directed to himself.

"Thanks!" said he, breaking open the seal. "Your father has brought this from Uxbridge, I suppose?"

"He has, sir. He sent me with it; and bid me ask you if there be an answer to go back. As you were not at the house, I brought it here. I hope I have done right, sir!"

"Oh, certainly! But how did you know where to find me? My tongueless attendant, Oriole, could not have told you?"

"He made sign, sir, that you had taken this road. I thought I should meet you here; and father said it might be important for you to have the letter at once."

The red blood mantled higher upon the girl's cheeks, as she offered this explanation. She knew she had exceeded her father's instructions; which had been, simply, to leave the letter at "Stone Deans," the residence of Henry Holtspur.

The cavalier, occupied with the epistle, noticed neither her blushes nor embarrassment.

"'Tis very considerate of you;" said he, turning gratefully towards the girl, as he finished reading the letter. "Your father has guessed correctly. It is of the greatest importance that I should have had this letter in good time. You may tell him that it needs no reply. I must answer it in person, and at once But say, Mistress Betsey; what return can I make to you for this kind service? You want a ribbon for your beautiful black hair? What color is it to be? I think blue—such as those flowers are—does not so well become you. Shall it be a red one?"

The words, though courteously intended, fell with an unpleasant effect upon the ear of her to whom they were addressed. They were not the speeches to which she would fain have listened.

"Thanks, sir;" said she, in a tone that betrayed pique, or some other unlooked-for emotion. "A fine ribbon would scarce suit my coarse common hair. These flowers are good enough for it!"

" Ah Mistress Betsey! Your beautiful tresses can bear this disparagement; you know they are neither coarse nor common Nay, if you refuse the ribbon, you must accept the price of one. I cannot allow that the essential service you have done me should go unrewarded. Take this piece of gold, and make purchase with it to suit yourself—scarf, gown or gloves—which ever you please.''

Somewhat to the cavalier's surprise, his liberal largess was rejected —not with scorn, but rather with an air of sadness—sufficiently marked to have been noticed by him, had he not been altogether unsuspicious of the cause.

" Well, well,'' said he, putting back the coin into his purse, " I am sorry you will not permit me to make some amends for your kindness. Perhaps I may find an opportunity on some future occasion. Meanwhile I must be gone. The letter you have delivered summons me hence—without delay. Many thanks, Mistress Betsey, and a fair good morning to you. ''

A touch of the spur caused his chafing steed to spring out into the middle of the road; and the rider, heading him for the highway that conducted towards Uxbridge, soon swept round the corner—at the same instant becoming lost to the sight of the dark-eyed damsel— whose glance, full of passion and disappointment, had followed him to the point of his disappearance.

CHAPTER III.

A SUSPICIOUS LOVER.

The girl listened awhile to the departing hoofstrokes, as they came back with clear resonance from the hard causeway. Then dropping her eyes to the ground, she stood silent under a tree—her swarth complexion still further darkened by sombre shadows, now over-spreading every feature of her face.

Not long did she continue in this silent attitude.

"I would have taken the ribbon,'' muttered she, "as a gift—if he had meant it that way. But it wasn't so. No. It was only as wages he offered it to me; and his money—that was worse! Had it been a lock of his hair. Ah! I would rather he gave me that than all the gold coins in his purse, or all the silks in the shops of Uxbridge.

"He called my hair beautiful; twice he said so!

"Did he mean it? Or was it only mocking of me? I am sure I do not think so myself; though others have told me the same. I wish it were fair, instead of dark, like that of Mistress Marion Wade. Then, perhaps it would be beautiful!

"Blue don't become me, he says. Lie there, despised color! Never more shall blue blossom be seen in the hair of Bet Dancey."

As she said this, she plucked the bunch of harebells from behind her comb; and flung the flowers at her feet.

"It was Will, that gave them to me;" she continued. "He only gathered them an hour ago. What if he were here to see them now? Ah! what care I?—what should I care? I never gave him reason-- not the least bit. They were worn to-day, not to please *him*; but in hopes of pleasing one I do care for. Had I thought that that one liked not blue, there were plenty of red ones in the old garden of Stone Dean. I might have gathered some as I came through it. What a pity I didn't know the color he likes best!"

"Ha!" she exclaimed, starting forward upon the path; and bend-ing down over the spot where the flowers had fallen—and where the dust showed signs of having been recently disturbed. "That is not the track of *his* horse. That little shoe—I know it—Mistress Marion Wade!"

For a second or two the speaker preserved her stooping attitude, silently regarding the tracks. She saw they were fresh—that they had been made fresh that morning—in fact, within the hour.

Her father was a forester—a woodman by calling—at times, a *stealer of deer*. She had been born in the forest—brought up under the shadow of its trees. She was capable of interpreting that sign— too capable for the tranquillity of her spirit.

"Mistress Marion has been here," she muttered. "Of late, often have I seen these tracks, and twice the lady herself. What brings her along this lonely road? What has she been doing here this morn-ing? Could it be to meet *him*?"

She had no time to conjecture a response to this self-asked inter-rogatory.

As the words passed from her lips, her attention was attracted to the sound of hoofs—a horse moving at a gallop along the main road

Could it be the cavalier coming back?

No. It was a peasant on a sorry steed—the same who had passed the other way scarcely an hour before—the same who had given chagrin to Mistress Marion Wade.

It was the woodman, Will Walford.

The girl appeared desirous of shunning him; but he had caught sight of her crimson cloak, and an encounter was unavoidable.

"Aw, Bet! be it thee, girl?" he cried out, as he came within speaking distance. "Why it beeant all o' an hour since I left thee at thy hum! What's brought thee this way?"

"Father got home soon after you left. He came by the wood path, and missed you, I suppose."

"Like enough for that part of the story," replied the man, appearing to suspect prevarication; "but that an't gieing an answer to my question. I asked as how you yerself coomed this way?"

"Oh, me you mean, Will?"

"Ees—myself, Bet!"

"Father brought a letter from Uxbridge for Master Holtspur. He was tired when he got home; and as you had the old horse, he sent me over to Stone Dean with it."

"But Stone Dean an't here—not by a good half mile."

"I went there first. Master Holtspur wasn't at home; and as the dummy made signs that he was gone along the road, and would soon be back, I followed him. Father said the letter was important, and told me to give it to Master Holtspur at once."

"You seed Holtspur, then?"

"I did, Will. I overtook him where he was stopping here under the old beech tree."

"And what did thee then?"

"Give him the letter—what else should I do?"

"Ay, what else? Dang it, Bet Dancey, thee art too fond o' runnin' after other people's business, an' this Master Holtspur's in particklar—that's what thee be."

"It was my father's business. What had I to do with the letter but deliver it, as I was told?"

"Never mind about it, then," rejoined the surly sweetheart, whose incipient jealousy was somewhat appeased by the explanation. "Jump up, an' ride behint! I han't got the pillion; but you won't mind that, since it's your own nag, and knows it's you, Bet. He'll make his old rump as soft as a cushion for you. Hi—hullo! where's the blue blossoms I gied you for your hair? Dang me if that beant them scattered over the ground thear!"

"Indeed!" said Bet, with a feigned look of surprise, "so it is. They must have fallen out as I was fixing my comb. Father started me off in such a hurry, I hadn't half time to put it in its place. This hair of mine's a bother, anyhow. It's by half too thick, and gives me constant trouble to keep it pinned up. I shall have it cut short I think, like those Puritan people, who are getting to be so plenty. How would you like that Will?"

"Dang it! not at all. It would never do to crop thy bonny locks that fashion. 'Twould complete spoil it. Never mind them flowers, lass. Thear be plenty more where they coom from; an' I'm a bit hurried just now to see thy father. Yee up, then; an' let us haste hom'ard."

The girl, not without some show of reluctance, obeyed what appeared as much a mandate as a request; and, climbing to the croup, she extended her arms round the waist of him who, though calling himself her lover, was to her an object of fear rather than affection.

CHAPTER IV.

THE COUSINS.

Having re-entered the gates of the park, Marion Wade checked her palfrey into a walk; and, at this pace, continued on towards the paternal mansion.

The scarlet that late tinted her cheeks had become subdued There was pallor in its place. Her lips even showed signs of blanching.

In her eye there was a cowed look—as if she had committed crime, and feared discovery! But gazing on that face, you could scarce think of crime. It was too fair to be associated with sin.

She sat negligently in her saddle—the undulating outlines of her majestic form rendered more conspicuous by the movements of her palfrey; as it straired up the acclivity of the hill.

The hawk had been restored to its perch; but the gauntlet no longer shielded her wrist; and the *pounces* of the bird, penetrating

the tender skin, had drawn blood. A tiny stream laced the silken
epidermis of her hand, and trickled to the tips of her fingers.

She felt not the wound. She beheld not the blood. The emotions
of her soul deadened the external senses; and, absorbed in the contemplation of her rash act—half repenting of it—she was conscious
of naught else, till her palfrey came to a stop under the windows of
the dwelling.

Giving her bridle to a groom, she dropped lightly to her feet; and
glided silently towards a side door of the house—intending to enter
unobserved. In her own chamber, she might more securely give way
to that tumult of thoughts and passions, now agitating her bosom.

Her design was frustrated. As she approached the portal, a clear
voice, ringing along the corridor, called her by name; and the instant
after a fair form—almost as fair as her own—issuing forth, glided up
by her side.

It was Lora—the cousin spoken of in her late soliloquy—Lora
Lovelace.

"Give me the little pet," cried Lora, reaching forward, and lifting
the hawk from its perch. "Oh, Marion!" continued she, drawing
back at sight of the blood. "What is this? You are wounded?"

"Ah! indeed, yes. I did not notice it before. The kestrel must
have caused it. The wicked jade! Her claws need coping. Don't
trouble about it, child. It's nothing."

"But where is your gauntlet, Marion? If it had been on your
hand, you would not have got scratched in this fashion!"

"Ah! the gauntlet? Where is it? Let me see."

Marion made search about her dress—in the crown of her beaver
—everywhere that might give concealment to a glove. An idle search.

"I must have dropped it!" added she, feigning surprise. "Perhaps it is sticking somewhere about the saddle? If not, I must have
lost it upon the road. It don't signify. I must buy me a new pair
--that's all."

"Dearest cousin!" said Lora, speaking in a tone of earnest appeal; "the sight of blood always makes me think of danger. I am
never happy when you are out alone on these distant hawking excur-
sions. Marion, you should take attendants with you; or remain
within the enclosure. I am sure there is danger outside."

"Danger outside! Ha! Ha! Perhaps you are right there,
little Lora. Perhaps it's that which lures me beyond the palings of
the park! When I go forth to hawk or hunt, I don't care to be

scooped up by enclosures. Give me the wild game that has free range of the forest!"

"But think, Marion! You know what we've heard about the highwaymen? It's true about the lady being stopped on Red Hill—in her carriage, too. Uncle says it is; and that these robbers are growing bolder every day, on account of the bad government. Oh, cousin, take my advice! and don't any more go out alone."

"Good counsel, daughter; though it be given you by one younger than yourself. I hope you will set store by it; and not leave me under the necessity of strengthening it by a command."

The tall middle-aged gentleman, of noble serious mien—who, stepping forth, had entered thus abruptly into the conversation—was Sir Marmaduke Wade, the father of Marion, and uncle of Lora.

"Your cousin speaks truly," continued he; "and it's well I am reminded of it. There's no longer any safety on the roads. Not much in one's own house, so far as that goes: for there are two kinds of robbery just now rife in this unhappy land—in the King's court, as on the King's highway. Henceforth children, confine your rambles within the limits of the park. Even with attendants, you may not be safe outside."

"That is true," affirmed Lora. "The lady who was stopped had several attendants—I think you said so, uncle?"

"Six of different sorts, escorting her carriage. In sooth, a valiant escort! They all scampered off. Of course they did. How could they be loyal, with a corrupt administration, such as ours; destroying every vestige of honesty and loyalty in the realm? Men are sure to become vile if only to imitate their masters. But come, my children! Let us hope for better times; and, to keep up the character of merry Old England, I've planned an entertainment for you —one that all our friends and neighbors are to take part in."

"What is it?" asked Lora whose spirit was, at the moment, more highly attuned to the idea of pastime than that of her silent cousin.

"A fête champêtre."

"Where? Here? In our own park?"

"In our own park, of course."

"And who are to be invited, dear uncle?"

"Everybody for ten miles round; and farther, if they choose to come. I don't mind an ox or two extra for the occasion."

"Occasion! what, uncle? It isn't Christmas!—it isn't Whitsun tide! nor yet May-day!"

" Can you think of nothing except holidays ?   What say you to a birthday ? "

"Oh! true; Walter's will be next week. But, papa, is brother coming home ? "

"That's it. He is to arrive on the eve of his birthday. Poor lad! he's been a long while from us; not long enough, I hope, to get spoiled in a dangerous school. Well, we must give him a welcome worthy of old Bucks. And now, girls! go to work; and see that you do your share in making preparation for our guests."

With this parting injunction, the knight turned back into the house; leaving his niece and daughter to discuss the pleasant subject he had placed before them.

For some seconds after he was gone, there was no exchange of speech between the cousins. Each was absorbed in her own thoughts.

"Oh! 'twill be a happy day; for Walter will be here!" was the secret reflection of Lora.

Marion's, in a somewhat similar strain, was less affirmative :—
"Oh! 'twould be a happy day, if Holtspur should be here!"

CHAPTER V

WALTER WADE

Autumn was still in the sky; but it had passed its midtime; and the beechen forests of Bucks were enrobed in their livery of yellow-green.   The cuckoo had forsaken the copse; and the swallows were making rendezvous on the spire of the village church.   The ringdove sat silent in the dell; and the woodquests were gathering into groups. The pheasant ventured with her young brood beyond the cover-edge; the partridge carried her chicks across the stubble; and finch, sparrow, and linnet, were forming their respective families into full-fledged cohorts—in preparation for those dark, chill days, when they would need such companionship to cheer them.

In truth, it is a right fair land, this same shire of Bucks—lovely in its spring-tide; fair in its summer bloom; and fairer still in its

October. You may travel far, without beholding a spot more bewitch-
ing than the land of the beechen "weed;" and embosomed within the
undulating arms of the Chilterns, is many a spot worthy of wider re-
nown. The mountain you meet not, the lake is rare; but the softly
swelling hill, and deep romantic dale, are ever before and around you;
and the eye of traveler, or tourist, is continually attracted to scenes
of sylvan beauty, upon which it long delights to linger.

So thought a youthful stripling, astride a stout steed; as, emerging from the town-end of Uxbridge, he rode over the old bridge
crossing the Colne.

The sun was just sinking behind the Chiltern hills; whose forest-
clad spurs stretched down into the plain—as if to meet and welcome
him.

It was a fair landscape that unfolded itself before his eyes. Upon
the ridge of Red Hill, the rays of the descending sun slanted among
the leaves of the beeches; heightening their yellow sear to the hue of
gold. Here and there the wild cherry tree, of more radiant foliage;
the green oak, and the darker green of the holly, mottled the slope:
while on either flank, lying low among hills, the valleys of Alder-
l Chalfont were gradually becoming shrouded under the
purple shadow of the twilight.

Right and left meandered the Colne, through meadows of emerald
verdure—its broad unrippled surface reflecting the sapphire sky;
while on its banks appeared herds of sleek kine, slowly lounging
along the grassy sward, or standing motionless in the stream—as if
placed there to give the last touch to a scene typical of tranquillity
and contentment.

It was a scene worthy of Watteau or Cuyp—a picture calculated
to create a quiet joy, even in the breast of a stranger. So might
have thought Walter Wade; who, after a long absence from this his
native shire, now gazing on its wood-embowered hills and valleys,
recognized the *mise en scene* of his boyhood's home !

The young traveler felt such a happiness. On cresting the high
causeway of the old bridge—which brought the Chilterns full before
his view—he reined up his horse in the middle of the road; while at
the same time an ejaculation escaped from his lips, indicative of the
pleasure which the sight afforded.

"Dear old Chilterns ! " he exclaimed. "Friends you seem, with
arms outstretched to receive me ! How bright and fresh you look to
one coming from that sooty London'! What a pity I did not start as

hour earlier—so that I might have enjoyed this fine sunset from the summit of Red Hill! No matter. There will be moonlight anon; and that will do just as well. Sunlight or moonlight, give me a ride through the beechen woods of Bucks. Charming at all hours!"

"I' faith, I wonder," continued he, becoming more reflective in his soliloquy; "how any one can fancy a city life! I'm sure, I've been well enough placed to enjoy it. The queen has been very kind— very kind indeed. She has twice kissed me. And the king, too, has complimented me on my service—only at parting he was very angry with me. I don't know why. *I* did nothing to anger him.

"I wonder why I'm summoned home? Father don't say in his letter; but I suppose he'll tell me when I arrive there. No matter. I'm only too glad to get back to dear old Bulstrode. I hope that in veterate deer-stealer, Dick Dancy, hasn't killed off all our deer. I mean to go in for some grand stalking this winter—that do I.

"Let me see! Three years—no; it will be three come Christmas— since I took service at Court. I shouldn't be surprised if cousin Lora is grown a big girl by this; and sister Marion too? Ah! Marion was big enough when I left. Lora won't be as tall as she. No—she wasn't the make for that. Lora would be what the queen calls *petite*. For all that, I dare say she's got to be a grown woman. She was just my own age; and I think I may say, that I'm now a man. Heigho! How time passes!"

And, as if the reflection had suggested the necessity of making as much of the time as possible, the young horseman gave the whip to his steed, shot out from between the parapet walls of the bridge, and passed on at a canter.

Though Walter Wade had pronounced himself a man—somewhat modestly it must be admitted—the statement was scarcely correct; and the error must be attributed to a very common and pardonable weakness of boyhood, ambitious of entering upon manhood.

He was still only a stripling—a youth of nineteen—though well grown for his age; and in point of size might have passed muster among men. A slight moustache already appeared upon his upper lip. It was light-colored, like his hair—neither of which was red, but of that Saxon "yellow" so often associated with eyes of blue; and which, when met with in woman, presents the fairest type of female beauty.

The Greeks—themselves a dark people, above all others skilled in feminine charms—have acknowledged this truth, though by that acknowledgement ignoring the claims of their own race.

To the **spume** of the sea was the Cyprian goddess indebted for the whiteness of her skin— to the blue sky, for the color of her eyes— to the golden sun, for the hue of her hair. Among the classic ancients, the dark haired Venus elicited but little admiration. And not very different is the *partiality* of the moderns.

The belle of the ball-room is invariably a *blonde;* and even the *nymphe du pavé*, who trails golden pennants from under the rim of her coquettish hat, looks scornfully askance at the darker tresses of her sister in sin !

It is odd that blue eyes do not admire blue eyes— that light-colored tresses do not wish to be interwoven with those of a like hue. Is there an instinct of approximation between extremes ? Do contrasts possess an innate desire for contiguity? If so, it would explain the *penchant* of the dark Athenians for the fair-skinned Cytherea.

There are fair-haired youths whom men may admire ; and woman love. Walter Wade was such a one.

A forehead of fine expanse, crested with curling hair—a nose sufficiently aquiline to exhibit the true aristocratic breed—a chin prominent—lips typical of contempt for aught that was mean. Such were his features.

Gazing upon his face, you might not pronounce it handsome. For a man, it might appear too feminine. But if you were at all skilled in Saxon physiognomy, on seeing such a face, and knowing that the owner of it had a sister, you might safely set *her* down as a being of incomparable beauty.

It was not necessary to have overheard his soliloquy, to tell that he who made it, was the scion of some distinguished house. The good steed he bestrode, caparisoned in costly fashion ; the rich costume he wore ; his sharply chiseled features, and aristocratic bearing—all betokened the *filius nobilis*.

He was, in effect, the son of Sir Marmaduke Wade, of Bulstrode Park ; who could point to an ancestry older than the Conquest, and whose Saxon sires—along with the Bulstrodes, the Hampdens, and the Penns—had so doughtily defended their beechen woods and broad fields against the Norman invader, that the great Conqueror was pleased to compound with them for a continuance of their tenure It was a family with whom kings had never been favorites. It had figured among the barons, who had forced the tyrant John to set his signature to the celebrated Charter of English liberty ; and elsewhere have its representatives been found in the front rank of the champ ions of Freedom.

It may be wondered why young Walter Wade had been in the service of the Court—as declared in his soliloquy. That, however, is easily explained. An ambitious mother, of queenly inclinations—an uncle in high office near the throne—these will account for the son :f Sir Marmaduke having stood as a page in the Presence.

But the mother's influence was now at an end. She was no more. And that of her brother—the uncle—was not strong enough to prevent Sir Marmaduke recalling his son from a Court—whose immorality had become the theme of every tongue; and whose contamination the fond father but so justly dreaded.

This was why the stripling was on his return to the paternal mansion; and why the king had shown displeasure at parting with him. It was a bold act on the part of the knight; and it might need all the influence of his official brother-in-law, to avert from him the vengeance of Charles—that most contemptible of tyrants.

I; was not upon these things that Walter Wade was reflecting, as he rode onward. A pleasanter theme was the subject of his thoughts —his cousin Lora.

It was love's young dream—by some deemed the sweetest in life is perhaps the most evanescent.

With Walter, it had not been so very fleeting. Starting at sixteen, it was now nearly three years old. It had stood the test of a long absence; and under circumstances most unfavorable to love's endurance; amid smiling maids of honor, and dames of high degree. Yes; Walter's heart had nobly repelled the blandishments of more than one belle; and this, too, in a court famed for its *fair*.

That kiss, somewhat coyly granted by his cousin, "deep in a forest dell," where they had wandered in search of wild flowers—that soft pressure of Lora's little hand—those thrilling words, "Dear Walter," that on the same occasion had fallen from Lora's pretty lips—all were remembered, as if they had been incidents of yesterday.

Did *she* remember them with equal interest! This was the thought upon which Walter Wade had been dwelling ever since parting from the portals of Whitehall Palace.

During his two years of absence, he had not been left altogether uninformed of what was passing at Bulstrode. Though in those days letters were written at long intervals—and then only on mat ters of great importance—Walter had kept up a correspondence with Marion; with whom epistles had been exchanged regularly once a month. He dared not write to Lora—nor even *about* her. He knew what he said to his sister would be communicated to his little mis tress; and he feared to show himself too solicitous. Every word in his letters, relating to his cousin, had been carefully studied—as to the impression it might produce—for in this sort of strategy, young love is as cunning as that of older hearts. At times the boy courtier even affected indifference about his cousin's affairs; and more than once there was danger of a quarrel—or at least a coolness. This was more especially the case, when his sister—ignorant of the pain she was producing—spoke of Lora's great beauty; and the havoc it was making among the hearts of the country beaux

Perhaps had Marion passed these pretty compliments upon herself, she would have said nothing beyond what was true ; for, although Walter's cousin was beautiful, and a belle, his sister was at that time the acknowledged "belle of the shire "

CHAPTER VI.

"THE KING!"

For the first half mile after crossing the Colne, the thoughts of the young courtier had been given exclusively to his cousin. He recalled the old time—that scene in the silent dell—the kiss among the wild flowers -that proved her partiality for him. He remembered all these occurrences with a strong confidence in Lora's loyalty.

His fanciful reflections were suddenly, and somewhat rudely in-terrupted.

On arriving at an inn that stood by the roadside, a spectacle was presented to his eyes which turned his thoughts into a different channel.

In a wide open space in front of the hostelry was a troop of horse-men. By their armor and equipments, Walter knew them to be *cuirassiers*, in the service of the king.

There were about fifty in the troop; and from the movements of the men, and the condition of their horses—still smoking from the march—it was evident they had come to a halt only a few minutes before.

The troopers had dismounted. Some of them were still occupied with their horses, helping them to provender; while others, who had already performed this duty, were seated under a huge old elm tree—joyously, as well as noisily, regaling themselves with such cheer as the hostelry afforded.

A glance at these roisterers told the young cavalier who and what they were;—a troop of the returned army from the north; that had been lately, and somewhat clandestinely, brought southward by the king.

This corps had originally been recruited in the Low Countries; and among them were several foreigners. Indeed, the smaller number were Englishmen; while there were many countenances of the true Gallic type; and a still larger proportion of those famed hirelings—who figured so largely in the wars of the time—the *Walloons*

Amid the clamor of voices, with which the ears of the young courtier were assailed, he could hear French and Flemish commingled with his native tongue; while the oaths peculiar to all three nations, thickly interlarding the conversation, told him that he was in the presence of a remnant of that army that "swore so terribly in Flanders."

A crowd of the neighboring rustics had collected around the inn; and stood with mouths agape, and countenances expressing unlimited astonishment, at the sayings and doings of the strange steel-clad cavaliers who had dismounted in their midst.

To Walter Wade, there was nothing either new or surprising in the spectacle. He had seen the like in London; and often of late. He had been expecting such a sight—partly from having heard, in passing through Uxbridge, that a troop of horse was before him; and partly from having observed their tracks along the dusty road upon which he had been traveling.

He did not know why they were going down into Buckinghamshire; but that was the king's business, not his. In all likelihood they were on there way to Oxford, or some garrison town in the west; and were making their night halt at the inn.

Giving but a moment's thought to conjecture any of these, the young courtier was about riding past—without taking notice of the coarse

Jests flung towards him by the rough troopers under the tree—when a voice of very different intonation, issuing from the door of the hostelry, commanded him to halt.

Almost simultaneous with the command, two cavaliers stepped forth out of the inn; and one of them, having advanced a few paces towards him, repeated the command.

Partly taking by surprise at this rude summons—and partly believing it to proceed from some old Court acquaintance—Walter drew bridle, and stopped.

It was easy to tell that the two men, who had so brusquely brought themselves under his notice, were the officers in command of the troop. Their silken doublets—only partially concealed by the steel armor —their elegant Spanish leather boots, with lace ruffles at the tops; the gold spurs upon their heels; the white ostrich plumes waving above their helmets; and the richly chased scabbards of their swords —all indicated rank and authority. This was further made manifest by the tone of command in which they had spoken, and their bearing in presence of the troopers.

The latter, on seeing them come forth from the house, desisted from their jargon, and, though they continued to pass their beer cans, it was in a constrained and respectful silence.

The two officers wore their helmets; but the visors of both were open; and Walter could see their faces distinctly.

He now perceived that neither of them was known to him; though one of them he thought he had seen before, a few days before—only for a moment, and in conference with the Queen!

This was the older of the two, and evidently the senior in rank— the captain of the troop. He was a man of thirty, or thereabouts, with a face of dark complexion, and not unhandsome; but of a rakish expression that drink, and the indulgence of evil passions, will imprint upon the noblest features. His had once been of the noblest— and still were they such that a gentleman need not have been ashamed of—had it not been for a cast half cynical, half sinister, that could be detected in his eyes; sadly detracting from a face otherwise well favored. Altogether it was a countenance of that changing kind, that, smiling, might captivate the heart; but, scowling, could inspire it with fear.

The younger man—who from the insignia on his shoulder was a *cornet*—presented a very different type of physiognomy. Though still only a youth, his countenance was repulsive in the extreme. There was no need to scan it closely, to arrive at this conclusion. In that reddish round face, shaded by a scant thatch of straight hay-colored hair, you beheld at a glance a kindred compound of the stupid, the vulgar, and the brutal.

Walter Wade had never looked on that countenance before. It inspired him with no wish to cultivate the acquaintance of its owner. If left to his own inclinations, the young courtier would not have desired ever to look upon it again.

"Your wish? demanded he, rising proudly up in his stirrups, and so confronting the officer who had addressed him. "You have summoned me to stop—your wish?"

"No offence, I hope, young gallant?" replied the cuirassier captain "None meant, I assure you. By the sweat upon your horse—not a bad-looking brute by-the-way. A good nag. Isn't he, Stubbs?"

"If sound," laconically rejoined the cornet.

"Oh! sound enough, no doubt, you incorrigible jockey! Well, youngster, as I was saying, the sweat upon your horse proves that you have ridden fast and far. Both you and he stand in need of refreshment. We called to you, merely to offer the hospitality of the inn."

"Thanks for your kindness, replied Walter, in a tone that sufficiently expressed his true appreciation of the offer; "but I must decline availing myself of it. I am not in need of any refreshment; and as for my horse, a short five miles will bring him to a stable, where he will be well cared for."

"Oh! you are near the end of your journey, then?"

"By riding five miles further I shall reach it."

"A visit to some country acquaintance, where you can enjoy the balmy atmosphere of the beech forests—have new-laid eggs every morning for breakfast, and new-pulled turnips along with your bacon for dinner, eh?"

The choler of the high-bred youth had been gradually mounting upward, and might soon have found vent in angry words. But Walter Wade was one of those happy spirits who enjoy a joke—even at their own expense—and perceiving that his new acquaintances meant no further mischief than the indulgence in a little idle *badinage*, he repressed his incipient spleen, and replied in the same jocular and satirical strain.

After a sharp passage of words—in which the young courtier was far from being worsted—he was on the point of riding onward; when the captain of the cuirassiers again proffered the hospitality of the inn by inviting him to partake of a cup of burned sack which the landlord had just brought from the house.

The offer was made with an air of studied politeness · and Walter, not caring to appear churlish, accepted it.

He was about raising the goblet to his lips, when his entertainers called for a toast.

" What would you ?" asked the young courtier.

"Anything my gallant! Whatever is uppermost in your mind. Your mistress, I presume?"

"Of course," chimed in the cornet. "His mistress of course."

" My mistress, then!" said Walter, tasting the wine, and returning the cup to the hand from which he had received it.

"Some pretty shepherdess of the Chilterns—some sweet wood nymph, no doubt? well here's to her! And now," continued the officer, without lowering the goblet from his lips, "since I've drunk to your mistress, you'll not refuse the same compliment to my master —the king. You won't object to that toast, will you?"

"By no means," replied Walter. "I drink it willingly, though the king and I have not parted the best of friends."

"Ha, ha, ha! friends with the king! His Majesty has the honor of your acquaintance, eh!"

"I have been nearly three years in his service."

"A courtier?"

"I have been page to the queen."

"Indeed! perhaps you will have no objection to favor us with your name!"

Not the slightest. My name is Wade—Walter Wad .·-

"Son of Sir Marmaduke, of Bulstrode Park?"

"I am."

" Ho, ho," muttered the questioner, in a significant tone, and with a thoughtful glance at the young courtier.

" I thought so," stammered the cornet, exchanging a look of in telligence with his superior officer.

"Son to Sir Marmaduke, indeed!" continued the latter. "I · that case, Master Wade, we are likely to meet again, and perhaps you will some day favor me with an introduction to your sweet shepherd ess. Ha, ha, ha! Now for the toast of every true Englishman— The King!'"

Walter responded, though with no great willingness; for the tone of the challenger, as well as his words, had produced upon him an unpleasant impression. But the toast was one that, at the time, it was not safe to decline drinking; and partly on this account, and partly because the young courtier had no very particular reason for declining, he raised the goblet once more to his lips, as he did so repeating the words—"To THE KING."

The cornet drinking from a cup of his own, echoed the sentiment; and the troopers under the tree, clinking their beer measures together vociferated in loud acclaim—"THE KING—THE KING!"

CHAPTER VII.

"THE PEOPLE!"

After this general declaration of loyalty, there was a lull—an interval of profound silence—such as usually succeeds the drinking of a toast.

The silence was unexpectedly broken by a voice that had not yet mingled in the chorus, and which was now heard in clear firm tones, pronouncing a phrase of very different signification—"THE PEOPLE!"

A sentiment so antagonistic to the one so late issuing from the lips of the troopers, produced upon them an instantaneous commotion. The soldiers, seated under the tree, started to their feet; while the officers faced in the direction whence the voice had come—their eyes angrily flashing under the umbrils of their helmets.

He who had so daringly declared himself was not concealed. A horseman, of elegant appearance, had just ridden up, and halted in the middle of the road; where the landlord, apparently without orders, and as if accustomed to the service—was helping him to a goblet of wine. It was this horseman that called out—"The People!"

In the enthusiasm of their loyalty, his arrival had either not been observed by the troopers—or at all events no notice had been taken of it—until the emphatic pronunciation fell upon their ears like the bursting of a bomb. Then all eyes were instantly turned towards him.

As he gave utterance to the phrase, he was in the act of raising the wine cup to his lips. Without appearing to notice the effect which his speech had produced, he coolly quaffed off the wine and with like *sang froid* returned the empty goblet to the giver.

The defiant insolence of the act had so taking the troopers by surprise, that they stood in their places—just as they had started up—silent and apparently stupefied. Even the officers, after hurrying forward, remained speechless for several seconds—as if under the influence of an angry amazement. The only sounds for awhile heard were the voices of the spectators—tapsters, stable-helpers, and other idlers—who had clustered in front of the inn—and who now formed an assemblage, as large as the troop itself.

Despite the presence of the armed representatives of royalty, the sentiments of these were unmistakably the same, as that to which the strange horseman had given voice; and they were emphatically complimenting *themselves*, when they clinked their pewter pots, and in chorus proclaimed—"THE PEOPLE!"

Most of them, but the moment before, and with equal enthusiasm, had drunk "The King;" but in this sudden change of sentiment they only resembled most politicians of modern times, who have been dignified with the name of "Statesmen!"

But even among these tapsters and stable-helpers, there were some who had refrained from being forced into a lip loyalty; and who echoed the second sentiment with a fervent spirit, and a full knowledge of its everlasting antagonism to the first.

When the ultimate syllable of this sacred phrase had died upon the ear of the assembled croud, it was succeeded by a silence ominous and expectant. Two individuals commanded the attention of all—the captain of the cuirassiers, and the horseman who had halted upon the road; the toaster of the "King;" and the proposer of the "People!"

The soldier should speak first. It was to him that the challenge—if such he chose to consider it—had been flung forth.

Had it been a rustic who had uttered it—one of the assembled crowd—even a freehold farmer of puritanic pretensions—the cuirassier captain would have answered him on the instant, perhaps with steel added to the persuasion of his tongue. But a cavalier, of broad bands, and gold spurs buckled over the Spanish leather boots, astride a noble steed, with a long rapier hanging handy anent his hip, was an individual not to be ridden over in such haste; and one whose "argument" called for consideration.

2*

"Zounds, sir!" cried the captain of the cuirassiers, stepping a space or two forward, "from what Bedlam have you broken loose? Methinks you've been tasting too freely of the St. Giles's tap; and 'tis that which makes your speech smell so rankly. Come, fellow, uncover your head, and tune your tongue to a different strain. You go not hence till you've purged your traitorous throat by drinking the toast of every true and loyal gentleman of England—'THE KING!'"

"Fellow indeed!" exclaimed the cavalier, looking scornfully askance at him who had dictated the insulting proposition. "A fellow!" he continued in a calm but satirical tone; "not in the habit of drinking toasts with strangers. Yours is not to his liking, any more than your fashion. If he had the fancy to drink to England's king, it would not be in the con   .y of those who have disgraced England's fame—at the ford of N   urn."

Gathering up his reins as he sp   . and giving utterance to a taunt ing laugh, the strange horseman   sed the spur against the sides of his splendid steed; and started f at a swinging gallop along the road.

It was only when that laugh r   in his ears that the cuirassier captain became roused to the full frenzy of rage; and with eyes on fire, and brow black as midnight, he rushed forward, sword in hand, in a frantic attempt to strike down the insulter.

"Disloyal knave!" cried he, lunging out to the full length of his arm; "thou shalt drink the king's health in thine own blood! Ha! stop him!" he continued, as the horseman glided beyond his reach —"My pistols!"

"Ho, there!" shouted he to his followers. "Your carabines! Fire upon him! Where are your weapons, you careless vagabonds? To horse, and follow!"

"An' ye take my advice, masters," put in the landlord of the inn —a sturdy tapster of independent speech—"ye'll stay wheer ye are. An' ye doan't, ye'll be havin' yeer ride for nothin'. Ye maw't as well gie chase to a wild goose. He'll be two mile frae this 'fore you can git astride o' your nags."

"What, varlet!" cried the cuirassier captain turning furiously upon the speaker—"you presume——'

"Only, great coronel, to gie ye a bit o' sound advice. Ye ma' folla it or no' an' ye pleeze; but f ye folla him ye won't catch him—not this night, I trow; though theer be a full moon to light ye on his track,"

The air of imperturbable coolness with which the Saxon Boniface made rejoinder, instead of increasing the fury of the officer, seemed rather to have the effect of tranquilizing him.

"You know him, then ? " demanded he, in an altered tone

"Well, e-es ! a leetlish bit only. He be one o' my customers; and have his drink occasional as he passes by here. I know his horse a bit better, mayhap. That be a anymal worth the knowin'. I've seed him clear that geeat—it be six feet high—moren once. Wee've seed him do it; ain' we, lads ? "

"That we have, Master Jarvis," replied several of the bystanders, to whom the appeal had been made.

"E-ees indeed, great coronel," continued the landlord, once more addressing his speech to the captain of the cuirassiers; "an if yer fellows want to folla him, they maun be up to ridin' cross country a bit, or else——"

"His name ! " eagerly interrupted the officer; "you know where the knave lives ? "

"Not exactly—neyther one nor t'other ;" was the equivocal reply. "As for his name, we only know him 'bout here as the *Black Horse-man*; an that he belongs some'ere among the hills up the Jarret's Heath way—beyond the great park o' Bulstrode."

"Oh! he lives near Bulstrode, does he ? "

"Somer bot theere, I dar say."

"I know where he lives," interposed one of the rustics who stood by. "It be a queery sort o' a place—a old red brick house; an' Stone Dean be the name o't. It lie in the middle o' the woods 'tween Beckenfield an' the two Chaffonts. I can take ye theer, master officer, if ye be a wantin' to go."

"Jem Biggs ! " said the landlord, sliding up to the last speaker, and whispering the words in his ear, "thee be a meddlin' 'ficious beggar. If thee go on such a errand, don't never agen show thy ugly mug in my taproom."

"Enough ! " impatiently exclaimed the officer; "I dare say we shall easily find the fellow. Dismount, men," continued he, turning to some of the troopers, who had sprung into their saddles. "Return your horses to their stalls. We may as well stay here for the night, he added in a whisper, to his cornet ; "it's no use going after him till the morning. As the old prattler says, we might have our ride for nothing. Besides, there's that little appointment in Uxbridge. By the angel Gabriel ! I'll find the knave, if I should have to scour every corner of the county. More wine, landlord!—burnt sack!—and beer for these thirsty vagabonds! We'll drink, 'The King' once more, with three times three. Ha! where's our courtier? Gone too?"

"He's just ridden off, captain;" answered one of the troopers, still seated in his saddle. "Shall I gallop after, and bring him back?"

"No," replied the officer, after a moment's consideration. "Let the stripling go his way. I know where he's to be found; and shall do myself the honor of dining with him to-morrow. The wine! Come! fill your cans, you right royal rascals, and drink—' The King!'"

"*The King—Hurrah!*"

CHAPTER VIII.

THE BLACK HORSEMAN.

Desirous of escaping from the disagreeable companionship—into which he had been so unceremoniously, as well as unwillingly, drawn—the young courtier had taken advantage of the confusion, and trotted quietly away.

On rounding a corner—beyond which the road was not visible from the inn—he put spurs to his horse, and urged the animal into a gallop.

Though he had given no offence, he was not without apprehension, that he might be followed, and summoned back; for the brace of bullies, from whom he had just parted, appeared quite capable of committing further outrage. He knew that, in the name of the king, excesses were of every day occurrence. The monarch's minions had become accustomed to insult the people with impunity. The soldiers, in particular, bore themselves offensively—more especially those hungry troopers; who, returning unpaid from the Northern campaign, were thrown idly upon the country. The disgrace they had fairly earned by fleeing before the Scots from the ford of Newburn, had deprived them of the sympathies of their own countrymen: as a natural consequence, provoking towards the latter a sort of swaggering and reckless hostility.

The incident which had occurred, and in which he had been an involuntary actor, inspired Walter Wade with some emotions that were new to him, and, as he slackened his pace, after a sharp canter, he fell into a train of reflections very different from those hitherto engaging his thoughts.

He was still too young to have entered into the politics of the time.

He knew that there was trouble between the king and his people; but breathing only the atmosphere of the "Presence," he could have other belief, than that the right was on the side of royalty.

He knew that the king, after an interregnum of eleven years, had summoned a Parliament, to settle the differences between himself and his subjects. He knew this from having been officially present at its opening. He knew, moreover, that this Parliament, after sitting only a few days, had been summarily dismissed; for he had been also present at its prorogation.

What should the young courtier care for such incidents as these—however significant they might be to the patriot, or politician?

To do him justice, however, Walter Wade, young as he was, was not altogether indifferent to what was passing. The spirit of his ancestry—that love of liberty, that had displayed itself at Runnymede—was not absent from his bosom. It was there; though hitherto held in check by the circumstances surrounding him. He had witnessed the punishments of the pillory—by summary sentence of Star Chamber and High Commission Court; he had been present at fearful spectacles of ear-croppings and other mutilations; and, although among companions, who beheld such scenes with indifference—or often regarded them as sources of amusement—more than once had he been profoundly affected by them. Stripling though he was, more than once had he reflected upon such royal wrongs. Circumstances, however, had placed him among the ranks of those, to whom the smiles of a tyrant were sweet; and he was still too young and unreflecting, to give other than a passing thought to the theme of Liberty.

That the enemies of the king suffered justly, was the belief that was breathed around him. He heard the statement on all sides; and from pretty lips—from the lips of a queen! How could he question its truth?

His encounter with the cuirassiers had produced an impression upon him, calculated to change his political sentiments—almost to change them.

"A scandal . " muttered he to himself. That these military bullies should be allowed to act as they please. I wonder the king per-
mits it. Perhaps it may be true what ' wicked Pym '—as the queen
calls him—said in the Parliament House : that his Majesty encour-
ages their insubordination. Ah ! if I had thought so, I should have
joined that brave fellow, who drank just now to *the people*. By-the-
by, who can *he* be? He's gone up the road—as if he lived our way. A
splendid rider ; and a horse worthy of him. I never saw either before.' If he be of Bulstrode neighborhood ; he must have come into it
since my time. Perhaps a traveler only ? And yet his horse looked
fresh, as if he had just stepped out of the stable. He could not have
ridden him farther than from Uxbridge ? "

"I thought those fellows were preparing to pursue him ; " continued he, glancing back over his shoulder. "They must have given up
the idea ; else I should hear them behind me. If they come on, I
shall slip aside among the trees, and let them pass. I don't want
any more converse with such companions as Captain Scarthe—that's
what his cornet called him, I think ; nor yet with Master Cornet
Stubbs himself. Stubbs indeed ! Surely there must be something in
names ?"

On finishing this series of reflections, the young courtier drew bridle ; and halted for the purpose of listening.

He could hear voices behind—at the inn—a chorus of rough voices
in loud vociferation. It was the "hip hurrah," of the troopers responding to the toast of "*the king.*" There was no other sound —
at least none to indicate that the pursuit was being continued.

"Good ! they are not following him. Prudent on their part, I
should say. If he has kept on as he started, he will be miles off by
this."

"There's no chance of my overtaking him ! " continued he, once
more heading his horse to the road. "My faith ! I wish I could.
Now that I remember the circumstances, I've heard there are robbers on this route. Sister wrote me about them not long since.
They stopped a lady's coach, and plundered it ; though they did no
hurt to the lady, beyond stripping her of her jewels—even to the rings
in her ears ! Only one of them—the captain I suppose—came near
the coach. The others stood by ; but said not a word. How very
funny of the fellows to act so ! Well, if it be my ill fortune to encounter robbers, I hope it may also be my good-fortune to find them equal-
y well-mannered. I don't mind giving them all I've got,—it's not

much—if they'll only let me pass on unmolested, like the lady. I' faith, I've been a fool to leave London so late; and that unlucky ad: venture at the inn has made it later. It's quite night. There's a beautiful moon, to be sure; but what of that, in this lonely place? It would only help to give light to the rascals; and enable them all the more easily to strip me of my trappings."

Notwithstanding his apparent indifference to an encounter with robbers, which these reflections might indicate, the young traveler was not without some apprehension. At the time, the roads of England were infested with highwaymen and footpads. Robberies were incidents of daily occurrence—even on the very skirts of the metropolis; and on the highways and byways, the demand for your purse was almost as common as the modern solicitation for alms.

In general, the "gentlemen of the road" were not sanguinary in their disposition. Some were even courteous. In truth, many of them were men, who, by the tyrannous exactions of the Sovereign, had been beggared in fortune; and forced to adopt this illegal mode of replenishing their exchequers. They were not all ruffians by instinct. Still there were some of them, with whom "Stand and deliver!" meant "Death if you do not!"

It was not without a feeling of nervousness, that Walter Wade scanned the long slope of road extending towards the crest of Red Hill—at the bottom of which he had now arrived. It was on this very hill—as stated in the correspondence of his sister—that the coach had been stopped, and the lady rifled of her rings.

The road running up the steep acclivity was of no great width—nothing resembling the broad macadamized "turnpike" of modern times. It was a mere track, just wide enough for wheels—bordered by a beechen forest, through which the path wound upward; the trees standing close along each side, and in some places forming arcades over it.

The young traveler once more reined up and listened. The voices from the inn no longer reached his ear—not even in distant murmering. He would have preferred hearing them. He almost wished that the pursuit had been continued. Little as he might have relished the companionship of Captain Scarthe, or cornet Stubbs, it would have been preferable to falling into that of a party of highwaymen or footpads.

He bent forward to catch any sound that might come from the road before him. He could hear none—at least, none of a character to make him uneasy. The soft monotone of the goatsucker fell upon his ear; mingled with the sharper note of the partridge, calling her young across the stubble. He heard, also, the distant barking of the watch-dog; and the sheep-bell tinkling in the fold; but these sounds, though characteristic of tranquil country life—and sweet to the ear so long hindered from hearing them—were not inconsistent with the presence either of footpad or highwayman; who, lurking concealed among the trees, need not interrupt their utterance.

Walter Wade was far from being of a timid disposition; but no youth of eighteen could be accused of cowardice, simply because he did not desire an encounter with robbers.

It did not, therefore, prove poltroonery on his part, when, proceeding along the road, his heart beat slightly with apprehension—no more, when on perceiving the figure of a horseman dimly outlined under the shadow of the trees, he suddenly came to a halt, and hesitated to advance.

The horseman was about a score of spaces from where he had stopped—moving neither one way nor the other, but motionless in the middle of the road.

"A highwayman!" thought Walter, undecided whether to advance, or to ride back.

"But no, it can scarce be that? A robber would not take stand so conspicuously. He would be more likely to conceal himself behind the trees—at least until——"

While thus conjecturing, a voice fell upon his ear, which he at once recognized as the same he had late heard so emphatically pronouncing "*The people!*"

Re-assured, the young traveler determined to advance. A man of such mien, as he who bestrode the black steed—and actuated by such a sentiment, as that he had so boldly announced—could scarcely be a disreputable person—much less a highwayman? Walter did not wrong him by the suspicion.

"If I mistake not," said the stranger, after the preliminary hail, "you are the young gentleman I saw, a short while ago, in rather scurvy company?'

"You are not mistaken, I am."

"Come on then! If you are my only pursuer, I fancy I shall incure no danger, in permitting you to overtake me? Come on young sir! Perhaps on these roads it may be safer for both of us, if we ride in company!"

Thus frankly solicited, the young courtier hesitated no longer; but, pricking his horse with the spur, rode briskly forward.

Together the horsemen continued the ascent up the hill.

Half way up, the road swerved towards the southwest. For a short distance the track was clear of trees, so that the moonlight fell full upon it. Here the two travelers, for the first time, obtained a distinct view of one another.

The stranger—who still retained his *incognito*—merely glanced towards his companion; and seeming satisfied with a slight inspection, allowed his eyes to wander elsewhere.

Perhaps during his halt before the hostelry he had made a more elaborate examination of the young courtier.

Walter, on the other hand, had at the inn caught only a glimpse of the black horseman. Now, though out of courtesy, looking furtively and askance, he proceeded to examine him more minutely.

The personal appearance of the latter was striking enough to court examination. Walter Wade was impressed with it—even to admiration.

He saw beside him, not a youth like himself, but a man in the full prime and vigor of manhood—perhaps over thirty years of age. He saw a figure of medium size, and perfect shape—its members knitted together, with a terseness that indicated true strength. He saw shoulders of elegant *tournure;* a breast of swelling prominence; a full round throat, with jaws that by their breadth proclaimed firmness and decision. He saw dark brown hair curling around a countenance, that in youth might have appeared under a fairer complexion; but was now bronzed, as if stained with the tan of travel. He saw eyes of dark hazel hue—in the moonlight shining softly, and mildly, as those of the dove. But Walter knew that those same eyes could flash like an eagle's; for he had seen them so fired, on first beholding them.

In short, the young courtier saw by his side, a man that reminded him of a hero of Middle Age romance—one, about whom he had been lately reading; and whose character had made a deep impression upon his youthful fancy.

The dress of the cavalier was in perfect keeping with his fine figure and face. It was simple, although of costly material. Cloak, doublet, and trunks were silk velvet, of dark maroon color. The boots were of the finest spanish leather; and his hat, a beaver—the brim in front coquettishly turned up, with a jeweled clasp, holding a black ostrich feather that swept backward to his shoulder. A scarlet sash, of China crape, looped around the waist—an embroidered shoulder belt crossing the breast, from whith dangled a rapier in richly chased sheath; buff-colored gloves, with gauntlets attached, cuffs of white lawn covering the sleeves of his doublet; and broad collar of the same, extending almost to his shoulders: fancy all these articles of costly fabric, fitted to the fashion of the time to a faultless manly figure, and you have a portrait of the cavalier whose appearance had won the admiration of Walter Wade.

The horse was in keeping with the rider—a steed of large size, and perfect proportions—such as an ancient paladin might have chosen to carry him upon a crusade. He was of the true color—a pure black, all except his muzzle, where the velvet-like epidermis was tinged with yellowish red, presenting the hue of umber. Had his tail been suffered to droop, its tip would have touched the ground; but even while going at a walk it swung diagonally outward, oscillating at each step. When in the gallop, it floated upon the air, spread, and horizontal.

The spotted skin of a South American jaguar, with housings of scarlet cloth, caparisoned the saddle; over the pommel of which hung a pair of holsters, screened by the thick glossy fur of the North American beaver.

The bit was a powerful mameluke—about that time introduced from the Spanish peninsula—which clanking between the teeth of the horse, constantly kept his mouth in a state of foam.

This beautiful steed had a name. Walter had heard it pronounced. As the young courtier road up, the horse was standing—his muzzle almost in contract with the road— and pawing the dust with impatience. The short gallop had roused his fiery spirit. To tranquilize it, its rider was caressing him—as he drew his gloved hand over the smooth skin of the neck, talking to him, as if he had been a comrade, and repeating his name. It was "Hubert."

After exchanging salutations, the two horsemen rode side by side for some moments, without vouchsafing further speech. It was the silence consequent upon such an informal introduction. The rider of the black steed was the first to break it.

"You are Walter Wade—son to Sir Marmaduke, of Bulstrode Park?" said he, less by way of interrogative than as a means of commencing the conversation.

"I am," answered the young courtier, showing some surprise "How learnt you my name, sir?"

"From your own lips."

"From my own lips! When, may I ask?" inquired Walter, with
a fresh scrutiny of the stranger's countenance. "I don't remember
having had the honor of meeting you before."

"Only within the last half-hour. You forget, young sir, having giv-
en your name in my hearing?"

"Oh true!—you overheard, then—you were present——?"

"I rode up just as you were declaring your identity. The son of
Sir Marmaduke Wade has no need to conceal his name. It is one to
be proud of."

"In my father's name, I thank you. You know him, sir?"

"Only by sight and—*reputation*," answered the stranger, musing-
ly. "You are in the service of the court?" he continued, after a
pause.

"No longer now. I took leave of it this very morning."

"Resigned?"

"It was my father's wish I should return home."

"Indeed! And for what reason? Pardon my freedom in asking
the question."

"Oh!" replied the young courtier, with an air of *naïveté*, "I should
make you free to the reason, if I only knew it myself. But in truth,
sir, I am ignorant of it. I only know that my father has written to
the king, asking permission for me to return home; that the king
has granted it—though, I have reason to think, with an ill grace;
since his Majesty appeared angry with me at parting, or, perhaps, I
should say, angry with my father."

The intelligence thus communicated by the *ci-devant* courtier, instead of eliciting any expression of regret from his companion, seemed
rather to gratify him.

"So far good!" muttered he to himself. "Safe upon our side.
This will secure him."

Walter partially overheard the soliloquized phrases, but without
comprehending their import.

"Your father," continued the stranger, "is likely to have a good
reasons for what he has done. No doubt, Master Walter, he has
acted for your best interests; though it may be rather unpleasant for
you to exchange the gay pleasures of a royal palace for a quieted life
in the country."

"On the contrary," replied the youth, "it is just what I was de-
siring. I am fond of hawking and hunting; not in the grand ceremonious fashion we've been accustomed to at Court—with a crowd of

squalling women to fright away the game—but by myself on the
quiet, among the hills here, or with a friend or two to take part.
That's the sport for me!"

"Indeed!" said the strange horseman, smiling as he spoke; "these
are heterodox sentiments for a courtier. It's rather odd to hear one
of your calling speak disparagingly of the sex; and especially the
ladies of the Court. The maids of honor are very interesting, are
they not? I have understood that our French queen affects being
surrounded by beauties. She has a long train of them, it is said?"

"Painted dolls!" scornfully rejoined the ex-courtier, "tricked in
French fashions. Give me a genuine English girl—above all, one
who keeps to the country and's got some color. And some conscience besides; for, by my troth, sir, there's not much about the
Court—except what's artificial!"

"Bravo!" exclaimed the stranger, " a Court satirist, rather than
a courtier. Well! I am glad to hear my sentiments so eloquently
expressed. Give me also the genuine English girl, who breathes only
the pure air of the country!"

"That's the style for me!" echoed Walter, in the warmth of youthful enthusiasm.

"Well! there are many such to be met with among these Chiltern
Hills. No doubt, Master Wade, you know some; and, perhaps, you
have one in particular before your mind's eye at this very moment?
Ha! ha! ha!"

The color came to Walter's cheeks as he stammered out a reply,
which only partially repudiated the insinuation.

"Your pardon!" cried the cavalier, suddenly checking his laughter. "I don't wish to confess you—I have no right to do so—I have
given you reason to think me unmannerly."

"Oh! not at all," said Walter; himself too free of speech to be
offended by that quality in another.

"Perhaps you will excuse the curiosity of a stranger," continued
the black horseman. "I have only been a short time resident in this
part of the country; and one is naturally curious to know something of
one's neighbors. If you promise not to be angry, I shall make bold
to ask you another question."

"I shall not be offended at any question one gentleman my ask of
another. You are a gentleman, sir?"

"I have been brought up as one; and, though I have parted with,
or rather been deprived of the fortune that attaches to such a title, I

hope I have not forfeited the character. The question I am about to put may appear rather trivial after so elaborate an introduction. I merely wished to ask, whether you are the only member of your father's family."

"Oh, dear, no !" frankly responded the youth; " I have a sister— sister Marion."

"Grown up, like yourself?"

"She should be by this. She wasn't quite grown when I saw her last; but that will be three years come Christmas. She's older than I; and, i'faith, I shouldn't wonder if she be taller too. I've heard say she's a great big girl—nearly the head taller than Lora."

"Lora?"

"Lora Lovelace—my cousin, sir."

" 'Tis his sister—'tis Marion. I thought as much. Marion Wade! A noble name. It has a bold clarion sound—in keeping with the character of her who bears it. Marion ! Now know I the name of her who for weeks I have been worshiping !—who for weeks——"

"My cousin," continued the candid young courtier, interrupting the silent reflections of his traveling companion, "is also a member of my father's family. She has been staying at Bulstrode Park now for many years ; and will remain, I suppose, until——"

The heir of Bulstrode hesitated—as if not very certain of the time at which the stay of his cousin was to terminate.

"Until," interrogated the cavalier, with a significant smile, "until when ?"

"Really, sir," said Walter, speaking rather confusedly, " I can't say how long our cousin may choose to remain with us. When she comes to be of age, I dare say her guardian will claim her. Papa is not her guardian."

"Ah ! Master Walter Wade, I'd lay a wager, that before Mistress Lora Lovelace be of age, she'll choose her own guardian—one who will not object to her staying at Bulstrode for the remainder of her life. Ha ! ha ! ha !"

Instead of feeling indignant, the cousin of Lora Lovelace joined in the laugh. There was something in the insinuation that soothed and gratified him.

Conversing in this jocular vein, the two travelers reached the summit of the sloping declivity; and continuing onward, entered upon a wild tract of country known as *Jarret's Heath.*

CHAPTER IX.

"STAND AND DELIVER!"

Jarret's Heath—now Gerrard's Cross Common—was, at the time of which we write, a tract of considerable extent—occupying an elevated *plateau* of the Chiltern Hills, and one of the largest. Commencing at the brow of Red Hill, it extended westward for a distance of many miles—flanked right and left by the romantic valleys of Chalfont and Fulmere.

At that time only the adjoining valleys showed signs of habitation. In the former stood the noble mansion of Chalfont House, with its synonymous village; while on the other side, quaintly embowered amid ancient trees, was the manorial residence of Fulmere. About two miles further to the westward, where the plateau is broken by a series of rounded undulations, stood the magnificent mansion of Temple Bulstrode, the residence of Sir Marmaduke Wade.

The elevated plain, lying between the above-named lordships, bore scarce a trace of human occupancy. Its name, Jarret's Heath, would indicate the condition of its culture. It was a waste—upon which the plough had never broken ground—thickly covered with high gorse and heather. Here and there appeared straggling groves and copses, composed chiefly of black and white birch trees, interspersed with juniper and holly; while on each side towards the valleys, it was flanked by a dense forest of the indigenous beech.

Lengthwise through this waste trended the King's highway—the London and Oxford road—beyond it impinging upon the Park of Bulstrode, and running alongside the latter towards the town of Beaconsfield.

In the traverse of Jarret's Heath the main road was intersected by two others—one passing from the manor house of Fulmere to the village of Chalfont St. Peter's; the other forming the communication between Chalfont and the country towards Stoke and Windsor. These were but bridle, or *packhorse* paths, tracked out irregularly among the trees, and meandering through the gorse wherever it grew thinnest. That running from Stoke to Chalfont was the most frequented; and an old inn—the *Packhorse*—standing upon the Chal font side of the waste, betokened traffic and travel. There was not much of either; and the hostelry bore only a questionable character.

Such as it was, however, it was the only sign of habitation upon Jarret's Heath—if we except the remains of a rude hovel, standing by the side of the London Road, just at the point where, going westward from Red Hill, it debouched upon the waste.

This hovel had been long untenanted. Part of the roof had fallen in; it was a ruin. An open space in front, through which ran the road, might once have been a garden; but it was now overgrown with gorse, and other indigenous shrubbery—only distinguishable from the surrounding thicket by its scantier growth.

It was a singular spot to have been selected as a residence! since it stood more than a mile from any other habitation—the nearest being the suspected hostelry of the Packhorse. Perhaps it was this very remoteness from companionship that had influenced its original owner in the choice of a site for his dwelling.

Whether or no, it had been at best but a miserable tenement. Even with smoke issuing out of its clay chimney, it would have looked cheerless. But in ruins, with its roof falling piecemeal upon the floor, tall weeds standing close by its walls, gorse overgrowing its garden, and black birches clustering thickly around, it presented an aspect of wild and gloomy desolation; the very spot where one might expect to be robbed, or even murdered.

Conversing, as we have described them, the two travelers had arrived near the edge of the opening in which stood this ruined hut. The moon was still shining brightly; and through the break in the brushwood, formed by the clear causeway of the road, they could distinguish—though still at the distance of a mile or more—the tops of the magnificent trees, oaks, elms, and chestnuts, that crowned the undulating ridges of Bulstrode Park. They could even see a portion of the noble mansion of Norman architecture, gleaming red and white, under the silvery sheen of the moonlight.

In ten minutes more Walter Wade would be at home.

It was a pleasant anticipation for the young courtier to indulge in. Home so near, after such a long protracted absence—home, that promised the sweet interchange of natural affection, and—something more.

The cavalier—whose journey extended farther up the road—was about congratulating his companion on the delightful prospect, when a rustling noise, heard to the right of the path, suddenly stopped their coเversation. At the same instant a harsh voice sounded in their ears, pronouncing the significant summons :—

"STAND AND DELIVER ! "

The two travelers had already ridden into open ground, in front of the ruined hut, out of which the voice appeared to proceed. But they had no time to speculate as to whence it came; for on the instant of its utterance, a man was seen rushing forward into the middle of the road, and placing himself in a position to intercept their advance.

His threatening attitude, combined with the mode in which he manipulated a long-handled pike—the point of which he held close to the heads of their horses—left no doubt upon the minds of the travelers, that to stop them was his determination.

Before either could make reply to his challenge it was re-pronounced in the same loud tone; and with a fresh gesture of menace—in which the pike played an important part.

"Stand and deliver ! " interrogated the cavalier, slowly repeating the stereotyped phrase. " That's your wish, is it, my worthy fellow ? "

" It is ! " growled the challenger, " an' be quickish, if ye've any consarn for yer skins."

"Well," continued the cavalier, preserving the most perfect *sang froid,* " you can't say but what we've been quick enough in obeying your first command? You see we have both come to a stand *instanter ?* As for your second, it requires consideration. Before *delivering,* we must know the why and wherefore—above all, to whom we are to unburthen ourselves. You won't object to oblige us with your name—as also your reason of making such a modest request ? "

" Curse yer palaver ! " vociferated the man, with an impatient flourish of the pike. " There be no names gi'en on the road, nor reasons neyther. Yer money, or yer blood ! It be no use yer tryin' to get out o' it. Look thear ! Ye see there be a dozen o' us! What's the good o' resistin' ? Ye're surrounded."

And as he said this, the robber with a sweep of his formidable weapon indicated the circle of shrubbery—near the centre of which the scene was being enacted.

The eyes of the two travelers involuntarily followed the pointing of the pike.

Sure' enough they *were* surrounded. Six or seven fierce-looking men, all apparently armed with the same sort of weapon as that is

the hands of their leader, stood at equal distances from each other
around the opening—their forms half concealed by the trees and
gorse. They were all standing perfectly motionless. Not even their
weapons seemed to stir; and not one of them had as yet spoken, or
stepped forward; though it might have been expected they would
have done so—if only to strengthen the demand made by their
spokesman.

"Keep yer places, comrades!" commanded the latter. "There's
no need for any o' ye to stir. These are civilish gentlemen. We
don't want to hurt them. They bean't agoin to resist."

"But they be," interrupted the cavalier, in a mocking but determined tone; at the same time whipping a pistol from its holster—"*I am*,
to the death; and so too will the gallant youth by my side."

Walter had drawn his rapier—the only weapon he possessed.

"What! yield to a pack of cowardly footpads?" continued the
cavalier, cocking his pistol, as he spoke. "No—sooner——"

"Yer blood be on yer own head then!" shouted the robber, at the
same time rushing forward, and extending his pike, so that its steel
point was almost in contact with the counter of the cavalier's horse.

The moonlight shone full upon the footpad, showing a face of fierce
aspect—features of wild expression—black beard and whiskers—a
thick shock of dark hair matted and tangled—eyes bloodshot, and
gleaming with a lurid light!

It was fortunate for their owner, that the moonlight favored the
identification of those fear-inspiring features—else that moment
might have been his last.

The cavalier had leveled his cocked pistol. His finger was upon
the trigger. In another second the shot would have been discharged;
and in all likelihood his assailant would have been lying lifeless at
the feet of his horse.

All at once the outstretched arm was seen to drop, while at the
same instant from the horseman's lips issued an exclamation of singular import.

"Gregory Garth!" cried he, "you a highwayman—a robber?
About to rob—to murder——"

"My old master!" gasped out the man, suddenly lowering the
point of his pike. "Be it ye? Pardon. O pardon, Sir Henry! I
didn't know 'twar ye."

And as the speaker gave utterance to the last words, he dashed his
weapon to the ground; and stood over it in a cowering and contrite

attidude—not daring to raise his eyes to the face of him who had brought the affair to such an unexpected ending.

" O, Master Henry! " he again cried, " will ye forgie' me? Brute as I ar', 'twould ha' broke me heart to a hurted a hair o' yer head. Curse the crooked luck that's brought me to this! "

For some moments there was a profound silence—unbroken by any voice. Even the companions of the robber appeared to respect the *situation ;* since not one of them moved or made remark of any kind!

Their humiliated chief was himself the first to put a period to this interval of embarrassment.

" O, Master Henry! " he exclaimed, apparently in a paroxysm of chagrin. "Shoot me! Kill me if ye like! Arter what's passed, I doant desarve no better than to die. There's me breast! Send yer bullet through it; an' put an' end to the miserable life of Greg'ry Garth! "

While speaking, the footpad pulled open the flap of his doublet— laying bare before the moonlight a broad sinewy breast, thickly covered with coarse black hair.

Advancing close to the cavalier's horse he presented his bosom, thus exposed—as if to tempt the death he had so strangely solicited. His words, his looks, his whole attitude, proclaimed him to be in earnest.

" Come, come, Garth! " said the cavalier, in a soothing tone—at the same time returning the pistol to its holster.

" You're too good a man—at least you *were once*—to be shot down in that off-hand fashion."

"Ah, *once* Master Henry. Maybe that's true enough. But now I desarve it."

"Spare your self-recrimination, Gregory. Your life like my own, has been a hard one. I know it; and can therefore look more leniently on what has happened now. Let us be thankful it's no worse; and hope it will be the means of bringing about a change for the better."

"It will, Master Henry; it will; I promise that."

" I'm glad to hear you say so; and doubt not but that you'll keep your word. Meanwhile give orders to your trusty followers—by-the-way a well-behaved band—not to molest us. To-morrow mo···· ing there will be travelers along this way, upon whom I have no' slightest objection that both you and yours should practise yo* tuliar avocation; and to your hearts' content. Please desire thos gentlemen to keep their distance. I don't wish them to make any nearer approach—lest I might have the misfortune to find in their ranks some other old acquaintance, who like yourself has fallen from the paths of virtue."

As the footpad stood listening to the request, a singular expression was observed to steal over his fierce features—which gradually gath ered into a broad comical grin.

"Ah! Master Henry," he rejoined. "I may order 'em to obieege ye, but they woant obey. Yer needn't be afeerd o' 'em for all that. Ye may go as near 'em as ye like—*they* ain't a going' to molest ye Ye may run yer sword through an' through 'em, an' never a one o' 'em's goin' to cry out he be hurt."

"Well, they seem patient fellows in all sincerity. But enough— what do you mean, Gregory?"

"That they be nobodies, Master Henry—reg'lar nobodies. They be only dummies—a lot 'o old coats and hats, that's no doubt done good sarvice to their wearers 'fore they fell into the hands o' Gregory Garth—aye, an' they ha' done some good sarvice since—o' a different kind, as ye see."

"So these fellows are scare-crows? I had my suspicions."

"Nothing more nor less, master. Harmless as I once war meself; but since that time—ye know—when the old hall war taken from ye, an' ye went abroad—since then I've been——"

"I don't want to hear your history, Garth," said his former master, interrupting him," at least not *since then*. Let the past be of the past, if you will only promise me to forsake your present profession for the future. Sooner or later it will bring you to the block.

"But what am I to do?" inquired the footpad, in a tone of humble expostulation.

"Do? Anything but what you have been doing. Get work— honest work."

"As I live, I've tried wi' all my might. Ah! Sir Henry, ye've been away from the country a tidyish time. Ye don't know how things be now. To be honest be to starve. Honesty ain't no longer o' any account in England."

"Some day," said the cavalier, as he sat reflecting in his saddle "Some day it may be more valued—and that day not distant Gregory Garth!" he continued, making appeal to the footpad in a more serious and earnest tone of voice, "You have a bold heart and

a strong arm. I know it. I have no doubt, too, that despite th
outlawed life you've been leading, *your sympathies are still on the
right side*. They have reason; for you, too, have suffered in your
way. You know what I mean?"

"I do, Sir Henry, I do," eagerly answered the man. "Ye're right
Brute as I may be, an' robber as I ha' been, I ha' me inclinin' in that
'ere. Ah! it's it that made me what I be!"

"Hear me then," said the cavalier, bending down in his saddle,
and speaking still more confidentially. "The time is not distant—
perhaps nearer than most people think—when a stout heart and a
strong arm—such as yours, Garth—may be usefully employed in a
better occupation, than that you've been following."

"D'ye say so, Sir Henry?"

"I do. So take my advice. Disband these trusty followers of
yours—whose *staunchness* ought to recommend them for better service. Make the best market you can of their cast-off wardrobes.
Retire for a time into private life; and wait till you hear shouted
those sacred words—

"GOD AND THE PEOPLE!"

"Bless ye, Sir Henry!" cried the robber, rushing up; and, with a
show of rude affection, clutching the hand of his former master. "I
hed heard o' yer comin' to live at the old house i' the forest up
thear; but I didn't expect to meet ye i' this way. Ye'll let me come
an' see ye. I promise ye that ye'll never meet me as a robber agin.
This night Greg'ry Garth takes his leave of the road."

"A good resolve!" rejoined the cavalier, warmly returning the
pressure of the outlaw's hand. "I'm glad you have made it. Good-
night, Gregory!" he continued, moving onward along the road.
"Come and see me, whenever you please. Good-night, gentlemen?"
and at the words he lifted the plumed beaver from his head; and, in
a style of mock courtesy, waved the dummies an adieu. "Good-night,
my worthy friends!" he laughingly repeated, as he rode through their
midst. "Don't trouble yourselves to return my salutation. Ha,
ha! ha!"

The young courtier, moving after, joined in the jocular leave-taking
and both merrily rode away—leaving the footpad to the companion
ship of his speechless "pals."

CHAPTER X.

An incident so ludicrous could not fail to tickle the fancy of the young courtier; and bring his risible faculties into full play. It produced this effect; and to such a degree, that for some minutes he could do nothing but laugh—loud enough to have been heard to the remotest confines of the Heath.

"I shouldn't wonder," said he, recalling to mind the contents of his sister's letter, "not a bit should I wonder if this fellow be the same who stopped the lady's coach. You've heard of it?"

"I have," laughingly replied the cavalier. "No doubt, Gregory Garth and the coach-robber you speak of are one and the same individual."

"Ha! ha! ha! to think of the six attendants!—there was that number, I believe, escorting the coach—to think of all six running away, and from one man!"

"You forget the band. Ha! ha! ha! It is to be presumed, that Gregory had six scare-crows rigged up for that occasion also. Truer men, by my troth, than the cavaliers who accompanied the lady. Ha! ha! But for the immorality of the act it's an artifice worthy of my old instructor in the art of *venerie*. After all, I should have expected better of the ex-forester than finding him thus transformed into a footpad. Poor devil! who knows what may have been his trials and temptations? There are wrongs daily done upon England's people, in the name—aye, and with the knowledge—of England's king that would make a criminal of the meekest Christian; and Gregory Garth was never particularly distinguished for the virtue of meekness. Something may have been done to madden and to drive him to this desperate life. I shall know anon."

"One thing in his favor," suggested the young courtier, who notwithstanding the rude introduction, appeared to be favorably inclined towards the footpad. "He did not ill-treat the lady, though left all alone with her. True he stripped her of her jewelry; but beyond that he behaved gently enough. I have just heard the sequel of the story, as I came through Uxbridge. Ha! ha! odd as the rest of the affair. It appears that before leaving her, he caught one of her runaway attendants; forced him back upon the box; and, putting the reins and whip into the varlet's hands, compelled him to continue the journey."

"All as you say, Master Wade I heard the same story myself; though little suspecting that the facetious footpad was my old hench-man Gregory Garth. That part of his performance was natural enough. The rogue had always a dash of gallantry in his compo-sition. I'm pleased to think it's not all gone out of him."

"He appears very repentant after——"

"After having been within an inch of taking the life of one who —rather should I say of losing his own. It was a lucky turn that brought the moonlight on that bearded visage of his; else he might now have been lying in the middle of the road, silent as his scare-crow companions. By my troth! I should have felt sorry to have been his executioner. I am glad it has turned out as it has— more especially since he has promised, if not actual repentance, at least some sort of reformation. It may not be too late. There's good in him—or was—if his evil courses have not caused its complete eradication. Well! I am likely to see him soon; when I shall submit his soul to the test, and find whether there is still in it enough of the old honesty to give hope of his regeneration. The entrance to your father's Park?"

The speaker nodded towards a sombre pile of ivy-grown mason work—in the centre of which could be seen a massive gate, its serried rails just discernible under the tall chestnuts, that in double row shadowed the avenue beyond.

The heir of Bulstrode did not need to be thus reminded. Three years of absence had not effaced from his memory the topographic details of scenes so much loved, so long enjoyed. Well remembered he the ways that led towards the paternal mansion; and already, ere his fellow traveler ceased speaking, he had pulled up opposite the oft-used entrance.

"My journey extends farther up the road," continued the cavalier, without having made more than a momentary pause in his speech. "I am sorry, Master Wade, to lose your agreeable company; but we must part."

"Not, sir," said Walter, looking earnestly towards him, "not I trust, till you have given me an opportunity of thanking you for the service you have rendered me. But for your companionship, the adventure, as well as my day's journey, might have had a different termination. I should certainly have been plundered—perhaps impaled upon the long pike of your quondam servitor. Thanks to you, that I am to reach home in safety. I hope, therefore, you will not object to my knowing the name of one, who has done me such an essential service."

"I have but slight claim to your gratitude," replied the cavalier. "In truth not any, Master Wade. By the merest accident have we been thrown together as *compagnons de voyage.*"

"Your modesty, sir," rejoined the young courtier—as he spoke bending gracefully towards his companion, "claims my admiration equally with that courage, of which I have now witnessed more than one display. But you cannot hinder me from feeling gratitude; nor yet from expressing it. If you deny me the privilege of knowing your name, I can at least tell my friends how much I am indebted to *Sir Henry the Unknown.*"

"*Sir* Henry! Ah! Garth styled me so. The old forester is fond of bestowing titles. My father was so called; and honest Gregory, in his lack of heraldic skill, thinks the title must be hereditary. It is not so, however, I have not received the honor of knighthood from the sword of sacred majesty. What's more, it's not likely I ever shall. Ha! ha!"

The words that concluded this speech—as well as the laugh that followed—were uttered in a tone of defiant bitterness; as if the speaker held such loyal honors in but slight estimation.

The young courtier thus balked in obtaining the name of his protector, remained for a moment without making rejoinder. He was thinking whether in the matter of names he could not claim a fair exchange of confidence—since he had freely given his own,—when the cavalier, as if divining his thoughts, again accosted him.

"Pardon me," resumed the latter, in a tone of apology. "Pardon me, Master Wade, for my apparent want of courtesy. You honor me by asking my name; and, since you have treated me so frankly, I have neither the right nor the wish to conceal it from you. It is plain Henry Holtspur—not *Sir* Henry, as you have just heard me designated. Furthermore, Master Wade; if you know anything of a rather dilapidated dwelling, yclept 'Stone Dean'—situated in the heart of the forest, some three miles from here—and think you could find your way thither, I can promise you a welcome, a mouthful or venison, a cup of Canary to wash it down; and—not much more]

fear. During most mornings I am at home, if you will take your
chance of riding over."

"Nay, you must visit me first," rejoined Walter. "I should ask
you in now; but for the lateness of the hour. I fear our people have
retired for the night. You will come again; and permit me to intro
duce you to my father. I am sure he would like to thank you for the
service you have done me; and my sister Marion too."

A thrill of sweet secret pleasure shot through the heart of Henry
Holtspur, as he listened to the last words. Thanks from Marion!
A thought from her—even though it were but given in gratitude!

Love! Love! sweet art thou in the enjoyment; but far more delicious is the dream of thy anticipation!

Had the young courtier been closely observing, he might, at that
moment, have detected on the countenance of Henry Holtspur, a peculiar expression—one which he appeared to be endeavoring to conceal.

The brother of his mistress is the last man to whom a lover cares
to confide the secret of his bosom. It may not be a welcome tale—
even when the fortunes are equal, the introduction *en règle*, and the
intentions honorable. But if in any of these circumstances there
chance to be informality, then becomes the brother the *bête noire* of
the situation.

Was some thought of this kind causing Henry Holtspur a peculiar
emotion—prompting him to repress or conceal it from the brother of
Marion Wade? On returning thanks for the promised introduction,
why did he speak with an air of embarrassment? Why upon his
countenance, of open manly character, was there an expression almost
furtive?

The young courtier, without taking note of these circumstances,
continued to urge his request.

"Well—you promise to come?"

"Some time—with pleasure."

"Nay, Master Holspur, 'some time' is too indefinite; but, indeed,
so has been my invitation. I shall alter it. You will come to-morrow? Father gives a *fête* in our park. 'Tis my birthday; and the
sports, I believe, have been arranged on an extensive scale. Say, you
will be one of our guests?"

"With all my heart, Master Wade. I shall be most happy."

After exchanging a mutual good-night, the two travelers parted—
Walter entered the gate of the park—while the cavalier continued
along the highway, that ran parallel to its palings.

CHAPTER XI.

A QUEER VALEDICTORY.

After seeing the two travelers ride off, the disappointed footpad stood listening, till the hoofstrokes of their horses died upon the distant road.

Then flinging himself upon a bank of earth; and having assumed a sitting posture—with his elbows resting upon his knees; and his bearded chin reposing between the palms of his hands—he remained for some moments silent as the Sphinx, and equally motionless.

His features betrayed a strange compound of expressions—not to be interpreted by any one ignorant of his history, or of the adventure that had just transpired. The shadow of a contrite sadness was visible upon his brow; while in his dark grey eye could be detected a twinkle of chagrin—as he thought of the pair of purses so unexpectedly extricated from his grasp.

Plainly was a struggle passing within his bosom. Conscience and cupidity had quarreled—their first outfall for a long period of time. The contending emotions prevented speech; and, it is superfluous to say, his companions respected his silence.

In the countenance of Gregory Garth, despite his criminal calling —even in his worst moments—there were lines indicative of honesty. As he sat by the roadside—that roadside near which he had so often skulked—with the moon shining full upon his face, these lines gradually became more distinctly defined; until the criminal caste completely disappeared from his features, leaving only in in its place an expression of profound melancholy. But for the *mise en scène*, and the *dramatis personæ* surrounding him, any one passing at the moment might have mistaken him for an honest man, suffering from some grave and recent misfortune.

But as no one passed, he was left free to indulge, both in his sorrow and his silence.

At length the latter came to an end. The voice of the penitent footpad—no longer in the stern accents of menace and command but in soft and subdued tones—once more interrupted the stillness of the night

" Oh, lor—oh, lor! " muttered he, " who'd a believed I shud hr holden my pike to the breast o' Master Henry? Niver a thought hed I to use it. Only bluster to make 'em yield up but he'll think as how I intended it all the same. Oh, lor—oh, lor! he'll niver forgive me; well, it can't a be holp now; an' here go to keep the promise I've made him. No more touchin' o' purses, or riflin o' fine ladies on this road. That game be all over."

For a moment the dark shadow upon his brow appeared to partake slightly of chagrin—as if there still lingered some regret for the promise he had made; and the step he was about to take. The strife between conscience and cupidity seemed not yet definitively decided.

There was another interval of silence, and then came the decision. It was in favor of virtue. Conscience had triumphed.

" I'll keep me word to him," cried he, springing to his feet, as if to give emphasis to the resolve. " I'll keep it, if I shud starve! "

" Disband! " he continued addressing himself to the silent circle, and speaking in a tone of mock command. " Disband! ye beggars! Yer cap'n, Greg'ry Garth, ha'n't no longer any need o' yer sarvices. Dang it, meeats! " added he, still preserving his tone of mock seriousness, " I be sorry to part wi' ye. Ye've been as true as steel to me; an' ne'er a' angry word 'as iver passed atween us. Well it can't be holp, boys—that it can't. The best o' friends must part, some time or other; but afore we separates, I'm a goin' to purvide for one an' all on ye. I've got a friend over theer in Uxbridge, who keeps a biggish trade goin' on—they call it panbrokin'. It's a money-makin' bizness. I dare say he can find places for all o' ye. Ye be sure o' doin' well wi' him. Ye'll be in good company; wi' plenty o' goold an' jewelltry all w' round ye. Don't be afeerd o' what'll happen to ye. I'll take duppleickets for yer seeurity; so that in case o' me needin' ye again——"

At this crisis the fantastic valedictory of the retiring robber was brought to a sudden termination, by his hearing a sound—similar to those for which his ear had been but too well trained to listen. It was the footfall of a horse, denoting the approach of a horseman—a traveler. It was neither of those who had just passed over the Heath; since it came from the direction opposite to that in which they had gone—up the road from Redhill.

There was but one horseman—as the hoof-stroke indicated. From the same index it could be told, that he was coming on at a slow pace —a walk in fact—as if ignorant of the road, or afraid of proceeding

at a rapid rate along a path which was far from being a smooth one.
On hearing the hoof-stroke, Gregory Garth instinctively, as instantly, desisted from his farcical apostrophe; and, without offering the
slightest apology to his well-behaved auditors, turned his face away
from them, and stood listening.

"A single horseman?" muttered he to himself, "crawlin' along at
snail pace? A farmer maby, who's tuk a drap too much at the Saracen's Head, an' 's fallen asleep in his seddle? Now I think o't, it
be market day in that thear town o' Uxbridge."

The instincts of the footpad—which had for the moment yielded
before the moral shock of the humiliating encounter with his old
master—began to resume dominion over him.

"Wonder," continued he, in a muttered tone—"wonder if the
chaw-bacon ha' got any cash 'bout him? Or heve he been an' drunk
it all at the inn? Pish! what do it matter whether he heve or no?
Ha'nt I gone an' promised Master Henry 'twould be my last night?
Dang it! I must keep my word."

"Stay!" he continued, after reflecting a moment. "I said that it
shud be my last *night?* That's 'zactly what ye sayed, an' nothin'
else, Greg'ry Garth! It wouldn't be breakin' no promise if I——
"The night be yooung yet! 'Taint much arter eleven o' the clock?
I've just herd Chaffont bells strikin' *eleven.* A night arn't over till
twelve. That's the 'law o' the land.'

"What's the use o'talkin'? Things can't be wuss wi' me than
they is already. I've stole the sheep; an' if I'm to swing for't, I
moat as well goo in for the hul flock. After all, Master Henry ha'nt
promised to *keep* me; an' I may starve for me honest intentions. I
ha'nt enough silver left to kiver a spittle wi'; an' as for these rags,
they ar'nt goin' to fetch me a fortune. Dash it! I'll stop chaw-bacon, an' see whether he ha'n't been a sellin' his beests.

"Keep yeer places, lads!" continued he, turning once more to his
dummies; and addressing them as if he really believed them to be
"lads." "Keep yeer places; an' behave jest the same as if nuthin' 'd
been sayed about our seperatin'!"

Concluding his speech with this cautionary peroration, the footpad
glided back under the shadow of the hovel; and silently placed himself in a position to pounce upon the unwary wayfarer, whose ill luck
was conducting him to the crossing of Jaret's Heath at that late hour
of the night.

CHAPTER XII.

STRIPPING A COURTIER.

The robber had not long to wait for his victim. The necessary preparations for receiving the latter occupied some time—enough for the slow-paced traveler to get forward upon the ground; which he succeeded in doing, just as Gregory Garth had secured himself an ambush, within the shadow of the hovel. There stood he, in the at· titude of a hound in leash, straining upon the spring.

When the horseman, emerging from under the arcade of the trees, rode out into the open ground, and the moonlight fell upon him and his horse, the footpad was slightly taken by surprise. Instead of a farmer, fuddled with cheap tipple obtained at the Saracen's Head, Garth saw before him an elegant cavalier, mounted upon a smoking but handsome steed, and dressed in a full suit of shining satin!

Though surprised, Gregory was neither dismayed, nor disconcerted. On the contrary, he was all the better satisfied at seeing—in the place of a drunken clod-hopper, perchance with an empty wallet—a gentleman whose appearance gave every promise of a plethoric purse; and one, also, whose aspect declared to the practiced eye of the footpad, that compelling him to part with it, would be an achievement neither difficult nor dangerous.

Without losing an instant, after making this observation, the robber rushed out from under the shadow of the hut; and, just as he had hailed the two horsemen half an hour before, did he salute the satin-clad cavalier.

Very different, however, was the response which he now received in return to the stereotyped demand, "Stand and deliver!" Such travelers as the black horseman were rare upon the road; and he of the smoking steed, and satin vestments, instead of drawing a pistol from his holsters, or a sword from its sheath, threw up both hands in token of surrender; and, in a trembling voice, piteously appealed for mercy.

"Hang it, master!" cried Garth, still keeping his pike pointed at the breast of the frightened traveler, "doant be so skeeart! they woan't

hurt ye, man. Nee'r a one o'em's goin' to lay a finger on ye--that
be, if ye doant make a fool o' yerself by showin' resistance. Keep
yeer ground, boys! The gentleman hain't no intention to gie
trouble."

"No—I assure you, no!" eagerly ejaculated the traveler. "I
mean no harm to anybody. Believe me, friends! I don't, indeed
You're welcome to what money I've got. It isn't much. I'm only
a poor messenger of the king."

"A messenger o' the king!" echoed the captain of the robbers,
showing a new interest in the announcement.

"An', if I may ask the quest'n," proceeded he, drawing nearer to
the traveler, and rudely clutching hold of his bridle-rein, "whither
be ye bound, good master?"

"Oh sir," replied the trembling courtier, "I am glad I've met
with some one who, perhaps, can tell me the way. I am the bearer
of a message from his gracious Majesty to Captain Scarthe, of the
King's Cuirassiers; who is, or should be, by this time, quartered
with Sir Marmaduke Wade of Bulstrode Park—somewhere in this
part of the county of Buckingham."

"Ho, ho!" muttered Gregory Garth, speaking to himself, "message from his majesty to Captain Scarthe!—Sir Marmaduke Wade!
Bulstrode Park! What the ole Nick be all this about?"

"You know Sir Marmaduke Wade, do you not, good friend?"

"Well, Master Silk-and-Satin," scornfully drawled the footpad,
"without having the pleasure o' knowin' ye, or the honor o' bein'
your good friend eyther, I think as how I mout say, that I does know
somethin' o' that very gentleman, Sir Marm'duke Wade; though it
be news to me that there be such an individual as Captain Scarthe,
eyther in the county o' Bucks, or in the kingdom o' England—to say
nothin' o' a troop of King's Kewrassers bein' quartered at Bulstrode
Park. All o' that there be Greek to Greg'ry Garth."

"Good friend! I assure you it's nothing but the truth. Captain
Scarthe and his troop have certainly arrived at Bulstrode Park by
this time; and if you will only conduct me thither——"

"Bah! that arn't my bizness. Conduct yerself. Bulstrode Park
ain't a step from here. As to Captain Scarthe, or the King's Kewrassers, I shouldn't know eyther one nor t'other from a side o' sole
leather. If ye've got e'er a message, yer can hand it over to me, and
along' wi' it whatever loose cash ye be carryin' on yer fine-clad carcass. Fork out!"

"Oh! sir; to my money you're welcome—my watch also, and the chain. But as you love our good king, let me ride on my errand, on which he has despatched me!"

"Maybe I *don't* love 'our good king,' so much as ye think for, ye spangled flunky! Come, out wi' all ye've got, or these fellows 'll strip ye to the skin. Never mind, boys! Keep yer ground; he an't agoin' to be troublesome."

"No, no, good friends. I promise you I shall not. I yield up everything. Here's my purse. For your sakes I'm sorry there's no more in it. Here's my watch. I had it a present from our most gracious queen. You see, sir, it's very valuable!"

The footpad eagerly clutched the time-piece; and, holding it between his great horny fingers, examined it under the light of the moon.

"It must be valleyable," said he, turning it over and over. "It appears to be kivered all over wi' presious stones. A presant from the queen,'ye say?"

"I had it from her majesty's own hands."

"Dang her for a French——! This be the way she spends our English money. She be a bigger robber than Greg'ry Garth—that she be—an' ye can tell her I said so, the next time ye ha' the chance o' palaverin' to her. Go on! Emp'y yer pockets o' everythin'."

"I've only this penknife; these tablets, and pencil—that's all, I assure you."

"What's that glitterin' thing," asked the footpad, pointing to something the courtier appeared anxious to conceal, "as hangs about yer neck? Let's have a squint at it?

"That, sir, that is a—a—a locket."

"A locket; what be that?"

"Well, it's—it's——"

"It be wounderful like a bit o' a watch. What be inside o' it?"

"Nothing."

"Nothin'. Then what do you carry it for?"

"Oh, there is something inside; nothing of value, however; it's only a lock of hair."

"Only hair? A lovelock I s'pose? Well, that arn't o'much valley sure enough—leastwise to me it arn't—and yer may keep the hair. But I'll trouble ye for the case. It look like it mout pawn for somethin'. Quick off wi' it."

The terrified courtier instantly complied with the demand—in his fright not even taking advantage of the permission granted him to preserve the precious love token; but delivering both lock and locket into the outstretched fingers of the footpad.

"Oh, sir," said he, in a supplicating tone, " that is everything— everything ! "

"No, it arn't," gruffly returned the robber, " ye've got a niceish doublet thear—satin spick-span—trunks to match ; boots an' spurs o' the first quality ; a tidyish hat and feathers ; an' a sharpish toad-sticker by yer side. I doant partickler want any o' these things for meself; but I've got a relation that I'd like to make 'em a present to. So, strip ! "

"What, sir ! would you send me naked on my errand ? You for-get that I'm the bearer of a message from the king ? "

"No, daang me if I do ; an' daang the king, too ! That ere's potery for ye. I've heerd ye be fond o' it at Court. I like prose better ; an' my prose be, dismount an' strip."

Notwithstanding the tone of raillery the footpad was pleased to express himself, the unfortunate courtier saw that he was all the while in serious earnest, and that there would be danger in resisting his demands.

Spite of his reluctance, therefore, he was compelled to slide down from his saddle, and disrobe himself in the middle of the road.

Not until he stood nearly stark naked, did the relentless robber let him desist—leaving to him little else than his shirt and stockings !

"Oh, sir ! you will not mount me thus ? " said the wretched man, appealing with upheld hands to the footpad. "Surely you will not send me in this guise—the bearer of a royal message ? What a figure I should cut on horseback, without my boots—without my hat or doublet—without——"

"Stash yer palaver!" cried Garth, who was busied making the cast-off clothes into a bundle. "Who said ye war goin' to cut a figger a-horseback ! Whar's yer horse, I sh'd like to know ! "

The courtier gave a doubting nod towards the steed.

"Oh," responded the footpad, coolly continuing his task, " most a been yer horse ten minutes agone. He is myen now. I have been afoot long enough, while ye an' yourn ha' been ridin'. It be my time to mount for a bit. That's only fair, turn an' turn, arn't it ? "

The dismounted messenger made no reply. Though surprise and terror had by this time well nigh deprived him of his senses, he had enough left to admonish him that all remonstrance would be idle. He said nothing, therefore; but stood with shivering frame and teeth

shattering like castanets; for it chanced to be one of those chill au
tumnal nights, when the cold is felt almost as sensibly as in December

The footpad took no further notice of him, until he had completed
the binding of the bundle. Then straightening himself up, face to
face with his victim, he surveyed him from head to foot with a half
quizzical, half serious look.

The latter at length predominated—as if some suspicious thought
had come uppermost in his mind.

"Cowardly as ye be, ye king's minion," said he, addressing the
trembling messenger in a tone of scornful bitterness, "thear mout be
cunnin' an' mischief in ye. I'll take care that ye doant goo furder
this night. Come along into the house here! Ye woan't object to
that—seein' as ye're so starved-like outside. Come along!"

And without waiting for either the assent or refusal of the individual thus solicited, the robber seized him by the wrist; and half led,
half dragged him over the threshold of the hovel.

Once inside the ruin, he proceeded to bind his unresisting victim
with cords, which he had taken in along with him. He had plenty
of light for his purpose; for a portion of the roof had fallen in, and
the moonlight shone brightly upon the thatch-strewn floor.

Expert in the handling of ropes, his task was soon performed; and
in a few minutes the king's messenger stood with his arms bound
behind his back, and his ancles lashed as tightly together as if he had
been a dangerous felon!

"Now," said the robber, after securing the last loop, apparently
to his satisfaction, "ye woan't come loose till somebody lets ye; an'
that ar'n't going to be me. I ha'n't no wish to be cruel to ye—tho'
ye are a king's flunkey, an' as ye'll be easier lying down than stannin' up I'll put ye i' that position."

As he said this, he let go his hold; and permitted the unfortunate
man to fall heavily on the floor.

"Lie thear, Master Messenger, till somebody lifts ye. I'll see to
the deliverin' o' yer message. Good Night!"

And with a mocking laugh, Gregory Garth strode back over the
threshold—leaving the astounded traveler to reflections that were
neither very lucid nor very pleasant.

After passing out of the hut, the footpad hastened to take his departure from the spot.

He led the steed of the messenger out into the middle of the road,
and tied the bundle he had made to the cantle of the saddle. He

then glided to the near side of the horse; and caught hold of the withers—as if about to mount.

Something, however, caused him to hesitate; and an interval elapsed, without his making any effort to get into the saddle.

"Dang it, old partners!" cried he, at length—addressing himself to his band of dummies, whom he had been for some time neglecting —"'twon't do for us to part this fashion. If Greg'ry Garth are promoted to be a highwayman, he ar'n't going to look down on his pals o' the path. No! Ye shall go 'long wi' me, one an' all. Though the hul o' ye put thegither ar'n't worth this shinin' ticker I've got in my fob, for all that I can make better use o' ye, than leavin' ye here to scare the crows o' Jarret's Heath. Come along, my boys! Ise boun' this stout charger from the royal mews be able to carry the hul on us, an' not think it much o' a looad neyther. I'll find room for all o' ye—some on the crupper, an' the rest on the withers. Come along, then!"

Without waiting for any reply to his proposal, he glided round the edge of the opening, and rapidly dismantling the dummies one after the other, he returned toward the horse with their ravished vestments.

Hanging the "old clo'" across both croup and withers—and there attaching them by strings—he at length climbed into the saddle lately occupied by the king's messenger, and rode gleefully away.

Just as he had cleared the crossing of the road, the clock of Chalfont St. Peter's tolled the hour of midnight.

"Exact twelve!" exclaimed he, in a tone of congratulation. "Well, 'twur a close shave; but I've kep my word to Master Henry! If I hed broke that, I could niver a looked him i' the face agin. Ha! Hear them old church bells! How sweet they sound on the air o' the night! They' mind me o' the time when I wur a innocent child. Ring on! ring on! ye bells o' Peter's Chaffont! Ring on, an' tell the world that Greg'ry Garth is biddin' good-by to the road!"

CHAPTER XIII.

THE FÊTE CHAMPÊTRE.

Were the Chiltern hills stripped of the timber, to this day screening a considerable portion of their surface, they would present a striking resemblance to those portions of the great North American steppe; known in the trapper parlance as "rolling prairies." With equal truthfulness might they be likened to the ocean, after a great storm; when the waves no longer carry their foaming crests; and the undulations of the swell have, to a certain extent, lost their parallelism. If you can fancy the liquid element then suddenly transformed into solid earth, you will have a good idea of the shape of the Chilterns.

From time immemorial have these hills enjoyed a peculiar reputation. In the forward march of England's agriculture, it was long ere their sterile soil tempted the touch of the plough; and even at this hour vast tracts of their surface lie unreclaimed in "commons" covered with heath, furze, or forests of beech-wood.

At various periods of our history, their fame has not been of the fairest. The wild woods, while giving shelter to the noble stag, and other creatures of the chase, also served as a choice retreat for the outlaw and the robber; and in past times, it became necessary to appoint a "steward or warden," with a body of armed attendants, to give safe conduct to the traveler passing through their limits. Hence the origin of that noted office—now happily a sinecure; though, unhappily, not the only sinecure of like obsolete utility in this grievously taxed land.

Near the eastern verge of the Chiltern country, is situated the noble park of Bulstrode. It is one of the most ancient enclosures in England; older than the invasion of the Norman; perhaps as old as the evacuation of the Roman. In the former epoch it was the scene of strife—as the remains of a Saxon encampment lying within its limits, with a singular legend attached—will testify.

Extending over an area of a thousand acres, there is scarce a rood of Bulstrode Park that could be called level ground—the camp enclosure, already mentioned, forming the single exception. The

surface exhibits a series of smooth rounded hills, and undulating
ridges, separated from each other by deep valley-like ravines—the·
concavities of the latter so resembling the convexities of the former,
as to suggest the idea that the hills have been scooped out of the
valleys; and placed in an inverted position beside them. The park,
itself, offers a fair specimen of the scenery of the Chilterns—the
ocean swell suddenly brought to a stand; the waves, and the
"troughs" between, having lost their parallelism. The valleys traverse in different directions, here running into each other; there
shallowing upward, or ending abruptly in deep romantic dells, thickly
copsed with hawthorn, holly, or hazel—the favorite haunts of the
nightingale. The ridges join each other in a similar fashion; or rise
into isolated hills, so smoothly coped as to seem artificial. Belts of
shrubbery; and clumps of gigantic trees—elm, oak, beech, and
chestnut—mottle the slopes, or crown their summits; while the
spaces between exhibit a sward of that vivid verdure—only to be
seen in the pastures and parks of England. Such was Bulstrode
Park in the seventeenth century; such with but slight changes, is it
at the present day—a worthy residence for the noblest family in the
land.

● ● ● ● ● ● ● ● ● ● ●

It is the morning of the fête arranged by Sir Marmaduke Wade
—to celebrate the anniversary of his son's birthday; and, at the
same time, to commemorate his return to the paternal mansion.

The red aurora of an autumnal morning has given promise of a
brilliant day; and as if to keep that promise, a golden sun, already
some degrees above the horizon, is gradually mounting into a canopy
of cloudless blue.

IIis beams, striking obliquely through the foliage of the forest, fall
with a subdued light upon the earth; but in the more open undulations of the park they have already kissed the dew from the grass;
and the verdant turf seems to invite the footstep—like some vast
carpet spread over the arena of the expected sports.

It is evident that the invitation of Sir Marmaduke had been exten-
sively circulated; and accepted. On every road and path tending in
the direction of his residence, and from a distance of many miles,
groups of rustics, in their gayest holiday dresses, have been seen from
an early hour in the morning, proceeding towards the scene of the fête
—old and young; fair and dark; comely and common-looking, all
equally joyous and gleeful.

Within the lines of the old Saxon encampment a large company has
assembled. There are thousands in all—some roaming over the
ground; some seated under shady trees, on the summit of the turf-
grown moat. Here and there may be seen large numbers forming a
"ring"—the spectators of some sport that is progressing in their
midst.

Of sports, there are many kinds carried on at the same time. Here
is played the game of "balloon;" a huge leathern ball, inflated with
hot air, and bandied about amidst a circle of players—the game being to keep the ball passing from one to the other.

There, you may see another party engaged in a game of "bowls,"
fashionable as the favorite of royalty; and further on, a crowd clustered around a contest of "single-stick," where two stout fellows are
cudgeling one another, as if determined on a mutual cracking of skulls
—a feat however, not so easy of accomplishment.

Not far off, you may behold the gentler sport of "kiss in the ring,"
where blue-eyed Saxon girls are pursued by their rustic beaux, and
easily overtaken.

At other places, you may witness a wrestling match; a game of
foot-ball, or quoits; with "pitching the stone;" racing; leaping; and
vaulting.

At a short distance off, and outside the encampment, may be seen
an *al fresco* kitchen, on an extensive scale; where the servants of Sir
Marmaduke are engaged in roasting immense *barons* of beef; and huge
hogs cleft lengthwise. An hour or two later, and this spot will be
the most attractive of all.

Not alone does the peasant world appear in the park of Sir Marmaduke Wade. Cavaliers picturesquely attired, in the splendid costumes
of the time, along with high-born dames, are seen standing in groups
over the ground. Some are spectators of the sports; though not a
few of both sexes occasionally take part in them. The *fête champêtre*
is a fashionable mode of amusement, where rank is, for the time, surrendered to the desire for simple enjoyment; and it is not altogether
outre for the mistress of the mansion to mingle with her maidens in
the "out-door race;" nor the squire to take a hand at "single-stick,'
or "bowls," with his rustic retainers.

Even royalty, in those days, was accustomed to such condescension.

Such was the gay spectacle exhibited in the park of Sir Marmaduke
Wade; to celebrate the anniversary of that happy day, that had given
him a son and heir.

CHAPTER XIV.

FORWARD—MARCH.

The bells of Uxbridge were tolling the hour of noon. Scarthe's cuirassiers were still by the roadside inn, though in full armor; and each trooper standing by the side of his horse, ready to take saddle.

It was a late hour to begin their march; but they had been detained. The freshly rasped hoofs of the horses might declare the cause of the detention. The forges of Uxbridge had been called into requisition for the shoeing of the troop.

There was no special need for haste. They had not far to go; and, the duty upon which they were bent, could be entered into at any hour. At twelve they were all ready for the route.

"To horse!" was uttered in the usual abrupt tone of command, and at the same instant the two officers were seen issuing from the doorway of the inn.

The clattering of the steel, as the cuirassiers sprang to their saddles, could be heard on the calm air of the autumn noon, to the distance of a mile. The shop-keepers of Uxbridge heard it; and were only too glad when told its interpretation. All night long, Scarthe's royal swashbucklers had been swaggering through the streets; disturbing the tranquillity of their town, and leaving many a score unsettled.

No wonder they rejoiced, when that clinking of sabres, and clashing of *cuirasses*, declared the departure of Captain Scarthe and his following from the hostelry of the Saracen's Head.

Their men having mounted, the two officers betook themselves to their saddles, though with less alertness. The cornet seemed to have a difficulty in finding his stirrup; and, after he had succeeded in getting into his seat, it appeared an open question whether he should be able to keep it. Stubbs was intoxicated.

His superior officer was affected in a similar fashion; though to a less degree. At all events, he did not show his tipsiness so palpably. He was able to mount into the saddle, without the hand of a helper; and when there, he could hold himself upright. Habit may have given him this superiority over his comrade; for Scarthe was an old soldier, and Stubbs was not.

The carouse of the preceding night had commenced at the roadside 'un—early in one evening.

The incident that had there occurred—not of the most comforting nature, either to Scarthe or his subaltern—had stimulated them to continue at their cups—only transferring the scene to the inns of Uxbridge. A stray cavalier or two, picked up in the town, had furnished them with the right sort of associates for a midnight frolic; and it was not till the blue light of morn was breaking over the meadows of Colne, that the wearied roisterers staggered over the old bridge; and returned to their temporary quarters.

While the horses of the troop were in the hands of the farriers, the two officers had passed an hour or two, tossing upon a brace of the best beds the inn afforded; and it was close upon twelve at noon when Scarthe awoke, and called for a cup of burnt sack to steady his nerves —quivering after the night's carouse.

A slight breakfast sufficed for both captain and cornet. This despatched, they had ordered the troop to horse; and were about to continue their march.

"Comrades!" cried Scarthe, addressing himself to his followers, as soon as he felt fairly fixed in the saddle. "We've been spending the night in a nest of rebels. This Uxbridge is a town of traitors— Quakers, Dissenters, and Puritans—alike disloyal knaves."

"They are, by Gec-gec-ged?" hiccuped Stubbs, trying to keep himself upright on his horse.

"They are; you speak true, captain—they all'er you say," chorussed several of the troopers, who had come away without settling their scores.

"Then let them go to the devil!" muttered Scarthe, becoming alike regardless of Uxbridge and its interests. "Let's look to what's before. No—not that. First what's behind us. No pretty girls in the inn here. Ah! that's a pity. Never mind the women, so long as there's wine. Hillo, old Boniface! Once more set your taps a-flowing. What will you drink, vagabonds? Beer?"

"Ay, ay—anything you like, noble captain."

"Beer, Boniface; and for me more sack. What say you, Stubbs?"

"Sack, sa-a-ck!" stammered the cornet. "Burnt sa-a-ck. Nothing like it, by Ge-ged!"

"Who pays?" inquired the landlord, evidently under some apprehension as to the probability of this ultimate order being for cash.

"Pays, knave!" shouted Scarthe, pulling a gold piece from his

doublet, and shying it in the landlord's face. "Do you take the king's
cuirassiers for highway robbers? The wine—the wine! Quick with
it, or I'll draw your corks with the point of my sword."

With the numerous staff, which an inn in those times could afford
to maintain; both the beer, and the more generous beverage, were
soon within reach of the lips of those who intended to partake of them
The national drink was brought first; but out of deference to their
officers, the men refrained from partaking of it, till the sack was poured
into their cups.

Scarthe seized the goblet presented to him; and, raising it aloft,
called out :—

"The King!"

"The King, by Ge-ged!" seconded Stubbs.

"The King—the king!" vociferated the half hundred voices of their
followers—the bystanders echoing the phrase only in faint murmur
ing.

"Goblets to the ground!" commanded the captain—at the same
time tossing his own into the middle of the road.

The action was imitated by every man in the troop—each throwing
away his empty vessel, till the pavement was thickly strewn with
pots of shining pewter.

"Forward—ma-r-ch!" cried Scarthe, giving the spur to his charger; and with a mad captain at their head, and a maudlin cornet in
the rear, the cuirassiers filed out from the inn; and took the road in
the direction of Red-hill.

Despite the wine within him, the captain of the cuirassiers was, at
the moment, in a frame of mind anything but contented. One of his
reasons for having drunk so deeply, was to drown the recollection—
yet rankling in his bosom—of the insult he fancied himself to have
suffered on the preceding night; and which he further fancied to have
lowered him in the estimation of his followers. Indeed, he knew this
to be the case; for as he rode onward at the head of his troop, his
whole thoughts were given to the *black horseman*; and the mode by
which he might revenge himself on that mysterious individual.

Scarthe was on the way to country quarters—near which he had
been told, the black horseman had his home—and he comforted himself with the thought, that should these prove dull, he would find
amusement in the accomplishment of some scheme, by which his vengeance might be satisfied.

Could his eye at that moment have penetrated the screen of foliage rising above the crest of Red-hill, he might have seen behind it the man he meant to injure—mounted on that sable steed from which he derived his *sobriquet*. He might have seen him suddenly wheel back from the bushes, and gallop off in the direction in which he and his cuirassiers were marching—towards Bulstrode Park—the residence of Sir Marmaduke Wade.

Though Scarthe saw not this, his mid-day march was not performed without his meeting with an incident—one worth recording, even for its singularity; though it was otherwise of significant interest to the cuirassier captain.

In front of a dilapidated hovel upon Jarret's Heath, both he and his troop were brought to a sudden stand, on hearing a strange noise which appeared to proceed from the ruin.   It was a groan—or rather a series of groans—now and then varied by a sharp scream.

On entering the hut, the cause of this singular *fracas* was at once discovered: a man lying upon the floor—stripped to his shirt, and bound hand and foot !   This semi-nude individual informed them, that he had just awakened from a horrid dream, which he now feared was no dream but a reality !   He proclaimed himself a courier of the king; bound to Bulstrode Park, with a despatch for Captain Scarthe; but the despatch was lost ; with everything else he had borne on his body, even to the horse that had borne *him !*

After the full explanation had been given, Scarthe's chagrin at the failure of the king's message was counterbalanced by the amusement caused by the misadventure of the messenger; and after remounting the unfortunate man, sending him whence he had come, he continued his march, making the wild waste of Jarret's Heath rir g with a loud and long-continued cachinnation.

CHAPTER XV.

THE BLACK HORSEMAN!

The great clock in the tower of Bulstrode mansion was tolling the hour of noon. The sports were in full progress—both actors and spectators at the maximum of enjoyment.

Here and there, a knot of sturdy yeomen might be seen, standing close together—so that their conversation might not be overheard—discussing among themselves some late edict of royalty; and generally in tones of condemnation.

The arbitrary exactions, of which one and all of them had of late been victims; the tyrannous modes of taxation—hitherto unheard of in England—*ship, coat,* and *conduct* money—forced loans under the farcical title of *benevolences*; and, above all, the billeting of profligate soldiers in private houses—on individuals, who by some slight act or speech had given offence to the king, or some of his satellites—these were the topics of the time.

Conjoined with these grievances were discussed the kindred impositions, and persecutions of that iniquitous council, the Court of High Commission; which for cruel zeal rivaled even the Inquisition—and the infamous Star Chamber, that numbered its victims by thousands.

These truculent tools of tyranny had been for ten years in the full performance of their flagitious work; but, instead of crushing out the spirit of a brave people—which was their real aim and end--they had only been preparing it for a more determined and effective resistance.

The trial of Hampden—the favorite of Buckinghamshire—for his daring refusal to pay the arbitrary impost of "ship money," had met with the approbation of all honest men; while the judges, who condemned him, were denounced on all sides as worse than "unjust."

To its eternal glory be it told, nowhere was this noble spirit more eminently displayed than in the shire of Bucks—nowhere, in those days, was the word *liberty* so often, or so emphatically, pronounced. Shall I say, alas, the change?

True, it was yet spoken only in whispers—low, but earnest—like

4

thunder heard afar off over the distant horizon—heard only in low mutterings; but ready, at any moment, to play its red lightnings athwart the sky of despotism.

Such mutterings might have been heard in the park of Sir Marmaduke Wade. In the midst of that joyous gathering, signs and sounds of a serious import might have been detected—intermingling with scenes of the most light-hearted hilarity.

It may be wondered why those sentiments of freedom were not more openly declared. But that is easy of explanation. If among the assemblage who assisted at the birthday celebration, there were enemies to court and king; there were also many who were not friends to the cause of the people. In the crowd which occupied the old camp, there was a liberal sprinkling of spies and informers—with eyes sharply set to see, and ears to catch ever word that might be tainted with treason. No man knew how soon he might be made the victim of a denunciation—how soon he might stand in the awe-inspiring presence of the "Chamber."

No wonder that men expressed their sentiments with caution.

Among the gentlemen present there was a similar difference of opinion upon political matters—even among members of the same family! But such topics of discussion were studiously avoided, as unbecoming the occasion; and no one, carelessly contemplating the faces of the fair dames and gay cavaliers grouped laughingly together, could have suspected the presence of any sentiment that sprang not from the most contented concordance.

There was one countenance an exception to this general look of contentment—one individual in that brilliant throng that had as yet taken no pleasure in the sports. It was Marion Wade.

She, whose smile was esteemed a blessing wherever it fell, seemed herself unblessed.

Her bosom was a chaos of aching unrest. There was wanting in that concourse one whose presence could have given it peace.

Ever since entering the enclosure of the camp had the eye of Marion Wade been wandering over the heads of the assembled spectators; over the fosse, and toward the gates of the park—where some late guests still continued to straggle in.

Evidently was she searching for that she failed to find; for her glance, after each sweeping tour of inquiry, fell back upon the faces around her, with an ill concealed expresion of disappointment.

When the last of the company appeared to have arrived, the expression deepened to chagrin.

Her reflections, had they been uttered aloud, would nave given a
clue to the discontent betraying itself on her countenance.
"He comes not—he wills not to come! Was there nothing in
those looks? I've been mad to do as I have done. And what will
he think of me? What *can* he? He took up my glove—perhaps a
mere freak of curiosity, or caprice—only to fling it down again in
disdain? Now I know he cares not to come—else would he have
been here. Walter promised to introduce him—to *me*—to *me!* Oh!
there was no lure in that. He knows he might have introduced himself. Have I not invited him? Oh! the humiliation!"
Despite her painful reflections, the lady tried to look gay. But the
effort was unsuccessful. Among those standing near there were
some who did not fail to notice her wan brow, and wandering glance;
dames envious of her distinction—gallants, who for one smile from her
proud, pretty lips would have instantly sacrificed their long *love-
locks*, and plucked from their hats those trivial tokens, they had
sworn so hypocritically to wear.
There was only one, however, who could guess at the cause; and
that one could only *guess* at it. Her cousin alone had any suspicion,
that the heart of Marion was wandering, as well as her eyes. A
knowledge of this fact would have created surprise—almost wonder—
in the circle that surrounded her. Marion Wade was a full grown
woman; had been so for more than a year. She had been wooed
by many—by some worshiped almost to idolatry. Wealth and title,
youth and manhood, lands and lordships, had been laid at her feet;
and all alike rejected—not with the proud flourish of the triumphant
flirt; but with the tranquil dignity of a true woman, who can only be
wed after being *won*.
Among the many aspirants to her hand, there was not one who
could tell the tale of conquest. More than once had that tale been
whispered; but the world would not believe it. It would have been a
proud feat for the man who could achieve it—too proud to remain
unproclaimed.
And yet it had been achieved; though the world knew it not. She
alone suspected it, whose opportunities had been far beyond those of
the world. Her cousin, Lora Lovelace, had not failed to feel surprised
at those lonely rides—lonely from choice—since her own companionship had been repeatedly declined. Neither had she failed to observe,
how Marion had chafed and fretted, at the command of Sir Marmaduke, requiring their discontinuance. There were other circumstan

ces besides the lost glove, and the bleeding wrist—the fevered sleep at night, and the dreamy reveries by day. How could Lora shut her eyes to signs so significant?

Lora was herself in love; and could interpret them. No wonder that she should suspect that her cousin was in a like dilemma; no wonder she should feel sure that Marion's heart had been given away; though when, and to whom, she was still ignorant as any stranger within the limits of the camp.

"Marion!" said she, drawing near to her cousin, and whispering so as not to be overheard; "you are not happy to-day?"

"You silly child! what makes you think so?"

"How can I help it? In your looks——"

"What of my looks, Lora?"

"Dear Marion, don't mind me. It's because I dread that others may notice them. There's Winifred Wayland has been watching you; and, more still, that wicked Dorothy Dayrell. She has been keeping her eyes on you like a cat upon a mouse. Cousin! do try to look different; and don't give them something to talk about: for you know that's just what that Dorothy Dayrell would desire."

"Look different! How do I look pray?"

"Ah! I needn't tell you how. *You know how you feel;* and from that you may tell how you look."

"Ho! sage counselor, you must explain. What is it in my appearance that has struck you? Tell me, chit."

"You want me to be candid, Marion?"

"I do—I do."

The answer was given with an eagerness that left Lora no wish to withold her explanation.

"Marion," said she, placing her lips close to the ear of her who was alone intended to hear it, "*you are in love?*"

"Nonsense, Lora. What puts such a thought in your silly little head?"

"No nonsense, Marion; I know it by your looks. I don't know who has won you, dear cousin. I only know he's not here to-day You've been expecting him. He hasn't come. Now!"

"You're either a great big deceiver or a great little conjuror, Lora. In which of these categories am I to place you?"

"Not in the former, Marion; you know it. Oh! it needs no conjuring for *me* to tell that. But pray don't let it be so easy for others to read your secret, cousin! I entreat you——"

"You are welcome to your suspicions," said Marion, interrupting her. "And now I shall relieve you from them, by making them a certainty. It is of no use trying any longer to keep that a secret, which in time you would be sure to discover for yourself—I suppose. *I am in love.* As you've said, I'm in love with one who is *not* here. Why should I feel ashamed to tell it you? Nay, if I only thought he loved me as I do him, I'd care little that the whole company knew it—and much less either Winifred Wayland or Dorothy Dayrell. Let them——"

Just then the voice of this last-named personage was heard in animated conversation—interspersed with peals of laughter, in which a large party was joining.

It was nothing new for Dorothy to be the centre of a circle of laughing listeners; for she was one of the wits of the time. Her talk might not have terminated the dialogue between the cousins, but for the mention of a name—to Marion Wade of all absorbing interest.

Walter had just finished relating his adventure of the preceding night.

"And this wonderful cavalier," asked Dorothy, "who braved the bullying captain, and frightened the fierce footpads—did he favor you with his name, Master Wade?"

"Oh, yes!" answered Walter, "he gave me that—Henry Holtspur."

"Henry Holtspur! Henry Holtspur!" cried several in a breath, as if the name was not new to them, but had some peculiar signification.

"It's the cavalier who rides the black horse," explained one. "The *black horseman,*' the people called him. One lately come into this neighborhood. Lives in the old house of Stone Dean. Nobody knows him."

"And yet everybody appears to be talking of him! Mysterious individual! Some troubadour returned from the East?" suggested Winifred Wayland.

"Some trader from the West, more like," remarked Dorothy Dayrell, with a sneer, "whence, I presume, he has imported his leveling sentiments; and, a savage for his servant, too, 'tis said. Did you see aught of his Indian, Master Wade?"

"No," said the youth; "and very little of himself: as our ride together was after night. But I have hopes of seeing more of him to day. He promised to be here."

" And is not ? "

" I think not. I haven't yet encountered him. 'Tis just possible he may be among the crowd over yonder; or somewhere through the camp. With your permission, ladies, I shall go in search of him."

" Oh, do! do!" exclaimed half a score of sweet voices. " By all means, Master Wade, find the gentleman. You have our permission to introduce him. Tell him we're all dying to make his acquaintance."

Walter went off among the crowd; traversed the camp in all directions; and came back without the object of his search.

" How cruel of him not to come!" remarked the gay Dayrell, as Walter was seen returning alone. " If he only knew the disappointment he is causing! We might have thought less of it, Master Wade if you hadn't told us he intended to be here. Now I for one shall fancy your fête very stupid without him."

" He may still come," suggested Walter. " I think there are some other guests who have not arrived."

" You are right, Master Wade," interposed one of the bystanders; " yonder's somebody—a man on horseback—on the heath, outside the palings of the park. He appears to be going towards the gate."

All eyes were turned in the direction indicated. A horseman was seen upon the heath outside, about a hundred yards distant from the enclosure; but he was *not going towards the gate.*

" Not a bit of it," cried Dorothy Dayrell. He's changed his mind about that. See! he heads his horse at the palings. Going to take them? He is, in troth! High—over! There's a leap worth looking at.

And the fair speaker clapped her pretty hands in admiration of the feat.

There was one other who beheld it with an admiration; which, though silent, was not less enthusiastic. The joy that had shone sparkling in the eyes of Marion Wade, as soon as the strange horseman appeared in sight, was now heightened to an expression of proud triumph.

" Who is he?" asked half a score of voices, as the bold horseman cleared the enclosure.

" It is he—the cavalier we have just been speaking of," answered Walter, hurrying away to receive his guest; who was now coming on at an easy gallop towards the camp.

" *The black horseman—the black horseman!* " was the cry that rose up from the crowd; while the rustics rushed up to the top of the moat to give the new comer a welcome.

" *The black horseman! huzza!* " proclaimed a voice with that peculiar intonation that suggests a general cheer—which was given; as the cavalier, riding into their midst, drew his steed to a stand.

" *They* know him, at least," remarked the fair Dayrell, with a toss of her aristocratic head. " How popular he appears to be! Can any one explain it? "

" It's always the way with *new* people," said a sarcastic gentleman who stood near, " especially when they make their *début* a little mysteriously. The rustic has a wonderful relish for the unknown."

Marion stood silent. Her eyes sparkled with pride, on beholding the homage paid to her own heart's hero. The sneering interrogatories of Dorothy Dayrell she answered only in thought.

" Grand and noble! " was her reflection. " That is the secret of his popularity. Ah! the instincts of the people rarely err in their choice. He is true to *them*. No wonder they greet him as their god!"

For Marion, herself, a sweet triumph was in store.

The curiosity of the crowd, that had collected on the arrival of the black horseman, was passing away. The people had returned to their sports; or, with admiring looks, were following the famous steed to his stand under the trees. From an instinct of delicacy, peculiar to the country people, they had abandoned the cavalier to the companionship of his proper host—who was now conducting him towards the promised presentation.

They had arrived within a few paces of the spot where Marion was standing. Her face was averted, as if she knew not who was advancing. But her heart told her he was near. So, too, the whisperings of those who stood around. She dared not turn towards him. She dreaded to encounter his eye, lest it might look slightingly upon her

That studied inattention could not continue. She looked towards him at last. Her gaze became fixed—not upon his face, but upon an object which appeared conspicuous upon the brow of his beaver—. a *white gauntlet!*

Joy supreme! Words could not have spoken plainer. The token had been taken up; and treasured. Love's challenge had been accepted!

CHAPTER XVI.

THE LOVE TOKEN

A glove, a ribbon, a lock of hair, in the hat of a gentleman, was but the common affectations of the cavalier times; and only proclaimed its wearer the recipient of some fair lady's favor. There were many young gallants on the ground, who bore such adornments; and therefore no one took any notice of the token in the hat of Henry Holtspur—excepting those for whom it had a peculiar interest.

There were two who felt this interest; though from different motives. They were Marion Wade, and Lora Lovelace. Marion identified the glove with a thrill of joy; and yet the moment after she felt fear. Why? She feared it *might* be identified by others. Lora saw it with surprise. Why? Because it *was* identified. At the first glance Lora recognized the gauntlet; and knew it to have belonged to her cousin.

It was just this, that the latter had been dreading. She feared not its being recognized by any one else—not even by her father. She knew the good knight had more important matters upon his mind; and could not have told one of her gloves from another. But far different was it with her cousin; who, having a more intelligent discrimination in such trifles, would be likely, just then, to exercise it.

Marion's fears were fulfilled. She perceived from Lora's looks that the gauntlet—cruel and conspicuous tell-tale—was under her eye and in her thoughts.

"It is yours, Marion!" whispered the latter, pointing towards the plumed hat of the cavalier; and looking up, with an air more affirmative than inquiring.

"Mine! what, Lora? Yonder black beaver and plumes? What have I to do with them?"

"Ah! Marion, you mock me. Look under the plumes? What see you there?"

"Something that looks like a lady's glove. Is it one I wonder?"

"It is, Marion."

"So it is, in troth! This strange gentleman must have a mistress, then. Who would have thought of it?'

"It is yours, cousin."

"Mine? My glove do you mean? You are jesting, little Lora?"

"It is you who jest, Marion. Did you not tell me you had lost your glove?"

"I did. I dropped it. I must have dropped it—somewhere."

"Then the gentleman must have *picked it up!*" rejoined Lora, with significant emphasis.

"But, dear cousin; do you really think yonder gauntlet is mine?"

"O Marion, Marion! *you know it is yours!*"

Lora spoke half upbraidingly.

"How do you know you are not wronging me?" rejoined Marion, in an evasive tone. "Let me take a good look at it. Aha! My word, Lora, I think you are right. It does appear, as if it were my gauntlet—at least it is very like the one I lost the other day, when out a-hawking; and for the want of which my poor skin got so badly scratched. It's wonderfully like my glove!"

"Yes; so like, that it is the same."

'If so, how came it yonder?" inquired Marion, with an air of apparent perplexity.

"Ah, how?" repeated Lora.

"He must have found it in the forest?

"It is very impudent of him to be wearing it, then?"

"Very; indeed very."

"Suppose any one should recognize it as yours? Suppose uncle should do so?"

"There is no fear of that," interrupted Marion. "I have worn these gloves only twice. You are the only one who has seen them on my hands. Father does not know them. You won't tell him, Lora?"

"Why should I not?"

"Because—because—it may lead to trouble. May be this strange gentleman has no idea to whom the glove belonged. He has picked it up by the roadside; and stuck it in his hat—out of caprice, or conceit. I've heard many such favors are born with no better authority. Let him keep it, and wear it—if it so please him. I care not—so long as he don't know whose it is. Don't you say anything about it to any one. If father should know, or Walter—ah! Walter, young as he is, would insist upon fighting him; and I have no doubt that this *black horseman* would be a very dangerous antagonist."

4*

"O Marion!" cried Lora, alarmed at the very thought of such a contingency. "I shall not mention it—nor you. Do not for the world! Let him keep the glove, however dishonorably he may have come by it, I care not, dear cousin—so long as it does not compromise you."

"No fear of that," muttered Marion, in a confident tone; apparently happy at having so easily escaped from a dilemma she had been dreading.

The whispered conversation of the cousins was at this moment interrupted by the approach of Walter, conducting the cavalier into the midst of the distinguished circle.

The youth performed his office of introducer with true courtly grace, keeping his promise to all; and in a few seconds Henry Holtspur had added many new names to the list of his acquaintances.

It is no easy part to play—and play gracefully—that of being conspicuously presented; but the same courage that had distinguished the cavalier in his encounter with Garth, and his footpads, was again exhibited in that more imposing—perhaps more dangerous—presence.

The battery of bright eyes seemed but little to embarrass him; and he returned the salutations of the circle with that modest confidence which is a sure test of the true gentleman.

It was only when being presented to the last individual of the group —strange that Marion Wade should be the last—it was only then, that aught might have been observed beyond the ceremonious formality of an introduction. Then, however, a close observer might have detected an interchange of glances that expressed something more than courtesy; though so quickly and stealthily given, as to escape the observation of all. No one seemed to suspect that Marion Wade and Henry Holtspur had ever met before; and yet ofttimes had they met— ofttimes looked into each other's eyes—had done everything but speak!

How Marion had longed to listen to that voice, that now uttered in soft, earnest tones, sounded in her ears, like some sweet music!

And yet it spoke not in the language of love. There was no opportunity for this. They were surrounded by watchful eyes; and ears eagerly bent to catch every word passing between them. Not a sentiment of that tender passion, which both were eager to pour forth— not a syllable of it could be exchanged.

Under such constraint, the converse of lovers is far from pleasant It even becomes irksome; and scarce did either regret the occurrence of an incident, which, at that moment, engaging the attention of the crowd relieved them of their mutual embarrassment.

CHAPTER XVII.

The incident, thus opportunely interfering, was the arrival upon the ground of a party of *morris dancers* who, having finished their rehearsal outside the limits of the camp, now entered, and commenced their performance in front of the elevated moat—upon which Sir Marmaduke and his friends had placed themselves, in order to obtain a view of the spectacle.

The dancers were of both sexes—maidens and men—the former dressed in gay bodice and kirtle; the latter in their shirt sleeves, clean washed for the occasion—their arms and limbs banded with bright ribbons; bells suspended from their garters; and other adornments in true *Morisco* fashion.

There were some among them wearing character dresses: one representing the bold outlaw Robin Hood; another his trusty lieutenant, Little John; a third the jolly Friar Tuck, and so forth.

There were several of the girls also in character costumes. "Maid Marian," the "Queen of the May," and other popular personages of the rural fancy, were personified.

The morris dancers soon became the centre of general attraction. The humbler guests of Sir Marmaduke—having partaken of the cheer which he had so liberally provided for them—had returned into the camp; and now stood clustered around the group of Terpsichoreans with faces expressing the liveliest delight.

Balloons, bowls, wrestling, and single-stick were for the time forsaken; for the morris dance was tacitly understood, and expected, to be the chief attraction of the day.

It is true, that only peasant girls were engaged in it, but among these was more than one remarkable for a fine figure and comely face —qualities by no means rare in the cottage homes of the Chilterns.

Two were especially signalized for their good looks—the representatives of Maid Marian and the Queen of the May—the former a dark brunette of the gipsy type—while the Queen was a contrasting blonde, with hazel eyes, and hair of flaxen hue.

Many a young peasant among their partners in the dance—and also in the circle of spectators—watched the movements of these rustic belles with interested eyes. Ay, and more than one cavalier might have been observed casting sly glances towards Maid Marian, and the Queen of the May.

While those were bestowing their praises upon the peasant girls, in stereotyped phrases of gallantry, some of the stately dames standing around, might have found cause to be jealous; and some *were so.*

Was Marion Wade among the number?

Alas! it was even so. New as the feeling was, and slight the incident that called it forth, that fell passion had sprung up within her heart. It was the first time it had been touched with such a sting; for it was her first love, and too recent to have met with a reverse. A pang never felt before, she scarce comprehended its nature. She only knew its cause.

Holtspur was standing in the front rank of spectators—almost close to the ring in which the morris dancers were moving. As the beautiful Bet Dancey—who represented Maid Marian—went whirling voluptuously through the figures of the dance, her dark gipsy eyes, gleaming with amorous excitement, seemed constantly turned upon him. Marion Wade could not fail to observe the glance; for it was recklessly given. It was not this, however, that caused that pain to spring up within her bosom. The forest maiden might have gazed all day long upon the face of Henry Holtspur, without exciting the jealousy of the lady—had her gaze failed to elicit a return. But once as the latter turned quickly towards him, she fancied she saw the glance of the girl given back, and the passionate thought reciprocated!

A peculiar pang, never felt before, like some poisoned dart, pierced to the very core of her heart—almost causing her to cry out. In the rustic belle she recognized a rival!

The pain was not the less poignant, from its being her first experience of it. On the contrary, it was, perhaps, more so; and from that moment Marion Wade stood, cowed and cowering, with blanched brow—her blue eye steadily fixed upon the countenance of Henry Holtspur—watching with keen anxiety every movement of his features.

The dark doubt that had arisen in her mind was not to be resolved in that hour. Scarce had she entered upon her anxious surveillance when an incident arose, causing the morris dance to be suddenly interrupted.

Amidst the shouts, laughter, and cheering that accompanied the spectacle, only a few who had strayed outside the enclosure of the camp caught the first whisperings of a strange, and, to them, inexplicable sound. It appeared to proceed from some part of the road—outside the main entrance of the camp, and resembled a continued tinkling of steel implements, mingled with the hoof-strokes of a multitude of horses—not going at will, but ridden with that cadenced step that betokens the passage of a squadron of cavalry.

They who first heard it had scarce time to make this observation, much less to communicate their thoughts to the people inside the camp, when another sound reached their ears—equally significant of the movement of mounted men. It was the call of a cavalry bugle commanding the " Halt."

At the same instant the hoof-strokes ceased to be heard; and, as the last notes of the bugle died away in the distant woods, there was an interim of profound silence, broken only by the soft cooing of the woodquest, or the shriller piping of the thrush.

Equally within the camp was the silence complete. The cheers had been checked, and the laughter subdued, at that unusual sound. The ears of all were bent to listen for its repetition, while all eyes were turned in the direction whence it appeared to have proceeded.

There was something ominous in the sudden interruption of the sports, by a sound unexpected as it was ill understood; and some faces, but the moment before beaming with joy, assumed a serious aspect.

"Soldiers!" exclaimed several voices in the same breath; while the crowd, forsaking the spectacle of the morris dance, rushed up to the top of the moat and stood listening as before.

Once more came the clear tones of the cavalry trumpet, this time directing the "Forward;" and before the signal had ceased to echo over the undulations of the park, the files of a squadron of cuirassiers were seen passing between the massive piers of the main entrance, and advancing along the drive that led toward the mansion.

File followed file in regular order—each horseman, as he debouched from under the shadow of the trees, appearing to become a-blaze through the sudden flashing of the sunbeams upon the plates of his polished armor.

As the troop, riding by twos, had half advanced into the open ground, and still continued advancing, it presented the appearance of some gigantic snake gliding through the gateway—the steel armor representing its scales, and the glittering files answering to the vertabræ of the reptile.

When all had ridden inside and commenced winding up the slope that conducted to the dwelling, still more perfect was this resemblance to some huge serpent—beautiful but dangerous—crawling slowly on to the destruction of its victim.

"*The cuirassiers of the king.*"

There were many in the camp who needed not this announcement to make known to them the character of the new comers. The cuirass covering the buff doublet—the steel cap and gorget—the cuisses on the thighs—the pauldrons protecting the shoulders—the rear and vam-braces on the arms—all marked the mailed costume of the cuirassier; while the royal colors, carried in front by the cornet of the troop, proclaimed them the cuirassiers of the king.

By the side of this officer rode another, whose elegant equipments and splendidly caparisoned horse announced him to be the officer in command—the captain.

"The cuirassiers of the king!" What wanted they in the park of Sir Marmaduke Wade? Or what was their business at his mansion; for thither were they directing their march.

This question was put by more than one pair of lips, but by none less capable of answering it than those of Sir Marmaduke himself.

The spectacle of the morris dance had been altogether abandoned. Both actors and spectators had rushed promiscuously towards the moat—on that side fronting the park—and having taken stand upon its crest, were uttering exclamations of astonishment, or exchanging interogatories about this new interlude not mentioned in the programme of the entertainments.

At this moment the bugle once more brayed out the "Halt," and in obedience to the signal the cuirassiers again reined up.

As by this the head of the troop had arrived opposite to the old camp, and was at no great distance from it, some words that passed between the two officers could be heard distinctly by the people standing upon the moat.

"I say, Stubbs," called out the captain, spurring a length or two out from the troop and pointing towards the camp, "What are those rustics doing up yonder? Can you guess?"

"Haven't the most distant idea," answered the individual addressed.

"They appear to be in their holiday toggery—best bibs and tuckers. Is't a Whitsun-ale or a May-making?"

"Can't be either," rejoined Stubbs. "Isn't the season. No, by Ged."

"By the smoke of Venus! there appear to be some pretty petticoats among them. Mayn't be such dull quarters after all."

"No, by Ged! Anything but dull, I should say."

"Ride within speaking distance, and ask them what the devil they are doing."

The cornet, thus commanded, clapped spurs to his horse; and after galloping within fifty paces of the fosse, pulled up.

"What the devil are you doing?" cried he, literally delivering the order with which he had been entrusted.

Of course to such a rude interrogatory, neither Sir Marmaduke nor any of those standing around him vouchsafed response. Some of the common people in the crowd, however, called out—"We're merry-making. It's a fête—a birthday celebration."

"Oh! that's it," muttered the cornet, turning and riding back to communicate the intelligence to his superior officer.

"Let's go up and make their acquaintance," said the latter, as Stubbs delivered his report. "We shall reconnoitre the rustic beauties of Bucks, giving them the advantage of their holiday habiliments. What say you, Stubbs?"

"Agreeable," was the laconic reply of the cornet.

"*Allons!* as they say in France. We may find something up there worth climbing the hill for. As they also say in France, *nous verrons!*"

Ordering the troopers to dismount and stand by their horses— their own being given to a brace of grooms—the two officers, in full armor as they were, commenced ascending the slope that led to the Saxon encampment.

CHAPTER XVIII.

THE DEFIANCE

"So, good people!" said Scarthe, as soon as he and his companion had entered within the enclosure, "holding holiday, are you? An admirable idea in such fine weather—with the azure sky over your heads, and the green trees before your faces. Pray don't let us interrupt your Arcadian enjoyment. Go on with the sports! I hope you have no objection to our becoming spectators?"

"No, no!" cried several voices in response, "you are welcome, sirs, you are welcome."

Having thus spoken their permission, the people once more dispersed over the ground; while the two officers, arm in arm, commenced strolling through the encampment—followed by a crowd of the lower class of peasants, who continued to gratify their curiosity by gazing upon the steel-clad strangers.

Sir Marmaduke and his friends had returned to their former stand upon the elevated crest of the moat, and at some distance from the causeway where the two officers had entered. The latter saunteringly proceeded in that direction, freely flinging their jests among the crowd who accompanied them, and now and then exchanging phrases of no very gentle meaning with such of the peasant girls as chanced to stray across their path.

The host of the *fête* had resolved not to offer the intruders a single word of welcome. The rude demand made by the cornet, coupled with the coarse dialogue between the two officers—part of which he had overheard, had determined Sir Marmaduke to take no notice of them until they should of themselves declare their errand.

He had ordered the morris dance to be resumed. In front of where he stood the dancers had re-formed their figures, and with streaming ribbons and ringing bells were again tripping it over the turf.

"By the toes of Terpsichore, a morris dance," exclaimed the captain of cuirassiers, as he came near enough to recognize the costume and measure. "An age since I have seen one."

"Never saw one in my life," rejoined Stubbs, "except on the stage. Is it the same?"

No doubt Stubbs spoke the truth. He had been born in the ward of Cheap, and brought up within the sound of Bow-bells.

"Not quite the same," drawled the captain, "though something like,—if I remember aright. Let's forward and have a squint at it."

Hastening their steps a little, the two officers soon arrived on the edge of the circle; and without taking any notice of the "people of quality," who were stationed upon the platform above, they commenced flinging free jibes among the dancers.

Some of these made answer with spirit, especially Little John and the Jolly Friar, who chanced to be fellows of a witty turn, and who, in their own rude fashion, gave back to the two intruders full value for what they received.

Bold Robin—who appeared rather a surly representative of Sherwood's hero—bore their sallies with an indifferent grace, more especially on perceiving that the eye of the cuirassier captain became lit up with a peculiar fire while following Maid Marian through the mazes of the dance.

But the heart of the pseudo outlaw was destined to be further wrung. A climax was at hand. As Marian came to the close of one of her grandest *pas*, the movement had inadvertently brought her close to the spot where the cuirassier captain was standing.

"Bravo! beautiful Marian," cried the latter, bending towards her, and clasping her rudely around the waist. "Allow a thirsty soldier to drink nectar from those juicy lips of thine."

And without finishing the speech, or waiting for her consent—which he knew would be refused—he protruded his lips through the visor of his helmet till they came in contact with those of the girl.

A blow from a clenched feminine fist, received right in his face, neither disconcerted nor angered the daring libertine, who answered it by a loud reckless laugh, in which he was joined by his cornet and chorused by some of the less sentimental of the spectators.

There were others who did not seem inclined to treat the affair in this jocular fashion.

Cries of "Shame!" "Pitch into him!" "Gie it him, Robin!" were heard among the crowd, and angry faces could be seen mingled with the merry ones.

The idol of England's peasantry needed not such stimulus to stir him to action. Stung by jealousy and the insult offered to his sweetheart, he sprang forward, and raising his crossbow—the only weapon he carried—high overhead, he brought it down with a "thwack" upon the helmet of the cuirassier captain, which caused the officer to stagger some paces backward ere he could recover himself.

"Take that, dang thee!" shouted Robin, as he delivered the blow. "Take that; an' keep thy scurvy kisses to thyself."

"Low-born peasant!" cried the cuirassier, his face turning purple as he spoke, "if thou wert worth a sword, I'd spit thee like a red herring. Keep off, churl, or I may be tempted to take thy life!"

As he uttered this conditional threat, he drew his sword and stood with the blade pointing towards the breast of bold Robin.

There was an interval of profound silence. It was terminated by a voice among the crowd crying out,—"Yonder comes the man that'll punish him!"

All eyes were turned towards the elevated platform, on which stood the "people of quality." There was a commotion among the cavaliers. One, who had separated from among the rest, was seen hurrying down the sloping side of the moat, and making direct for the scene of the contention.

He had only a dozen steps to go; and before either the pseudo-outlaw of Sherwood forest or his mailed adversary could change their relative positions, he had glided in between them.

The first intimation the cuirassier had of a true antagonist was, when a bright sword-blade rasped against his own, striking sparks of fire from the steel; and he beheld in front of him no longer a "low-born peasant," clad in Kendal green, but a cavalier in laced doublet, elegantly attired as himself, and equally as determined.

This new climax silenced the spectators as suddenly as if the wand of an enchanter had turned them into stone; and it was not till after some seconds had elapsed that murmurs of applause rose round the ring, coupled with that popular cry, "*Huzza for the black horseman!*"

For a moment the captain of cuirassiers seemed awed into silence. Only for a moment; and only by the suddenness of the encounter Swaggerer as he may have been, Scarthe was no coward; and under the circumstances even a coward must have shown courage. Though still under the influence of a partial intoxication, he knew that bright eyes were upon him; he knew that high-born dames were standing within ten paces of the spot; and though hitherto, for reasons of his own, pretending to ignore their presence, he knew they had been spectators of all that had passed. He had no intentions, therefore, of showing the white feather.

Perhaps it was the individual who had thus presented himself, as much as his sudden appearance, that held him for the moment speechless; for in the antagonist before him, Scarthe recognized the cavalier who, in front of the roadside inn, had daringly drunk—

"To the People!"

The souvenir of this insult, added to this new defiance, furnished a double stimulus to his resentment—which at length found expression in words.

"You it is, disloyal knave? You!"

"Disloyal or not," calmly returned the cavalier, "I demand reparation for the slight you have offered to this respectable assemblage. Your free fashions may do for Flanders—where I presume you've been practicing them—but I must teach you to salute the fair maidens of England in a different style."

"And who are you, who propose to give the lesson."

"No *low-born peasant*, Captain Richard Scarthe. Don't fancy you can screen yourself behind that coward's cloak. You must fight, or apologize!"

"Apologize!" shouted the soldier, in a furious voice, "Captain Scarthe apologize! Ha, ha, ha! Hear that, Cornet Stubbs? Did you ever know *me* to apologize?"

"Never, by God!" muttered Stubbs, in reply.

"As you will then," said the cavalier, placing himself in an attitude to commence the combat.

"No, no!" cried Maid Marian, throwing herself in front of Holtspur, as if to screen his body with her own. "You must not, sir. It is not fair. He is in armor, and you, sir——"

"No—it arn't fair!" proclaimed several voices; while at the same moment a large fierce-looking man, with bushy black beard, was seen pushing his way through the crowd towards the spot occupied by the adversaries.

"'Twoan't do, Master Henry," cried the bearded man, as he came up. "You mustn't risk it that way. I know ye're game for any man on the groun', or in England eyther; but it arn't fair. The soger captain must peel off them steel plates o' his, and let the fight be a fair'n'. What say ye, meeats?"

This appeal to the bystanders was answered by cries of " Fair play, fair play! The officer must take off his armor."

"Certainly," said Walter Wade, at this moment coming up. "If these gentlemen are to fight, the conditions must be equal. Of course, Captain Scarthe, you will not object to that?"

"I desire no advantage," rejoined the cuirassier captain. "He may do as he likes; but I shall not lay aside my armor on any account."

"Then your antagonist must arm also," suggested one of the gentlemen who had accompanied Walter. "The combat cannot go on till that be arranged."

"No, no!" chimed in several voices, "both should be armed alike."

"Perhaps this gentleman," said one, pointing to the cornet, "will have no objection to lend his for the occasion? That would simplify matters. It appears to be about the right size."

Stubbs looked towards his captain, as much as to say, "Shall I refuse?"

"Let him have it," said Scarthe, seeing that the proposal could not well be declined.

"He's welcome to it!" said the cornet, who instantly commenced unbuckling.

There were hands enough to assist Henry Holtspur in putting on the defensive harness, and in a few minutes time he was encased in the steel accoutrements of the cornet—cuirass and gorget, pauldrons, cuisses and braces—all of which fortunately fitted as if they had been made for him.

The helmet still remained in the hand of one of the attendants, who made a motion towards placing it upon Holtspur's head.

"No," said the latter, pushing it away. "I prefer wearing my beaver." Then pointing to the trophy set above its brim, he added: "It carries that which will sufficiently protect my head. An English maiden has been insulted, and under the glove of an English maiden shall the insult be rebuked."

"Don't be so confident in the virtue of your pretty trophy," rejoined Scarthe, with a sarcastic sneer. "Ere long I shall take that glove from your hat, and stick it in the crest of my helmet. No doubt I shall then have come by it more honestly than you have done."

Time enough to talk of wearing, when you have won it;" quietly retorted the cavalier. "Though, by my troth," added he, returning sneer for sneer, "you should strive hard to obtain it; you stand in need of a trophy to neutralize the loss of your spurs, left behind you in the ford of Newburn."

The "Ford of Newburn" was Scarthe's especial fiend. He was one of that five thousand horsemen, who under Conway had ignominiously retreated from the Tyne—spreading such a panic throughout the whole English army, as to carry it without stop or stay far into the heart of Yorkshire. Once before had Holtspur flung the disgraceful souvenir in his teeth; and now to be a second time reproached with it, before a crowd of his countrymen, before his own followers —many of whom had by this time entered within the camp—but, above all, in presence of that more distinguished circle of proud and resplendent spectators, standing within earshot, on the moat above— that was the direst insult to which he had ever been subjected. As his antagonist repeated the taunting allusion, his brow, already dark, grew visibly darker; while his thin lips whitened, as if the blood had altogether forsaken them.

"Base demagogue!" cried he, hissing the words through his clenched teeth; "your false tongue shall be soon silenced. On the escutcheon of captain Scarthe there is no stain, save the blood of his enemies; and the enemies of his King. Yours shall be mingled with the rest."

"Come!" cried Holtspur, with an impatient wave of his weapon. "I stand not here for a contest of tongues; in which no doubt the accomplished courtier Scarthe would prove my superior. Our swords are drawn; are you ready, sir?"

"No," responded Scarthe.

"No?" interrogated his antagonist with a look of surprise. "What—"

"Captain Scarthe is a cuirassier. He fights not afoot.'

"You are the challenged party!" put in Stubbs; "You have the right of a choice, captain."

"Our combat, then, shall be on horseback."

"Thanks for the favor, gentlemen!" responded Holtspur, with a pleased look. "My own wish exactly; though I had scarce hoped to obtain it. You have said the word—we fight on horseback."

"My horse!" shouted Scarthe, turning to one of his troopers "Bring him up; and let the ground be cleared of this rabble."

There was no necessity for the order last issued. As soon as it had become known that the combat was to be fought on horseback, the people scattered on all sides—rushing towards the crest of the moat; and there taking their stand—most of them delighted at the prospect of witnessing a spectacle, which, even in those chivalrous times, was of uncommon occurrence.

CHAPTER XIX.

THE PRELUDE.

From the commanding eminence, on which were clustered the "quality folks," the preparations had been watched with a vivid interest; and with emotions varying in kind.

"Splendid! exclaimed Dorothy Dayrell, as the sword-blades were seen clashing together. Beats the morris-dancers all to bits! Just what I like! One of those little interludes not mentioned in the programme of the entertainment. Surely we're going to see a fight."

Lora Lovelace trembled, as she listened to these speeches

"Oh, Dorothy Dayrell!" said she, turning upon the latter an upbraiding look. "'Tis too serious for jesting. You do not mean it."

"But I do mean it, Mistress Lovelace. I'm not jesting. Not a bit of it. I'm quite in earnest, I assure you."

"Surely you would not wish to see blood spilled?"

"And why not? What care I, so long as it isn't my own blood; or that of one of my friends. Ah! Ah! Ah! What are either of these fellows to you, or me? I know neither. If they're angry with each other, let them fight it out. Poh, poh! They may kill one another, for aught I care."

"Wicked woman!" thought Laura, without making rejoinder.

Marion Wade overheard the unfeeling utterances; but she was too much occupied with what was passing on the plain below, to give heed to them. That incipient suspicion, though still unsatisfied, was not troubling her now. It had given place to a feeling of apprehension for the safety of him who had been its object.

"My God!" she murmured in soliloquy, her hands clasped over her bosom—the slender white fingers desperately entwining each other. "If he should be killed! Walter! dear Walter!" she cried, earnestly appealing to her brother; "go down, and stop it! Tell him—tell them they must not fight. Oh father, you will not permit it?"

"Perhaps I may not be able to hinder them," said Walter, springing out from among the circle of his acquaintances. "But I shall go down. You will not object, father? Mr. Holtspur is alone, and may stand in need of a friend."

"Go, my son!" said Sir Marmaduke, pleased at the spirit his son was displaying. "It matters not who, or what, he be. He is our guest, and has been your protector. If they are determined on fighting, see that he be shown fair play."

"Never fear, father!" rejoined Walter, hurrying down the slope. "And if that drunken cornet dare to interfere," continued he, half speaking to himself—"I'll give *him* a taste of *my* temper, very different from what he had last night."

As he gave utterance to this threat, the ex-courtier passed through the crowd, followed by several other gentlemen; who, from different motives, were also hastening towards the scene of contentation.

"Come, Mistress Marion Wade?" whispered Dorothy, in a significant way. "It is not your wont to be thus tender-hearted. What is it to us, whether they fight or no! It isn't *your* quarrel. This elegant cavalier, who seems to set everybody beside themselves, is not *your* champion, is he? If any one has reason to be interested in his fate, by my trow, I should say it was the Maid Marian—*alias* Bet Dancey. And *certes*, she does seem to take interest in him. See! What she's doing now, the modest creature? By my word, I believe the wench is about to throw herself upon his breast, and embrace him!"

These words entered the ears of Marion Wade with stinging effect. Suddenly turning, she looked down upon the sea of faces, that had thickened, and was swerving around the two men; who were expected soon to become engaged in deadly strife. Many of the cuirassiers had arrived upon the ground, and their steel armour now glittered conspicuously among the more sombre vestments of the civilian spectators.

Marion took no note of these; nor of aught else, save the half-score figures that occupied the centre of the ring. Scarthe and his cornet, Henry Holtspur, Robin Hood, the Little John, and the Friar were there; and there, too, was Maid Marian!

What was *she* doing in the midst of the men?

She had thrown herself in the front of the cavalier—between him and his adversary. Her hands were upraised—one of them actually resting upon Holtspur's shoulder! She appeared to be speaking in earnest appeal—as if dissuading him from the combat!

" In what way could the daughter of Dick Dancy be interested in the actions of Henry Holtspur ?"

The question came quickly before the mind of Marion Wade, though it rose not to her lips.

" Bravo! cried Dorothy Dayrell, as she saw that the cavalier was being equipped. " It's going to go on! A combat in full armor! " Won't that be fine? It reminds one of the good old times of the troubadours?"

" Oh, Dorothy!" said Lora, " to be merry at such a moment!"

Hush! " commanded Marion, frantically grasping the jester by the arm, and looking angrily into her eye. " Another word, Mistress Dayrell—another trifling speech—and you and I shall cease to be friends."

" Indeed!" scornfully retorted the latter. " What a misfortune that would be for me!"

Marion made no rejoinder. It was at this moment that Scarthe had flung out his taunt about the glove in the hat of his antagonist.

Maid Marian heard the speech, and saw the action.

" Whose glove! " muttered she, as a pang passed through her heart.

Marion Wade heard the speech, and saw the action.

" My glove!" muttered she, as a thrill of sweet joy vibrated through her bosom.

The triumphant emotion was but short-lived. It was soon supplanted by a feeling of anxious apprehension; that reached its climax, as the two cavaliers, each bestriding his own steed, spurred their horses toward the centre of the camp—the arena of the intended combat.

With the exception of that made by the horsemen, as they rode trampling over the turf, not a movement could be observed within or around the enclosure of the camp. The dark circle of human forms, that girdled the ground were as motionless, as if they had been turned into stones; and equally silent—men and women, youths and maidens, all alike absorbed in one common thought—all voicelessly gazing.

The chirrup of a grasshopper could have been heard throughout the encampment.

This silence had only commenced, as the combatants came forth upon the ground, in readiness to enter upon action. While engaged in preparation, the merits of both had been loudly and freely discussed and bets had been made, as if the camp were a cockpit; and the cavaliers a main of game birds, about to be unleashed at each other.

The popular feeling was not all at one side; though the "black horseman" was decidedly the favorite. There was an instinct on the part of the spectators that he was the *people's friend;* and, in those tyrannous times, the phrase had an important signification.

But the crowd was composed of various elements; and there was more than a minority who, despite the daily evidence of royal outrages and wrongs, still tenaciously clung to that, the meanest sentiment that can find home in the human heart—loyalty. I mean *loyalty to a throne.*

In the captain of cuirassiers, they saw the representative of that thing they had been accustomed to worship and obey—that mysterious entity, which they had been taught to believe was as necessary to their existence as the bread which they ate, or the beer they drank —a thing ludicrously styled "heaven-descended"—deriving its authority from God himself—*a king.*

Notwithstanding the insult he had put upon them there were numbers present ready to shout—

"Huzza for the cuirassier captain!"

Notwithstanding his championship of their cause, there were numbers upon the ground ready to vociferate—

"Down with the black horseman!"

All exhibitions of this sort, however, had now ceased; and, in the midst of a profound silence, the mounted champions, having ridden clear of the crowd, advanced towards each other with glances reciprocally expressive of death and determination.

CHAPTER XX.

THE COMBAT.

It was a terrible sight for the soft eye of a woman to look upon. The timid Lora Lovelace would not stay; but ran off towards the house, followed by many others. Dorothy Darell called after them, jerring at their cowardice!

Marion remained. She could not drag herself from the approaching spectacle; though dreading to behold it. She stood under the dark shadow of a tree; but its darkness could not conceal the wild look of apprehension with which she regarded the two mailed horsemen moving from opposite sides of the camp, and frowningly approaching one another.

Out rang the clear notes of the cavalry bugle, sounding the "charge." The horses themselves understood the signal; and, needed no spurring to prompt their advance.

Both appeared to know the purpose for which they had been brought forth. At the first note they sprang towards one another —snorting mutual defiance—as if they, like their riders, were closing in mortal combat!

It was altogether a duello with swords. The sword, at that time, was the only weapon of the cuirassier cavalry, excepting their pistols; but by mutual agreement these last were not be used.

With blades bare, the duellists dashed in full gallop towards each other, Scarthe crying out: "*For the King!*" while Holtspur, with equal energy raised the antagonistic cry: "*For the People!*"

At their first meeting, no wound was given, or received. As the steeds swept past each other, the ring of steel could be heard—sword blades glinting against cuirass and corslet—but neither of the combatants appeared to have obtained any advantage.

Both wheeled almost at the same instant; and again advanced to the charge.

This time the horses came into collision. That of the cuirassier was seen to stagger at the shock; but although, during the momentary suspension of the gallop, the sword-blades of the combatants were busy in mutual cut and thrust, they separated as before, apparently without injury on either side.

The collision, however, had roused the ire both of horses and riders; and, as they met for the third time, the spectators could note in the eyes of the latter the earnest anger of deadly strife.

Again rushed the horses together in a charging gallop, and met with a terrific crash—both weapons and defensive armor colliding at the same instant. The steed of the cuirassier recoiled from the impetus of his more powerful adversary. The black horse swept on unscathed; but as he passed to the rear, the hat of Holtspur was lifted upon the breeze; and fell behind him upon the grass.

Trifling as was the incident, it looked ominous. It was the first that had the appearance of a triumph; and elicited a cheer from the partisans of the cuirassier captain.

It had scarce reached its climax, ere it was drowned by the more sonorous counter-cheer that hailed the performance of the black horseman.

Having wheeled his horse with the rapidity of thought, he rode back; and, spitting his beaver upon the point of his sword, he raised it up from the ground, and once more set it firmly upon his head!

All this was accomplished before his antagonist could turn to attack him; and the *sang froid* exhibited in the act, along with the graceful equitation, completely restored the confidence of his supporters.

The fourth encounter was final—the last in which the combatants met face to face.

They closed in full gallop; thrust at each other; and then passed on as before.

But Holtspur had now discovered the point in which he was superior to his adversary; and determined to take advantage of it.

The steeds had scarce cleared one another, when that of the cavalier was seen suddenly to stop—reined backward, until his tail lay spread upon the grass. Then turning upon his hind hoofs, as on a pivot, he sprang out in full gallop after the horse of the cuirassier.

The black horseman, waving his sword in the air, gave out a shout of triumph—such as he had erst often uttered in the ears of Indian foemen—while the horse himself, as if conscious of the advantage thus gained, sent forth a shrill neigh, that resembled the scream of a jaguar.

With a glance over his shoulder, Scarthe perceived the approaching danger. By attempting to turn, he would expose himself sideways to the thrust of his adversary's sword.

There was no chance to turn just then. He must make distance to obtain an opportunity. His only hope lay in the fleetness of his steed, and trusting to this, he sank the spur deeply, and galloped on.

This new and unexpected manœuvre had all the appearance of a retreat; and the camp rang with cries of—"Coward!" "He is conquered!" "Huzza for the black horseman!"

For a moment Marion Wade forgot her fears. For a moment proud pleasant thoughts swept through her breast. Her bosom rose and fell under the influence of triumphant emotions. Was he not a hero —a conqueror—worthy of that heart she had wholly given him?

She watched every spring of the two steeds. She longed to see the pursuer overtake the pursued. She was not cruel; but she wished it to be over; for the suspense was terrible to endure.

Marion was not to be tortured much longer. The climax was close at hand.

On starting on that tail-on-end chase, the cuirassier captain had full confidence in his steed. He was a true Arab; possessing all the strength and swiftness of his race.

But one of the same race was after him; stronger, and swifter than he. Like an arrow from its bow, the steed of the cuirassier shot across the sward. Like another arrow, but one sent with stronger nerf, swept the sable charger in pursuit. Across the camp —out through the cleared causeway—over the open pasture of the park—galloped the two horsemen, as if riding a race. But their blazing armor, outstretched shining blades, angry looks and earnest attitudes—all told of a different intent.

Scarthe had been for some time endeavoring to gain distance, in order to have an opportunity of turning face to his antagonist. With the latter clinging closely behind him, he knew the manœuvre to be dangerous if not impossible—without subjecting himself to the thrust of Holtspur's sword. He soon began to perceive another danger— that of being overtaken.

The spectators had discontinued their shouts; and once more, a profound silence reigned throughout the camp. It was like the silence that precedes some expected catastrophe—some crisis inevitable.

From the beginning his pursuer had kept constantly gaining upon him. The fore hoofs of the sable charger now appeared at every bound to overlap the hind heels of his own horse. Should the chase continue but a minute longer, he must certainly be overtaken; for the blade of the cavalier was gleaming scarce ten feet behind his back. The climax was near.

"Surrender, or yield up your life!" demanded Holtspur in a determined voice.

"Never!" was the equally determined reply. "Richard Scarthe never surrenders—least of all to——"

"Your blood on your own head, then!" cried the black horseman, at the same instant urging his horse to a final burst of speed.

The latter gave a long leap forward; bringing him side by side with the steed of the cuirassier. At the same instant, Holtspur's sword was seen thrust horizontally outwards.

A cry went up from the crowd, who expected next moment to see the cuirassier captain impaled upon that shining blade. The cuirass of the time consisted only of the breast-plate; and the back of the wearer was left unprotected.

Undoubtedly in another instant, Scarthe would receive his death wound; but an accident saved him. As Holtspur's horse leaped forward, the hind heels of the other struck against his off fore leg, causing him slightly to swerve; and thus, changing the direction of the sword-thrust. It saved the life of Scarthe; though not his limbs: for the blade of his antagonist entering his right arm, just under the shoulder, passed clear through—striking against the steel rear-brace in front; and sending his own sword shivering into the air.

The cuirassier captain, dismounted by the shock, in another instant lay sprawling upon the grass; while his horse, with trailing bridle, continued his onward gallop, wildly neighing as he went.

"Cry quarter, or die!" shouted the cavalier, flinging himself from his saddle; and with his left hand grasping the cuirassier by the gorget, while in his right he held the threatening blade. "Cry quarter or die!"

"Hold!" exclaimed Scarthe. "Hold!" he repeated, with the addition of a bitter oath. "This time the chance has been yours. I take quarter."

"Enough," said Holtspur, as he restored his sword to its sheath. Then, turning his back upon his vanquished antagonist, he walked silently away

The spectators descended from their elevated position; and, clustering around the conqueror, vociferated their cheers and congratulations. A girl in a crimson cloak ran up, and, kneeling in front, presented him with a bunch of flowers. It was the insulted maiden, who thus gracefully acknowledged her gratitude.

There were two pairs of eyes that witnessed this last episode, with an expression that spoke of pain: the blue eyes of Marion Wade, and the green ones of Will Walford—the representative of England's outlaw. The original Robin could never have been more jealous of the original Maid Marian.

Marion Wade witnessed the presentation of the flowers, and their reception. She saw that the gift was acknowledged by a bow, and a smile—both apparently gracious. It never occurred to her to ask herself the question: whether the recipient, under the circumstances, could have acted otherwise?

She stayed not to witness more; but, with brain distraught, and bosom filled with fell fancies, she glided across the glacis of the old encampment; and, in hurried steps, sought the sacred shelter of her father's roof.

Though *hors de combat*, Scarthe was not fatally hurt. He had received only the one thrust—which, passing through his right arm, had disabled him for the time; but was not likely to do him any permanent injury.

He was worse damaged in spirit than in person; and the purple gloom that overshadowed his countenance told his followers, and others who had gathered around him, that no expression either of sympathy, or congratulation, would be welcome.

In silence, therefore, assistance was extended to him; and, in silence was it received.

As soon as the braces had been stripped from his wounded arm, and the semi-surgeon of his troop having stemmed its bleeding, had placed it in a sling, he forsook the spot where he had fallen; and walked direct towards the place occupied by Sir Marmaduke and his friends.

The ladies had already taken their departure—the sanguinary incident having robbed them of all zest for the enjoyment of any further sports.

The knight had remained upon the ground—chiefly for the purpose of discovering the object of Captain Scarthe's presence in his park.

He was determined no longer to remain in ignorance as to the cause of the intrusion; and was about starting out to question the intruder himself, when the approach of the latter admonished him to keep his place.

From Scarthe's looks, as he came forward, it was evident that an *éclaircissement* was at hand.

Sir Marmaduke remained silent—leaving the stranger to commence the colloquy, which was now inevitable.

As soon as Scarthe had got within speaking distance, he demanded, in an authoritative tone, whether Sir Marmaduke Wade was present upon the ground.

The interrogatory was addressed to the rustics standing upon the sward below.

They, perceiving that Sir Marmaduke had himself heard it, kept silence—not knowing whether their host might desire an affirmative answer to be given.

The tone of impertinence prevented Sir Marmaduke from replying, and the interrogatory was repeated.

Sir Marmaduke could no longer preserve silence.

"He *is* present," said he, without qualifying his answer by any title, or salutation. "*I* am Sir Marmaduke Wade."

"I am glad of it, good sir. I want to speak a word with you. Shall it be private? I perceive you are in company."

"I can hold no private conversation with strangers," replied the knight, drawing himself proudly up. "Whatever you have to say, sir, may be spoken aloud."

"As you wish, Sir Marmaduke," acquiesced Scarthe, in a tone of mock courtesy. "But if, to my misfortune, you and I have been hitherto strangers to each other, I live in hope that this unpleasant condition of things will soon come to an end; and that henceforth we shall be better acquainted."

"What mean you, sir? Why are you here?"

"I am here, Sir Marmaduke, to claim the hospitality of your house. By-the-way, a very handsome park, and apparently a commodious mansion. Room enough for all my people, I should think! It would scarce be courtesy between us if, eating, drinking, and sleeping under the same roof, we should remain strangers to one another!"

"Eating, drinking and sleeping under the same roof! You are merry, sir!"

"With the prospect of such pleasant quarters, would you expect me to be otherwise, Sir Marmaduke ? "

"After the lesson you have just received," replied the knight, returning irony, " one might expect to find you in a more serious frame of spirit."

"Captain Scarthe can show too many scars to trouble himself about such a trifle as that you allude to. But we are wasting time, Sir Marmaduke. I am hungry: so are my troopers; and thirsty. We feel inclined to eat and drink."

"You are welcome to do both one and the other. You will find an inn three miles farther up the road."

"Nearer than that," rejoined Scarthe, with an insulting laugh, "that's our inn."

And as he said this, he pointed to the mansion of Sir Marmaduke, standing proud and conspicuous on the crest of the opposite hill.

"Come sir ! said the knight, losing patience, "speak no longer in enigmas. Declare openly, and at once, what you are driving at."

"I am only too desirous to oblige you, Sir Marmaduke. Standing in need of refreshments as I do, I can assure you I have no wish to procrastinate this unseemly interview. Cornet Stubbs ! " he continued, turning to his subaltern; "if I am not mistaken, you carry a piece of royal parchment in your pocket. Please draw it forth; and do this worthy gentleman the favor to make him acquainted with its contents."

The cornet, who had re-incased himself in his suit of steel, inserted his fingers under the breast-piece of his cuirass ; and presently produced a folded parchment, upon which a large red seal was conspicuous. Unfolding it, he read aloud—

" *The King to Sir Marmaduke Wade.*

" *His Majesty hearing by good report of ye loyalty of Sir Marmaduke Wade, of Bulstrode Park, in ye shire of Buckingham, doth hereby entrust to him ye keep and maintenance of ye Captain Scarthe and his troop of horse till such time as his Majesty may need ye same for ye service of his kingdom ; and furthermore, his Majesty do recommend ye said Captain Scarthe to ye hospitality of Sir Marmaduke as a worthy and gallant officer and gentleman, who has done good service to his country and king.*

" *Given under ye great seal of his Majesty, at Whitehall Palace, this 15th day of October, Anno Domini,* 1640.

CAROLUS REX."

CHAPTER XXI.

The traveler, journeying among the Chiltern Hills, will often find himself on the summit of a ridge, that, sweeping round upon itself, encloses a deep basin-like valley, of circular shape.

Many of these natural concavities are of considerable size—having a superficial extent of several hundreds of acres. Often a farm homestead may be seen nestling within their sheltered limits; and not unfrequently a noble mansion, surrounded by green pastures—these again bordered by a belt of forest trees, cresting the summit of the surrounding ridge—the whole appearing like some landscape picture, set in a circular frame.

Such a picture was presented in the valley of Stone Dean; a fair mansion in the centre of a smiling park, with a rustic framework of beeching forest, coping the hills that encircled it.

The day was when the park and mansion of Stone Dean may have been kept in better repair. At the period of which we write, about both was visible an air of neglect—like a painting that has hung unheeded against the wall, till tarnished by dust and time.

Both dwelling and outbuildings exhibited evidences of decay; and but little sign of occupation. But for the smoke rising out of one of its tottering chimneys—and this not always to be seen—one viewing the house from the ridge above would have come to the conclusion that it was uninhabited. The shrubbery had become transformed into a thicket; the pastures, over-grown with gorse, genista, and bramble, more resembled a waste than a park enclosure; while the horned cattle wandering over them, appeared as wild as the deer browsing by their side; and, when startled by the step of the intruder, were equally alert in seeking the concealment of the surrounding forest.

Neither domesticated quadruped, nor bird appeared about the walls or within the enclosures; where a human voice was rarely heard to interrupt the shrill screech of the jay from the bordering woods; the clear piping of the blackbird amid the neglected shrubbery; and

5*

the monotonous cawing of the rooks upon the tops of the tall elm trees, that, holding hundreds of their nests, darkly overshadowed the dwelling.

In truth, Stone Dean had been a long time untenanted, except by one of those peculiar creatures termed " caretakers;" a grey-headed old veteran, who appeared less an occupant than a fixture of the place. He, his dog—old like himself—and a cat equally venerable, had for many years been the sole denizens of the " Dean."

No one in the neighborhood knew exactly to whom the estate belonged. Even its last occupier had been only a tenant at will; and the real owner was supposed to reside somewhere abroad—in the plantations of Virginia, it was believed.

There were not many who troubled their heads by conjectures upon the subject; for Stone Dean lay so much out of the line of the ordinary roads of the country, that but few persons ever found occasion to pass near it. Few could say they had ever been in sight of it. There were people living within five miles of the place that did not even know of its existence; and others who had once known and forgotten it.

Of late, however, the "Old house of Stone Dean " had become a subject of some interest; and at the fairs, and other village gatherings, its name was often pronounced. This arose from the circumstance: that a new tenant had displaced the old fixture of a caretaker —the latter disappearing from the place as quietly and inexplicably as he had occupied it!

About the new comer, and his domestic menage, there was an air of peculiarity approaching the mysterious. Such of the peasants, as had found pretext for visiting the house, reported that there was but one servant in the establishment—a young man, with a copper-colored skin, and long straight black hair, who answered to the name of " Oriole;" and, who appeared to be of the race of American Indians—a party of whom from the Transatlantic Plantations had about that time paid a visit to England.

It was further known that Oriole, either could not speak English, or would not. At all events, the visitors to Stone Dean had not been able to elicit from the servant any great amount of information respecting the master.

The master himself, however, was not long resident in the of Bucks before he became well enough known to his

He was in the habit of meeting them at their markets, and

makings; of entering into free converse with them on many subjects —more especially on matters appertaining to their political welfare and seemed to lose no opportunity of giving them instructive hints in regard to their *rights* as well as *wrongs*.

Such sentiments were neither new nor uncongenial to the dwellers amongst the Chilterns. They had long been cherished in their hearts; but the dread of the Star Chamber hindered them from rising to their lips. The man, therefore, who had the courage to give speech to them could not fail to be popular among the worthy yeomanry of Bucks; and such, in reality, had become the occupant of Stone Dean, in a few short weeks after taking up his residence in their county.

This individual possessed other claims to popular favor. He was a gentleman—nobly born, and highly bred. His appearance and behavior proclaimed these points beyond cavil; and in such matters, the instinct of the rustic is rarely incorrect. Furthermore, the stranger was a person of elegant appearance; perhaps not regularly handsome, but with that air of *savoir faire*, and bold bearing, sure to attract admiration. Plainly but richly dressed; a splendid horseman, and riding a splendid horse withal; frank and affable, not as if condescending—for at this the instinct of the rustic revolts—but distinguished by that simple unselfish spirit, which characterizes the true gentleman, how could Henry Holtspur fail to be popular?

Such was the cavalier, who had conquered the arm of Captain Scarthe, and the heart of Marion Wade.

*　　　*　　　*　　　*　　　*　　　*　　　*

It was the night of that same day, on which the *fête* had been held in the Park of Sir Marmaduke Wade. The unexpected arrival of the cuirassiers—with the exciting circumstances that succeeded—had brought the sports to an early termination.

After incidents of so tragical a character, it was not likely that any one should care to continue the tame diversion of quoits, or balloon. Even single-stick, and wrestling appeared insipid—succeeded to that strife, that had well-nigh proved deadly.

Long before night, the old camp had become cleared of its crowd. Though groups lingered later in the park, it was not in pursuance of sport, but out of curiosity; and to converse about what was passing at the mansion—whither the cuirassier captain and his troopers had transported themselves, after reading that ironical appeal to the hospitality of its owner.

Among the earliest who had left the ground was the conqueror in the equestrian combat. He could not have gone direct home; or he must have again ridden abroad, since at a late hour of the night—his horse dappled with sweat and foam—he was seen turning out of the king's highway into the bridle-road already described, as running over the ridges in the direction of Stone Dean.

As the woods extended nearly the whole of the way, he rode in shadow—though a bright moon was beaming in the heavens above. He rode in silence too. But the subject of his thoughts may be easily conjectured. Treading a track oft hallowed by her presence, what but Marion Wade could he be thinking of?

More unerringly might his sentiments be divined, when, on reaching the open glade, he stopped under the spreading beech, raised his beaver from his head, and gazed for some seconds upon the white glove, glistening beneath its *panache* of black plumes.

As he did so, his features exhibited a mingled expression—half fondness, half fear—as if his mind was wavering between confidence and doubt. It was an expression difficult to read; and no one ignorant of the circumstances of his life—perhaps no one but himself —could have given it the true interpretation.

Henry Holtspur had more than one thought to sadden his spirit; but the one which most troubled him then was, that she, who had given the glove—for he fondly clung to the belief that it had been a gift—that she had ceased to think either of it or of him. It was now six days since that token had been received; and excepting at the *fête*, he had not met her again. She came no more outside the enclosure of the park—no more was the track of her palfrey impressed upon the forest path

Why had she discontinued those lonely rides—those wanderings in the wood, that had led to such sweet encounters?

For days past, and every hour of the day, had Holtspur been asking himself this question; but as yet it remained unanswered.

Little did young Walter Wade suspect the profound, though well-concealed pleasure with which his fellow-traveler had heard, and accepted his proffered hospitality. The promised introduction on the morrow would surely enable the lover to obtain some explanation—if only a word—to resolve the doubt that had begun to torture him?

That morrow had arrived. The introduction had been given. The interview had ended; ill-starred he might deem it; since the conduct of Marion remained inexplicable as ever. Her speeches during the brief dialogue held between them had appeared even cold. With more pain than pleasure did Holtspur now recall them.

Man of the world as he was—far from being unskilled in woman's heart, or the way of winning it—he should have reasoned differently. Perhaps had the object of this new passion been an ordinary woman, he might have done so. Many had been his conquests; maidens of many climes, and of many shades of complexion—dark and fair, brunette and blonde—all beautiful, but none so brilliantly beautiful as that blue-eyed, golden-haired Saxon girl, who had made conquest of *his* heart, and held even his reason in captivity.

He gazed upon the glove with a glance at once tender and inquiring —as if he might obtain from it an answer to that question of all-absorbing interest;—whether, under the shadow of that sacred tree, it had fallen to the ground by accident, or whether it had been dropped by design?

His steed struck the turf with impatient hoof, as if demanding a reply.

"Ah! Hubert," muttered his rider, "much as I love you—even despite the service you have this day done me—I should part with you, to be assured, that I ought to esteem this spot the most hallowed upon the earth. But, come, old friend! that's no reason why you should be kept any longer out of your stall. You must be tired after your tournament, and a trot of twenty miles at its termination. I' faith, I'm fatigued myself. Let us home, and to rest!"

So saying, the cavalier, by a slight pressure of his knees against the side of his well-trained steed—a signal which the latter perfectly understood—once more set Hubert in motion; who carried him silently away from that scene of uncertain souvenirs.

CHAPTER XXII.

THE FOOTPAD'S CONFESSION.

It was late at night when Harry Holtspur passed between the ivy-mantled piers that supported the dilapidated wooden gate of Stone Dean Park. The massive door of the old mansion was standing open, as he rode forward to it. A light, faintly flickering within the hall, showed in dim outline the wide doorway, with its rounded arch of Norman architecture.

Midway between the jambs could be distinguished the figure of a man—standing motionless—as if awaiting his approach

The moon was shining upon this individual with sufficient clearness to show that he was a young man of medium stature, straight as a lance, and habited in a sort of tunic, of what appeared to be dressed deerskin. His complexion was a reddish brown—darker from the shadowing of a shock of jet-black hair; while a pair of eyes, that glistened against the moonlight, like two circular discs of highly polished ebony, exhibited no appearance of surprise at the approach of the horseman

Something resembling a turban appeared upon the young man's head; while his legs were wrapped in leggings of similar material to that which composed the tunic; and his feet were also encased in a *chaussure* of buckskin. A belt around his waist showed a pattern of colored embroidery; with a short knife stuck behind it, resting diagonally over the region of the heart.

Up to the moment that the horseman made halt in front of the doorway, this individual had neither spoken nor moved—not even as much as a finger; and with the moonlight full upon his face, and revealing his dusky complexion, it would not have been difficult for a stranger to have mistaken him for a statue of bronze—the stoop of the doorway appearing as its pedestal, and the arch above answering to the alcove, in which it had been placed. It was only after the horseman had fairly checked his steed to a stand, that the statue condescended to step down from its niche!

Then, gliding forward with the stealthy tread of a cat, the Indian —for such was this taciturn individual—caught hold of the bridle rein; and stood waiting for his master to dismount.

"Walk Hubert about for five minutes," said the latter, as he leaped out of the saddle. "That ruined stable's too damp for him after the exercise he has had. See that he's well rubbed down, and freely fed, before you leave him."

To these directions, although delivered in his own native language, the copper-colored groom made no verbal response.

A slight motion of the head alone indicated that he understood, and consented to obey them.

His master, evidently looking for no other sort of reply, passed on towards the doorway.

"Has any one been after me, Oriole?" inquired he, pausing upon the steps.

Oriole raised his right arm into a horizontal position, and pointed towards the open entrance.

"Some one inside?"

The interrogatory was answered by a nod in the affirmative.

"Only one, or more?"

The Indian held up his hand with all the fingers closed except one.

"One only? Did he come afoot, or on horseback?"

Oriole made answer, by placing the fore and middle fingers of his right hand astride of the index finger of the left.

"A horseman!" said the cavalier, translating the sign. "'Tis late for a visitor—especially as I did not expect any one to-night. Is he a stranger, Oriole?"

The Indian signaled an affirmative, by spreading his fingers, and placing them so as to cover both his eyes.

"Does he appear to have come from a distance?"

The pantomimic answer to this was the right arm extended to its full length; with the forefinger held in a vertical position—the hand being then drawn slowly in towards the body.

The horseman had come from a distance—a fact that the Indian had deduced from the condition of his horse.

"As soon as you have stalled Hubert, show the stranger into my sitting-room. Be quick about it; he may not intend to stay."

Oriole, leading off the steed, passed out of sight as silently as if both had been the images of a dissolving view

"I hope it is one from London," soliloquized the cavalier, as he entered the house. "I want a messenger to the City, and cannot spare either Dancey or Walford. Likely enough Scarthe's coming down is known there before this; but Sir Marmaduke's accession to the cause will be news, and good news, both to Pym and Hampden

"I shall not wait for Oriole to show him into my room," he continued, after a moment's reflection. "He will be in the old dining-hall, I suppose. I shall go to him at once."

So reflecting, the cavalier entered the room where he expected to salute his nocturnal visitor.

Finding it empty, he proceeded to explore another apartment, into which Oriole might have ushered the stranger; and then another; and at last the library—the apartment habitually used by himself, and where he had desired his guest to be shown in to him.

The library was also found untenanted. No visitor was there.

The cavalier was beginning to feel surprised; when a light glimmering from the kitchen, and a sound heard from it, led him to proceed in that direction.

On entering this homely apartment, he beheld the individual, who had done him the honor to await his coming home at such a late hour of the night. A glance inside betrayed the presence of Gregory Garth.

The ex-footpad was stretched along a large beechwood bench, in front of the fire; which, though originally a good one, was now in a somewhat smoldering condition—the half-burnt fagots having parted in twain, and tumbled down on each side of the *andirons*

There was no lamp; but from the red embers, and the blaze that intermittently twinkled, there came light enough to enable the cavalier to identify the form and features of his visitor.

Their owner was as sound asleep, as if in his own house, and reclining under the coverlet of his own couch; whilst a stentorian snore, proceeding from his spread nostrils, proclaimed a slumber from which it would require a good shaking to arouse him.

"So, Gregory Garth!" muttered the cavalier, bending over the sleeper, and gazing, with a half-quizzical expression, into the countenance of his quondam retainer, "It's you, my worthy sir, I have the honor of entertaining?"

A prolonged snore—such as might proceed from the nostrils of a rhinoceros—was the only response.

"I wonder what's brought him here to-night, so soon after——

Shall I awake him and ask; or leave him to snore away all the morning?"

Another trumpet-like snort seemed intended to signify the assent of the sleeper to the latter course of proceeding.

"Well," continued the cavalier, "I'm rather pleased to find him here. It looks as if he had kept his promise· and disbanded those terrible brigands of his. I trust he has don p. There's a spark of good in the rascal, or used to be; thoug/ ho knows whether it hasn't been trampled out before this. Juri_ g from the soundness of that slumber, one can scarcely think tl . ._'s anything very heavy upon his conscience. Whatever he has d ⁄ , it's to be hoped he has kept clear of ——"

The cavalier hesitated to pronounce th ·. .rd that had come upper-most in his thoughts.

"Holding a ten-foot pike within twe inches of a man's breast, is ugly evidence against him. Who k .. /s what might have been the result, if L hadn't identified those·· · tures in time?

"Shall I let him sleep on? It's ra.:.ur a hard couch; though I've often slept upon no better myself; and I dare say, Gregory hasn't been accustomed to the most luxurious style of living. He'll take no harm where he is. I shall leave him till the morning."

Gregory's former master was about turning away—with the intention of retiring to his own chamber—when something white in the hand of the sleeper caught his eye, causing him to step nearer and examine it.

Touching up the embers with the toe of his boot, and starting a blaze; he saw that the white object was a piece of paper, folded in the form of a letter.

It was one of goodly dimensions, somewhat shriveled up between the fingers of the ex-footpad, that were clutching it with firm muscular grasp. A large red seal was visible on the envelope which the cavalier—on scrutinizing it more closely—could perceive to bear the impress of the royal arms.

"A letter from the king!" muttered he, in a tone of surprise. "To whom is it directed, I wonder? And how comes this worthy to have been so suddenly transformed from a robber on the king's highway into a king's courier?"

The first question might have been answered by reading the super-scription; but this was hidden by the broad horny palm against which the back of the letter rested.

To obtain the solution to either mystery, it would be necessary to arouse the sleeper; and this the cavalier now determined upon doing.

"Gregory Garth!" cried he, in a loud voice, and placing his lips within an inch of the footpad's ear; "Gregory Garth! Stand and deliver!"

The well-known summons acted upon the sleeper like an electric shock—as when often pronounced by himself it had upon others—though perhaps with a different significance.

Starting into an erect attitude—and nearly staggering into the fire, before he could get upon his legs—Garth instinctively repeated the phrase:

"Stand and deliver!"

Then, in the confusion of his half-awakened senses, he continued his accustomed formula :—

"Yer money or yer life! Keep yer ground, comrades! They won't resist. They're civil gents——"

"Ha! ha! ha!" interrupted the cavalier, with a shout of laughter, as he seized his cidevant servitor by the shoulder, and pushed him back upon the bench. "Be quiet, Gregory; or you'll scare the rats out of the house."

"O Lor—O Lord! Master Henry—ye it be! I war a dreamin' —I ar'n't awake yet—a thousand pardons, Master Henry!"

"Ha! ha! ha! Well, Gregory—fortunately there's nothing but the rats to listen to these dreams of yours; else you might be telling tales upon yourself that would lead to the losing of your new commission."

"My new commission! What mean ye by that, Master Henry?"

"Why, from that which you carry in your hand," replied the cavalier, nodding significantly towards the letter. "I take it, you've turned king's courier?"

"Ah! now I understan' ye, Master Henry. King's cooreer, I'deed! That 'ud be a tidyish bizness for Gregory Garth. If I bean't that meself tho', I've been and met one as is. It war all 'bout this bit o' a letter I coomed over here the night—else I'd a made me call at a more seezonable hour."

"Is it for me?"

"Well, Master Henry, it ain't 'zactly 'dressed to ye, nor written to ye' neyther; but, as far as I'm able to make out the meenin' o't, I think as how there be somethin' in't ye ought'r know about. But ye can tell better arter ye ha' read it."

Gregory handed the letter to the cavalier; who now perceived that, although the seal was intact, the envelope had been torn open at the edges.

"A king's despatch   And you've opened it, Gregory?"

"Ye-es, Master Henry," drawled the footpad. "It coomed some-how apart atween my fingers. Maybe I've done wrong? I didn't know it war a king's despatch. And maybe if I hed knowed," he added in an under tone, "I shud a opened it all the same."

The cavalier looked at the superscription:—

For
    Ye Captain Scarthe,
  Command: H. M. Royal Cuirassiers
        Bulstrode Park,
      Shire of Buckingham.

"This is not for me, Garth. It is addressed to——"

"I know all that, Master Henry; though I didn't last night when I got the thing. I heerd o' their coomin' up the road this mornin', but——"

"But how came you by the despatch?"

"How coomed I by it?"

"Yes, who gave it to you?"

"Well, Master Henry—I got it—a gentleman I met last night—he —he gin it to me."

"Last night, you say? At what hour?"

"Wal, it war lateish—considerable lateish i' the night."

"Was it before, or after——"

"I met ye, Master Henry? That be what ye would be askin? Well, it war a leetlish bit arter."

Gregory hung his head, looking rather sheepish, as he made the stammering acknowledgment. He evidently dreaded further cross-questioning.

"What sort of a gentleman was he?" inquired the cavalier, with an air of interest, that had something else for its cause than the backslidings of the footpad.

"He war wonderfull fine dressed, an' rode a smartish sort o' beest —he did. 'Ceptin that ere black o' yourn, Master Henry, I han't seed a better hoss for some time to coom. As for the gent hisself, he sayed he war jest what ye ha' been a callin' me—a king's cooreer."

"And so you took this from the king's courier?"

"Oh! Master Hen——"

"I am sure he did not *give* it to you?"

"Well, Master Henry, it's no use me tellin' ye a lie 'bout it. I acknowledge I *tuk* the letter from him."

"And something else, no doubt. Come, Garth! no beating about the bush. Tell the whole truth!"

"Good lor! master; must I tell ye all?"

"You must; or you and I never exchange words again."

"Lor—O Lord! I'll tell ye, then, everything that happened atween us. Ye see, Master Henry," continued he, disposing himself for a full confession; "ye see, the gent hed such fine things about him—as a king's cooreer ought'er hev, I s'pose—a watch an' chain, an' fine clothes, an' a goold pencil, an' a thing he called a locket, to say nothin' o'——"

"I don't want the inventory, Garth," interrupted the cavalier. "I want to know what *you* did to him. You stripped him of all these fine things, I suppose?"

"Well, Master Henry, since I must tell ye the truth o't, I woan't deny but I tuk some on 'em from him. He didn't need 'em nigh as much as meself—that hedn't got nothin' in the world but them old duds as ye seed stuck up on sticks. I eased him o' his trumpery; that I confess to."

"What more did you do to him?"

This question was asked in a tone of stern demand.

"Nothin' more, I declare it, Master Henry—only—to make sure agin' his follerin' o' me—I tied him, hand and foot; and left him in the old hut by the roadside—whar there would be less danger o' his catching cold i' the night air."

"How considerate of you! Ah, Gregory Garth! Gregory Garth! All this after what you promised me, and so emphatically, too!"

"I swar, Master Henry, I ha'n't broke my promise to ye. I swar it!"

"Haven't broken your promise! Wretch! you only make matters worse by such a declaration. Didn't you say just now, that it was after parting with me, you met this messenger?"

"That's true; but ye forget, Master Henry, I promised to ye *that night* shud be my last upon the road: an' it hez been, an' will be."

"What mean you by this equivocation?"

"'Twar jest *eleven*, when ye an' yer young friend rode off. Thear war still a hour o' the night to the good; and, as ill luck would a't

jest then the feller kim ridin' up, glitterin' all ov'r i' spangles an'
satin, like a pigeon, as kep' sayin' ' Come an' pluck me!' What
cud I do? He wanted pluckin,' an' I hedn't the heart to refuse
him. I did it; but I swar to ye, Master Henry—an' I swar
it, as I hope for mercy hereafter—that I hed him stripped *afore it
struck twelve.* I heerd the bells o' Peters Chaffont a ringin' that
hour, jest as I war ridin' away from the ruin."

"*Riding* away! You took his horse, then?"

"Sure, Master Henry, ye wou'dn't a hed me to walk, wi' a beast
standin' ready seddled on the road afore me? He couldn't a been ne
use howsomedever to the cooreer: as he warn't a-goin' any furrer
that night. Besides, ye see, I hed all them clothes to carry. I
couldn't leave *them* behind; not knowin' as they mightn't some day
betray me arter I had turned honest."

"Garth! Garth! I doubt that day will never come. I fear you
are incorrigible."

"Master Henry!" cried the ex-footpad, in a tone in which serious
sincerity was strangely blended with the ludicrous " did ye iver know
o' me to break a promise? Did ye iver in yer life?"

"Well, in truth," answered the cavalier, responding to the earnest
appeal which his old servitor had addressed to him; "in the *letter*
I do not remember that I ever have. But in the *spirit*—alas!
Gregory——"

"Oh! master; doan't reproach me no more. I can't abear it
from ye! I made that promise t'other night, an' ye'll see if I
don't keep it. Ah! I'll keep it if I shud starve. I will by——"

And the ex-footpad, uttering an emphatic phrase, as if more fixedly
to clinch his determination, struck his right hand forcibly against
his ribs—his huge chest giving out a hollow sound, as though it had
received the blow of a trip-hammer.

"Gregory Garth," said the cavalier, speaking in a serious tone,
"if you would have me believe in the sincerity of your conversion,
you must answer me one question, and answer it without evasion.
I do not ask it either out of idle curiosity, or with any wish to use
the answer, whatever it be, to your prejudice. You know me,
Gregory, and will not deceive me?"

"Trust me for that, Master Henry—niver. niver. Ask yer quest'n.
Whatsomever it be, I'll gie ye a true answer."

"Answer it only, if you can say, yes, If your answer must be in
the negative, I dont want to hear it. Your silence will be sufficient."

"Put it, Master Henry; put it: I ain't afeerd."

The cavalier bent forward, and whispered the interrogatory:—

"Is your hand clear of—*murder?*"

"Oh Lord!" exclaimed the footpad, starting back with some show of horror, and a glance half reproachful. "O lor, Master Henry! Could ye a suspeecioned me o' such a thing? Murder—no—no—niver! I can swar to ye, I niver thort o' doin' such a thing; an' my hands are clear o' blood as them o' the infant in its kreddle. I've been wicked enough 'ithout that. I've robbed as ye know—war a-goin' to rob yerself an' yer friend——"

"Stay, Garth! what would you have done, had I not recognized you!"

"Run, Master Henry! run like the old Nick! I'd a tuk to my heels the next minnit, arter I see'd ye war in 'arnest; an' if yer pistol hedn't a put a stop to me, I'd a left my comrades to yer mercy. Oh! Master Henry; there ain't many travelers as would heve beh'ved like ye. It be the first time I iver hed to do more than threeten, an' bluster a bit; an' that war all I intended wi' ye an' yer friend."

"Enough, Gregory!" said the cavalier, apparently satisfied that his old henchman had never shed innocent blood.

"And now," continued he, "I hope you will never have even *threatening* to reproach yourself with in the future—at least so far as travelers are concerned. Perhaps ere long I may find you adversaries more worthy of your redoubtable pike. Meanwhile, make yourself comfortable here, till the morning. When my attendant returns from the stable, he will see to getting you some supper, and a better bed than you've just been roused from."

"Oh, Master Henry!" cried Garth, seeing that Holtspur was about to retire. "Doan't go! please doan't, till ye've read what's inside that ere dokyment. It concarns weighty matters, Master Henry; an' I'm sure it must be ye among others as is spoken o' in it."

"Concerns me, you think? Is my name mentioned in it?"

"No, not yer name; but thar's some orders about somebody; an' from what I know o' ye meself, I hed a suspeecion, as soon as I read it,—it mout be ye."

"Gregory," said the cavalier, drawing nearer to his old servant, and speaking in a tone that betrayed some anxiety as to the effect of his words, "what you know of me, and mine, keep to yourself

Not a word to any one of my past history; as you expect secrecy for your own. Here my real name is not known. That I go by just now is assumed for a time, and a purpose. Soon I shall not care who knows the other; but not yet, Gregory, not yet. Remember that!"

"I will, Master Henry."

"I shall read this despatch, then," continued the cavalier, "since you say that it contains something that may interest me; and especially, since I do not commit the indiscretion of breaking it open. Ha! ha! Your imprudence, worthy Garth, will save my conscience the reproach of that."

With a smile playing upon his countenance, the cavalier spread out the dispatch; and, holding it down to the light of the blazing logs, soon made himself master of its contents.

CHAPTER XXIII.

A DISPATCH FROM JOHN.

The purport of the king's missive to Scarthe did not appear to take Henry Holtspur much by surprise. His bearing betokened, that part of what it contained was known to him already; and the other part he might have been expecting. Enough, however, appeared in his manner to convince Gregory Garth, that he had given no offence to his old master in having stripped the courier of his dispatch.

Whilst Holtspur was still poring over the paper, the Indian youth entered; and after standing a moment or two in solemn silence—as if to see whether he was required for any particular purpose—he took a lamp from the table. Having lighted it at the blaze of the fire, he again withdrew. He departed as silently as he had entered, leaving Gregory Garth gaping in true Saxon astonishment, and wondering what part of the world had given birth to this wordless foreigner.

The cavalier after reading the dispatch folded it up; and deposited it under the breast of his doublet, as something to be carefully kept. Then turning to the ex-footpad, and pointing significantly to some viands that appeared upon the shelf, he strode out into the corridor, and took his way towards the library—into which Oriole, with the lamp, had already preceeded him.

This was a large room, plainly and somewhat scantily furnished. An oaken table stood in the centre, with some chairs of like construction, set scatteringly around the sides. Against the walls were suspended a number of paintings—their subjects scarce distinguishable under an envelope of long neglected dust. Here and there stood book-cases; their shelves close-packed with huge antique tomes, equally the victims of long neglect. Other objects, lying negligently around, appeared to have seen more recent service. There were arms, accoutrements, riding gear, traveling valises, and such like paraphernalia—placed *sans façon* on chairs, tables, or on the floor; and giving evidence that the house was tenanted by one who contemplated only a temporary sojourn.

There was no one in the room as the cavalier entered it. The Indian, after depositing his lamp on the table, had gone out again; and was now seen standing on the stoop of the front entrance—silent and statue-like, as at the moment of his master's return

"So so," muttered the cavalier, seating himself by the table; and once more perusing the dispatch. "Scarthe sent down to recruit! And for what purpose? Not for a new campaign against the Scots? I think his Majesty has had enough of that enemy. There's another may soon claim his attention—nearer home. Perhaps he is growing suspicious; and this may explain his instructions to the cuirassier captain. Well, let *him* obey them, if he can. As to recruiting, I fancy I've been before him in that work. He'll not add many files to his troop in this county—if peasants' promises are worth relying upon. Hampden's persecution and popularity have now secured Buckinghamshire for the good cause—the yeomanry to a man; and as for the peasantry, I have got *them* into the right way of thinking. The gentry, one after another, come round to us. This day has decided Sir Marmaduke Wade; converting him from a passive spectator to an active partisan—conspirator, if the name rings better. Ah! Sir Marmaduke! henceforth I shall love you, almost as much as I love your daughter. No, no, no. That is a love that passes all comparison; for which I would sacrifice everything upon the earth—aye, *even the cause!*

"No one hears me; I am speaking to my own heart. It is .lle to attempt deluding it. I may disguise my love from the world; but not from myself, no, nor from *her*. She must know it ere this? She must have read it in my looks and actions. Not an hour passes that she is not in my mind—not a minute. Even in my dreams do I behold her image—as palpably before me, as if she were present—that glorious image of feminine grace, crowned with red roses and yellow gold!

"Can it be an illusion? Could it have been *all accident?* Have those encounters been fortuitous—on my side only designed? And the last and dearest of all,—when was suffered to fall to the ground that snow-white souvenir, I have pinned so proudly to my beaver--tell me, ye spirits who preside over the destinies of Love—say that I am not the victim of a fancy, false as it would be fatal to my happiness!

"I saw her—I spoke to her—I dared not ask herself. Though yearning for the truth—as the soul yearns for a knowledge of *hereafter*—I dared not trust myself to demand it. I dreaded the answer, as one building castles in the air may dread the tempest that in an instant may destroy them.

"O God! I feel that if this structure be destroyed—this last love of my life—I shall perish amid the ruins."

The cavalier paused, a deep sigh causing his bosom to heave upward—as if in terror at the contemplation of such a contingency.

After a moment he resumed the thread of his reflections.

"She must have seen her glove so conspicuously placed? She could not fail to recognize it? She could not mistake the motive of my wearing it? If, after all, *her* act was not intentional—if the gauntlet was really *lost*—then am *I* lost. I shall pass in her eyes as an impertinent—a presumptuous trickster. Instead of her love, I shall be the object of her contempt—not pitied, but scorned! Even Scarthe, despite his defeat, will be thought worthier than I!

"I am mad to think of her! More than mad to hope she should think of me! Worse than wicked to wish it. Even if she *should* love me, how can it end? *Only in her undoing!* Heaven keep me from the crime!

"Heaven is my judge, I have endeavoured to avoid it. I have tried *not* to love her; at times wished she should not love me. This was at first; but, alas! no longer can I resist the sweet fascination. My heart has leaped beyond my control; and both soul and body must

now obey its inclinings. Without the love of Marion Wade, I care
not how soon my life may come to an end—nor much either in what
way—an ignominious gallows, or an honored grave.

"Sir Marmaduke I must speak to in person. Even a letter might
not now reach him. 'Tis monstrous, this act of his *Gracious
Majesty!*" The cavalier pronounced the last words with a scornful
emphasis. "Monstrous, as on the king's part, stupidly foolish.
It cannot fail to effect good service for our side; and I should rejoice
were it any other than Sir Marmaduke. But, to think of this man
in his house—Richard Scarthe—the wily courtier—the notorious
profligate—under the same roof with Marion Wade—in the same
room—seated by the same table—in her presence at all hours, by
night as by day—wielding that dangerous power that springs from an
attitude of authority. O Heavens!"

The painful thoughts which this train of reasoning produced, caused
the cavalier to start to his feet, and rapidly pace the room—in hope
of allaying his agitation.

"Will Sir Marmaduke remain at Bulstrode?" he continued, after
a time. "He cannot help himself? To go elsewhere, would only
bring down upon him the wrath of this queen-ridden tyrant—
perhaps, subject him to some still more severe infliction? But will
he keep his family there—exposed among the swaggering soldiery—
perhaps to be insulted—perhaps · ·

"Surely he will send them away—somewhere, anywhere, until a
better time? Thank Heaven, there is hope of a better!"

"I shall see Sir Marmaduke to-morrow. I promised him I should.
With *her*, too, shall I seek an interview; although it may end in
giving me chagrin—even if it should be my last."

Having muttered this somewhat reckless resolve, the cavalier once
more threw himself into a chair; and, with his elbows resting upon
the table, and the palms of his hands crossed over his forehead, he
seemed to give way to some profound and painful reflection.

*   *   *   *   *   *   *

Whatever it was, he was not allowed long to indulge in it. The
entrance of Oriole would scarce have aroused him from his reverie—
for the moccasined foot of the Indian made no sound upon the floor
—but at the same instant a noise of another kind was heard within
the apartment—the grinding of a horse's hoof on the gravel outside
the entrance door.

Oriole, after entering, had stopped in an attitude that told he had
something to communicate.

" What is it, Oriole ?   Another visitor ? "

The Indian nodded in the affirmative.

" On horseback ?   I need not ask : I hear the tread of his horse. A stranger ? "

With the same pantomime as he had used when interrogated before, the Indian made reply—adding also, by a repetition of his former signs, that the visitor had come from a distance.

"Show him in here; see to his horse, and find stabling fo. him The gentleman may perhaps make stay for the night."

Without any other acknowledgement that he understood the instructions, than by proceeding to obey them, the taciturn attendant turned on his heel, and glided out of the apartment.

The arrival of a guest at that, or any other hour, caused but little surprise to the host of Stone Dean.   There was nothing unusual in the circumstance.   On the contrary, more than a moiety of his visitors were accustomed to make their calls after midnight—not unfrequently taking their departure before morning.   Hence the " perhaps " in the orders given to Oriole.

"Who can he be ? " was Holtspur's self-interrogation, as his attendant passed out of the room.   "I expected no one to-night."

The grave, sonorous voice, at this moment interrogating the Indian furnished no clue to the speaker's identity.   Holtspur did not recognize it.

There was no reply on the part of Oriole; but, his silent gesticulation must have proved sufficient: for, shortly after, the tread of a heavy boot, accompanied by a slight tinkling of roweled spurs, sounded within the hall.   In another moment, a tall dark man made his appearance in the doorway; and, without waiting further invitation, or even taking off his hat, stepped resolutely into the room.

The individual, thus freely presenting himself, was a man of peculiar—almost rude—aspect.   He was dressed in a suit of coarse brown cloth ; a felt hat, without any feather, and strong trusset boots—the heels of which were furnished with iron spurs, exceedingly rusty. Instead of lace, he wore a band of plain linen of the narrowest cut which, with the closely trimmed hair above, betokened an affectation of the Puritan costume ; whatever may have been the religious proclivities of the wearer.

Notwithstanding the commonness of his attire, there was nothing, either in his countenance or demeanor, that proclaimed him a mere messenger, or servant.   On the contrary, the slight salute which he

vouchsafed to the cavalier; the non-removal of his hat; and the air
of cool confidence which he continued to preserve, after entering the
room, bespoke a man, who, whatever his rank in life, was not accustomed to cringe in the presence of the proudest.

The face was rather serious than sour. The hair was dark—the
skin slightly cadaverous—though the features were not disagreeable
to look upon. Though far from cheerful in their expression, they
were interesting from a certain cast denoting calmness and courage;
traits of character further confirmed by the determined glance of a
penetrating coal-black eye.

"By the dust upon your doublet, Master," said Holtspur, after re
turning the salutation of his visitor, "you have left some miles of
road behind you, since setting foot in the stirrup?"

"Twenty-five."

"That is just the distance to London. Thence, I presume?"

"From London."

"May I ask your errand?"

"I come from *John*," replied the stranger, laying a significant em
phasis on the name.

"You have a message for me?"

"I have."

There was a pause—Holtspur remaining silent—as if awaiting the
delivery of the message.

"Before declaring my errand," pursued the stranger, "I want a
word, to make sure you are he for whom it is intended."

"The John who sent you, is the same who nobly resisted payment
of the *ship money*."

"Enough!" said the messenger, taking a dispatch from under the
breast of his doublet; and, without further hesitancy, handing it to
his host.

There was no superscription upon the folded paper; but, as the
cavalier broke it open under the light of the lamp, at the head of the
page could be seen something that resembled an address—written in
hieroglyphics.

The body of the despatch was in plain English, and as follow:—

"*A cuirassier captain—Scarthe by name—has gone down with the
skeleton of a troop to your neighborhood. It is believed he has a commission to recruit. He is to be quartered on Sir Marmaduke Wade; but
you will know all this before our messenger reaches you. It is well·
Sir Marmaduke will surely hold out no longer! Make some excuse to*

him ; and ascertain how this BENEVOLENCE *acts. Do all you can, without compromising yourself, to make the recruiting unpopular. Call the friends together at the old rendezvous on the night of the 29th Pym and Martin, and I will be down; and perhaps young Harry Vane. If you could get Sir Marmaduke to attend, it would be a point. See that your invitations are conveyed with due secrecy, and by trusty hands. I give you but little time. Act with caution; for this cuirassier captain, who is a courtier of some note, is doubtless entrusted with other commissions, besides that of raising recruits. Keep your eye upon him; and keep his as much as may be off yourself. My Messenger returns here at once. Feed his horse, and despatch him. You may trust the man. He has suffered in the cause : as you may convince yourself by glancing under the brim of his beaver. Don't be offended if he insists on wearing it in your presence. It's a way he has. He will himself tell you his name, which for certain reasons may not be written here. The good work goes bravely on."*

So ended the dispatch.

There was no name appended. None was needed; for, although the handwriting was not that of the great patriot, Henry Holtspur well knew that the dictation was his. It was not the first communication of a similar kind that had passed between him and Hampden.

The first thing which he did, after having read the dispatch, was to cast a stealthy glance at the individual who had been its bearer; and directed towards that portion immediately under his hat.

Holtspur could observe nothing there—at least nothing to explain the ambiguous allusion in the letter of his correspondent. One circumstance, however, was singular. On both sides, the brim of the beaver was drawn down, and fastened in this fashion by a strap of leather passing under the chin, as if the wearer had caught cold in his ears, and wished to protect them from the night air.

The oddness of the style did not remain long a puzzle. He who had adopted it, noticed the furtive scrutiny of the cavalier; and answered it with a grim smile.

" You perceive that I wear my hat rather slouchingly—not to say ill-mannerly," said he. " It has been my fashion of late. Why I've taken to it would be explained by my uncovering; but, perhaps it would save trouble, if I tell you my name. I am William Prŷnne."

" Prynne! " exclaimed the cavalier, starting forward and eagerly grasping the Puritan by the hand. " I am proud to see you under my poor roof; and, such hospitality as I can show——"

"Henry Holtspur need not declare these sentiments to William Prynne," said the earless Puritan, interrupting the complimentary speech. "The friend of the oppressed is well known to all who have suffered; and I am of that number. I thank you for a hospitality which I can partake of for but a few minutes. Then I must bid you adieu, and be gone. The work of the Lord must not tarry. The harvest is fast ripening; and it behooves the reapers to get their sickles in readiness."

The cavalier was too much alive to the necessity of the times, to spend a moment in idle speech. Directing the messenger's horse to be well cared for—a duty which the ex-footpad took upon himself to perform—he ordered Oriole to place a repast before his visitor.

To this the hungry Puritan, notwithstanding his haste, proceeded to do ample justice; while Holtspur, throwing open his desk, hurriedly indited an answer to the letter of his correspondent.

Like the dispatch, it was neither directed nor signed by any name, that could compromise either the writer, or him for whom it was intended. The greatest danger would be to him who was to be entrusted with its delivery. But the staunch partisan of religious liberty recked little of the risk. The great cause, glowing in his zealous heart, rendered him insensible to petty fears; and, after finishing his hurried meal, he once more betook himself to the saddle; shook the hand of his host with cold yet fraternal grasp; bade adieu to Stone Dean; and rode swiftly and silently away.

CHAPTER XXIV

A TRIO OF COURIERS.

Before the hoof-strokes of the Puritan's horse had ceased grinding on the graveled path, Holtspur summoned the ex-footpad into his presence.

During the interval that had elapsed, the latter had not been idling his opportunity, as was indicated by the condition of the haunch of cold venison of which he had been invited to partake; and which was the same set before the traveler who had just taken his departure. A huge *crevasse* scooped crosswise out of the joint, told incontestably that Garth had supped to his satisfaction; while a tankard of strong ale, which accompanied the missing meat, had set his spirits in a very satisfactory state.

As he had previously obtained sufficient sleep—to compensate for his loss for that necessary restorative on the preceding night—he was now ready for anything—according to his own declaration "anything from pitch and toss up to manslaughter!"

It was fortunate he was in this prime condition; since his services —though not for any sanguinary purpose—were just then needed.

"Garth!" began the cavalier, as his old retainer entered the room "I hinted to you, that a good cause might stand in need of you soon. It needs you *now.*"

"I'm ready, Master Henry, to do yer biddin'; an' though I never cut throat i' me life, if *you* say the word——"

"Shame—shame! Gregory! Don't, my good fellow, allow your thoughts to run into such frightful extremes. Time enough to talk of throat-cutting when——" here the cavalier paused in his speech; "never mind when," he continued—"I want you just now for a purpose altogether pacific."

"Oh, anythin' ye like, Master Henry. I'm ready to turn Puritan, an' go a preechin', if ye're i' the mind to make a missioner o' me. I had a word or two wi' that theer'un, whiles ye war a writin' im out his answer; an' he gied me a consid'rable insight into theer way o' translatin' the Scripter. I reckon it be the right way; though 'tain't accordin' to old Master Laud an' his Romish clargy."

"Come, Garth!" said the cavalier, speaking impatiently; "the service for which I want you has nothing to do with religious matters. I'm in need of a messenger—one who knows the country—more especially the residences of a number of the gentry, to whom I have occasion to send letters. How long have you been living in Buckinghamshire?"

"Well, Master Henry, I've been in an' about old Bucks a tidyish time—off an' on I reckon for the better part o' the last ten year—i'deed, iver since I left the old place, ye know—but I han't niver been over a entire year i' the one partikler place at a time, d'ye see. My constitushun ha' been rather delicate at times, an' needed change o' air."

"You know the topography of the country, I suppose?"

"I doan't understand what ye mean by that ere topografy. It be a biggish sort o' a word. If ye mean the *roads*, I knows *them*, putty nigh as well as the man that made 'em—'specially them that runs atween here an' Oxford."

"Good! That's the very direction in which I stand in need of a trusty messenger. I have others I can send towards the north and south; but none who know anything of the Oxford side. You will do. If you are familiar with the roads in that direction, then you must also be acquainted with most of the residences near them—I mean those of the gentry."

"Oh! ye-e-s," assented Greorgy, in a thoughtful drawl. "I've heerd speak o' most on 'em; an' I dar say most o' 'em's heerd speak o' me."

"Could you deliver letters to H—— L——, to Sir K. F——, to young M——, son of Lord S., to R——M——, of Cheveley Park, and to Master G. O., a magistrate of the borough of High Wycombe?"

The cavalier, in putting this question, gave the names in full.

"Well," replied the ex-footpad, "I dare say I kud deliver letters to all the gents ye've made mention o', that be i' the order as ye've named 'em. But if I war to begin whar ye've left off, then I shud be obligated to leave off jest whar I hed begun."

"What! I don't understand you, Gregory."

"Why, it be simple enough, Master Henry. War I to carry a letter to that old pot-guts Justice o' High Wycombe, 'tain't likely I shud bring back the answer, much less get leave to go on to the t'others, as ye've named."

"How's that, Garth."

"Kase ye see Old Wyk an' I hae *had a leetlish bit o' a quarrel,* oncest on a time; an if he war to see me agin, he might remember that ere diff'rence atween us, an' *jug* me. I'll take yer letters to t'others; an' 'im last o' all, if ye insist on't; but if ye do, Master Henry, I won't promise to bring back any answers."

"Never mind *him*, then," said the cavalier, appearing to give up the idea of communicating with the Wycombe Justice. "You can safely visit *all* the others, I suppose?"

Gregory nodded assent.

"You must start at once. Ah! I did not think of it; you will stand in need of a horse!"

"No, I woan't," replied the footpad, with a significant smile, "I've got one."

"Oh! the horse you——"

The cavalier hesitated to finish the speech that had risen to his tongue.

"Why, ye-e-s," drawled the ex-footpad, "it's a anymal as has done the king sarvice; an' I doan't see why it shudn't now be employed in the sarvice o' the people. If I be allowed to ha' my guess, Master Henry, I shud say, that's the errant on which ye be sendin' me."

"It is," assented the cavalier, with emphasis.

"I am glad o' 't," exclaimed Garth, in a tone that betrayed a certain degree of enthusiasm. "Write yer letters, Master Henry, I'll take 'em whar they'er directed—even if one o' 'em be to *the jailer o' Newgate!*"

The cavalier, gratified by this ebulition, turned smilingly to the table, and commenced preparing the epistles.

In less than an hour, the ex-footpad was transformed into a postman; and mounted upon the stolen steed of the king's courier was making his way along the main road that runs between the city of London and the city of Colleges.

At his departure the Indian attendant was called into the room

"Oriole!" asked the cavalier. "Do you think you can find the way to the cottage of Dick Dancey—the woodman who comes here so frequently? You have been to the wigwam, haven't you?"

The Indian made a sign of assent.

"You know the way, then? The moon is still shining. I think you will have no difficulty in finding the place—although there's not a very clear path to it."

Oriole's only rejoinder to this was a slight scornful curling of the lip, as much as to say, "Does the pale-face fancy that I am like one of his own race—a fool to lose my way in the forest?"

"All right, my redskin!" continued the cavalier, in a jocular strain, "I see you can find the road to Dancey's. But I want you to go beyond. In the same direction, only half a mile farther on, there is another hut inhabited by another woodman. You have seen him here also—the young man with the hay-colored hair and white eyebrows?"

Oriole signified that he had seen the individual; though a certain expression—just discernible in the Indian's eye—betokened repugnance to the person so described.

"Very well," continued the cavalier, without appearing to notice the expression. "I want both Dancey and the light-haired man to come to me—as soon as you can summon them. Go to Dancey's first; and if you think you cannot find the other, Dancey will go along with you. Tell both to come prepared for a journey of two days. What a pity you can't talk, my poor fellow! But no matter for that; Dancey will understand your signs."

The Indian, as if he either did not hear, or heeded not this expression of sympathy, turned towards the door; and without either sign or ceremony made his spectral-like departure.

"The night of the 29th," soliloquized Henry Holtspur, as he sat once more pen in hand before his writing-table. "Not much time have they given me. Dick and his prospective son-in-law must start at once. By-the-way, I don't know whether it's safe to trust this Walford—though the old deer-stalker believes in him. I'm always suspicious of white eyebrows. I've noticed something in his grey green eyes I don't like; and this very day—after I had espoused the quarrel of his sweetheart, too—I saw him looking at me with glances not altogether grateful! Jealous, perhaps, of the girl having given me those flowers? Ah! if he only knew how little her token was cared for, alongside that other token—if he knew how I myself was suffering—perhaps 'twould cure him of his spleen!

"After all he's but a brutal fellow—far from worthy of being the favorite of this bold forest bird, Bet Dancey. I' faith she's a hen-hawk that deserves an eagle for her mate; and I might have given this rough rustic cause to be uncomfortable, but that his black beauty is eclipsed under the glare of that dazzling sunbeam. Ah! Marion Marion! in thy presence—or absence either—all other faces seem ill favored. Charming or ugly, to my eyes all are alike!

"Come!" continued the cavalier, as the train of his reflections was interrupted by some thought prompting him to the necessity of action. "I must get these letters ready against the arrival of my messengers There are a dozen, and I'm but an indifferent scribe. Luckily, as they're only 'notes of invitation,' a word to each will be sufficient."

Saying this, he drew his chair nearer to the table; and proceeded to pen the epistles.

He did not desist from his task, until some ten or twelve letters— sealed and addressed to various individuals, all gentlemen of the county, lay on the table before him.

"These, I think, are all," muttered he, as he ran his eye over the addresses. "Along with those, whom Garth has gone to summon, a goodly array they will make, and all true friends to the cause of England's liberty!"

This soliloquy was succeeded by the entrance of the Indian, whose dark form came stealing like a shadow under the light of the lamp.

By a pantomimic gesture, his master was told that the two men he had gone to fetch, had arrived along with him and were waiting orders outside.

"Send them in here," commanded the cavalier. "One at a time. First, Dancey; the other after Dancey has gone out."

Oriole instantly vanished; and soon after the tread of a heavily shod foot was heard in the hall outside.

There was a single knock followed by the spoken permission to "come in."

The door opened; and the noted deer-stealer stepped into the apartment.

He was a man of immense body and large limbs, somewhat loosely put together; but from sheer size seemingly endowed with herculean strength.

About his face there was nothing to indicate any evil disposition. On the contrary, it had a cheerful honest look; which rather contradicted the character implied by the appellation of deer-stealer. As with his representative of modern days, the poacher, perhaps the stealing of a deer, as the snaring of a pheasant, could scarce have been looked upon in the light of a positive theft. At all events Dick Dancey, who was notorious in this line, was otherwise well regarded oy those who had dealings with him.

He was no ordinary man—either in physical or mental conforma- tion; and his huge muscular form, crowned by a capacious head, is which glanced a pair of dark-brown eyes, keen as an eagle's, gave him an imposing, if not a fearful aspect. He was dressed in a doublet of faded cotton velveteen, with trunks of coarser material reaching down to mid-thigh. From the bottoms of these to the tops of his heavy cow-skin boots, his limbs were protected by thick woolen hose; while on his head appeared a full-crowned cap made out of the skin of a spotted dog, the long hair ruffing out around the rim.

The accoutrements of this formidable forester were of the simplest. A skin wallet, suspended by a belt passing over his shoulders, hung by his right side; while as if to balance it, a heavy hanger, half sword, half knife, dangled against his left hip. A large knotted stick, carried in hand, completed his equipment for the journey, of the nature of which he seemed to have had some previous acquaintance.

"Dancey!" said the cavalier, as soon as the deer-stealer was fairly inside the room, "I want you upon a matter of business. You are an accomplished traveler, I know. Have you any objection to play errand-boy for a couple of days?"

"To carry any message for you, sir," rejoined the woodman, with a grotesque effort at a bow, "I'd esteem an honor, 'specially after what happened this day, sir; or I moat say yesterday, seein' it be now near the morrow mornin'. My daughter, sir, I can answer for Bet, she's a good-hearted gurl, sir, though maybe a little too forrard, or that sort; but she be wonderful obleeged, sir, to you, sir."

"Poh-poh, Dancey; I am not deserving of your daughter's thanks. What I did in her behalf was only a duty; which I should equally have felt bound to perform for the humblest individual on the ground. Indeed, your beautiful daughter did not seem to stand in need of my interference. She had already found a sufficiently chivalric champion in bold Robin Hood——"

"Ah! sir," interrupted the deer-stealer, bending down towards his patron, and speaking in a tone of serious confidence, "that's just where the trouble be. She han't thanked *him*, and the poor fellow's beside hisself, because she won't make more o' him. I do all I can to get her take on to him; for I believe Wull Walford to be a worthy lad; an' he mean well for my gurl. But 'taren't no use, sir, ne'er a bit on't. As the sayin' be, one man may take a horse to the water, but forty can't make the anymal drink, if he an't a mind to."

"I think, friend Dancey," quietly rejoined the cavalier, "you'll do well to leave your daughter free to follow her own inclinations— especially in a matter of the kind you speak of. Perhaps her instincts of what's best for her, in that regard, may be more trustworthy than yours."

"Ah! sir," sighed the fond parent of the beautiful Betsey, "if i'd leave her free to foller her own ways, she'd go clear to the devil—she *would*. Not that she's a bad sort, my Bet aren't. No, no—she be a good-hearted gurl, as I've already sayed; but she's too forrard, sir —too forrard, and proud enough to have inclinins for them as be far above her. That's why she looks down upon Wull: because ye see, sir, he be only a poor woodman; tho' that's as much as I be myself."

The cavalier might have suspected the beautiful Betsey of having other reasons for disliking "Wull Walford;" but it was not the time to talk upon such a theme; and without further parley, he changed the conversation to the business for which he had summoned the old woodman into his presence.

"Here are six letters I want you to deliver," said he, taking that number from the table.

"You perceive," he added, holding them up to the light of the lamp, "that I have numbered the letters—in the order in which you will arrive at the houses where you are to deliver them—so that there may be no mistake. I need not add, Dancey, that each is to be *delivered with your own hand, or else not at all*."

"I understand what you mean, sir. I don't part wi' ere a one o' 'em, 'cept to the party hisself. You can trust Dick Dancey for that."

"I know it, Dick; and that's why I'm giving you all this trouble. I only wish you could have taken these others; but it's impossible. They're for a different section of the country; and must go by another hand."

"Wull Walford's wi' me, sir. Ye sent for him, too, didn't ye?"

"I did. You say he can be trusted, Dancey?"

"Oh, sir! there's no fear o' him. He ha'n't no love for eyther Church, or King. He has been i' the stocks once too often for that."

"Ah! ah!" laughed the cavalier, "that is but slight recommendation of his trustworthiness. It don't matter, however. He shall not know much of the nature of his errand: and therefore, there will be no great danger in his carrying the letters."

Dancey saw that he was expected to take the road at once; and without further parley, he started off on his distant round of delivery; before leaving the house, however, having fortified himself against the raw air of the night, by a stoup of strong ale—with which Oriole had been directed to supply him.

Will Walford—who among the *dramatis personæ* of the morris dance had performed the *rôle* of Robin Hood—next presented himself to receive his chapter of instructions.

This worthy had doffed his tunic of Kendal green, and now figured in his proper costume—a jerkin of grey homespun russet, with wide petticoat breeches reaching to mid-thigh. The green woolen stockings, in which he had personated the outlaw, still appeared upon his legs—with a pair of heavy hob-nailed buskins on his feet. On his head was the high-crowned hat worn at the *fête*, with a portion of the plume of cock's feathers still sticking behind its band of scarlet colored tape.

Altogether the costume of the woodman was not inelegant; and the wearer affected a certain air of rustic dandyism, which showed him conceited of his personal appearance.

He had but slight reason for this vanity, however. At the *fête* he had proved himself but a poor representative of the chivalrous outlaw of Sherwood Forest; and, now that he stood partially plucked of his borrowed feathers, he looked altogether unlike the man, whom the beautiful Bet Dancey would have chosen for her champion.

It was a countenance, though naturally of an evil aspect, more sullen than sinister; while the glance of a watery otter-like eye, along with a certain expression of cowardice, betrayed insincerity.

Will Walford was evidently a man not to be trusted—very far.

He appeared like one who, to gratify a passion would turn traitor upon a partisan.

It was just such a suspicion of his character that hindered Henry Holtspur from revealing to him the secret contained within those half-dozen letters—which he now entrusted to him for delivery, after giving him the names of the gentlemen for whom they were intended.

With a promise to perform the duty—apparently sincere—the woodman walked out of the room; but, as he turned off into the shadowy hall, a glance flung back over his shoulder betrayed some feeling towards his patron, anything but friendly.

Still more surly was the look cast upon the young Indian, as the latter—apparently with an unwilling grace—presented him with the parting cup.

There was no word spoken, no health drunk—neither of master nor man. The ale vessel was emptied in sullen silence; and, then thanklessly tossed back into the hands from which it had been received.

A gruff "good-night," and Will Wa ford, striding off through the corridor, was soon lost to view.

Oriole turned back into the room accompanied by his master, and stopping near the door, stood waiting for the latter to look around. On his doing so, the Indian elevated his right arm; and holding it horizontally, with the back of his hand upwards, he described a wide curve in an outward direction from his body.

" Good, you say ?   Who is good ? "

The Indian made a motion, to signify that he had not finished his pantomime.

" Ah ! you've something to add ?   Go on."   -

The hand was again carried out from the body in a waving direction; but this time with the thumb turned upwards.

" No," said the cavalier, translating the sign, " *not good*, you mean to say ?   He who has just gone off ? "

Oriole nodded assent—at the same time placing his fore and middle fingers, joined together, over his mouth; and then separating them as he carried them away from his lips—thus signifying, that the words of the woodman would proceed in two directions : otherwise, that he was *double tongued*.

" A liar—a deceiver, you think, Oriole ?   I have some suspicion of it myself.   Do not be afraid ; I shall not trust him too far.   But come ' my faithful red-skin ; you must be tired sitting up ?   Close the door, to keep out the rats and robbers ; and get to your bed.   I hope we will have no more visitors to trouble us, till we've both had a good night's rest.   Go sleep, my lad."

So saying, the cavalier lifted up the lamp ; stepped forth from the library ; and betook himself to his own sleeping apartment.

CHAPTER XXV

IN COUNTRY QUARTERS

On the bold brow of one of the central hills of Bulstrode Park, stood the dwelling—a palatial structure of red brick, with facings of white stone—the latter transported over the sea from the quarries of Jaen.

The style of architecture was that known as "Norman"—with thick massive walls, having the circular Roman arch over the doors and windows.

In front was a space appropriated to the purposes of parterre and shrubbery; while to the rearward extended the stables and other offices—enclosing an extensive court-yard between them and the dwelling.

In the rear of the outbuildings was the garden—approached through the court-yard by a strong iron wicket; while encircling all—grounds, gardens, and houses—was a deep battlemented moat, which imparted to the mansion somewhat of the character of a fortified castle.

On the morning after the *fête* in Bulstrode Park, the court-yard of the dwelling presented an unusual spectacle. A stranger, entering through the great arched gateway, might have mistaken the square enclosure inside for the yard of a barrack. Horses were standing in rows around the walls—their heads tied up to hooks that had been freshly driven into the mason-work; while men in topped boots, wide hanging hose, and grogram shirts—with sleeves rolled up to the elbows—were engaged in grooming them.

Leathern buckets, containing water, stood by the heels of the horses —where the pavement appeared splashed and wet.

Other men, of similar appearance, might have been seen seated upon benches, or squatted upon the coarse woolen covers of their horses —occupying themselves with the cleaning of armor, furbishing steel cuirasses, cuisses, and helmets, to the sheen of silver, and then hanging them against the walls, under a sort of shed that had been specially erected for their reception.

Under the same shelter large demi-pique dragoon saddles had been placed in rows— astride of long trestles set up for the purpose.

Every available space upon the walls was occupied by a bridle, a
pair of spurs, pistols, or holsters, a sword with its belt, or some piece
either of offensive, or defensive, armor.

It is scarce necessary to say, that these horses and men—these
saddles, bridles, arms, and armor—were the component parts of Captain Scarthe's troop of cuirassiers, viewed *en déshabille.*

What with the neighing of steeds that did not belong to the place,
the barking of dogs that did; and the swearing and gibbering of three-
score men in half-a-dozen distinct languages; the usually quiet court-
yard of Sir Marmaduke's mansion had been transformed into a sort
of Pandemonium: for, to say nothing of any other sounds, the conversation usually carried on among Scarthe's cuirassiers was not unlike
what might be heard—could one only penetrate into that mythical
locality.

Notwithstanding their noted ruffianism, they appeared to be behaving better than was their wont—as if under some unusual restraint.
They were merry enough—no doubt from being installed in such comfortable quarters, but they did not appear to exhibit any offensive attitude toward the inmates of the mansion.

If by chance a pretty housemaid tripped across the court-yard, on
some errand to the garden, or elsewhere, she was sure of being
saluted by a volley of *jeux d'esprit* in French, Flemish, or English;
but beyond this, the behavior of the troopers was no worse than that
of most soldiers similarly quartered.

Moreover, the men, instead of being permitted within the mansion,
were contenting themselves to sleep in the out-houses; as testified by
the straw beds scattered over the floors of the granary and other
offices, in which they had passed the night.

This semi-courteous tolerance on the part of Captain Scarthe's
followers towards their involuntary host—unlike the character of the
former, as it was unexpected by the latter—requires some explanation; which the conversation between Scarthe himself and his cornet,
occurring at that very moment, will supply.

The two officers were in a large sitting-room, that had been assigned to them in the eastern wing of the dwelling.   It is scarce
necessary to say that the room was handsomely furnished; for the
mansion of Sir Marmaduke Wade, besides being one of the oldest,
was also one of the grandest of the time. The walls of the apartment specified were covered with Cordovan leather, stamped with
heraldic devices; the huge bay window was hung with curtains of

dark green velvet; while the pieces of massive furniture exhibited sculptural carvings not only elaborate, but perhaps of higher art than can be produced at the present time.

A massive round table in the middle of the floor was covered by a heavy cloth of rich Damascus pattern; while the floor itself in lieu of Brussels or Turkey carpet was hidden under a mattrass of smooth shining rushes, neatly woven into a variety of patterns.

Scarthe was seated, or rather reclining on a *fauteuil* covered with crimson velvet; while his cornet, who had just entered the room, stood in front of him—as if in the reception or delivery of a message.

Neither of the officers was in armor. The steel plates had been laid aside, or not fastened on for that day.

Scarthe himself was habited in all the fantastic frippery fashionable at the time. A doublet of yellow satin, with trunk hose of the same—the latter fringed at the bottoms with silk ribbons, tipped with tags of gold. A broad Vandyke collar of point lace, cuffs to correspond, and a scarlet sash, also weighted with golden tags, adorned the upper part of his body; while boots of yellow Cordovan leather, with snow-white lawn puffing out at the ample tops, completed the list of his habiliments.

Despite his pale face; despite a certain sinister cast of his countenance—not always to be observed—Richard Scarthe was a handsome man. The eyes of many a courtly dame had deemed him more than interesting; and as he reclined against the back of the *fauteuil* in an attitude of perfect ease, he looked not the less interesting that the scarlet scarf passed over his right shoulder was crossed by another of more sombre hue—acting as a *sling*, in which his right arm rested.

A wounded man—especially if the damage has been received in a duel—is a dangerous object for the eye of a sentimental young lady to rest upon. It might be that Captain Scarthe was acquainted with this not very recondite truth. It might be that some such thought had been in his mind that very morning, while making his toilette before the mirror.

The cornet was neither so handsome as his captain, nor so daintily dressed; and yet one previously acquainted with Stubbs' rather slovenly habit, could not have failed to notice on that particular morning that more than ordinary pains had been taken with his " make-up."

He was in a plain military suit of buff, but the collar and cuffs were clean; and so also was his plump, fresh-colored face—a condition in which it was not always to be found.

His hay-colored hair, too, exhibited something of a gloss—as though the brush had been recently and repeatedly passed through it.

There was a flush on Stubbs' cheek with a soft subdued light in his eye, that betokened some unusual emotion in his mind—some thought more refined than ordinarily held dominion there. In short, Stubbs had the look of a man who had been so unfortunate as to fall in love.

As we have said, the cornet was standing. He was silent also; as if he had already delivered his report and was awaiting the reply.

"I'm glad they're taking it so quietly," said the captain in rejoinder to whatever communication his cornet had made. "Our fellows are not used to sleeping in stables—with a fine house standing close by. But we're in England now, Stubbs; and it won't do to keep up the fashions of Flanders. By so doing we might get our good king into disgrace."

"We might, by Ged," stiffly assented Stubbs.

"Besides," continued the captain, speaking rather to himself than to his subaltern, "I've another reason for not letting them forage too freely, just now. The time may come, when it will be more profitable to put the screw on. The cat plays with the mouse before killing it. Did the vagabonds grumble at my order?"

"Not a bit. No, by Ged! They're too fond of you for that."

"Well, cornet; next time you go among them, you can promise them plenty of beef and beer. They shall have full rations of both, and double ones too. But no pickings and stealings. Tell them that the eighth commandment must be kept, and that nothing short of hanging will satisfy me if it be broken. They must be given to understand that we're no longer engaged in a campaign, though the Lord knows how soon we may be. From what I heard and saw yesterday among that rabble, I shouldn't wonder if the king sets us to cutting their throats before spring."

"Like enough," quietly assented Stubbs.

"I don't care how soon," continued the cuirassier captain, musing as he spoke. "I shouldn't care how soon—but—that, if it come to blows, we'll be called away from here; and after the infernal march-ings and countermarchings we've had for the last six months, I feel inclined for a little rest. I think I could enjoy the *dolce far niente* devilish well down here—that is, for a month or so. Nice quarters, a'n't they?"

"Are, by Ged!"

"Nice girls, too—you've seen them, haven't you?"

"Just a glimpse of them through the window, as I was dressing There were two of them out on the terrace."

"There are only two—a daughter and a niece. Come, cornet; declare yourself! Which?"

"Well, the little un's the one to my taste. *She's a beauty*, by Ged!"

"Ha! ha! ha! I might have known it," cried the captain. "Well—well—well!" he continued, speaking to himself in a careless drawl. "I believe, as I always did, that nature has formed some souls utterly incapable of appreciating her highest works. Now here is a man who actually thinks that dapper little prude more beautiful than her queenlike cousin; a woman that to me—a man of true taste and experience—is known to possess qualities—ah! such qualities! Ha! ha! ha! Stubbs sees but the boddice and skirt. I can perceive something more—never mind what—the soul that is concealed under them. He sees a pretty lip—a sparkling eye—a neat nose—a shining tress; and he falls over head and ears in love with one or other of these objects. To me 'tis neither lip, glance, nor tress; 'tis the *tout ensemble*—lips, nose, eyes, cheeks, and *chevelure*—soul and body all combined."

"By Ged! that would be perfection," cried Stubbs, who stood listening to the enraptured soliloquy.

"So it would, cornet."

"But where will you find such? Nowhere, I should say?"

"You are blind, cornet—stone blind, or you might have seen it this morning."

"I admit," said the cornet, "I've seen something very near it— the nearest it I ever saw in my life. I didn't think there was a girl in all England as pretty as that creature. I did'nt, by Ged!"

"What creature?"

"The one we've been speaking of, the little one—Mistress Lora Lovelace is her name. I had it from her maid."

"Ha! ha! ha! You're a fool, Stubbs, and it's fortunate you are so. Fortunate for me, I mean. If you'd been gifted with either taste or sense, we might have been rivals; and that, my killing cornet, would have been a great misfortune for me. As it is, our roads lie in different directions. You see something—I can't, nor can tell you what—in Mistress Lora Lovelace I see that in her cousin which I can, and *do* comprehend. I see perfection. Yes, Stubbs, this morning you have had before your eyes not only the most beautiful woman in the shire of Bucks, but, perhaps, the love-liest in all England. And yet you did not know it! Never mind, worthy cornet. *Chacun à son goût.* How lucky we don't all think alike!"

"Is, by Ged!" assented the cornet in his characteristic fashion, 'I like the little 'un best."

"You shall have her all to yourself. And now, Stubbs, as I can't leave my room with this wounded wing of mine, go and seek an interview with Sir Marmaduke. Smooth over the little rudenesses of yesterday; and make known to him, in a roundabout way—you understand—that we had a cup of sack too much at the inn. Say something of our late campaign in Flanders, and the free life we had been accustomed to lead while there. Say what you like; but see that it be the thing to soften him down and make him our friend I don't think the worthy knight is so disloyal, after all. It's something about this young sprig's being recalled from Court, that has got him into trouble with the king. Do all you can to make him friendly to *us*. Remember, if you fail, we may get no nearer to that brace of beauties, than looking at them through a window, as you did this morning. It would be of no use forcing ourselves into their company. If we attempt that, Sir Marmaduke may remove his chicks into some other nest; and then, cornet, our quarters would be dull enough."

"I'll see Sir Marmaduke at once?" said the subaltern, inter-rogatively.

"The sooner the better. I suppose they have breakfasted ere this. These country people keep early hours. Try the library. No doubt you'll find him there: he's reported to be a man of books."

"I'll go there, by Ged!"

And with this characteristic speech, the cornet hastened out of the room.

"I must win this woman," said Scarthe, rising to his feet, and striding across the floor with an air of resolution; "*I must win her,*

if *I should lose my soul!* Oh! beauty! beauty the true and only
enchanter on earth. Thou canst change the tiger into a tender lamb,
or transform the lamb into a fierce tiger. What was I yesterday
but a tiger? To-day subdued—tamed to the softness of a suckling.
'Sdeath! Had I but known that such a woman was watching—for
she was there, no doubt—I might have avoided that accursed encounter. She saw it all—she must have seen it! Struck down from my
hoise, defeated—'Sdeath!"

The exclamation hoarsely hissing through his teeth, with the fierce
expression that accompanied it, showed how bitterly he bore his
humiliation. It was not only the pain of his recent wound—though
that may have added to his irritation—but the sting of defeat that
was rankling in his soul—defeat under such eyes as those of Marion
Wade!

"'Sdeath!" he again exclaimed, striding nervously to and fro.
"Who and what can the fellow be? Only his name could they tell
me—nothing more—Holtspur! Not known to Sir Marmaduke before
yesterday! He cannot, then, have been known to *her?* He cannot
have had an opportunity for *that?* Not yet—not yet!"

"Perhaps," he continued, after a pause, his brow once more
brightening, "they have never met? She may not have witnessed
the unfortunate affair? Is it certain she was on the ground? I did
not see her.

"After all, the man may be married? He's old enough. But no,
the glove in his hat—I had forgotten that. It could scarcely be his
wife's! Ha! ha! ha! what signifies? I've been a blessed Benedict
myself; and yet while so, have worn my beaver loaded with love-
tokens. I wonder to whom that glove belonged. Ha! Death and
the devil!"

Scarthe had been pacing the apartment, not from side to side, but
in every direction, as his wandering thoughts carried him. As the
blasphemous exclamation escaped from his lips, he stopped suddenly
—his eyes becoming fixed upon some object before him.

On a small table that stood in a shadowed corner of the apartment
a glove was lying—as if carelessly thrown there. It was a lady's
glove, with gauntlet attached, embroidered with gold wire and bordered with lace. It appeared the very counterpart of that at the
moment occupying his thoughts—the glove that had the day before
decorated the hat of Henry Holtspur.

"By heaven, 'tis the *same!*" he exclaimed, the color forsaking his cheeks as he stood gazing upon it. "No—not the same," he continued, taking up the glove, and scrutinizing it with care. "Not the same, but its mate—its fellow! The resemblance is exact; the lace, the embroidery, the design—all. I cannot be mistaken."

And as he repeated this last phrase, he struck his heel fiercely upon the floor.

"There's a mystery," he continued, after the first painful pulsations of his heart had passed. "Not known to Sir Marmaduke until yesterday! Not known to Sir Marmaduke's daughter! And yet wearing her gauntlet conspicuously in the crown of his hat? Was it hers? Is *this* hers? May it not belong to the other—the niece? No—no—though small enough, 'tis too large for her tiny claw. 'Tis the glove of Marion!"

For some seconds Scarthe stood twirling the piece of doeskin between his fingers and examining it on all sides. A feeling far stronger than mere curiosity prompted him to this minute inspection; as would be divined by the dark shadows rapidly chasing each other over his pallid brow.

His looks betrayed both anguish and anger, as he emphatically repeated the phrase—"Forestalled, by heaven!"

"Stay there!" he continued, thrusting the glove under the breast of his doublet. "Stay there, thou devilish tell-tale—close to the bosom thou hast filled with bitter thoughts. Trifle as thou seemest, I may yet find thee of serious service."

And with a countenance in which bitter chagrin was blended with dark determination, he continued to pace excitedly over the floor of the apartment.

CHAPTER XXVI.

THE BOUDOIR.

The warm golden light of an autumn sun was struggling through the half-closed curtains of a window in the mansion of Sir Marmaduke Wade.

It was still early in the afternoon; and the window in question, opening from an upper story and facing westward, commanded one of the finest views of the park of Bulstrode. The sunbeams slanting through the parted tapestry lit up an apartment, which by its light luxurious style of furniture and costly decoration proclaimed itself to be a boudoir or room exclusively appropriated to the use of a lady.

At that hour there was other and better evidence of such appropriation, since the lady herself was seen standing in the embayment of its window, under the arcade formed by the drooping folds of the curtains.

The sunbeams glittered upon tresses of a kindred color—among which they seemed delighted to linger. They flashed into eyes as blue as the canopy whence they came; and the rose-colored clouds they had themselves created in the western sky were not of fairer effulgence than the cheeks they appeared so fondly to kiss.

These were not in their brightest bloom. Though slightly blanched neither were they pale. The strongest emotion could not produce absolute pallor on the cheeks of Marion Wade—where the rose never altogether gave place to the lily.

The young lady stood in the window looking outward upon the park. With inquiring glance she swept its undulating outlines, traced the softly-rounded tops of the chestnut trees, scrutinized the curving lines of the copses, saw the spotted kine roaming slowly o'er the lea, and the deer darting swiftly across the sward; but none of these sights were the theme of her thoughts, or fixed her attention for more than a passing moment.

There was but one object within that field of vision upon which her eyes rested for any length of time, not constantly, but with glances straying from it only to return. This was a gate between two massive piers of mason-work, grey and ivy-grown. It was not the principal entrance to the park, but one of occasional use, which opened near the western extremity of the enclosure into the main road. It was the nearest way for any one going in the direction or Stone Dean, or coming thither.

There was nothing in the architecture of those ivy-covered piers to account for the almost continuous scrutiny given to it by Mistress Marion Wade, nor yet in the old gate itself—a mass of red-colored rusty iron. Neither was new-to her. She had looked upon that entrance—which opened directly in front of her chamber window—every day, almost every hour of her life. Why, then, was she now so assiduously gazing upon it?

Her soliloquy will furnish the explanation.

"He promised he would come to-day. He told Walter so before leaving the camp—the scene of his conquest over one who appears to hate him—far more, over one who *loves him!* No. The last triumph came not then. Long before was it obtained. Ah me! it must be love, or why should I so long to see him?"

"Dear cousin, how is this? Not dressed for dinner? 'Tis within five minutes of the hour."

It was the pretty Lora Lovelace who, tripping into the room, asked these questions—Lora fresh from her toilette and radiant with smiles.

There was no heaviness on *her* heart—no shadow on her countenance. Walter and she had spent the morning together, and whatever may have passed between them, it had left behind no trace of a cloud.

"I do not intend dressing," rejoined Marion; "I shall dine as you see me."

"What, Marion! and these strange gentlemen to be at the table!"

"A fig for the strange gentlemen! It's just for that I won't dress. Nay, had my father not made a special request of it, I should not go to the table at all. I'm rather surprised, cousin, at your taking such pains to be agreeable to guests thus forced upon us. For which of the two are you setting your snare, Little Lora—the conceited captain or his stupid subaltern?"

"Oh!" said Lora, with a reproachful pouting of her pretty lips, "you do me wrong, Marion. I have not taken pains on their account. There are to be others at the table besides the strangers."

"Who?" demanded Marion.

"Why—why,"—stammered Lora, slightly blushing as she made answer, "why, of course there is uncle Sir Marmaduke."

"That all?"

"And—and—cousin Walter, as well."

"Ha! ha! Lora, it's an original idea of yours to be dressing with such studied care for father and Walter. Well, here goes to get ready. I don't intend to make any further sacrifice to the rigor of fashion than just pull off these sleeves, dip my fingers into a basin of water, and tuck up my tresses a little."

"O Marion!"

"Not a pin, nor a ribbon, except what's necessary to hold up my troublesome horse-load of hair. I've a good mind to cut it short Sooth! I feel like pulling some of it out through sheer vexation."

"Vexation—with what?"

"What—what—why, being bored with these blustering fellows—especially when one wants to be alone."

"But, cousin, these gentlemen cannot help their being here. They have to obey the commands of the king. They are behaving very civilly. Walter has told me so. Besides, uncle has enjoined upon us to treat them with courtesy."

"Aha! they'll have scant courtesy from me. All they'll get will be a yes and a no; and that not very civilly, unless they deserve it."

"But if they deserve it?"

"If they do——"

"Walter says they have offered profuse apologies and regrets."

"For what?"

"For the necessity they are under of becoming uncle's guests."

"I don't believe so—no, not a bit. Look at their rude behavior at the very beginning—kissing that bold girl, Bet Dancey, in the presence of a thousand spectators! Ha! well punished was Captain Scarthe for his presumption. He feel regret! I don't believe it, Lora. That man's a hypocrite. There's falsehood written in his face, along with a large quantity of conceit; and as for the cornet—the only thing discernible in his countenance is—stupidity."

As Marion pronounced the last word, she had completed her toilette—all that she had promised or intended to make. She was one who needed not to take much trouble before the mirror. Dressed or in *déshabille* she was the same—ever beautiful. Nature had made her in its fairest mould, and art could not alter the design.

Her preparations for the dinner table consisted simply in replacing her morning boddice by one without sleeves—which displayed her snow-white arms nearly to the shoulders. Having adjusted this, she inserted one hand under her wavy golden hair, and adroitly turning its profuse tresses round her wrist, she rolled them into a spiral coil, which by means of a pair of large hair-pins she confined at the back of her head. Then dipping her hands into a basin of water, she shook off the crystal drops from the tips of her roseate fingers, wiped them on a white napkin, flung the towel upon the table, and cried "Come on!"

Followed by the light-hearted Lora, she descended to the dining-hall, where the two officers were already awaiting their presence.

A dinner-party under such circumstances as that which assembled round the table of Sir Marmaduke Wade—small in numbers though it was—could not be otherwise than coldly formal.

The host himself was polite to his uninvited guests—studiously so; but not all his habitual practice of courtly manners could conceal a certain embarrassment that now and then exhibited itself in incidents of a trivial character.

On his part, the cuirassier captain used every effort to thaw the ice that surrounded him. He lost no opportunity of expressing his regret at being the recipient of such a peculiar hospitality; nor was he at all backward in censuring his royal master for making him so.

But for an occasional distrustful glance visible under the shaggy eyebrows of the knight—visible only at intervals, and to one closely watching him—it might have been supposed that Sir Marmaduke was warming to the words of his wily guest. That glance, however, told of a distrust, not to be removed by the softest and most courteous of speeches.

Marion adhered to her promise and spoke only in monosyllables, though her fine open countenance expressed neither distrust nor dislike. The daughter of Sir Marmaduke Wade was too proud to appear otherwise than indifferent. If she felt contempt, there was no evidence of it—neither in the curling of her lip, nor the cast of her eye.

Equally in vain did Scarthe scrutinize her countenance for a sign of admiration. His most gallant speeches were received with an air of frigid indifference -his wittiest sallies elicited only such smiles as courtesy could not refuse.

If Marion at any time showed sign of emotion, it was when her glance was turned towards the window, apparently in quest of some object that *should* be visible outside. Then her bosom might be seen swelling with a suppressed sigh—as if her thoughts were dwelling on one who was absent.

Slight as were these manifestations, they did not escape the observation of the experienced Scarthe.

He saw and half interpreted their meaning—his brow blackening under bitter fancies thus conjured up.

Though seated with his back to the window, more than once he turned half round to see if there was any one in sight.

When the wine had been passed several times, making him less cautious, his glances of admiration became bolder, his speeches less courteous and reserved.

The cornet talked little.

It was enough for him to endorse the sentiments of his superior officer by an occasional monosyllable.

Though silent, Stubbs was not altogether satisfied with what was passing. The by-play between Walter and Lora, who were seated together, was far from pleasing to him. He had not been many minutes at the table before discovering that the cousins had an amiable inclination towards each other, which carried him to the conclusion that in the son of Sir Marmaduke Wade he would find a very formidable rival.

Even on the blank page of his stolid countenance soon became discernible the lines that indicate jealousy, while in his white skewbald eyes could be detected a glance not a whit more amiable than that which flashed more determinedly from the dark orbs of the cuirassier captain.

The dinner passed without any unpleasant *contretemps*. The party separated after a reasonable time—Sir Marmaduke excusing himself upon some matter of business—the ladies having already made their courtesy to their stranger guests.

Walter, rather from politeness than any inclination, remained a while longer in the company of the two officers, but as the companionship was kept up under a certain feeling of restraint, he was only too well pleased to join them in toasting *The King!*—which, like our modern lay of royalty, was regarded as the *finale* to every species of entertainment.

Walter strayed off in search of his sister and cousin—most likely only the latter; while the officers, not yet invited into the sanctuary of the family circle, retired to their room—to talk over the incidents of the dinner, or plot some scheme for securing the indulgence of those amorous inclinations with which both were now thoroughly imbued.

CHAPTER XXVII.

UNDER THE TREES.

Marion Wade was alone—as before, standing in her window under the arcade of parted tapestry—as before, with eyes bent on the iron gate and ivy-wreathed portals that supported it.

Everything was as before: the spotted kine lounging slowly over the lea; the fallow deer browsing upon the sward; and the birds singing their sweet songs, or winging their way from copse to copse.

The sun only had changed position. Lower down in the sky, he was sinking still lower—softly and slowly, upon a couch of purple-colored clouds. The crest of the Chilterns were tinted with a roseate hue; and the summit of the Beacon-hill appeared in a blaze, as when by night its red fires had been wont to give warning of the approach of a hostile fleet by the channels of the Severn.

Brilliant and lovely as was the sunset, Marion Wade saw it not; or, if seeing, it was with an eye that stayed not to admire.

That little space of rust-colored iron and grey stone-work—just visible under the hanging branches of the trees—had an attraction for her far outstripping the gaudy changes of the sunset.

Thus ran her reflections:—" Walter said he would come—perhaps not before evening. 'Tis a visit to papa—only him! What can be its purpose! Maybe something relating to the trouble that has fallen upon us? 'Tis said he is against the king; and for the people. 'Twas on that account Dorothy Dayrell spoke slightingly of him

For that shall not I? No—never—never! She said he must be peasant born. 'Tis a false slander. He is gentle, or I know not a gentleman.

"What am I to think of yesterday—that girl, and her flowers? I wish there had not been a fête. I shall never go to another!

"I was so happy when I saw my glove upon his beaver. If 'tis gone, and those flowers have replaced it, I shall not care to live longer—not a day—not an hour!"

A sudden change came over both the attitude and reflections of Marion Wade.

Some one had opened the gate! It was a man—a rider—bestriding a black horse!

An instinct stronger than ordinary aided in the identification of this approaching horseman. The eyes of love need not the aid of a glass; Marion saw him with such.

"It is he!" she repeated in full confidence, as the cavalier, emerging from the shadow of the trees, commenced ascending the slope of the hill.

Marion kept her eyes bent upon the advancing horseman, in straining gaze; and thus continued until he had arrived within a hundred yards of the moat that surrounded the mansion. One might have supposed that she was still uncertain as to his identity.

But her glance was directed neither upon his face nor form, but towards a point higher than either—toward the brow of his beaver—where something white appeared to have fixed her regard. This soon assumed the form and dimensions of a lady's gauntlet—its slender fingers tapering towards the crown of the hat, and outlined conspicuously against the darker back-ground.

"It is the glove—my glove!" said she, gasping out the words, as if the recognition had relieved her from some terrible suspense. "Yes, it is still there. O joy!"

All at once the thrill of triumph became checked, by a contrary emotion. Something red was seen protruding from under the rim of the beaver, and close to the glove. Was it a *flower?*

The flowers given by Maid Marian were of that color. Was it one of them?

Quick as the suspicion had arisen did it pass away. The red object sparkled in the sun. It was not a flower; but the garnet clasp that held the gauntlet in its place. Marion remembered the clasp. She had noticed it the day before.

She breathed freely again. Her heart was happier than ever. She was too happy to gaze longer on that which was giving her content. She dreaded to exhibit her blushing cheek to the eyes of the man, whose presence caused it to blush; and she retired behind the curtain, to enjoy unobserved a moment of delicious emotion.

Her happiness did not hinder her from once more returning to the window; but too late to see the cavalier as he passed across the parterre. She knew, however, that he had entered the house; and was at that moment below in the library—holding with her father the promised interview.

She knew not the purpose of his visit. It could not have reference to herself. She could only conjecture its connection with the political incidents of the time; they were talked of in every house—even to dividing the sentiments of the family circle, and disturbing the tranquillity of more than one erst happy home.

She was aware that the visit of Henry Holtspur was *only to her father*. He had come, and might go as he had come, without the chance of her exchanging speech with him; and as this thought came into her mind, she half regretted having retired from the window. By so doing, she had lost the very opportunity long desired—often wished for in vain.

Only a word or two had been spoken between them on the day before—the stiff ceremonial phrases of introduction—after which the incident of the duel had so abruptly parted them.

Now that Holtspur had been presented by a brother—and with the sanction of a father—what reason was there for reserve! Even prudery could not show excuse for keeping aloof. She should have spoken to him from the balcony. She should have welcomed him to the house. He must have seen her at the window? What reflection might he have, about her retiring—as if to hide herself from his gaze? He would scarce consider it courtesy? He might fancy he had given her some offense—perhaps in that very act which had produced such an opposite impression—the triumphant exposure of her glove?

Perhaps he might take offense at her coy conduct, and pluck the token from its place? How could she convey to him the knowledge of her happiness at beholding it there? How tell him that he was not too welcome to wear it?

"If I could find the other," she soliloquized in low murmuring, I should carry it in some conspicuous place, where he might see it on my hand—my breast—in the frontlet of my coif, as he wears its fellow in his beaver. If only for a moment, it would tell him what I wish, without words. Alas! I've lost the other. Too surely have I lost it. Everywhere have I searched in vain. What can I have done with it? Bad omen, I fear, to miss it at such a time!"

"If he go forth as he has come," continued she, resuming her mental soliloquy, "I shall not have the opportunity to speak to him at all—perhaps not even to exchange salutation. He will scarce ask to see *me*. He may not look back. I cannot call after him. What is to be done?"

There was a pause, as if her thoughts were silently occupied in forming some plan.

"Ha!" she exclaimed at length, pretending to look inquiringly out of the window. "Lora and Walter are wandering somewhere through the park? I shall go in search of them?"

The motive thus disclosed was but a mere pretense—put forth to satisfy the natural instinct of a maiden's modesty. It ended the struggle between this and the powerful passion that was warring against it.

Marion flung the coifed hood over her head; drew the coverchief forward to shade the sun from her face—perchance also to hide the virgin blush which her thoughts had called forth; and, gliding downstairs, passed out on her pretended errand.

If she had either desire or design; to find those she went forth to seek, she was destined to disappointment. Indeed, her search was not likely to have been successful; for on issuing from the house, she went only in one particular direction—the most unlikely one for Walter and Lora Lovelace to have taken at that hour; since it was a path that led directly to the western entrance of the park.

Had she sought the old Saxon camp, it is probable she would have found the missing pair; though more than probable, that neither would have thanked her for her pains.

As it was, she took the opposite way; and, after traversing a long stretch of avenue with slow, lingering steps, she found herself near that old ivy-ground gateway that opened upon the Oxford high-road.

Apparently terrified at having strayed so far, at such a late hour, for the sun was now hidden behind the trees, she faced round; and commenced retracing her steps towards the mansion.

True, there was an expression upon her face resembling fear; but it was not that of alarm at the late hour, nor the distance that lay between her and the dwelling, rather was it the fear one feels in doing some act that may expose to censure or shame.

Marion Wade was upon the eve of committing such an act. She had long since abandoned the idea of that self-deception, with which upon starting forth she had tried to still the scruples of her conscience. She was no longer looking for Lora Lovelace or Walter Wade; but for one who was now dearer to her than either cousin or brother. She was waiting for Henry Holtspur—that noble cavalier, whose graceful image had taken complete possession of her heart—waiting and watching for him, with all the eagerness that a powerful passion can inspire.

* * * * * * * * * *

It was still only twilight; and any one, coming down the avenue, might have noticed a white object, appearing at intervals round the stems of the trees that skirted the path. This object would remain stationary for a moment, and be then withdrawn, to appear again at another point, a little nearer to the house. A good eye might have told it to be the head of a woman, wearing a white hood, the graceful coif or coverchief of the time.

Henry Holtspur observed it as he rode down the slope of the hill, after having taken leave of Sir Marmaduke Wade. He simply supposed it to be some peasant girl coming up the path, for in such a light, and at such distance, who could tell the difference between a cottager and a queen?

Had he known who it was—had he suspected the bright object moving like a meteor from tree to tree was the beautiful Marion Wade, it would have sent the blood tingling from the stirrups under his feet to the crown of his head.

No such suspicion was in his mind. He was too busy chafing at the disappointment of having left the house, without seeing her, to imagine for a moment such a splendid fortune was still in store for him.

And the blood *did* tingle from the stirrups beneath his feet to the crown of his head, thrilled through every vein of his body, as arriving opposite to the advancing form, he perceived it to be no peasant, but the peerless Marion Wade, she so exclusively occupying his thoughts.

To check his steed to a stand, as if threatened by some sudden danger, to raise the beaver from his head, and bow to the peak of his saddle, were acts that proceeded rather from instinct than any reasoned design.

At the same instant escaped from his lips, partially in salute, and partially as if elicited by surprise, the words—

"Mistress Marion Wade!"

There was an interval of embarrassment: how could it be otherwise?

It was brief. Henry Holtspur was over thirty years of age, and Marion Wade had escaped from her teens. The passion that had sprung up between them was not the fond fancy of boyhood or girlhood. On his side, it was the love of manhood; on hers, an affection with a man for its object, a man mature, with a pass to be proud of, one in whose face and features could be traced the souvenirs of gallant deeds, whose romantic mien betrayed a type of heroism not to be mistaken.

With Marion it was her first affection, the first that could be called real: With Holtspur, perhaps, it was to be the last love of his life, ever the strongest; since the heart then can hope for no other.

It was not the place of the maiden to speak first; and, though scarce knowing what to say, Holtspur made an effort to break the spell of that hesitating silence.

"Pardon me; for interrupting your walk!" said he, seeing that she had stopped, and stood facing him. "It is but fair to confess that I have been wishing for an opportunity of speaking with you. The unlucky incident of yesterday, of which, I believe, you were a spectator, hindered me from meeting you again; and I was just reflecting upon having experienced a similar misfortune to-day, when you appeared. I hope, Mistress Wade, you will not be offended at being thus waylaid?"

"Oh! certainly not;" answered she, slightly surprised, if not piqued, by the somewhat business-like candor of his speech. "You have been on a visit to my father, I believe?"

"I have;" replied the cavalier, equally chilled by the indifferent character of the question.

"I hope, sir," said Marion throwing a little more warmth into her manner, "you received no hurt from your encounter of yesterday?"

"Thanks, Mistress Marion! not the slightest; except, indeed——"

"Except what, sir?" inquired the lady, with a look of alarm.

"Only that I looked for fair eyes to smile upon my poor victory."

"If mine deceived me not, you were not dissappointed. There was one who not only smiled upon it, but seemed desirous to crown it with flowers! It was but natural: since it was in her defense you drew your sword."

"Ah!" responded the cavalier, appearing for the first time to remember the incident of the flower presentation. "You speak of the peasant girl who represented Maid Marian! I believe she did force some flowers into my hand; though she owed me less gratitude than she thinks for. It was not to champion her that I took up the quarrel; but rather to punish a swaggerer. In truth, I had quite forgotten the episode of the flowers."

"Indeed!" exclaimed Marion, a flush of joy suffusing her face, which she seemed endeavoring to conceal. "Is it thus you reward gratitude? Methinks, sir, you should value it at a higher price!"

"It depends," said the cavalier, rather puzzled for a reply,"on whether gratitude has been deserved. For my part, I consider myself as altogether without any claim of gratitude of the girl. The conduct of the cuirassier captain was a slight to all on the ground. But now, since I have come to confession, I should say that it was in the interest of others I *took up the gauntlet* against him."

Marion glanced at the little glove set coquettishly in the crown of the cavalier's hat. She fancied that he laid a significant emphasis on the figurative phrase, "took up the gauntlet." Her glance, however, was quick and furtive—as if fearful of betraying the sweet thoughts his words had suggested.

There was a pause in the conversation—another interval of hesitating silence, then neither knew what to say—each fearing to risk the compromise of a trivial remark.

Marion had recalled the introductory speech of the cavalier. She had it upon her tongue to demand from him its meaning; when the latter relieved her by resuming his discourse.

"Yes," he said, "there are occasions when one does not deserve gratitude even for what may appear an honest act; as, for instance, one who has found something that has been lost, and returns to the owner, only after long delay, and with great reluctance."

As Holtspur spoke, he pointed to the glove in his hat. Marion's face betrayed a strange mixture of emotion—half distressed, half triumphant.

She was too much embarrassed to make answer

The cavalier continued his figurative discourse.

"The finder, having no right to the thing found, it should be given up. That is but simple honesty; and scarce deserving of thanks

For example, I have picked up this pretty gauntlet; and however much I might wish to keep it—as a souvenir of one of the happiest moments of my existence—I feel constrained, by all the rules of honor and honesty, to restore it to its rightful owner—unless 'hat owner, knowing how much I prize it, will consent to my keeping it."

Holtspur bent low in his saddle, and listened attentively for the rejoinder.

"Keep it!" said Marion, abandoning all affectation of ignorance as to his meaning; and accompanying the assent with a gracious smile. "Keep it, sir, if it so please you."

Then, as if fearing that she had surrendered too freely, she added, in a tone of *naïveté*,—"It would be no longer of any use to me—since I have lost the other—its fellow."

This last announcement counteracted the pleasant impression which her consent had produced, and once more precipitated Henry Holtspur into the sea of uncertainty.

"No longer of any use to her," thought he, repeating her words. "If that be her only motive for bestowing it, then will it be no longer of any value to me."

He felt something like chagrin. He was almost on the point of returning the doubtful token.

"Perhaps," said he, hesitatingly, "I have offended by keeping it so long without your consent, and more by displaying it as I have done. For the former, I might claim excuse, on the plea that I had no opportunity of restoring it. But, for the latter, I fear I can offer no justification. I can only plead the promptings of a vain hope—of a passion that I now believe to be hopeless, as it will be deemed presumptive."

The tone of despondency in which this speech was delivered, struck sweetly on the ear of Marion Wade. It had the true ring of love's utterance, and she intuitively recognized it. She could scarce conceal her joy, as she made rejoinder—

"Why should I be offended, either at your detaining the glove, or wearing it?" As she said this, she regarded the cavalier with a forgiving smile. "The first was unavoidable; the other I ought to esteem an honor. Setting store by a lady's favor is not the way, sir, to offend her."

"Favor! Then she has meant it as such!"

Along with the unspoken thought, a gleam of returning confidence shot over the cavalier's countenance.

"I can no longer endure the doubt," muttered he, "I shall speak to her more plainly. Marion Wade!"

Her name was uttered aloud; and in a tone of appeal that caused her to glance up with some surprise. In her look there was no trace of displeasure at the familiar mode of address.

"Speak, sir," she said, encouragingly. "You have something to say?"

"A question to ask—only one; and oh! Marion Wade, answer it with candor! You promise?"

"I promise."

"You say you have lost the other glove?"

Marion nodded an affirmative.

"Tell me then, and truly; did you *lose* this one?"

The cavalier, as he spoke, pointed to the white gauntlet.

"Your meaning, sir?"

"Ah! Marion Wade, you are evading the answer. Tell me, if it fell from your fair hand unknown—unnoticed; or was it dropped by *design?* Tell me —oh, tell me truly."

He could not read the answer in her eyes, for the long lashes had fallen over them, hiding the blue orbs beneath. The red blood mantling upon her cheeks, and mounting up to her forehead, should have aided him to it, had he been closely observing. Her silence, too, might have served to enlighten him as to the reply she would have made, had her modesty permitted speech.

"I have been candid with you," he continued, urging his appeal by argument; "I have thrown myself upon your mercy. If you care not for the happiness of one who would risk his life for yours, then do I adjure you, as you care for truth, to speak the truth! Dropped you this glove by accident or design?"

With the silence of one who awaits to hear the pronouncing of his sentence, Henry Holtspur sat listening for her answer.

It came like an echo to his speech; but an echo that only repeated the final word.

"*Design!*" murmured Marion Wade, in a low soft voice, whose very trembling betokened its truth.

The abyss of ceremony no longer lay between them. That one word had bridged it.

Henry Holtspur sprang from his saddle, and glided in among the trees.

In another instant their arms were entwined, their lips in mutual contact, and their hearts pressed close together, beating responses, sweet as the pulsations of celestial life.

    *   *   *   *   *   *   *

"Adieu! sweet Marion, adieu!" cried the lover, as she glided from his arms, reluctant to let her leave.

"She will be the last love of my life," he muttered, as he leaped into his saddle almost without touching stirrup.

The trained steed stood at rest till his rider was fairly fixed in the seat. He had remained silent and motionless throughout that sweet interview of the lovers—its sole witness. Proudly champing his bit, he seemed exulting in the fair conquest his master had made—as he had shown himself after the triumph of yesterday. Perhaps Hubert had some share in achieving the victory of love, as of war?

The steed stirred not till he felt the spur; and even then, as if participating in the reluctance of his rider, he moved but slowly from the spot

CHAPTER XXVIII.

A JEALOUS EAVESDROPPER.

If no eye beheld the meeting between Marion Wade and Henry Holtspur, there was one that witnessed their parting with a glance that betokened pain. It was the eye of Richard Scarthe.

On leaving the dinner table, some details of military duty had occupied the cuirassier captain for an hour or two, after which, having no further occupation for the evening, he resolved to seek an interview with the ladies of the house, more especially with her who, in the short space of a single day, had kindled within him a passion that, honorable or not, was at least ardent.

He was already as much in love with the lady as it was possible for such a nature to be. A month in her company could not have

more completely enamored him. Her cold reception of his complimentary phrases—as yet only offered to her with the insinuating
delicacy of an experienced seducer—instead of chilling his incipient
desires, had only served to add fuel to the flame. He was too well
exercised in conquering the scruples of maiden modesty to feel despair
at such primary repulses.

"I shall win her in spite of this monosyllabic indifference," muttered he to Stubbs, as they returned to their sitting-room. "Pshaw :
'tis only pretense before strangers. By my troth, I like this sort of
a beginning. I'm fashed of facile conquests. This promises to be a
little difficult, and will enable me to kill the *ennui*, which otherwise
might have killed me in these rural quarters. I shall win her as I
have won others—as I should Lucretia herself, had she lived in our
time."

To this triumphant boast his satellite spoke assent in his characteristic fashion.

"Safe to do it, by Ged," said he, as if convinced of the invincibili-
ty of one, who more than once had spoiled his own chances in the
game of love-making.

Scarthe was determined to let but little time elapse before entering
upon his amour. His passion prompted him to immediate action;
and the first step was to seek an interview with the woman he had
resolved upon winning.

It was one thing, however, to desire an interview with the daughter
of Sir Marmaduke Wade, another to obtain it. The cuirassier
captain was not in the position to demand, or even seek it by request.
Any attempt on his part to force such an event might end in his discomfiture; for although he could compel Sir Marmaduke to find bed,
board, and forage for himself and his troopers, the tyranny of the
king did not, or rather dared not, extend so far as to violate the
sanctity of a gentleman's family. That of his household had been
sufficiently outraged by the act of *benevolence* itself.

These circumstances considered, it was clear to Scarthe that the
desired interview must be brought about by stratagem, and appear
the result of simple accident.

In pursuance of this idea, about half an hour before sunset, he
sallied forth from his room, and commenced strolling through the
grounds, here stopping to examine a flower, there standing to scrutinize a statue, as if the science of botany and the art of sculpture
were the only subjects in which, at the particular moment, he felt
any interest.

One near enough to note the expression upon his features might easily have told that neither a love of art nor an admiration of nature was there indicated. On the contrary, while apparently occupied with the flower or the statue, his eyes were turned towards the house, wandering in furtive glance from window to window.

In order not to compromise his character for good breeding, he kept at some distance from the walls along the outer edge of the shrubbery. In this way he proceeded past the front of the mansion, until he had reached that side facing to the west.

Here his stealthy reconnaissance was carried on with increased earnestness; for although not certain what part of the house was occupied by the female members of the family, he had surmised that it was the western wing. The pleasant exposure on this side—with the more careful cultivation of the flower-beds and turf-sward, plainly proclaimed it to be the *sacred precinct*.

One by one he examined the windows—endeavoring to pierce the interior of the apartments into which they opened; but, after spending a full quarter of an hour in this fantastic scrutiny, he discovered nothing to repay him for his pains—not the face of a living creature.

Once only, he caught sight of a figure inside one of the rooms on the ground floor; but the dress was dark; and the glimpse he had of it, told it to be that of a man. Sir Marmaduke it was, moving about in his library.

"The women don't appear to be inside at all," muttered he, with an air of discontent. "By Phœbus! what if they should have gone for a stroll through the park? Fine evening—charming sunset. I' faith, I shouldn't wonder but that they're out enjoying it. If I could only find *her* outside, that would be just the thing. I'll try a stroll myself. Perhaps I may meet her. 'Tis possible."

So saying, he turned away from the statue—which he had been so long criticising—and faced to the foot-bridge that spanned the fosse.

As he laid his hand upon the wicket gate—with the intention of opening it—an object came under his eyes—that caused the blood to leap into his cheeks, and mantle upwards upon his pale forehead.

The elevated causeway of the bridge had placed him in a position, from which he could view the long avenue leading down to the road. Far down it, near the gateway, a steed, saddled and bridled—as if ready for a rider to mount, was standing on the path.

There was no one holding the animal, no one looking after him, no one near.

It was not the circumstance of seeing a horse thus caparisoned, and uncared for, though this was odd enough, that flushed the cheek of the cuirassier captain, and caused his fingers to tremble on the uplifted latch. It was the sight of *that* particular horse which produced such effect: for the curving neck and sable coat of the animal, visible even through the gray gloaming of the twilight, enabled Scarthe to recognize the steed, that had played so conspicuous a part in his own humiliation.

"Holtspur's horse, by heaven?" were the words that fell mechanically from his lips. "The man must be there himself, behind the trees. There, and what doing there?"

"I shall go down, and see," he muttered, after a moment of inde cision.

Opening the wicket gate, he passed through; quickly traversed the remaining portion of the causeway; and continued on towards the spot where the steed was standing.

He did not go in a direct path towards the object that had thus interested him, which would have been the avenue itself, but proceeded in a circuitous direction, through some copse-wood that skirted the slope of the hill.

He had reason for thus deviating.

"Holtspur in the park of Sir Marmaduke Wade!" muttered he, as he crept through the thicket with the cautious tread of a deerstalker. "Where is Sir Marmaduke's daughter?"

As the suspicion swept across his brain, it brought the blood scorching like fire through his veins. His limbs felt weak under him. He almost tottered, as he trod the sward.

His jealous agony was scarce more acute, when, on reaching the row of chestnuts that bordered the avenue, and craning his neck outward to get a view, he saw a man come out from among the trees, and step up to the side of the steed; while at the same instant a white object, like a lady's coverchief or scarf fluttered amid the foliage that overhung the path.

The man he recognized: Henry Holtspur! The woman, though seen less distinctly, could be only the one occupying his thoughts—only Marion Wade!

Though not a coward—and accustomed to encounters abrupt and dangerous—Scarthe was at that crisis the victim of fear and indecision. In his chagrin he could have rushed down the slope, and stabbed Holtspur to the heart, without mercy or remorse. But he

had no intention of acting in this off-hand way. The encounter of
the day before—of which the torture of his wounded arm emphati·
cally reminded him—had robbed him of all zest for a renewal of the
black horseman's acquaintance.

He only hesitated as to whether he should screen himself behind
the trees, and permit the lady to pass on to the house; or remain in
ambush till she came up, and then join company with her.

He was no longer uncertain as to who it was. The white-robed
figure, that now stood out in the open avenue, was Marion Wade.
No other could have shown that imposing outline under the doubtful
shadow of the twilight.

It was not till the horseman had sprung into the saddle, turned
his back upon the mansion, and was riding away, that Scarthe recovered from his irresolution.

He felt sensible of being in a state of mind to make himself ridiculous; and that the more prudent plan would be to remain out of
sight.   But the bitter sting was rankling in his breast—all the more
bitter that he suspected an *intrigue*.   This fell fancy, torturing him
to the heart's core, stifled all thoughts of either policy or prudence,
and impelled him to present himself.

With an effort such as his cunning, and the control which experience had given him over his passions, enabled him to make—he
succeeded in calming himself sufficiently for a pretense at courteous
conversation.

At this moment, Marion came up.

She started on seeing Scarthe glide out from among the trees.
The wild passion gleaming in his eyes was enough to cause her alarm
though she made but slight exhibition of it.   She was too highly
bred to show emotion, even under such suspicious circumstances.
Her heart at that moment thrilling with supreme happiness, was too
strong to feel fear.

" Good even, sir," she simply said, in return to the salute which
Scarthe had made as he approached.

" Pardon my question, Mistress Wade," said he, joining her, and
walking by her side.   " Are you not afraid to be out alone at this
late hour—especially as the neighborhood is infested with such
ferocious footpads as your brother has been telling me of ?   Ha!
ha! ha! "

" Oh ! " said Marion—answering the interrogatory in the same
spirit in which it appeared to have been put—" That was before

Captain Scarthe and his redoubtable cuirassiers came to reside with us Under their protection, I presume, there will no longer be anything to fear from footpads, or even highwaymen!"

"Thanks for your compliment, lady! If I could only flatter myself that our presence here would be considered a protection by Mistress Marion Wade, it would be some compensation for the unpleasantness of being forced as a guest upon her father."

"You are gracious, sir," said she, bowing slightly in return to the implied apology.

Then casting a quick but scrutinizing glance at the countenance of the speaker, she continued in thought—"if this man be honest, the devil's a witch. If he be, I never saw look that so belies the heart."

"Believe me, Mistress Wade," proceeded the hypocrite, "I keenly feel my position here. I know that I cannot be regarded in any other light than that of an intruder. Notwithstanding the pleasure it may be, to partake of the hospitality of your noble house, I would gladly forego that happiness, were it in consonance with my duty to the king —which of course is paramount to everything else."

"Indeed!"

"To an officer of his majesty's cuirassiers it should be."

"In France, perhaps, or in Flanders, where I understand you've been campaigning. In England, sir, and in the eyes of an English woman, there are higher duties than those owing to the king. Did it ever occur to you that you owe a duty to the *people?* or if you prefer the expression, *to the State.*"

"*L'état est roi. L'état est moi?* That is the creed of Richard Scarthe!"

"Even if your king be a tyrant?"

"I am but a soldier. It is not mine to question the prerogatives of royalty, only to obey its edicts."

"A noble creed! Noble sentiments for a soldier! Hear mine, sir!"

"With pleasure, Mistress Wade!" replied Scarthe, cowering under her scornful glance.

"Were I a man," she continued, her eyes sparkling with enthusiasm, "rather would I shave my crown, and cover it with the cowl of a friar, than wear a sword to be drawn in no better cause than that of an unscrupulous king! Ha! There are men rising in this land, whose fame shall outlive the petty notoriety of its princes. When these have become obscured behind the oblivion of ages, the names of

Vane and Pym, and Cromwell and Hampden, and Holt——," she bu half pronounced the one she held highest—"shall be household words!"

"These are wild words, Mistress Wade!" rejoined Scarthe, his loyalty—along with a slight inclination of anger—struggling against the admiration which he could not help feeling for the beautiful enthusiast; "I fear you are a rebel ; and were I as true to the interests of my king as I should be, it would be my duty to make you a captive." "Ah!" he continued, bending towards the proud maiden, and speaking in a tone of ambiguous appeal, "to make *you* a captive, *my* captive, that would indeed be a pleasant duty for a soldier, the recompense of a whole life."

"Ho!" exclaimed Marion, pretending not to understand the *inuendo*, "since you talk of making me a captive, I must endeavor to escape from you. Good evening, sir."

Flinging a triumphant smile towards the disappointed wooer, she glided rapidly beyond his reach ; and, nimbly tripping over the footbridge, disappeared from his sight amid the shrubbery surrounding the mansion.

CHAPTER XXIX.

AN ESCORTED COURIER.

On parting from Marion Wade, Henry Holtspur should have been the happiest of men. The loveliest woman in the *shire*, to his eyes in the *world*, had declared to him her love, and vowed eternal devotion. Its full fruition could not have given him firmer assurance of the fact.

And yet he was not happy. On the contrary, it was with a heavy heart that he rode away from the scene of that interview with his splendid sweetheart. He knew that the interview *should not have occurred, that Marion Wade ought not to be his sweetheart!*

After riding half a dozen lengths of his horse, he turned m his sad. dle, to look back, in hopes that the sight of the loved form migh! tranquilize his conscience.

Happier for him had he ridden on.

If unhappy before, he now saw that which made him miserable Marion had commenced ascending the slope. Her light-colored gar ments rendered her easily recognizable through the dimness of the twilight. Holtspur watched her movements, admiring the queenly grace of her step, distinguishable despite the darkness and distance

He was fast recovering composure of mind, so late disturbed by some unpleasant thought, and no doubt would have left the spot with contentment; but for an incident, which at that moment transpired under his view.

Marion Wade had got half-way up the hill, and was advancing with rapid step. Just then some one, going at a quicker pace, appeared in the avenue behind her.

This second pedestrian must have passed out from among the trees : since but the moment before the receding form of the lady was alone in the avenue.

In a few seconds she was overtaken; and the two figures were now seen side by side. In this way they moved on—their heads slightly inclined towards each other, as if engaged in familiar conversation!

The dress of the individual who had thus sprung suddenly into sight was also of a light color, and might have been a woman's. But a red scarf diagonally crossing the shoulders—a high-peaked hat with plume of ostrich feathers—and, more than all, the tallness of the figure, told Henry Holtspur that it was a man who was walking with Marion Wade.

The same tokens declared he was not her brother; Walter was not near so tall. It could not be her father; Sir Marmaduke was ac customed to dress in black.

The rows of chestnuts that bordered the walk came to a termination near the top of the hill. The figures had arrived there. Next mo ment they moved out from the shadow of the trees, and could be seen more distinctly.

" 'Tis neither her father, nor brotner—'tis Scarthe."

It was Holtspur who pronounced these words, and with an intona tion that betokened both surprise and chagrin.

" He has forced himself upon her ! He came skulking out from the trees, as if he had been lying in wait for her ! I shouldn't won der if 'twas so. What can I do ? Shall I follow and interrupt the interview ? "

" There is danger here," he continued, after a pause. " Ah ! villain ! " he exclaimed standing erect in his stirrups, and stretching out his clenched hand in the direction of the departing figures ; " if you but dare—one word of insult—one ribald look, and I am told of it— the chastisement you've already had will be nothing to that in store for you."

" O God ! " he exclaimed, as though some still more disagreeable thought had succeeded to this paroxysm of spite ; " a dread spectacle it is ! The wolf walking by the side of the lamb !

" He is bowing and bending to her ! See ! She turns towards him ? She appears complacent ! O God ! is it possible ? "

Involuntarily his hand glided to the hilt of his sword—while the spurs were pressed against the ribs of his horse.

The spirited animal sprang forward along the path—his head turned towards the mansion ; but, before he had made a second spring, he was checked up again.

" I'm a fool ! " muttered his rider ; " and you, too, Hubert. At all events I should have been thought so, had I ridden up yonder. What could I have said to excuse myself ! 'Tis not possible. If it were so, I should feel no remorse. If it were so, there could be no ruin ! "

" Ha ! they have reached the bridge. She is leaving him. She has hurried inside the house. He remains without, apparently forsaken ! "

" Oh Marion, if I've wronged thee, 'tis because I love thee madly— madly ! Pardon ! pardon ! I will watch thee no more ! "

So saying, he wheeled his steed ; and, without looking back, galloped on towards the gateway.

Even while opening the gate and closing it behind him, he turned not his eye towards the avenue ; but, spurring into the public road, continued the gallop which the gate had interrupted.

The head of his horse was homeward—so far only as the embouchure of the forest path that opened towards Stone Dean. On reaching this point he halted ; and, instead of entering upon the by-way, remained out into the middle of the high road—as if undecided as to his course.

He glanced towards the sky—a small patch of which was visible between the trees, on both sides overarching the road.

The purple twilight was still lingering amid the spray of the forest; and through the break opening eastward, he could perceive the horned moon cutting sharply against the horizon.

"Scarce worth while to go home now," he muttered, drawing forth his watch, and holding the dial up to his eyes. "How swiftly the last hour has sped—ah ! how sweetly ! In another the men will be there. By riding slowly I shall just be in time ; and you, Hubert, can have your supper in a stall at the Saracen's Head. Aha ! a woman in the window ? By heavens, 'tis Marion ! "

The exclamatory phrases were called forth, as turning towards the park, he caught sight of the mansion, visible through an opening between the chestnuts.

Several windows were alight ; but the eye of the cavalier dwelt only on one ; where, under the arcade of the curtains, and against the luminous background of a burning lamp, a female form was discernable. Only the figure could be traced at that far distance ; but this—tall, graceful, and majestic—proclaimed it to be the *silhoutte* of Marion Wade.

After a prolonged gaze, commencing with a smile, and terminating in a sigh, Holtspur once more gave Hubert the rein, and moved silently onward.

The ruined hut on Jarret's Heath was soon reached, conspicuous under the silvery moonlight, as he had last viewed it ; but no longer the rendezvous of Gregory Garth and his fierce footpads. The dummies had disappeared, even to the sticks that had served to support them and naught remained to indicate, that in that solitary place the traveler had ever listened to the unpleasant summons : "Stand and deliver ! "

Holtspur could not pass the spot without smiling ; and more : for as the ludicrous incident came more clearly before his mind, he drew up his horse, and leaning back in the saddle, gave utterance to a loud laugh

Hubert, on hearing his master in such a merry mood, uttered a responsive neigh. Perhaps Hubert was laughing too ; but man and horse became silent instantly, and from precaution.

More than one neigh had responded to that of Holtspur's steed, which the cavalier knew were not echoes, but proceeded from horses approaching the spot.

Suddenly checking his laughter, and giving his own steed a signal to be still, he remained listening.

The neighing of the strange horses had been heard at a distance as if from some cavalcade coming up the road by Red Hill. In time, there were other sounds to confirm the surmise : the clanking of sabres against iron stirrups and the hoof-strokes of the horses themselves

"A troop!" muttered Holtspur. "Some of Scarthe's following, I suppose, from an errand to Uxbridge? Come, Hubert! They must not meet us."

A touch of the spur, with a slight pull upon the bridle rein, guided the well-trained steed behind the hovel; where, under the shadow of some leafy boughs, he was once more brought to a stand.

Soon the hoof-strokes sounded more distinctly; as also the clank of the scabbards, the tinkling of the spur-rowels, and curb-chains.

The voices of the men were also mingled with these sounds; and both they and their horses, soon after, emerged from the shadows of the thicket, and entered the opening by the hut.

There were seven of them; the odd one in advance of the others, who were riding two and two behind him.

A glance at their habiliments proclaimed them to be men of military calling, an officer accompanied by an escort.

As they arrived in front of the hovel, the leader halted, commanding the others to follow his example.

The movement was sudden, apparently improvised on the part of the officer, as unexpected by his following. It was evidently the appearance of the ruin that had caused it to be made.

"Sergeant!" said the leader of the little troop, addressing himself to one of the men who rode nearest to him; "this must be the place where the king's courier was stopped! There's the ruined hovel he spoke about; and this I take to be Jarret's Heath. What say you?"

"It must be that place, major," replied the sergeant; "it can't be no other. We've come full four miles from Uxbridge, and should now be close to the park of Bulstrode. This be Jarret's Heath for sure."

"What a pity those rascals don't show themselves to-night   I'd give something to carry them back with me bound hand and foot. It would be a satisfaction to poor Cunliffe, whom they stripped so clean; leaving him nothing but his stockings. Ha! ha! ha! I should like to have seen that noted court dandy, as he must have appeared just here—under the moonlight. Ha! ha! ha!"

"I fancy I heard the neighing of a horse in this direction?" continued the leader of the little troop. "If the fellows who plundered the courier hadn't been footpads, we might have hoped to encounter them——"

"**You forget**, major," rejoined the sergeant, "that Master Cunliff's horse was taken from him. Maybe the captain of the robbers is no longer a footpad, but mounted!"

"No—no," rejoined the officer, "the neighing we heard was from some farmer's hack running loose in the pastures. Forward! we've already lost to much time. If this be Jarret's Heath, we must be near the end of our errand. Forward!"

Saying this the leader of the band, close followed by the treble file of troopers, dashed forward along the road—their accoutrements, and the hoofs of their horses, making a noise that hindered them from hearing the scornful, half involuntary laugh sent after them from the cavalier concealed under the shadow of the hut.

"Another king's courier for Scarthe!" muttered Holtspur, as he headed his horse once more to the road. "No doubt the duplicate of that precious dispatch! Ha! ha! His Majesty seems determined that this time it shall reach its destination. An escort of six troopers! Notwithstanding with all that, and the bravado of their leader, if I had coughed loud enough for them to hear me, I believe they'd have scampered off a little faster than they are now going. These conceited satellites of royalty—'*cavaliers*,' as they affectedly call themselves—are the veriest poltroons; brave only in words. Oh! that the hour were come, when Englishmen may be prevailed upon to demand their rights at the point of the sword; *the only mode by which they will ever obtain.them*! Then may I hope to see such swaggerers scattered like chaff, and fleeing before the soldiers of liberty! God grant the time may be near! Hubert let us on and hasten it!'

Hubert, ever willing, obeyed the slight signal vouchsafed to him; and spreading his limbs to the road, rapidly bore his master to the summit of Red Hill; then down its sloping declivity; and on through the fertile, far-stretching meadows of the Colne.

CHAPTER XXX.

THE SARACEN'S HEAD

The Saracen's Head stood on an exact half mile from the Colne river, and the end of Uxbridge town. To reach it from the latter, it was necessary to cross over the quaint old bridge, whence the place derives its name.

It was a roadside inn, old as the bridge itself—perhaps ancient as the Crusades, from which its cognomen had come. It was the inn at which Scarthe and his cuirassiers had made their night halt, when proceeding to Bulstrode Park ; the same afterwards known—as it is to the present day—by the appellation of *Queen's Head.* The altered lettering on its sign-board was not the act of the honest Saxon Boniface, who held it at the time of the first Charles ; but of a plush-clad proprietor, who succeeded him during the servile days of the Restoration.

While in Master Jarvis' occupancy it might have born a title equally as appropriate, and perhaps more significant than either— the *King's Head*; since under its roof, this phrase was frequently whispered—sometimes loudly pronounced—with a peculiar significance—one very different from the idea usually attached to it. It may be, that words spoken, and thoughts exchanged within the walls of the old hostelry led to a king's losing his head; or, at all events. precipitated that just and proper event.

On the same night that Henry Holtspur was riding down Red Hill, with the Saracen's Head as the declared goal of his journey, and about the same hour, a number of pedestrians, not all going together, but in scattered groups of two, three, and four, might have been seen crossing the Colne river at Uxbridge ; who, after clearing the causeway of the bridge, continued on up the road, in the direction of the inn.

On reaching it—one group after the other—they were seen to enter, after giving a preliminary challenge or greeting to its host, who received them by the door as they came up.

This reception continued, until at least fifty men had glided inside the ivy-grown portico of the Saracen's Head.

They were all men, nothing in woman's shape or apparel appearing amongst them.

They were men in the humbler walks of life, though not the very humblest. Their dresses betokened them to be artizans, and of different callings, as proclaimed by the various costumes; for in those days the costume told the trade.

Nor did they appear to be habited for any particular occasion. The butcher was in his long leathern boots, redolent of suet; the miller, in white cap, hoary with the "stoor" of the mill; the blacksmith, with wide hose hidden under an apron of singed sheepskin; and the tailor's *jour*, with his bowed legs encased in a covering of cotton velveteen.

In some of the groups there were individuals of a more pretentious appearance: men who wore beaver hats, and doublets of superior quality, with sound russet boots, white linen cuffs and collars. Still was there about their garments a certain commonness of cut that proclaimed the wearers to be of the class of small shop-keepers—in modern days miscalled *tradesmen*.

On any evening—especially if the weather chanced to be fine—a few such individuals might have been seen seeking the hospitality of the Saracen's Head, for its tap was one of the most popular, and attracted customers even from Uxbridge. On the night in question, however, the great number of guests—as well as the lateness of the hour at which they were seeking the noted rendezvous—told of some purpose more important than merely to imbibe Master Jarvis' celebrated brewage.

There was an air of business about the men as they marched along the road; and in their muttered conversations could be distinguished a tone of earnestness that betokened some serious subject. They did not loiter, like men strolling out for an evening's pastime, but walked briskly forward as bent upon an errand, or keeping some preconcerted appointment.

As already stated, the landlord of the inn received the different groups. There was something mysterious in this worldless welcome —so unusual at the Saracen's Head, the more so as on the broad open countenance of its owner there was no trace of churlishness. Equally mysterious might have appeared a circumstance observed as the guests came up to the door:—each raising his right hand within a few inches of Master Jarvis' nose, with the thumb bent inward, holding the hand a second or two in that position, and then withdrawing it.

The mystery could only be explained by presuming that this was a signal, and the slight assenting nod with which it was answered was simply a permission to enter.

It might have been observed, moreover, that the guests so signal ing, instead of going towards the common or tap-room of the inn, proceeded through a long corridor—leading to the interior of the establishment—where a large and much better appointed apartment had been arranged to receive them.

Others who entered the house without giving the *thumb signal*, greeted the landlord in a different way, and were shown towards the tap-room, or walked on, as was their wont, without invitation.

For more than an hour these groups of men continued to arrive up the road from Uxbridge. At the same time other men—though not in such numbers—might have been seen coming down the same road from the direction of Red Hill, and Denham; and also along by-paths from the villages of Harefield and Iver.

Some difference might have been noticed between these, and the men who came from Uxbridge—the former by their style of dress and general appearance being evidently denizens of the country—grasiers or farmers—and not a few of them having the substantial look of independence that bespoke the *freeholder*.

All, however, were moving towards the inn with a like motive—as each of them upon entering was seen to offer to its owner that silent masonic salute, which admitted them into the secret interior of the establishment.

Of those who came in from the country, not a few were on horseback, as if they had ridden from a distance; and the ample stables were soon almost as well filled—and perhaps more profitable—than when Scarthe and his cuirassiers had honored the inn with their patronage.

Among the last who rode up was a horseman of distinguished mien, whose dress and equipments—but still more the steed he bestrode, and the style of his equitation—proclaimed him to be different from all the others. Even under the deceptive light of the moon there was no mistaking him for a common man. His free, graceful bearing, declared the cavalier.

To the landlord, and a few others just entering the inn, he was individually known. These, as he rode forward to the door, could be heard whispering to one another that phrase that had lately become of almost cabalistic import—*the black horseman*.

He dismounted; and without hesitancy entered along with the rest—simply nodding to them as he passed.

It was not necessary for *him* to hold up his thumb before the eyes of the stalwart door-keeper. This precaution against the admission of traitorous spies was not required in the case of Henry Holtspur. The owner of the hostelry knew the master of the ceremonies about to be performed under its roof; and the latter, passing him with a significant smile, kept on unattended along the dimly lit corridor—as one who had oft trodden it before.

With like familiarity, he opened the door of the inner apartment, now filled with men—whose manifold voices mingling with earnest conversation could be heard even to the entrance outside.

Suddenly the sounds became hushed; but only for an instant. Then arose something more than a murmur of applause—amidst which could be heard, in many an enthusiastic repetition, the name of him who had entered and the sobriquet by which to most of them he was better known.

Though the massive door of oak closing again hindered the voices from being any longer heard outside, the conversation was not discontinued. Only was it conducted into its true channel—the master mind of that enthusiastic assemblage guiding it in its course.

It might have been termed treasonable—if such phrase can be applied to speech condemning the conduct of the uxorious tyrant. Freely were the acts of the king commented upon, and his late edicts discussed; until some of the speakers, becoming inspired—partly by the intoxicating tap of the Saracen's Head, which, at the cost of the cavalier, circulated without stint, and partly from the smart of some recent wrong—shook their clenched fists in the air, to render more emphatic their vows of vengeance.

On that night, in the conclave held in the hostelry of the Saracen's Head, was foreshadowed a spectacle—not long after to be realized and even witnessed by some there present—*a king standing upon a scaffold!*

"Thank the Lord!" muttered Holtspur to himself, as he sprang into his saddle, and headed Hubert for the hills. "Thank the Lord for all His mercies!" added he, in the phraseology of some of his Puritan co-conspirators late ringing in his ears. "There can be no mistaking the temper of these fellows. After ten years of tyrannical usurpation they're aroused at last. The time is come, not only for the dethronement of a tyrant, but for establishing in dear old

England the only form of government that is not a mockery of common sense—the only one upon which Liberty may rely—the Republic!"

After he had given utterance to this speech, a smile—half of regretful bitterness, half of contempt—not only for his fellow countrymen, but his fellow men—cynically shadowed his countenance: for the sentiment so expressed naturally led him to reflect how few there were in his own country who shared it with him!

Holtspur lived in a time when the word *republic* was scarcely ever heard; or, when heard, only ill-understood, and scoffed at as a dream of the enthusiast. Not that he had himself any doubt as to its true signification. Perfectly did he comprehend its import—awful—grand—including the whole theory of human happiness, and man's misery. Even in those times of tyrannical persecution—when Laud lorded it over the souls, and Strafford over the bodies of men—or even, still later, when, with impunity, the Waldense Protestant could be impaled upon the spear of the Inquisition—there were men and minds who could not be coerced to deny the divine origin of democracy, and believe in the pseudo "divine right" of kings.

Not in those times alone, but in all ages; for *time* cannot alter *truth*. A circle was a circle, before God made man to trace its curvature! and when God made men, he intended them to govern themselves uncontrolled by tyrants.

That they have not done so, does not prove an error in the intention. The circumference of the circle, imperfect by some interruption, does not argue the non-existence of the curve. No more in early ages—no more in mediæval times, no more *now*, does the non-existence of the pure republic prove that it is not the proper form. It *is* the proper form, the only one recognized by the laws of right and truth. He who does not acknowledge this must be the owner either of a *bad head* or a *bad heart*. On either horn of the dilemma does he hang who denies the *republic!*

Is there such a man, or thing in human shape! I cannot think there is. Thinking so, I could not avoid imitating my hero, in that scornful contempt that expressed itself on his countenance, while reflecting how few there were who participated in his sentiments.

Ah! had he lived in the present time, he would have witnessed strange proofs of their truth. He would have recognized, as I do, in what others call the failure of republican institutions, their proudest triumph. He would have seen thirty millions of men, comparatively with the rest of their race, transformed into giants, by the influence of less than a century of republican training! He would have seen them divided into two parties, warring against each other like Titans of the olden time; and seeing this, he could have come to no other conclusion, than that, united these thirty millions of republican people would have been a match for the whole monarchial world.

Henry Holtspur did not need to dive into futurity for facts to substantiate his belief in a republican form of government. His conviction came from the past, from the sources of eternal truth. The sarcasm expressed upon his features was caused by the contempt which a noble soul must naturally feel, for those things in human shape who believe, or pretend it, in the "divine right" of kings.

The cloud lingered, until he had turned into the forest road, and came in sight of the old beech, that tree whose umbrageous branches overshadowed, to him, the sweetest and most sacred spot upon earth.

Once again he drew up under its canopy, once again gazed upon the white gauntlet, till love absorbed his every thought, even to the exclusion of that political passion, *the republic.*

CHAPTER XXXI.

DANCEY'S DAUGHTER.

The domicile of Dick Dancey could scarce with correctness be called a house. Even cottage would be too dignified a name for the wooden hovel, in which the woodman and his family habitually found shelter from the rain and wind.

To the latter the house itself was but little exposed; for, when a tempest raged, before striking on the frail structure, its fury was expended upon the giant beeches of Wapsey's Wood, that stretched their protecting arms over and around it.

It was a cabin of rough logs, clayed between the chinks, and roofed with a thatch of rushes, such, excepting the roof, as might be seen at the present day in the backwoods of America.

A narrow doorway, barely wide enough to admit the big body of the woodman himself; two or three small windows, with diminutive panes of glass set in lead; an enclosure of limited dimensions, girt with a flimsy paling, designed for a garden, but grown into a weed-bed; a stack of fire fagots; a shed that gave occasional shelter to a scraggy cob; a clay-bedaubed kennel containing a large fierce-looking mongrel, the cross between sheep-dog and deer-hound; these were the principal features in the external aspect of Dick Dancey's household.

The interior view was equally rude, and equally simple. A kitchen with a clay floor, and clay-plastered walls, against which stood upon shelves, or hung upon pegs, a sparse collection of utensils; some dingy old prints on common paper, and in cheap frames; a string of onions; another of rabbit-skins; and close by, the freshly-flayed hide of a fallow deer. Traps, gins, nets, and other implements for taking forest game and fish were visible in a corner by themselves; and in another corner lay a large wooden. ax, the implement of the owner's proper calling. On the floor stood a beech-wood table, with half a dozen rush-bottomed chairs, and some culinary utensils of red earthenware; while in the cavity, representing a fire-place, two large stones did duty for andirons.

The kitchen was everything—the two rooms, the only others in the house—were both bed-chambers; and both of very limited divisions. Each contained only a single bed; but one of the rooms was furnished a little better than its fellow;—that is, the bed had sheets and a coverlet; while the other was only a shakedown of straw rushes, with some rags of coarse grogram, and a couple of deer-skins for bed-clothes.

In the first chamber there was a chair or two, and a small table placed against the wall. Over this glistened a piece of broken mirror, attached to the plastered surface, by a couple of rusty nails bent against the edges of the glass. A cotton pin-cushion; two or three common side-combs for holding up the hair; a small brush of bristles; a pair of white linen cuffs, that showed signs of having been more than once worn since washing; with some minor articles of female apparel, all lying upon the table, told the occupant of the chamber to be a woman.

It was the sleeping-room of Bet Dancey—the daughter of the deer-stalker, and the only member of his family. The other apartment was the dormitory of Dick himself.

The bed-rooms, however, were of inferior importance: since both Dick and his daughter lived habitually in the kitchen. They were both to be found there on the fourth day after the *f te,* at which the beautiful Betsey had cut such a conspicuous figure.

Dick was seated at the table, engaged in the agreeable occupation of eating. A mug of beer, the fragments of a loaf of bread, and some ribs of roast venison, were the viands before him.

It was his breakfast; though the sun shining down through the tops of the beeches betokened it near dinner-time; and Bet had breakfasted some hours earlier. But Dick had returned home late the night before—fatigued after a long journey—and in consequence had snored upon his shakedown of straw, until the bells of Bulstrode were tolling twelve.

From the conversation carried on between him and his daughter, it was evident that, up to that hour, not many words had passed between them since his coming home.

" Ha theer be'd any un here, gurl? "

"Yes. One of the soldiers from the Park has been here—twice."

"One o' the sogers!" muttered Dick, in a tone that betrayed unpleasantness. "Dang it, that's queery! Did he tell thee his errand? "

"Only that he wanted to see *you.*"

" Wanted to see me! Art sure o' that, gurl? "

" He said so, father."

" Thou'rt sure he didn't come to see *thee* ? "

The woodman as he asked this question, gazed scrutinizingly upon the countenance of his daughter.

"Oh, no, father!" replied Betsey, without flinching from his gaze. "What could he want with me? He said he had a message for yourself; and that his captain. wished to speak with you on some business."

" Bizness wi' his captain! Hech! Did he say nothin' o' what it be'd about? "

" No."

" Nor made no inquiries o' any kind? "

" He only asked me if I knew Mr. Henry Holtspur, and where he lived."

" What did'st thee tell him? "

" I said that *you* knew him; and that he lived at the old house of Stone Dean."

The beautiful Betsey did not think it necessary to inform her father that the cuirassier had said a good deal more; since it was in the shape of gallant speeches, and related only to herself.

"Makin inquiries 'bout *him!*'" muttered Dancey to himself. "I shudn't wonder if theer be somethin' afit. Muster Holtspur must be told o't an' at once. I'll go over theer soon's I've ate my breakfast. Wull's been here too," he continued, once more addressing his daughter, though not interrogatively. "I see'd him last night, when I got to Muster Holtspur's. He told me he'd been."

"Yes—*he* has been twice. The last time he came was when the other was here. They had some angry words."

"Angry words, eh! What be'd they about, gurl?"

"I am sure I can't tell, father. You know Will always gets out of temper, when any one speaks to me. Indeed, I can't bear it; and won't any longer. He taunted me that day; and said a many things he'd no right to."

"I tell thee, gurl, Wull Walford have a right to talk to thee as he pleases. He is thy friend, gurl; and means it only for thy good. Thou beest too short wi' the lad; and say'st things, for I've heard thee myself, that would aggruvate the best friend thee hast i' the world. Thou wilt do well to change thy tone; or Wull Walford may get tired o' thy tricks, an' go a speerin' som'ere else for a wife."

"I wish he would!" was the reply that stood ready on the tip of Bet's tongue; but which from a wholesome dread of the paternal temper—more than once terribly exhibited on this subject—was left unspoken.

"I tell thee, gurl, I've see'd Wull Walford last night, I've talked wi' him a bit, an' I reckon as how he'll ha' somethin' seerus to say to thee 'fore long."

The dark cloud that passed over the countenance of the girl told that she comprehended the nature of the "something" thus conjecturally foreshadowed.

"Now, Bet," added the woodman, having laid bare the roasted rib, and emptied the beer-mug; "bring me my old hat, and the long hazel staff. I be a gooin' over to the Dean; an' as that poor beest be well-nigh done up, I maun walk. Maybe Muster Holtspur moat coom here, while I be gone theer. I know he wants to see me early, an' I ha' overslept myself. He sayed he might coom. If he do, tell im I'll be back in a jiff—if I doan't find 'im over theer, or meet 'im on the way "

And with this injunction, the gigantic deer-stealer squeezed himself through the narrow doorway of his hovel; and, turning in the direction of Stone Dean, strode off under the shadowy boughs of Wapsey's Wood beeches.

He was scarce out of sight when Bet, stepping back from the door, glided into her little chamber; and, seizing the brush of bristles, began drawing it through the long tresses of her hair.

In that piece of broken glass, with a disc not bigger than a dinner plate, was reflected a face with which the most critical connoisseur of female beauty could scarce have found fault.

The features were of the true gipsy type, the aquiline nose, the wild hawk-like eye, the skin of golden brown, and thick crow-black hair overshadowing all. There was a form, too, beneath, which, though muscular almost as a man's, and with limbs large and vigorous, was, nevertheless, of tempting *tournure*. It was no wonder that Marion Wade had deemed it worthy the admiration of Henry Holtspur—no wonder that Henry Holtspur had deemed Will Walford unworthy of possessing it.

"*He* coming here! And to find me in this drabby dress, with my hair hanging like the tail of father's old horse! I should sink through the floor for very shame!

"I trust I shall be in time to titivate myself. Bother my hair! it's a yard too long, and a mile too thick. It takes as much trouble to plait as would weave a hank of homespun.

"It'll do now. Stick where I stick you, ye ugly comb! Will's gift. Little do I prize it, troth!

"Now for my Sunday gown, my cuffs and ruffs. They're not quite so grand as those of Mistress Marion Wade; but I flatter myself they're not amiss. If I were only allowed to wear gloves—pretty gauntlets, like those I've seen on her hands, small and white as the drifted snow! Ah! there, I'm far behind her: my poor hands are red and big; they've had to work and weave; while hers, I dare say, never touched a distaff. Oh! that I could wear gloves to cover these ugly fingers of mine. But no—I daren't. The village girls would laugh at me, and call me a ——. I won't say the word. Never mind for the gloves. Should he come, I'll keep my hands under my apron, so that he shan't see a finger."

Thus soliloquized Bet Dancey in front of her bit of broken looking-glass.

It was not Will Walford who had summoned up her ludicrous soliloquy; nor yet the cuirassier—he who had called twice. For

neither of these was the dark-haired damsel arraying herself in her
flaunting finery. The lure was being set for higher game—for
Henry Holtspur.

"I hope father mayn't meet him on the way. He'll be sure to
turn him back if he do; for father likes better to go to Stone Dean
than for him to come here. Luckily there's two paths; and father
always takes the short cut—by which *he* never comes.

"Ha! the dog barks! 'Tis some one! Mercy on me! If't be
him I'm not half ready to receive him. Stay in, you nasty comb!
It's too short in the teeth. Will's no judge of combs, or he'd a
bought me a better. After all," concluded she, bending down before
the bit of glass, and taking a final survey of her truly beautiful
face, "I think I'll do. Perhaps I'm not so pretty as Mistress
Marion Wade; but I'm sure I'm as good-looking as Mistress Dorothy Dayrell. The dog again! It must be somebody; I hope
'tis ——"

Leaving the name unpronounced, the girl glided back into the
kitchen; and, crossing it with quick step, stood once more within
the doorway.

As yet there was no one in sight. The dog was barking at something that had roused him either by scent or sound. But the girl
knew that the animal rarely erred in this wise; and that something
—either man or beast—must be approaching the hut.

She was not kept long in suspense, as to who was the coming
visitor; though the hope, to which she had given thought, had well
nigh departed before that visitor came within view. The dog was
making his demonstration *towards the south*. The path to Stone
Dean led *northward* from the cottage. Henry Holtspur, if coming
from home, should appear in the latter direction.

The girl knew of another visitor who might be expected by the
southern path, and at any hour. In that direction dwelt Will Walford. It might be he?

A shadow of disappointment swept over her face, accompanying
this conjecture. It seemed to say, how little welcome just then
would Will Walford be.

Such must have been its signification: for at sight of this individual—the moment after advancing along the path—the shadow on her
countenance sensibly deepened.

"How very provoking!" muttered she. "At such a time, too—
just as I had hopes of seeing *him*. If *he* should come, too—even

though his errand be to father—I shouldn't wonder if Will was to make some trouble. He's been jealous ever since he saw me give Master Holtspur the flowers—worse about him than any one. Will's right there; though the other's not to blame—no, no—only myself. I wish he were a little in fault. Then I shouldn't mind Will's jealousy; nor he, I'm sure. Oh! if he loved me, I shouldn't care for aught, or anybody, in the wide world!"

Having made this self-confession, she stepped back into the doorway; and, standing upon the stoop, awaited the unwelcome visitor with an air of defiant indifference.

"Mornin', Bet!" saluted her suitor, in a curt, sulky fashion, to which "Bet" made an appropriate response. "Thou beest stannin' in the door as if thou wast lookin' for some'un? I doan't suppose it are for me, anyhow."

"No, indeed," answered the girl, taking but slight pains to conceal her chagrin. I neither expected you, nor do I thank you for coming. I told you so, when you were here last; and now I tell you again."

"Wall, you consated thing!" retorted the lout, with a pretense at being indifferent; "how do thee know I be come to see thee? I may have bizness wi' Mast' Dancey, mayen't I?"

"If you have, he's not at home."

"Where be he gone?"

"Over to Stone Dean. He's only left here a minute ago. He went by the short cut across the woods. If you keep on, you'll easily overtake him."

"Bah!" ejaculated the woodman, "I beant in such a hurry. My bizness wi' your father 'll keep till he coom back; but I'se also got somethin' to say to thyself as woan't keep much longer. Thee be done up wonderful fine this mornin'! Be theer another *fîte* to come off? 'Tain't day o' a fair, be it?"

"My doing up, as you call it, has nothing to do with either *fîte*, or fair. I'm dressed no different from other days, I'm sure. I've only put on my new skirt and boddice—because—because——"

Notwithstanding her readiness, Mistress Betsey appeared a little perplexed to find an excuse for her being habited in her holiday attire.

"Because," interrupted the woodman, noticing her confusion "because thee wast looking out for some 'un. That's the because Bet Dancey!" continued he, his increased jealousy stimulating him to bolder speech: "doan't try to deceive me. I arn't such a blind fool as you think I be. You've put on your finery to receive some 'un as you ha' been expectin'. That swaggerin' soger, I 'spose? Maybe the fine gentleman o' Stone Dean hisself; or I wouldna' wonder if 't mout be that ere Indyen dummy o' his. You beant partickler, Bet Dancey; not you. All's fish as comes to thy net—all's one."

"Will Walford!" cried the girl, turning red under his taunts, "I shall not listen to such talk, either from you or any one. If you've nothing else to say to me, you may pass on."

"But I hev' somethin' else to say to thee; an' I mean to say't now, Bet."

"Say it, then, and have done with it," rejoined the girl, as if desirous of hurrying the interview to an end. "What be it?"

"It be this, then," replied the woodman, moving a little nearer to her, and speaking in a more serious tone than he had assumed; "Bet Dancey, I needn't be tellin' thee how I be in love wi' thee. Thou know'st it well enoo."

"You've told it me a hundred times. I don't want to hear it again."

"But thou shalt. An' this time, I tell thee, will be the last."

"I'm glad to hear that."

"What I be goin' to say," continued the suitor, without heeding her repeated interruptions, "be this, Bet Dancey. I see'd thy father last night; an' he an' me talked it over atween us. He's gie'd me his full consent."

"To what, pray?"

"Why, to ha'e thee for my wife."

"Indeed!" exclaimed the girl, with a scornful laugh. "Ha! ha! ha! That's what you had to tell me, is it? Now, Will Walford, hear me in return. You've told me a hundred times that you loved me, and you've now promised that it will be the last time. I've said to you a hundred times it was no use; and I promise you this will be *my* last saying it. Once for all, then, I declare to you, that I *shall never be your wife—never! never!*"

The last words were pronounced with a stern emphasis, calculated to carry conviction; and the rustic suitor shrank under them, as if they had annihilated the last remnant of his hopes.

Only for an instant did he preserve his cowering attitude. His was not a nature to be stung without turning; and the recoil soon came.

"Then dang it!" cried he, raising his long ax, and winding it round his head in a threatening manner, "if thee doan't be my wife, Bet Dancey, thou shalt never be the wife o' any other. I swear to thee, I'll kill the first man thee marriest; an' thyself along wi' him if I ever live to see the day that makes two o' ye one!"

"Away, wretch!" cried the girl, half terrified, half indignant. "I don't want to listen to your threats. Away, away!"

And, saying this, she retreated inside the hut—as she did so, slamming the door in his face.

"Dang thee, thou deceitful slut!" apostrophized the discarded suitor; "an' I'll keep my threet, if I ha' to swing for it!"

As he gave utterance to this fell menace, he threw the ax over his shoulder; sprang across the broken palings; and strode off among the trees—once more muttering as he went: "I'll keep my threet, if I ha' to swing for it!"

For some minutes the door of the cottage remained closed. It was also barred on the inside; for the girl had been a good deal frightened, and feared the fellow's return. The wild look that had gleamed from under his white eyebrows would have caused fear within the bosom of any woman; and it had even terrified the heart of Bet Dancey.

On barring the door, she glided up to one of the windows and watched. She saw him take his departure from the place.

"He is gone, and I am glad of it for *two* reasons," soliloquized she. "What a wicked wretch! I always thought so. And yet my father wants me to marry that man! Never—never! I shall tell father what he has said.

"Maybe that may change him.

"Heigho! I fear *he* is not coming to-day! and when shall I see him again? There's to be another *fête* at Michaelmas; but that's a long time; and it's such a chance meeting him on the road—where one mayn't speak to him, perhaps. Oh! if I could think of some errand to Stone Dean! I wish father would send me oftener. Ah me! what's the use? Master Holtspur's too grand to think of a poor peasant girl. *Marry* me he could not, perhaps he *would* not— I don't want that, if he'd only *love* me!"

The lurcher, who had kept silent during the stormy interview between Bet and her rustic admirer, now broke out in a fresh brewer of baying.

"Is it Will again?" cried the girl, gliding back to the window and looking out. "No it can't be him: the dog looks the other way. It's either father coming back, or——. 'Tis he! 'tis he!

"What am I to do? I must open the door. If he sees it shut he may not think of coming in; I wish him to come in!"

As she said this, she glided up to the doorway, and pushing back the bar, gently drew up the door.

She did not show herself in the entrance. A quick instinct hindered her. Were she to do so, the visitor might simply make an inquiry; and, being answered that her father was not at home, might turn back or pass on. This would not suit her purpose: *since she wished him to come in.*

He was afoot. That augured well. She watched him through the window as he drew near. She watched him with a throbbing bosom.

CHAPTER XXXII.

THE DISPATCH AT LAST.

Richard Scarthe, Captain of the King's Cuirassiers and confidant of the Queen, was seated in his apartment in the mansion of Sir Marmaduke Wade.

A small table stood within the reach of his hand, on which was a decanter containing wine and a silver goblet. He had thrice filled the latter and thrice drained its contents to the last drop. But the intoxicating fluid, even thus liberally imbibed, had failed to give solace to the chagrin with which his spirit was affected.

It was now the third day of his residence under the roof of Sir Marmaduke Wade, and he had made scarce any progress in the programme he had sketched out—of ingratiating himself with the knight and his family.

On the part of these a rigorous etiquette continued to be kept up; and it appeared probable that beyond what necessity demanded of them, only the slightest intercourse might ever occur between them and their uninvited guests.

Of these circumstances, however, the soldier made not much account. He might expect in time to smooth over the unpleasant occurrences that had inaugurated his introduction. He knew himself to have a tongue that could wheedle with the devil; and with this he hoped at no distant day to remove the hostile impression, and establish an intimacy—if not altogether friendly—that would at least give him the opportunity he desired. Indeed, he even flattered himself that he had already made some progress in this direction; and it was not that was causing the extreme acerbity of spirit he now strove to soothe with copious libations from the wine cup.

His chagrin sprang from a different cause. What at first was only a suspicion had now become almost a certainty,—that he was forestalled in the affections of a beautiful woman whom he already loved with an indescribable ardor—forestalled, and by the very man who, in her eyes, had so horribly humiliated him.

Notwithstanding this belief, he had not abandoned hope. Richard Scarthe was a courtier of too much confidence in his own prowess to yield easily to despair. He had succeeded oft before in the estrangement of hearts already prepossessed, and why should he not again?

As the wine mounted to his brain, his mind began to contend against the conviction with which his late act of espionage had so unhappily supplied him. The evidence of the glove was, after all, inconclusive. The one he had picked up was no doubt the glove of Marion Wade; but what reason was there for believing that it was its fellow he had seen in the hat of Henry Holtspur? A glove of white doe-skin leather was a fashion of the time—so, too, the gold and lace ornaments upon the gauntlet. The daughter of Sir Marmaduke Wade was not the only lady who wore white gloves. Why should it be hers?

Every reason had he to arrive at the contrary conclusion. He had ascertained that his antagonist was a stranger to the family, introduced to Marion scarce an hour before the combat, and not speaking to her afterwards.

Thus in his own mind would Scarthe have disposed of the circumstance of the two gloves: deeming it an accidental coincidence.

But then there was the interview in the park—that interview of which he had been a witness. Could *it* have been accidental? Or for some other purpose than that of a love meeting?

There was but little probability in these conjectures. For all that, the jealous Scarthe, under the influence of the wine, earnestly indulged in them until he began to feel a sort of hope of their being true. It was but for a moment—short and evanescent—and again did his mind relapse into a doubting condition.

Henry Holtspur had by this time become the *bête noire* of his existence, against whom his bitterest hostility was henceforth to be directed. He had already taken some steps to inform himself of the position and character of his rival; but in this he had met with only slight success. A mystery surrounded the movements of the *black horseman*; and all that Scarthe could learn in relation to him was that he was a gentleman of independent means who had lately taken up his residence in the neighborhood, his domicile being an old mansion known by the quaint appellation of "Stone Dean."

Scarthe ascertained, also, that Holtspur was a stranger to most, if not all, the distinguished families of the neighborhood; though it was believed that he associated with others at a greater distance, and that he had hitherto stood aloof from those near him, not from any want of the opportunity of being introduced, but rather from the absence, on his part, of the inclination.

It was rumored that he had spent a portion of his life in the colonies of America; and the fact that he was occasionally seen accompanied by a young Indian in the capacity of body servant gave confirmation to the rumor.

Scarthe had learnt nothing more in relation to his conqueror, excepting that two men of the neighborhood were occasionally employed by him in matters of service. These were a woodman of the name of Dancey, and another of the like ilk—a younger man, called Walford.

The cuirassier captain had not taken the trouble to collect this information without some glimmering of a design, though as yet he saw not very clearly in what way he could benefit by the knowledge. In fact, Captain Scarthe had never in his life felt more powerless to rid himself of a rival who had so rudely crossed his path.

To challenge his late antagonist and fight him again was not to be thought of—after such a termination to the first combat. The life of Scarthe had been conceded to him; and the laws of honor would have precluded him from seeking a second affair –had he been so inclined. But the touch of the cavalier's steel had taught him its sharp quality, and he had not the slightest inclination to tempt it again. Though yearning fiercely for vengeance, he had no thought of seeking it in that way, and in what fashion he was to find it, he had as yet conceived no distinct idea.

The *séance* with his own thoughts had been protracted for more than an hour, and the cloud that still sat upon his brooding brow betokened that it had been unsuccessful. The wine, quaffed spasmodically, had been quaffed in vain. His vengeance, even so stimulated, had failed to suggest a scheme for its satisfaction.

length an idea seemed to occur to him that called for the presence the second personage. He rose to his feet, and striding to the doo sed rapidly out of the room.

In a few ds he re-entered, followed by one of his troopers—a young fellow whose countenance might have appeared pleasing enough but for an expression of softness, almost silliness, that marked it.

"Well, Withers?" inquired the officer, as soon as the two had got fairly within the room, "you have seen the two woodmen?"

"Only one, captain. The old one, Dancey, hadn't come home yet; but his daughter said she was expectin' him the night."

"And the other?"

"Wull Walford? Yes, captain, I seen him, and delivered your message."

"Well; he's coming to see me, is he not?"

"I'm afeard not, captain."

"Why not?"

"He's a queery sort, is Wull Walford. I knew him 'fore I left the county to list in the troops. He's a ill-tempered cur; that's what *he* is."

"But why should he show temper with me? He don't know but that I may intend kindness to him?"

"After what's happened, he's afeard to see you, captain. That's why I think he won't come."

"After what's happened! And what *has* happened? You mystify me, my man!"

"I mean, captain, the little affair as occurred between you and him—in the old camp over there."

"Between me and him? Who are you thinking of, Withers! Not the 'black horseman,' as the rustics call this——"

"No, captain; Wul Walford, I mean."

"And pray what has occurred between Master *Wull* Walford and myself? I remember ... individual of the name."

"You remember Robin Hood, captain—he as had the 'dacity to strike at your honor with his bow?"

"O-o-h! that's the difficulty, is it. So, so," continued Scarthe, in half soliloquy. "Wull Walford of Wapsey's Wood and the bold outlaw of Sherwood Forest are identical individuals, are they? No wonder the fellow has some scrup ... 'bout seeing me again. Ha! ha! I dare say I shall be able to overcome them. A crown or two will no doubt suffice to satisfy Master Walford for what he may have considered a slight to his sweetheart; and as to the blow over my own crown, I can the more easily pardon that since I believe he broke the stock of his weapon in dealing it. So, Robin Hood it is. Well, if I'm not mistaken, he and I may be fast friends yet. At all events, from what I observed on that occasion, he is not likely to be on the friendliest terms with my enemy. Withers!"

"Captain!" said the trooper, making a fresh salute, as if in the expectation of receiving some order

"I shall want you to guide me to the domicile of this Walford. I suppose he has a house somewhere; or does he, like his prototype, roam anywhere and everywhere, and sleep under the shadow of the greenwood tree?"

"He lives in a poor sort o' cottage, captain—not very far from that of Dick Dancey."

"Then we may visit both at once, and as the older woodman is expected to return home to-night I shall not go until to-morrow. How far is it to this Wapsey's Wood?"

"Scant two miles, captain. It's up the road in the direction of Beaconsfield."

"Enough. I shall go on horseback. After morning parade, see that you have the grey horse saddled, and your own as well. Now, be off to your quarters; say nothing to any of your comrades what duty you are going on, nor to any of your country acquaintances neither, else you may get yourself into trouble. Go!"

The trooper, making a salute, expressive of assent to the caution thus delivered, betook himself from the presence of his commanding officer.

"He's but a silly fellow, this Withers," muttered the latter, as the soldier had gone out of hearing. "Not the man for my purpose

His knowledge of the neighborhood—the only one of my vagabonds who has ever been in it before—makes it a necessity to employ him in this matter. Perhaps in Wull Walford, I may find a more intel ligent *aide-de-camp. Nous verrons!*"

And with this conjectural reflection, Scarthe threw himself back in his chair; and once more gave way to the gloomy surmises that had already tormented his unhappy mind.

Again did they torment him as before; and it was a relief to him when the door once more turned upon its hinges, and his subaltern stepped into the room.

Not that Stubbs had any cheering news to communicate; nor was there just·then anything encouraging in his countenance. On the contrary, the cornet looked but little less lugubrious than his captain; and he had been in that mood ever since morning.

Lora Lovelace would scarce condescend to exchange a word with him; and when by chance he had been twice or thrice in her com· pany, it was only to find himself the subject of a slight or a satire, and the next moment to receive the cold shoulder. All this, too, so delicately done, that Stubbs could find no opportunity for retaliation; unless by allowing a license to his vulgar spite, which Scarthe had cautioned him against. In fact the cornet felt that the young lady, on more than one occasion, had made a butt of him—he did, by Ged!

He had at an earlier hour communicated to his captain the ill success of his wooing: but the latter was too much absorbed in his own schemes, to offer him either advice or assistance.

The entrance of his subaltern turned the thoughts of Scarthe into a new channel, as testified by his speech.

"So, then, there's no one arrived from London yet?" he said, interrogatively, as he saw the cornet proceeding to seat himself.

A simple negative was the reply.

"'Tis very odd that the message—whatever it was—has not been delivered in duplicate before this time?"

"Very odd!—'tis by Ged!"

"I shouldn't wonder if the fellow, frightened as he was by those precious footpads, has taken leave of his senses altogether; and, instead of carrying back my letter, has climbed into a tree, and hanged himself thereon."

"Like enough, by Ged!"

"Had I only slipped in a postscript, giving the king a hint about the character of the rascals to whom his courier so tamely surren- dered, perhaps the best thing he could have done would have been to string himself up. I haven't the slightest doubt about its being the band of scarecrows that stopped the son of Sir Marmaduke. Of course, it must have been; since it was on the same night, and the same spot. Ha! ha! ha! In all of my campaigns I never heard of a more clever bit of strategy. Ha! ha! ha!"

"Nor I," said Stubbs, joining in the laugh.

"I'd give a month's pay to get hold of the comical villain that planned it. If he felt inclined to join our cuirassiers, I'd make a corporal of him without asking a question."

"He'd make a first-rater. He would, by Ged!"

"I should like, also, to get hold of him for another reason," continued Scarthe, changing to a more serious tone. "We might recover the lost dispatches—which, no doubt, are still in the doublet he stripped from the chicken-hearted courier. Ha! ha! ha! What a pickle we found him in! A pigeon completely plucked and trussed. Oh! how the queen will laugh when she reads my report to her. I hope she won't tell it to the king. If she do blab, it'll be no laughing matter for the poor devil of a messenger!"

"It won't, by Ged!"

"Particularly if the dispatches contained anything of importance. I wonder what they were about—sent so soon after us; hope it wasn't a countermand."

"By Ged! I hope not."

"I'm not tired of our country quarters just yet: and won't be, till I've tried them a little longer. Rather icy these girls are, Stubbs? Don't repine, lad. Perhaps they'll thaw, by and by."

"I hope so," said Stubbs, his stolid features brightening up at the idea. "If it wasn't for that young sop of a cousin, 'twould be all right. I believe it would, by Ged?"

"Pooh! pooh! Don't make your mind uneasy about him It appears to be a kind of kittenly affection that's between them. He's just come home, after a three years' absence from her apron-string; and it's natural she should like to play with him a bit. Only as a toy, Stubbs. She'll soon tire of him, and want another. Then will be your turn, my killing cornet."

"Do you think so, captain?"

"Think so! Sure of it. Ha! if it were my game, I shouldn't want an easier to play. Mine's a different affair—very different. It will require all the skill of— of Captain Scarthe to win in that quarter. Ho! Who's there? Come in!"

The interrogatory had been called forth by a knock heard outside. At the command to enter, the door was opened, showing a cuirassier standing upon the stoop, with his hand raised to his helmet.

"Your business, sergeant?" demanded the captain.

"A messenger has arrived escorted by three files of dragoniers."

"Whence?"

"From London."

"Show him in; and see that his escort are taken care of outside."

The sergeant disappeared to execute the order.

"This should be the bearer of the duplicate dispatch?" said Scarthe, conjecturally; "and if it contains a countermand, I hope it has been also lost."

"I doubt it," rejoined the cornet; "the three files of dragoniers ought to have been a match for the dozen dummies!" and as Stubbs said this, he smiled conceitedly at the pretty speech he had perpetrated.

The courier came in—a cavalier by his costume and bearing; but of a type very different from the one rifled by the robber. He was a grizzled old veteran, armed from the toes to the teeth; and his steel-grey eye, shining sagely through the bars of his helmet, betokened a character not likely to have been duped by Gregory Garth and his scare-crows. Had this individual been bearer of the original dispatch instead of the copy, in all likelihood the repentant footpad would have committed no other crime on that memorable night; and would have been saved the sin of breaking the promise he had made to his master.

"A courier from the king?" said Scarthe, bowing courteously as the cavalier came forward.

"A dispatch from his majesty," returned the messenger, with an official salute, at the same time holding out the document. "It is the copy of one sent three days ago, and lost upon the road. Captain Scarthe, I believe, is already acquainted with the circumstance."

A slight twinkling in the steel-grey eye of the speaker, while making the concluding remark, told that he had heard of the adventure, and was not insensible to its ludicrous nature.

"Oh, yes!" assented Scarthe. "I hope the bearer of the original has not come to grief through his misadventure."

"Dismissed the service," was the formal rejoinder.

"Ah! I am sorry for that. The fright he had was, I should think, punishment enough; to say nothing of the loss of his horse, purse, watch, and love locket. Ha! ha! ha!"

The hearty laugh in which the captain indulged, chorussed by Stubbs, sanctioned only by a grim smile on the part of grey-eye, told that the sympathy of the latter for the disgraced courier was not very profound.

"Cornet Stubbs," said Scarthe, turning to his subaltern, and waving his hand towards the messenger, "see that this gentleman does not die of hunger, and thirst. Excuse me, sir, while I peruse the King's dispatch. Perhaps it requires to answer."

The cornet, inviting the courier to follow him, passed out of the room; while Scarthe, stepping into the embayment of the window, broke open the royal seal, and read:

"His Majestie the King to Captain Scarthe, commanding ye Cuirassiers in the County of Bucks.

"In addition to ye orders already given, Captain Scarthe is hereby commanded to raise by recruit in ye county of Bucks as many men as may be disposed to take service in his Majestie's regiment of Cuirassiers; and he is by these same presents empowered with ye King's authority to offer to each and every recruit a bounty as prescribed in ye accompagnying schedule.

"Furthermore, it having come to ye ear of his Majestie, that divers disloyal citizens of said shire of Bucks have of late shown symptoms of disaffection to his Majestie's Government, in the holding of secret meetings, and divers other and like unlawful acts, and by speeches containing rebellious doctrines against his Majestie's Government and person, as likewise against the well-being of ye State and ye Church; therefore, his Majestie do command his loyal and trusted servant, ye Captain Scarthe aforesaid, to search, discover, and take cognizance of all such dissentious persons; and if he find good and substantial proof of their disloyalty, then is he hereby enjoined and commanded to communicate ye same to ye Secretary of his Majestie's Council of State, in order that such rebellious subjects be brought to trial before ye Star Chamber, or ye High Commission Court, or such other court or courts as may conform to the nature of their offence and punishment

"Given at our palace of Whitehall.

(signed)   *CAROLUS REX."*

"Pish!" exclaimed Scarthe, as he concluded reading the dispatch "That's a pretty duty to put *me* on! Making a spy of me! The king forgets that I am a gentleman'

"I shall obey the first command readily enough. My troop wants recruiting; and I suppose, along with the increased numbers, I may get that colonelcy I ought to have had long ago. As to my eaves-dropping about inns, and listening for every silly speech that Jack makes to Jame, and Jem repeats to Collin—with the usual embellish-ments of the rural fancy—I'll do nothing of the sort;—unless," added he, with a significant smile, "unless the *queen commands me*. To gratify her sweet grace, I'll turn potboy, and wait upon the gossips of the tap. Ho! what's this?—more writing; a postscript! Per-haps, as in the letters of ladies, the most important part of the epistle?

"*Since the above dispatch, his Majestie hath been further informed that one of his Majestie's subjects—by name Holtspur—and bearing the Christian name of Henry, hath more than any other been of great zeal in promoting the subversive doctrines aforementioned; and it is believed that the said Holtspur is an active instrument and co-adjutor among the enemies of his Majestie's Government. Therefore Captain Scarthe is directed and enjoined to watch the goings and comings of ye said Holtspur, and if anything do appear in his conduct that may be deemed sufficient for a charge before ye Star Chamber, then is Captain Scarthe directed to proceed against and arrest the said individual. His Majestie in ye matter in question will trust to the discretion of Captain Scarthe to do nothing on slight grounds—lest the arrest of a subject of his Majestie, who might afterwards be proven innocent, bring scandal on ye name and government of his Majestie.*
"*C. R.*"

"Spy!" exclaimed Scarthe, starting to his feet as he finished read-ing the postscript. "Spy, you say? I thank you for the office. Fear me not, kind king. I'll play the part to perfection."

"Did I not say so?" he continued, striding to and fro across the floor, and waiving the paper triumphantly over his head. "The wo-men are wise: they keep their best bit for the last. Henceforth of a letter give me the postscript.

"So, Master Henry Holtspur, I thought there was something not sound about you—ever since you drank that toast to taunt me Aha!

9

If I don't have you on the hip· · as Will Shakespeare says—then I'm not Dick Scarthe, captain of the king's cuirassiers.

Stay, I must go gently about this business—gently and cautiously. The king counsels it so. No fear for my rashness. I know when to be stormy, and when to be tranquil. Proofs are required. That won't be difficult, I ween—where a red rebel stands before the bar.

"I'll find proofs. Never fear, your Majesty. I'll find, or *frame* them—proofs that will satisfy that scrupulous tribunal, the Star Chamber! Ha! ha! ha!"

And, as he gave utterance to the satirical laugh, he passed rapidly out of the room—as if starting off in search of those proofs he so confidently expected to obtain.

CHAPTER XXXIII

WILL WALFORD.

We left the beautiful Bet Dancey, with her eye fixed on the man she admired, waiting his entrance into her father's cottage, and with a throbbing bosom.

Hers were not the only eyes that were watching Henry Holtspur—nor the only bosom throbbing at the approach. There was one other beating as wildly as hers, though with emotions of a far different kind. It was that of her discarded suitor.

On parting with his cruel sweetheart, Will Walford had walked on among the trees, not caring what direction he took. The horoscope of a happy life, as the husband of Bet Dancey—which he had long been contemplating—had become dim and dark by the very decided dismissal he had just received ; and the young woodman's world, circumscribed though it might be, was now, to his view, a waste chaos.

For a time he could find no other occupation for either thought or speech, than to repeat the revengeful phrase with which he had signalized his departure.

Only for a short time, however, did he continue in this reckless mood. The fact of his sweetheart being done up in her holiday dress, once more recurred to him—along with the suspicion that she must be expecting some one.

This thought checked his steps—bringing him to an instantaneous halt.

Despite his ungracious dismissal—despite the hopelessness of his own suit—he determined on discovering who was the happy rival; who it was for whom that bodice had been buttoned on.

That there was such an individual he could scarce have a doubt. The girl's manner towards himself—her air of anxiety while he stayed in her presence—the desire she had expressed for him to follow, and overtake her father—and finally, the banging of the door in his face—all pointed to a wish on her part to get rid of him as soon as possible. Even the dull brain of the brute was quick enough to be convinced of this.

If he had any doubting hope upon the subject, it was determined by the baying of the lurcher, which at this moment broke upon his ear. The dog could no longer be barking at him? Some other rival must have engaged the animal's attention; and who could that other be, but the man for whom Bet's black tresses had been so coquettishly coifed?

The jealous rustic faced around and commenced returning towards the hut, as if the bark of the dog had been a command for him to do so.

Very different, however, was the attitude exhibited on his backward march. Instead of the reckless devil-me-care swagger with which he had taken his departure, he now made approach with the instinctive caution of one accustomed to the woods; sheltering himself behind the trunks of the trees, and gliding from one to the other—as if afraid of being shot at by somebody lying in wait within the cottage.

After arriving upon the edge of the open ground, that extended some yards outside the enclosure, he came to a final stop—crouching down behind a bush of holly, whose thick dark foliage appeared sufficient to screen him from the observation of any one—either in the cottage, or in front of it.

The first glance which he gave, after getting into position, discovered to him the individual whose arrival had set the dog to barking

Had it been the coarse cuirassier—Bet's latest conquest—or even the officer who at the *fête* had made so free with her lips, Will Walford would have been pained by the presence of either. But far more dire were his thoughts, on perceiving it was neither one nor the other; but a rival infinitely more to be dreaded—his own patron—the protector of Maid Marian.

Had it been any other who was making approach, Will Walford might have sprung from his hiding-place, and shown himself upon the instant—perhaps commanded their instantaneous departure. But after witnessing that combat in the Saxon camp—combined with other knowledge he possessed of the character and qualities of the "black, horseman"—a wholesome fear of this individual counseled him to keep his place.

The dog soon ceased his angry demonstrations; and springing gleefully upon his chain, commenced wagging his tail in friendly recognition of the new arrival. It was evident the cavalier was not coming to the cottage of Dick Dancey for the first time.

As Walford reasoned thus, the cloud upon his countenance became darker—the agony in his heart more intense. Still more agonizing were his emotions when he saw Henry Holtspur step inside the hut, and heard his voice in free conversation with that of the girl. The tone appeared to be of two persons who had talked in confidence—*who understood one another!*

The shadow of a fell intent showed itself on the beetling brow of Will Walford. Despite his dread of such a powerful adversary, jealousy was fast urging him to a dark deed—to do, or dare it. No doubt, in another instant, it would have stimulated him to the wielding of that terrible wood-ax, but for an unexpected incident that turned him from his intention.

The dog again gave out his howling note of alarm; but soon changed it into a yelp of recognition, on perceiving that it was his own master who was coming along the path.

At the same instant Walford recognized the old woodman. Instead of showing himself, he crept closer in among the glabrous leaves of holly, and lay crouching there—more like a man who feared being detected, than one bent on detection.

It was not till the cavalier had stepped forth from the cottage, and apparently entering into serious conversation with its owner, walked off with him into the woods, that Walford stole out from his hiding place under the holly.

Then, shaking his ax in the direction in which they had gone—with a gesture that seemed to signify only the adjournment of his fiendish design—and still keeping the bush between his own body and the windows of the hovel, he sneaked sulkily away.

He did not go in silence, but kept muttering as he went; at intervals breaking out into louder enunciations—as some thought especially exasperating struck into his excited brain.

Again he repeated the menace made on his first departure from the cottage.

"Ees, dang me! I'll keep my threet, if I shud ha' to hang for't."

This time, however, the "threet" applied to a special victim—Holtspur. It is true that he still mentally reserved a condition; and that was, should his suspicions prove correct. He was determined to play the spy upon his sweetheart by day and by night; and should he discover good grounds for his jealousy, nothing should then stay his hand from the fell purpose already declared—to kill.

This purpose—fully resolved upon as he walked through the wood—had some effect in tranquilizing his spirit; though it was far from giving it complete contentment.

His steps were turned homeward; and soon brought him to a hut standing only a few hundred yards from that of Dick Dancey—of even humbler aspect than the domicile of the deer-stealer. It looked more like a stack of fagots than a house. It had only one door, one window, and one room; but these were sufficient for his owner, who lived altogether alone.

"The "plenishing" was less plentiful, and of a commoner kind than that in the cottage of the deer-stealer; and the low truck-bed in the corner, with its scanty clothing, looked as if the hand of woman had never spread sheet, or coverlet, upon it.

The appearance of poverty was to some extent deceptive. However obtained, it was known that Walford possessed money; and his chalk score in the tap-room of the "Packhorse" was always wiped out upon demand. No more did his dress betray any pecuniary strait. He went well habited; and could even afford a fancy costume when occasion called for it—to represent Robin Hood, or any other popular hero of the peasant fancy.

It was this repute of unknown, and therefore indefinite, wealth, that in some measure sanctioned his claim to aspire to the hand of the beautiful Bet Dancey, the aknowledged belle of the parish; and though his supposed possession of property had failed to win over the heart of the girl herself, it had a deal to do in making him the favorite of her father.

Already slightly suspicious of Bet's partiality for the black horseman, what he witnessed that morning rendered him seriously so. It is true, there was still nothing ascertained—nothing definite. The cavalier might have had some object in visiting Dancey's cottage, other than an interview with Bet; and Walford was only too willing to think so.

But the circumstances were suspicious—sufficiently so to make sad havoc with his happiness; and had Dancey not returned at the time he did, there is no knowing what might have been the *dénouement* of the interview he had interrupted.

On entering his unpretentious dwelling, Walford flung his ax into a corner, and himself into a chair—both acts being performed with an air of recklessness, that betokened a man sadly out of sorts with the world.

His thoughts, still muttered aloud, told that his mind dwelt on the two individuals whose names constantly turned up in is soliloquy— Bet Dancey and Henry Holtspur. Though Bet was at intervals most bitterly abused, the cavalier come in for the angrier share of his denunciations.

"Dang the interloper!" he exclaimed, "why doan't he keep to his own sort? Ridin' about wi' his fine horse on' his fine feathers an' pokin' hisself into poor people's cottages, where he have no bizness to be? Dang him!

"What's brought him into this neighborhood anyhow? I shud like to know that. An' what's he doin' *now?* I shud like to know that. Gatherin' a lot o' people to his house from all parts o' the country, an' them to come in the middle o' the night! I shud like to know that.

"Theer be somethin' in it *he* doan't want to be know'd: else why shud those letters I carried—ay, an' opened an' read 'em too—why shud they have told them as I tuk 'em to, to come 'ithout bringin' theer own grooms, an' at that late hour o' the night? Twelve o'clock the letters sayed—one an' all o' them!

"I shud like to know what it's all about. That's what I shud.

"Ay! an' maybe I know some'un else as wud like to know. That fellow as fought wi' him at the feeat. I wish he'd run him through the ribs, instead o' gettin' run through hisself. Dang it! what can *he* be wantin' wi' me? Can't be about that thwack I gin him over the skull cap? If't are anything consarnin' that, he would'nt a' sent after me as he's done? No, he'd a sent a couple o' his steel-kivered sogers, and tuck me at once. Withers sayed he meant well by me; but that Withers an't to be depended on. I never knew *him* tell the truth afore he went sogerin'; an' it an't like he be any better now. Maybe this captain do mean well, for all that? I'd gie somethin' to know what he *be* wantin'.

"Dang it!" he again broke forth, after pondering for a while; "it mout be somethin' about this very fellow—this black horseman? I shud say that 'ere captain 'ill be thinkin' o' him, more'n about anybody else. If he be—ha!"

The last ejaculation was uttered in a significant tone, and prolonged, as if continuing some train of thought that had freshly started into his brain.

"If't be that—it may be? Dang me! I'll know! I'll go an' see Master Captain Scarthe—that's what they call him, I b'lieve. I'll go this very minnit."

In obedience to the resolve thus suddenly entered upon, the woodman rose to his feet; seized hold of his hat; and made towards the door.

Suddenly he stopped, looked outward upon some sight, that seemed to cause him some surprise and gratification.

"I've heerd say," he muttered, "that when the devil be wanted he beeant far off. Dang it; the very man I war goin' to see be comin' to see *me*! Ees—that be the captain o' the kewressers, an' that's Withers as be a ridin' ahint him!"

Walford's announcement was but the simple truth. It was Captain Scarthe and his confidant Withers, who were approaching the hovel.

They were on horseback; but did not ride quite up to the house. When within a hundred yards of the door the officer dismounted; and having given his bridle to the trooper, advanced on foot and alone.

There was no enclosure around the domicile of Will Walford—not even a ditch; and his visitor, without stopping, walked straight up the door, where the woodman was standing on the stoop to receive him.

With the quick eye of an old campaigner, Scarthe saw that on the ugly face of his late adversary there was no anger. Whatever feeling of hostility the latter might have entertained at the fête, for some reason or other, appeared to have vanished; and the captain was as much surprised as gratified at beholding something like a smile, when he expected to have been favored with a frown.

Almost intuitively did Scarthe construe this circumstance. The man before him had an enemy that he knew to be his also—one that he hated more than Scarthe himself.

To make certain of the justness of this conjecture was the first move on the part of the cuirassier captain.

"Good morrow my friend!" began he, approaching the woodman with the most affable air. "I hope the little incident that came so crookedly between us, and which I most profoundly regret, I hope it has been equally forgotten and forgiven by you. As I am an admirer of bravery, even in an adversary, I shall feel highly complimented if you will join me in a stoup of wine. You see I always go prepared—lest I should lose my way in these vast forests of yours, and perhaps perish of thirst."

As he approached the conclusion of this somewhat jocular peroration, he held up a flask, suspended by a strap over his shoulders, and unconcernedly commenced extracting the stopper.

His *ci-devant* adversary, who seemed both surprised and pleased at this brusque style of soldering a quarrel, eagerly accepted the proffered challenge; and after expressing consent in his rough way, invited the cavalier to step inside his humble dwelling, and be accommodated with a seat.

Scarthe gave ready assent; and in an other second had planted himself on one of the two dilapidated chairs which the hovel contained.

The wine was soon decanted into a pair of tin cups, instead of silver goblets; and in less that ten minutes' time Captain Scarthe and Will Walford were upon as friendly terms as if the former had never touched the lips of Maid Marian, nor the latter broken a cross-bow over his head.

"The fact is, my bold Robin!" said Scarthe, by way of a salvo, "I and my companion, the cornet, had taken a little too much of this sort of stuff on that particular morning and you know when a man——"

"Dang it, yes!" rejoined the rustic, warming to his splendid companion, who might likely become a powerful patron, "when one has got a drap too much beer i' the head, he arn't answerable for every bit o' mischief in the way. I know 't was only in sport that ye kissed the lass. Dang it! I'd ha' done the same myself. Ay, that I would."

" Ah ! and a pretty lass she is, this Maid Marian   Your sweetneart,
I take it, Master Walford ? "

" Oh ! e-es—Betsey be somethin' o' that sort," replied the woodman, rather vain in the avowal.

" A fortunate fellow you are ! I dare say you will soon be married
to her ? "

Walford's reply to this interrogatory was ambiguous and indistinct.

" As one," continued the captain, " who has a good deal of experience in marrying matters—for I've had a wife or two myself—I'd
advise you—that is, after the fair Betsey becomes Mistress Walford
—not to permit any more presents of flowers ? "

" Dang it ! " ejaculated the jealous lover, " what do you mean by
that, master ? "

" Why, only that I was witness to that little affair in the old
camp; and to say the truth, was not a little surprised. If any one
deserved those flowers from Maid Marian, it was surely the man who
first took up her quarrel. That was yourself, Master Walford : as
my skull-case—which still aches at the remembrance—can truly
testify."

" Dang me, if I didn't ! The black horseman had no business to
interfere, had he ? "

" Not a bit ! You and I could have settled *our* little difference
between ourselves ; and I was just upon the eve of asking your for-
giveness—for I felt I had been foolish—when this fellow stepped in.
He interfered, for no other reason, than to figure well in the eyes of
the girl. I could see plain enough it was that; though I knew nothing of either party at the time. But I've learnt something *since*,
that puts the matter beyond dispute."

" Learnt somethin' since—you have ? " gasped Walford, springing up
from his chair, and earnestly stooping towards the speaker. " If thee
know'st anything anent Maid Marian—Bet Dancey, I mean, an' *him*
—tell it me, an'——"

" Keep cool, Walford. Resume your seat, pray. I'll tell you all I
know ; but before I can make sure that I have been correctly informed, it is necessary for me to know more of this person, whom you
style the *Black Horseman*. Perhaps you can tell me something,
that will enable me to identify him with the individual whose name
I have heard, in connection with that of Maid Marian, or Bet Dancey
—as you say the beauty is called."

"What do you want .o know o' him?" as&ed Walford, evidently
ready to impart all the intelligence regarding Holtspur of which he
was himself possessed.

"Everything," replied Scarthe, perceiving that he need not take
trouble to keep up even a show of reserve. "As for myself, I know
only his name. After all it may not have been him—who——"

"Who what?" quickly inquired the impatient listener.

"I tell you presently, Master Walford; if you'll only have a little
patience. Where does this black horseman hold out!"

"Hold out?"

"Ay, where's his hostelry?"

"I've seen him oftener than anywhere else at the Saracen's Head,
down the road nigh on to Uxbridge."

"Zooks? my brave Robin, that isn't what I mean. Where does
he live?"

"Where's his own home?"

"Ah! his home."

"Tain't very far off from here, just a mile t'other side o' Wapsey's
Wood, in a big hollow i' the hills. Stone Dean the place be called.
It be a queery sort o' a old dwellin', and a good lot out o' repairs, I
reckon."

"Does he see any company?"

"Wall, if you mean company, sich as fine ladies an' the like, I
doan't think he ever do hev that sort about him. And not much of
any sort, whiles the sun be a shinin'. After night——"

"Ah! his friends generally visit him by night," interrupted
Scarthe, with a glance that betokened satisfaction. "Is that your
meaning, Master Walford?"

"No, not gen'rally, ye mout say altogether. I have been to Stone
Dean more'n twenty times, since he coomed to live at the old house,
at all hours I've been, an' I never seed a soul there i' the day-time,
'ceptin myself and Dick Dancey. There be a' odd sort o' a sarvint
he brought with him, a Indyen they calls him."

"But Master Holtspur has visitors in the night-time, you think?"

"Ay! that he have—lots o' 'em."

"Who are they?"

"Doan't know neer a one o' 'em. They be all strangers to these
parts—least-wise they appear so—as they come ridin', kivered wi'
mud an' dust, like after makin' a goodish bit o' a journey. There'll
be a big gatherin' o' 'em theer nex' Sunday night—considerin' the

letters that's gone. I took six myself, an' Dick Dancey as many
more—to say nothing o' a bunch carried to the west end o' the country by a fellow I doan't know nothin' about. It be a meeting o' some
sort, I take it."

"On next Sunday night, you say?"

The question was evidently asked with a keen interest; for the revelations which Will Walford was making, had all at once changed
the jocular air of his interrogator into one of undisguised eagerness

"Next Sunday night!"

"At what hour?".

"Twelve o' the clock."

"You are sure about the hour?"

"I ought to be; since I ha' got to be theer myself, along wi' Dick
Dancey, to look to the gentlemen's horses. A big crowd o' 'em ther'll
be for the two o' us to manage; as the gentlemen be comin' 'ithout
theer grooms. But what was it, Master?" inquired the woodman,
returning to the torturing thought that was still uppermost; "you
sayed you knowed somethin' as happened atween Bet Dancey an'
him? If he's been an' done it, then, dang me—I'll keep my threet,
if I shud ha' to swing for it!"

"Done what?"

"Made a fool o' Bet—that's what I meean. What is't ye know,
Mister Captain? Please to tell me that!"

"Well, then," replied the tempter, speaking slowly and deliber-
ately—as if to find time for the concoction of some plausible tale.
"For myself, I can't say I know anything—that is, for certain—I
have only heard—altogether by accident, too—that your Maid Marian was seen—out in the woods with a gentleman—and at a very
unreasonable hour of the night."

"What night?" gasped the woodman.

"Let me see! Was it the night of the *fête*? No. It was the
next after—if I remember aright."

"Damn her! The very night I war gone over to Rickmans'orth
wi' them letters. Augh!"

"I shouldn't have known it was this fellow, Holtspur: as the person who gave me the information didn't say it was him. It was only
told me that the man, whoever he might be, was dressed in fine velvet doublet, with a beaver and black plumes; but from what I've
seen myself, and from what you've just now told me, I think it very
likely that the black horseman was the individual. It was in the

woods, near Stone Dean, where they were seen. You say he lives there. It looks suspicious, don't it?"

"'Twar him! I know it, I be sure o't. Augh! If I don't ha' revenge on him, and her, too! Dang the deceitful slut! I will! I will!"

"Perhaps the girl's not so much to blame. He's a rich fellow, this Holtspur, and may have tempted her with his money. Gold goes a great way in such matters."

"Oh! if 't were only money, I could abear it better. No! It ain't that, master, it ain't that! I'm a'most sure it ain't. She's done it, damn her!"

"Perhaps we may be mistaken. Things may not have gone so far as you think. At all events, I should advise you to let the girl alone and confine your revenge to the villain who has wronged her."

"Him first—him first! And then, if I find she's let herself be made a fool o'——"

"Whether or not, he deserves no thanks from you for having made the attempt."

"I'll thank him!—I will, whenever I gets the chance. Wait till I gets the chance."

"If I am not mistaken, you may have that—without waiting long."

Misinterpreting these words, the woodman glanced towards his ax with a significant and savage leer, that did not escape the keen eye of Scarthe.

"True," said the latter, in a tone of disapproval, "you might have *that* chance almost at any hour. But there would also be a chance of failure, with a considerable risk of your getting run through the ribs. If what you've told me be as I suspect, there will be no need to resort to such extreme measures. Perhaps I may be able to point out a surer and safer method for you to rid yourself of this rival."

"Oh, Mister Captain! If you would only do that—only tell me how—I'll—I'll——"

"Have patience! Very likely I may be able to assist you," interrupted Scarthe, rising to take his departure. "I've something in my mind will just suit, I think. But it requires a little reflection—and —some preliminary steps that must be taken elsewhere. I shall return here to-night, after sunset. Meanwhile, stay at home; or if you go abroad, keep your tongue behind your teeth.. Not a word to any one of what has passed between us. Take another pull at the flask, to keep up your spirits. Now, Walford, good day to you."

Having pronounced these parting words, the officer walked out of the hut; and returning to his horse, leaped lightly into the saddle, and rode off—followed by his attendant Withers.

He did not communicate to the latter aught of what transpired between him and the woodman. The muttered words that escaped him, as he trotted off among the trees, were spoken in a slow, measured soliloquy.

"No doubt one of the very meetings of which his majesty has spoken so opportunely in his dispatch? Richard Scarthe shall make one at this mid-night assembly—uninvited though he be. Ah, if I can only find a fair opportunity to play eavesdropper, I promise Master Holtspur a more substantial dwelling than he now inhabits! Ho, have no fear, kind King Carolus. Right willingly shall I play the spy! Ha, ha, ha!"

Elated by the high hope with which his new-gained knowledge had inspired him, he gave the spur to his grey, while Wapsey's Wood gave back the echoes of his joyous laughter

CHAPTER XXXIV.

A SUSPICIOUS DEPARTURE.

It was Michaelmas night over merry England; but at that late hour when the rustic—weary with the revels incidental to the day—had retired to rest and dream. In other words, it was midnight.

Though at a season of the year when a clear sky might be expected, the night in question chanced to be an exception. The canopy of bright blue usually smiling over the Chiltern Hills was obscured by black cumulous clouds, that hung in motionless masses, completely shrouding the firmament. Not a ray of light, from either moon or stars, was shed upon the earth; and the narrow bridle-path as well as the wider highway could with difficulty be discerned under the hoof of the traveler's horse.

Notwithstanding the almost complete opacity of the darkness, it was not continuous. Gleams of lightning at intervals flashed over the sward, or in fitful coruscation illumined the deep arcades of the forest—the beeches for a moment appearing burnished by the blaze. Though not a breath of air stirred among the trees, nor a drop of rain had as yet fallen upon their leaves, those three sure foretellers of the storm—clouds, lightning and thunder—betokened its proximity. It was such a night as a traveler would have sought shelter at the nearest inn, and stayed under its roof unless urged upon an errand of more than ordinary, importance. Despite the darkness of the paths and the lateness of the hour—despite the tempest surely threatening in the sky—some such errand had tempted forth at least two travelers on that very night.

As Marion Wade and Lora Lovelace sat conversing in their chamber on the eve of retiring to rest, two horsemen heavily cloaked might have been seen passing out from under the windows and heading towards the high road, as if bent upon a journey.

It was Marion's sleeping apartment that was occupied by the brace of beautiful maidens—whose intention it was to share the same couch.

It had not been their habit to do so, for each had her separate chamber. But an event had occurred making it desirable that on that particular night they should depart from their usual custom. Lora required the confidence of her cousin, older than herself, and her counsel as well, in a matter so serious as to demand the privacy of a sleeping apartment.

Indeed, two events had happened to her on the day preceding, both of which called for the interposition of a friend. They were matters too weighty to be borne by a single bosom.

They were somewhat similar in character, if not altogether so; both being avowals of love, ending in offers of marriage.

There was, however, a considerable dissimilarity in the individuals from whom the tender declarations had proceeded. One was her own cousin—Walter Wade—the other, it is scarce necessary to say, being Cornet Stubbs.

Lora had not hesitated as to the reply she should make to either. It was not for this she was seeking the counsel of her cousin. The answers had been given frankly and freely on the same instant as the asking. To Walter an affirmative; to Stubbs a negative. If not indignant, at least final and emphatic

That point had been settled before the sun went down; and Marion's advice was only sought in order that the little Lora—her junior in years as well as womanly experience—might become better acquainted with the details relating to that most important ceremony of a woman's life—the *nuptial*.

Alas for Lora, her cousin proved but a poor counselor. Instead of being able to give advice, Marion needed rather to receive it; and it was from a vague hope that Lora might suggest some scheme to alleviate her own unpleasant reflections that she had so gladly listened to the proposal of their passing the night together.

What had occurred to disquiet the thoughts of Marion Wade?

Nothing—at least nothing but what is known already, and from that some may think she should have been *very* happy. She had met the man she loved—had received from his own lips the assurance that her love was reciprocated—had heard it in passionate speech, sealed and confirmed by a fervent kiss and a close and rapturous embrace.

What more wanted she to confirm her in the supremest happiness that can be enjoyed outside the limits of Elysium?

And yet Marion Wade was far from being happy!

What was the cause of her disquietude?

Had aught arisen to make her jealous? Did she doubt the fidelity of her lover?

A simple negative will serve as the answer to both questions.

She felt neither jealousy nor doubt. The mind of Marion Wade was not easily swayed by such influences. Partly from a sense of self-rectitude; partly from a knowledge of her own beauty, for she could not help knowing that she was beautiful: and partly, perhaps, from an instinctive consciousness of the power consequent on such a possession; hers was not a love to succumb readily to suspicion. Previous to that interview with her lover, the first and last properly deserving the name, she had yielded a little to this unpleasant emotion. But that was while she was still uncertain of Holtspur's love, before she had heard it declared by himself, before she had listened to his vows, plighted in words, in all the earnestness of eternal truth.

Since that hour no doubt had occurred to her mind. Suspicion she would have scorned as a guilty thing. She had given her own heart away—her heart and soul—wholly and without reserve, and she had no other belief than that she had received the heart of Henry Holtspur in return.

Her unhappiness sprang from a different cause, or rather causes, for she had three sources of disquietude.

The first was a consciousness of having acted wrongly—of having failed in filial duty; and to a parent whose generous indulgence caused the dereliction to be all the more keerly felt.

The second was a sense of having transgressed the laws of social life—the unwritten but well understood statutes of the high-class society in which the Wades had lived and moved since the Conquest —and in all likelihood long before that hackneyed era of historic celebrity.

To have challenged the acquaintance of a stranger,—perhaps an adventurer,—perhaps a vagabond; ah! more than challenged 'his acquaintance,—provoked the most powerful passion of his soul; *thrown down the gauntlet to him,*—token of love as of war. When did ever Wade, a female Wade, commit such an indiscretion?

It was a bold act, even for the bold and beautiful Marion. No wonder that it was succeeded by an *arri:re pens!e* slightly unpleas- ant.

These two causes of her discomfort were definite, though perhaps least regarded.

There was a third, as we have said, which, though more vague, was the one that gave her the greatest uneasiness. It pointed to peril—the peril of her lover.

The daughter of Sir Marmaduke Wade was not indifferent to the events of the time, nor yet to its sentiments. Though separated from the Court, and well that she was so, she was not ignorant of its trickery and corruption. In the elevated circle by which she was surrounded these were but the topics of daily discourse, and from the moderate yet liberal views held by her father she had frequent opportunities of hearing both sides of the question. A soul highly gifted as hers could not fail to discern the truth, and long before that time she had imbibed a love for true liberty in its republican form, a loathing for the effete freedom to be enjoyed under the rule of a king. In political light she was far in advance of her father, and more than once had her counsel guided his wavering resolves; influ- encing him perhaps even more than the late outrage of which he had been the object, to that determination to which he had at last yielded himself,—to declare for the Parliament and people.

Marion had been gratified by the resolve; joyed to see her father surrendering to the exigencies of the times, and becoming one of the popular party that had long owned her admiration.

A heart thus attuned could not fail to perceive in Henry Holtspur
its hero, its immaculate idol; and such to the mind of Marion Wade
did he seem. Differing from all the men she had ever known; un
like them in motives, action and aspect, in joys and griefs, passions
and powers; contrasting with those crawling sycophants, pseudo
cavaliers who wore long love-locks and prated eternally of court and
king, in him she beheld the type of a heroic man, worthy of a woman's love, a woman's worship!

She saw, and worshiped!

Notwithstanding the fervor of her admiration, she did not believe
him immortal, nor yet invulnerable.   He was liable to the laws of
humanity,—not its frailties, thought she, but its dangers.

She suspected that his life was in peril.   She suspected it from the
rumors that from time to time had reached her of his bold, almost
reckless, bearing on matters inimical to the court.   Only in whispers
had she heard these reports previous to the day of the *fête* in her
father's park, but then had she listened to that loud proclamation
from his own lips, when, charging upon Scarthe, he had cried out
'*For the People!*'

She loved him for that speech; but she had done so even before
hearing it, and she could not love him more.

"Cousin Lora," said she, while both were in the act of disrobing,
you ought to be very happy. What a fortunate little creature you are!

"Why, Marion?"

"To be admired by so many, and especially by the man you yourself admire."

"Dear me! If that be all, I *am* contented. So should you, Marion, for the same reason. If I'm admired by many, all the world
pays homage to you. For my part, I don't want the world to be in
love with me—only one."

"And that's Walter. Well, I think you're right, coz. Like you
I should never care to be a coquette. One heart well satisfies me—
one lover."

"And that's Henry Holtspur."

"You know too much, child, for me to deny it."

"But why should I be happier than you? You've your cavalier
as well as I. He loves you no doubt as much as Walter does me;
and you love him, I dare say, though I can't be certain of that, as
much as I love Walter. What then, Marion?"

"Ah, Lora! your lover is sure, safe, certain to become yours for
life. *Mine is doubtful and in danger.*"

"Doubtful? What mean you by that, Marion?"

"Suppose my father refuse to acknowledge him, then——"

"Then I know what his daughter would do."

"What *would* she do?"

"Run away with him; I don't mean with the venerable parent the knight, but with the lover, the *black horseman*. By-the-way. what a romantic thing it would be to be abducted on that splendid steed! Troth, Marion! I quite envy you the chance."

"For shame, you silly child! Don't talk in such foolish fashion!"

Marion colored slightly as she uttered the admonition. The thought of an elopement was not new to her. She had entertained it already; and it was just for this reason she did not desire her cousin to dwell upon it, even in jest. With her it had been considered in serious earnest, and might be again if Sir Marmaduke should prove intractable.

"But you spoke of danger?" said Lora, changing the subject. "What danger?"

"Hush!" exclaimed Marion, suddenly starting back from the mirror, with her long yellow hair sweeping like sunbeams over her snow-white shoulders; "did you hear something?"

"The wind?"

"No! it was not the wind. There is no wind; though, indeed, it's dark enough for a storm. I fancied I heard horses going along the gravel walk. Extinguish the light, Lora, so that we may steal up to the window and see."

Lora protruded her pretty lips close up to the candle and blew it out. The chamber was in utter darkness.

All unrobed as she was, Marion glided up to the casement, and cautiously pulling aside the curtain, looked out into the lawn.

She could see nothing; the night was dark as pitch.

She listened all the more attentively, her hearing sharpened by the idea of some danger to her lover, of which, during all that day, she had been suffering from a vague presentiment.

Sure enough she *had* heard the hoof-strokes of horses on the graveled walk, for she now heard them again, not so loud as before, and each instant becoming more indistinct.

This time Lora heard them, too

It might be colts straying from the pastures of the park? But the measured fall of their feet, with an occasional clinking of shod hoofs, proclaimed them, even to the inexperienced ears that were listening, to be horses guided and ridden.

"Some one going out. Who can it be at this hour of the night?
'Tis nearly twelve !"

"Quite twelve, I should think," answered Lora. "That game
of lansquenet kept us so long. It was half-past eleven before
we were through with it. Who should be going abroad so late, I
wonder?"

Both maidens stood in the embayment of the window, endeavoring
with their glances to penetrate the darkness outside.

The attempt would have been vain had the obscurity continued,
but just then a vivid flash of lightning shooting athwart the sky
illuminated the lawn, and the park became visible to the utmost
limit of its palings.

The window of Marion's bedchamber opened upon the avenue
leading out to the west. Near a spot to her suggestive of pleasant
memories she now beheld, by the blaze of the electric brand, a sight
that added to her uneasiness.

Two horsemen, both heavily cloaked, were riding down the avenue,
their backs turned towards the house, as if they had just taken their
departure from it. They looked not round. Had they done so at
that instant they might have beheld a tableau capable of attracting
them back.

In a wide-bayed window, whose low sill and slight mullions scarce
offered concealment to their forms, were two beautiful maidens, lovely
virgins, robed in the negligent costume of night, their heads close
together, and their nude arms mutually encircling one another's
shoulders, white as the chemisettes draped carelessly over them.

Only for an instant was this provoking tableau exhibited. Sudden
as the recession of a dissolving view, or like a picture falling back out
of its frame, did it disappear from the sight, leaving in its place only
the blank vitreous sheen of the casement.

Abashed by that unexpected exposure, though it was only to the
eye of heaven, the chaste maidens had simultaneously receded from
the window before the rude glare that startled them ceased to flicker
against the glass.

Sudden as was their retreating movement, previous to making it
they had recognized the two cloaked horsemen who were holding
their way along the avenue.

" Scythe !" exclaimed Marion.

" Scythe !" ejaculated Lora.

CHAPTER XXXV

A TREASONOUS ASSEMBLY.

The astonishment of the cousins at seeing two travelers starting forth so late, and upon such a dismal night, might have been increased, could they have extended their vision beyond the palings of the park and surveyed the forest-covered country for a mile or two to the northwest of it.

On the ramification of roads and bridle-paths that connected the towns of Uxbridge and Beaconsfield with the flanking villages of Fulmer, Stoke, Hedgerly and the two Chalfonts, they might have seen, not two, but twenty travelers, all on horseback and riding each by himself, in a few instances only two or three of them going together.

Though upon different roads and heading in different directions, they all appeared to be making for the same central bourn; which, as they neared it, could be told to be the old house of Stone Dean.

One by one they kept arriving at this point of convergence; and passing through the gate of the park, one after another, they rode silently on to the dwelling, where they as silently dismounted.

There delivering up their horses to three men who stood ready to take them, the visitors stepped unbidden within the open doorway, and following a dark-skinned youth who received them without saying a word, were conducted along the dimly-lighted corridor and ushered into an inner apartment.

As they passed under the light of the hall lamp, or had been seen outside during the occasional flashes of the lightning, the costume and bearing of these saturnine guests proclaimed them to be men of no mean degree, while their travel-stained habiliments told that they had ridden some distance before entering the gates of Stone Dean.

It might have been remarked as strange that such cavaliers of quality were thus traveling unattended, for not one of them was accompanied by groom or servant of any sort. It was also strange that no notice was taken of this circumstance by the men who led off their horses towards the stables, all three performing their duty without the slightest exhibition of either curiosity or surprise.

None of the three wore the regular costume of grooms or stable servants, nor had any of them the appearance of being accustomed to act in such a capacity. The somewhat awkward manner in which they were fulfilling their office plainly proclaimed that it was new to them; while their style of dress, though different in each, declared them to belong to other callings.

Two were habited in the ordinary peasant garb of the period, with a few touches that told them to be woodmen, and, as the lightning flashed upon their faces, it revealed these two personages to be Dick Dancy, and his co-adjutor, Will Walford.

The dress of the third was not characteristic of any exact calling; but appeared rather a combination of several styles: as though several individuals had contributed a portion of their apparel to his make-up. There was a pair of buff-leather boots, which, in point of elegance, might have encased the feet and ancles of a cavalier—the wide tops turned down over the knees, showing a profusion of white lining inside. Above these dangled the legs of a pair of petticoat breeches of coarse kersey, which strangely contrasted with the costly character of the boots. Over the waistband of the breeches puffed out a shirt of finest linen, though far from being either spotless or clean; while this was again overtopped by a doublet of homespun woolen cloth, of the kind known as "marry-muffe"—slashed among the sleeves with the cheapest of cotton velveteen. Surmounting this, in like contrast, was the broad lace collar band of a cavalier, with cuffs to correspond, both looking as if the last place of deposite had been the buck-basket of a washerwoman, and the wearer had taken them thence, without waiting for their being submitted to the operations of the laundry.

Add to the above-mentioned habiliments a high-crowned felt hat, somewhat battered about the brim, with a tarnished tinsel band, but without any pretense at a plume ; and you have the complete costume of the third individual who was acting as an extemporized stable-helper at the dwelling of Stone Dean.

Had there been light enough for the travelers to have scrutinized his features, no doubt they would have been somewhat astonished at this queer-looking personage, who assisted in disembarassing them of their steeds. Perhaps some of them, seeing his face, might have

thought twice before trusting him with the keeping of a valuable horse
for, in the tall stalwart figure, that appeared both peasant and gen
tleman in alternate sections, they might have recognized an old and
not very trustworthy acquaintance, the famed footpad, Gregory
Garth.

In the darkness, however, Gregory ran no risk of detection, and
continued to play his *improvised* part without any apprehensions of
an awkward encounter.

By the time that the great clock in the tower of Chalfont Church
had ceased tolling the hour of twelve, more than twenty of the noctural visitors to Stone Dean had entered within the walls of that
quaint old dwelling ; and still the sound of shod hoofs, clinking occasionally against the stones upon the adjacent road, told that an odd
straggler had yet to arrive.

About this time two horsemen, riding together, passed in through
the gate of the park. Following the fashion of the others, they continued on to the front of the house, where like the others, they also
dismounted, and surrendered their horses to two of the men who
stepped forward to receive them.

These animals, like the others, were led back to the stables; but
their riders, instead of entering the house by the front door, as had
been done by all those who had preceded them, in this respect deviated slightly from the programme.

As soon as the two grooms, who had taken their horses, were fairly out of sight, they were seen to act in obedience to a sign given
by the third; who whispering to them to follow him, led the way first
along the front of the house, and then around one of its wings, towards the rear.

Even had there been moonlight, it would have been difficult to identify these new comers, who were so mysteriously diverted from making entrance by the front door. Both were muffled in cloaks, more
ample and heavy than the quality of the night seemed to call for.
Scarcely could the threatening storm account for this providence on
their part.

On rounding the angle of the building, the man preceding them
made a stop, at the same time half facing about.

A gleam of lightning disclosed the countenance of their conductor.
It was the woodman—Walford.

His face was paler than wont—of that ghastly hue that denotes the
consciousness of crime, while his deep-set watery eyes, shining from

beneath his white eyebrows and hay-colored hair, gave to his ill-favored features an expression almost demoniac.

The countenances of the two cavaliers were also for an instant illuminated. One was the handsome face of Captain Scarthe, appearing like that of the guide unnaturally pale under the unearthly glare of the electric light. The other was the stolid, but rubicund, countenance of his subaltern, Stubbs.

While the light lasted, Walford was seen beckoning them to follow faster.

"Coom on, masters!" muttered he, in an earnest, hurried tone, "there's ne'er a minute to be lost. That 'ere duminy o' an Indyer has got his eyes everywhere. If he sees ye, he'll want to take ye in side among the rest; an' that won't answer yer purpose, I reckon."

"No! that would never do," muttered Scarthe, hastening his steps; "*our* presence inside would spoil this pretty pie. Go on, my good fellow! We'll follow you, close as the skirt of your doublet."

Without another word the trio moved on, the guide keeping a pace or two in advance; Stubbs clumsily staggering in the rear.

In this order they continued around the right wing of the house, all three making their way with as much silence and caution, as if they had been a band of burglars about to enter upon the ceremony of "cracking a crib."

The almost amorphous darkness would have hindered them from being observed, even had there been any one in the way. But there was not—no one to see them stealing along that sombre-colored wall —no eye to witness their entrance within the private side-door that admitted them by a narrow passage into the unused apartments of the house,—no eye to behold them as they stood within that small dark chamber, that commun ated by a window of dingy glass with the large hall in which the guests of Henry Holtspur were assembled.

"Just the place!" whispered Scarthe, as glancing through the glass, he saw the forms of men, moving confusedly over the floor of a well-lit apartment, and listened to the murmur of voices. "The very observatory I wished for. Now go, my good fellow!" he continued, transferring his whisper to the ear of Walford. "In twenty minutes from this time steal our horses out of the stables, and have them ready. We shall go back by the front entrance. Your worthy confrères will never know but that we've issued from the hive inside there. If they should suspect anything, I've got two sorts of metal upon my person, one or other of which will be sure to keep them quiet."

Half pushing his late conductor back into the passage, Scarthe
quietly closed the door behind him; and drew Stubbs up to the cob-
web-covered window. Behind it both silently took their stand,
crouching like a pair of gigantic spiders, that had placed themselves
in expectation of prey!

Neither made the slightest stir. They no longer talked to each
other even in whispers. They were well aware of the danger they
would incur, if detected in their eavesdropping—aware that they
might have to pay for it with their lives, or at the very least, suffer
severe punishment, by a castigation upon the spot, and the consequent disgrace due to their dastardly conduct... The act they were
committing was of no trifling character, no child's play of hide and
seek; but a bold and dangerous game of espionage, in which not only
the personal liberty, but even the lives of many individuals might be
placed in peril, these too, among the highest in the land.

Scarthe was conscious of all this; and but that he was impelled to
the act by the most powerful passion of man's nature, the promptings of a profound jealousy, he might have hesitated before placing
himself in such a position. His mere political proclivities would
never have tempted him to the committal of such an imprudent act.
Much as he inclined towards the king, he was not the man to play
spy over a conference of conspirators, such as he believed this assembly to be, from motives of mere loyalty. The thought stimulating
him was stronger by far.

He had not placed himself in that position blindly trusting to chance.
Like a skilled strategist, as he was, he had well reconnoitred the
ground before entering upon it. His co-adjutor, Walford, acting under
a somewhat similar motive, had freely furnished him with all the information he required. The woodman—from an acquaintance with
the old "care-taker," who had held charge of the house previous to
Holtspur's occupation—had a thorough knowledge of the dwelling
of Stone Dean— its ins and its outs—its trap-doors and sliding-
panels—every stair and corner, from cellar to garret. Walford had
assured the spies, that the chamber in which he secreted them was
never entered by any one; and that the glass-door communicating
with the larger apartment could not be opened, without breaking it to
pieces. Not only was its lock sealed with the rust of time, but the
door itself was nailed fast to the post and lintels.

There was no fear of their being seen. The cobwebs precluded the
possibility of that. As to their being heard, it would depend upon

their own behavior; and under the circumstances, neither captain nor cornet were likely to make any noise that might attract attention

For the rest the affair had been easy enough. Among a crowd of unknown guests arriving at the house—even under the supervision of a staff of regular domestics—it was not likely that a distinction should be made between the invited and those unasked; much less under the *outre* circumstances foreseen and well understood by Scarthe and his companion.

Neither Dancey nor Garth were supposed to know the persons of either. Nor had Oriole ever seen them; though Walford was far more concerned about the instincts of the Indian, than the observations of his fellow-helpers.

So far, however, he had succeeded in baffling both.

Scarthe commenced by wiping off enough of the cobwebs, to give him a clear disc of vision, of about the size of a crown piece.

With his eye close to the glass he commanded a view of the adjoining apartment, as well as the company it contained.

As to hearing, there was no difficulty about that. Even the ordinary conversation could be heard plainly through the panes; but when any one spoke louder than the rest, every word could be distinguished.

Scarthe had not been very long occupied in his surveillance, before perceiving that he was playing the spy upon a company of gentlemen. None present were of the peasant type.

Soon also did he become acquainted with the general tenor of the discourse; and convinced of the correctness of his conjetcture: that the meeting was an assembly of conspirators. This was the name given to it by the loyalist captain; though rather did it merit to be called a conference of patriots—perhaps the purest that ever assembled on the earth.

The subjects discussed were various; but all relating to two matters of chief moment:—the liberty of the subject; and the encroachments of the sovereign. Out of doors, or inside, these were the topics of the time.

Three or four of the speakers appeared to be regarded above the rest; and when one or other of these stood up, an air of silent respect pervaded the assembly.

Scarthe had no personal knowledge of these distinguished individuals. He little suspected, when that man of noble mien rose up—he for whom the hum of conversation became suddenly hushed—and upon whom every eye was turned with a regard that seemed that of a brotherly affection—little suspected the sneaking spy of a Court, that he was listening to the most disinterested patriot England has ever produced—that glorious hero of the Chilterns, John Hampden.

As little knew he that in the speaker who followed, a man of mature age, and perhaps of more eloquent tongue, he beheld the future accuser of Strafford, the bold prosecutor who successfully brought this notorious renegade to the block.

Neither did Scarthe recognize in that young but grave gentleman, who spoke so enthusiastically in favor of a nonconformist religion, the self-denying nobleman, Sir Harry Vane; nor in him who had a quick answer for every opponent, and a jest for every occasion, the elegant, whose appearance of superficial dandyism concealed a heart truely devoted to the interests of English liberty, Harry Martin of Berks.

From his concealment Scarthe saw all these noble and heroic men, without identifying them. He cared not for one or the other, what they did, or what they said. His eye was set, and his ear bent, to see one who had not yet presented himself, to hear one who had not yet spoken.

The host of the house, he who had summoned these guests together, was the man whom Scarthe desired to see and hear. Though the royalist spy felt satisfied, that what had passed already would be proof sufficient against Holtspur, he wanted one speech from his own mouth, one word that would more surely convict him.

He was not disappointed. In that congregation Henry Holtspur was not expected to be silent. Though regarded more in the light of an actor than an orator, there was those who waited to hear him with that silent eagerness that tells of a truer appreciation than the mere ebullition of a noisy enthusiasm. As the host of the house he had hitherto modestly remained in the background, until forced to take his turn; and his turn at length came.

In a speech which occupied more than an hour, Pym had set before the assembly a full list of the grievances under which the nation groaned, a sort of epitome of the famous oration that afterwards ushered in the attainder of Strafford. Its effect upon all, was to strengthen them in the determination to oppose, with greater energy than ever, the usurpations of the Court; and many of the gentlemen present declared their willingness to make any sacrifice, either personal or pecuniary, rather than longer submit to the illegal exactions of the monarch.

"Why," said Holtspur, rising to his feet and standing conspicuously before his guests; " why should we continue to talk in enigmas? I, for one, am tired of keeping up this pretense of hostility towards the subordinates, whilst the real enemy is allowed to escape all accusations of criminality. It is not Strafford, nor Laud, nor Finch nor Mainwaring, nor Windebank, who are the oppressors of the people. These are but the tools of the tyrant. Destroy them to-day, and to-morrow others will be found to supply their place, as fitting and truculent as they. To what end, then, are our protests and prosecutions? The hydra of despotism can only be crushed *by depriving it of its head*. The poisonous tree of evil is not to be destroyed by here and there lopping off a branch. It can be rendered innoxious only by striking at its roots!

"Some gentlemen here seem to think, that, by surrounding the king with good counselors, we may succeed in bringing him to rule with justice. But good counselors, under the influence of an unscrupulous Court, may any day change their character; and then the work will have to be done over again. Look at Strafford himself! Ten years ago, had we met as we meet to-night, Thomas Wentworth would have been with us, foremost in our councils. See the baneful effects of royal favor! It will ever be so, as long as men set up an idol, call it a king, and fall down upon their faces to worship it!

" For my own part I scorn to palter with words. I see but one criminal worthy our accusations: and he is neither counselor, nor secretary, nor bishop; but the master of all three. In my mind, gentlemen, it is no longer a question of whether we are to be ruled by a good king or a bad king; *but whether we are to have a king at all !*"

" My sentiments!" cried Henry Martin, and several others of the younger and bolder spirits; while a general murmur of approbation was heard throughout the room.

These were wild words, even within that secret assemblage. The question of *king or no king* had begun to shape itself in the minds of a few men; but this was the first time it had risen to the lips of any one. It was the first *spoken* summons invoking the dark shadow that hovered over the head of Charles Stuart, until his neck lay bleeding on the block!

"Enough!" gasped out Scarthe, in an almost inaudible whisper, as he recovered his long-suspended breath; "enough for *my* purpose. You heard it, Stubbs?"

"I did, by Ged!" replied the subordinate spy, taking care to imitate his superior in the low tone in which he made answer.

"We may go now," said Scarthe. "There's nothing more to be seen or done—at least nothing I need care for. Ha! who's speaking now? That voice? Surely I've heard it before!"

As he said this, he placed his eye once more to the disc of cleared glass.

Suddenly drawing himself back, and clutching his associate by the arm, he muttered—

"Who do you think is there?"

"Can't guess, captain."

"Listen then!" and placing his lips close to the ear of his companion he whispered in slow syllables, "Sir Mar-ma-duke Wade."

"Do you say so?"

"Look for yourself: look and listen! Do both well: for the words you hear *may yet win you your sweetheart.*"

"How, captain?"

"Don't question me now," hurriedly replied the latter, at the same time returning to his attitude of attention.

It was in truth Sir Marmaduke Wade, who was addressing the assembly. But his speech was a very short one; for the worthy knight was no orator; and it was nearly finished by the time Scarthe and the cornet had succeeded in placing themselves in a position to have heard him.

Enough reached the ears of the former to give him all he required for a fell purpose; which even at that moment had commenced taking shape in his diabolical brain.

In the few words that dropped from the lips of his host, Scarthe could discover sufficient evidence of disloyalty. Indeed, the presence of Sir Marmaduke in that place—coupled with, perhaps, something more than suspicion which the king already entertained towards him —would be proof enough to satisfy the Star Chamber.

"We may go now," whispered Scarthe, stealing towards the door, and drawing his subaltern after him. "Softly, cornet!" continued he, as hand in hand they retraced the dark passage. "Those boots of yours creak like a ship in a swell! Fancy you are treading on eggs!"

As he made this facetious remark, they emerged into the open air; and whispering mutual congratulations, went skulking onward, like a brace of felons making their escape from the confinement of a prison.

"If this fellow," said Scarthe, "can only succeed in extricating our horses, I think we may flatter ourselves, that we have made a successful job of it. Come on."

And Scarthe led the way along the wall, towards the front of the dwelling.

They proceeded with as much caution as ever. Though outside, they were not yet safe from having their presence discovered, and their purpose suspected.

The sky was clearer than when they had last looked upon it: for the thunder-storm, now over, had scattered the clouds, and deluged the earth with rain.

At the angle of the building they could make out the figure of a man, standing under the shadow of a tree. It was Walford. On seeing them, he stepped forth, and advanced to meet them.

"Theer be nobody by the front door," he muttered, when near enough to be heard. "Stay by the steps, but don't show yer faces. I'll ha' the horses round in a twinkle."

Saying this, the traitor left them; and disappeared in the direction of the stables.

Obedient to his instructions, they took their stand; and still conversing in whispers, awaited his return.

True to his promise, almost in an instant the two horses were brought round—one led by himself, the other by Dancey.

The latter was too much occupied by the gold piece, glistening within his palm, to think of scrutinizing the countenance of the giver

"Odds luck, Wull!" said he, turning to his comrade, after the two horsemen had ridden off; "stable keepin' appear to be a better bizness than winin' the wood-ax. If they be all as liberal as these 'uns we shall ha' a profitable night o't."

Walford assented with a shrug of the shoulders, and a significant grin, which in the darkness was not noticed by the unsuspicious deerstealer.

Just then, George Garth coming up armed with a tankard of ale, perhaps surreptitiously-drawn from the cellar, interrupted the conversation, or rather changed it in a different channel; for it was still carried on to the accompaniment of a copious imbibing of the home-brewed.

CHAPTER XXXVI.

AN ARREST RESOLVED UPON.

The two spies moved silently away, neither speaking above his breath, till they had regained the road, outside the gates of Stone Dean; then, no longer fearing to be overheard, they talked in louder tones.

"What a grand *coup* it would be," observed Scarthe, partly in soliloquy, and partly addressing himself to his companion.

"What, captain?" inquired Stubbs.

"To capture this whole nest of conspirators."

"It would, by Ged!"

"It would get me that colonelcy, true as a trivet; and you, my worthy cornet, would become Captain Stubbs."

"Zounds! why not try to take 'em, then?"

"Simply because we can't. By the time we should get our vagabonds in their saddles, and ride back, every knave of them would be gone. I saw they were about to break up; and that's why I came so quickly away. Yes—yes!" continued he, reflectingly, "they'd be scattered to the four winds, before we could get back. Besides, besides, he might slip off through the darkness, and give trouble to find him afterwards. What matters to me about the others? I must make sure of *him;* and that will be best done in the daylight. To-morrow he shall be mine; and the day after, the lieutenant of the Tower shall have him; and the Star Chamber; and then—*the scaffold!*"

"But, captain," said Stubbs, in answer to the soliloquized speech, only a portion of which he had heard, "what about our worthy host, Sir Marmaduke? Can't you take *him?*"

"At any time—ha, ha, ha! And hark you, Stubbs! I've a word for you on that delicate subject. I've promised you promotion. The queen, on my recommendation, will see that you have it. But you get my endorsement, only on conditions, on conditions, do you hear?"

"I do. What conditions, captain?"

"That you say nothing, either of where you've been, what you've heard, or what you've seen this night, till I give you the cue to speak."

"Not a word, by Ged! I promise that."

"Very well. It'll be to your interest, my worthy cornet, to keep your promise, if you ever expect me to call you *captain*. In time you may understand my reasons for binding you to secrecy; and in time you shall. Meanwhile, not a whisper of where we've been tonight, least of all to Sir Marmaduke Wade. Ah! my noble knight! " continued the captain, speaking to himself; "I've now got the sun shining that will thaw the ice of your aristocratic superciliousness! And you, indifferent dame! If I mistake not your sex and your sort, ere another moon has flung its mystic influence over your mind, I shall tread your indifference in the dust, make you open those loving arms, twine them around the neck of Richard Scarthe, and cry, "Be mine, dearest! mine for ever !""

The speaker rose exultingly in his stirrups, as if he had already felt that thrilling embrace; but, in a moment after, sank back into his saddle, and sat in a cowed and cowering attitude.

It was but the natural revulsion of an over-triumphant feeling, the reaction that succeeds the indulgence of an unreal and selfish conceit.

His sudden start upward had roused afresh the pain in his wounded arm. It recalled a series of circumstances calculated to humiliate him; his defeat, the finding of the glove, his suspicion of a rival, that assignation scene, that almost made it a certainty.

All these remembrances suggested by the sting of the still unhealed sword-wound, as they came simultaneously rolling over his soul, swept it clear of every thought of triumph; and, despite the success of his strategy, he re-entered the park of Sir Marmaduke Wade as heavy in heart, and perhaps poorer in hope, than any tramping mendicant that had ever trodden its tree-shaded avenues.

He knew the situation of Marion's sleeping chamber. He had made it his business to ascertain that. He gazed upon the window as he rode forward; he fancied he saw a form receding behind the curtain, like some white nymph dissolving herself into the world of ether.

He checked his steed; and for a long time kept his eyes fixed upon the casement; but nothing appeared to impart consolation. There was no light in the chamber; the cold glitter of the glass was in consonance with the chill that had crept over his spirits; and he moved on, convinced that his imagination had been mocking him.

And yet it was not so. It was a real form, and no illusion that he had seen receding from the window—the form of Marion Wade, that more than once had appeared since his departure.

The lamp so opportunely extinguished, had not been re-lit. The cousins, grouping their way through the darkness, had betaken themselves to bed.

What else could they do? Even though what they had seen might forbode evil to some one, what power had they to avert it?

Had there been a certainty of danger, it is true—and to him who was the chief subject of her apprehensions—Marion Wade could not have gone tranquilly to sleep.

Neither did she; for although the midnight excursion of the cuirassier captain and his cornet might have no serious significance, coupled with the presentiment from which she was already suffering, she could not help fancying that it had.—

The hour was too late for an adventure, either of gayety or gallantry, in a rural neighborhood, where all the world—even the wicked —should have long ago retired to rest.

For more than an hour the cousins had lain side by side—conferring on the incident that had so unexpectedly transpired. Of other confidences they had unbosomed themselves—though much of what they intended to have said remained unspoken; on account of the distraction caused to their thoughts by this new circumstance.

Both had been perplexed—alike unable to discover the clue to the mysterious movement of Scarthe and his cornet.

After more than an hour spent in shaping conjectures, and building hypotheses, they had arrived no nearer to a rational belief, than when commencing their speculations on the subject.

Finally, Lora, less interested in the event or its consequences, laid her head complacently on the pillow, and fell off into a sleep—determined no doubt, to dream of Walter.

For Marion there was no such solace; no rest for her that night— with the image of Henry Holtspur hovering over her heart; and her bosom filled with vague apprehensions about his safety.

She had not tried to sleep. She had not even kept to her couch; but stealing silently from her unconscious cousin, she had repeatedly sought the window; and gazed forth from it.

After going several times to and fro, she had at length stationed herself by the casement; and there crouching in its embayment, her form shrouded by the silken tapestry, had she remained for hours, eagerly listening to every sound, listening to the rain, as it plashed heavily on roof, terrace, and trees, watching the lightning's flash, straining her eyes while it glared adown the dark arcade between the chestnuts, that bordered the path by which the noctural excursionists might be expected to re-appear.

Her vigil was not unrewarded. They came back at length, as they had gone, Scarthe and Stubbs, together and by themselves.

"Thank Heaven!" muttered Marion, as she caught sight of the two forms returning up the avenue, and saw that they were alone. "Thank Heaven! Their errand, whatever it may have been, is ended. I hope it had no reference to *him!*"

Holding the curtain, so as to screen her form, she stayed at the window until the two horsemen had ridden up to the walls. But the darkness outside, still impenetrable except when the lightning played, prevented observation; and she only knew by the sound of their horses' hoofs, that they had passed under her window towards the rear of the mansion. and entered the courtyard, whose heavy gate she could hear closing behind them.

Then, and not till then, did she consent to surrender herself to that god puissant as love itself; and, gently extending her white limbs alongside those of Lora, she entered upon the enjoyment of a slumber, perhaps not so innocent as that of her unconscious cousin, but equally profound.

Little did Scarthe suspect, that the snow-white vision so suddenly fading from his view, was the real form of that splendid woman, now weirdly woven around his heart. Had he suspected it, he would scarce have retired to his couch; which he did with embittered spirits, and a vile vow, instead of a prayer, passing from his lips. It was but the repetition of that vow, long since conceived, to win Marion Wade, to win and wed her, by fair means or by foul.

He resought his couch, but not with the intention of going to sleep.

With a brain, so fearfully excited, he could not hope to procure repose.

Neither did he wish it. He had not even undressed himself; and his object in stretching his limbs upon a bed, was that he might the more effectually concentrate his thoughts upon his scheme of villainy.

In his homeward ride he had already traced out his course of immediate action; which in its main features comprehended the arrest of Henry Holtspur, and sending him under guard to the Tower of London. It was only the minor details of this preliminary design that now occupied his mind.

Before parting with his subaltern, he had given orders for thirty of his troopers to be ready to take saddle a little before daybreak; the order being accompanied by cautionary injunctions—that the men were to be aroused from their slumbers without any noise to disturb the tranquillity of the mansion—that they were to "boot and sa'ldle" without the usual signal of the bugle; in short, that they were to get ready for the route with as much secrecy and silence as possible.

There would be just time for the cornet to have these commands executed; and, knowing the necessity of obedience to his superior, Stubbs had promptly proceeded to enforce them.

One by one the men were awakened with all the secrecy enjoined in the order; the horses were saddled in silence; and a troop of thirty cuirassiers, armed *cap-à-pied*, ready to mount, stood in the church-yard, just as the first streak of grey light—denoting the approach of dawn—became visible above the eastern horizon.

Meanwhile Scarthe, stretched along his couch, had been maturing his plan. He had but little apprehension of failure. It was scarcely probable that his enemy could escape capture. So adroitly had he managed the matter of the espionage, that Henry Holtspur could have no suspicion of what had occurred.

Scarthe had been sufficiently familiar with Walford and his ways, to know that this traitor would be true to the instincts of jealousy and vengeance. There was no fear that Holtspur would receive warning from the woodman; and from whom else could he have it? No one.

The arrest would be simple and easy. It would be only necessary to surround the house, cut off every loophole of escape, and capture the conspirator—in all probability in his bed. After that the Tower —then the Star Chamber; and Scarthe knew enough of this iniquit-ous tribunal, to feel sure that the sentence it would pass would for-ever rid not only Walford, but himself, of a hated rival. It would also disembarass the king of a dangerous enemy; though of all the motives, inspiring Scarthe to the act, this was perhaps the weakest

His hostility for Holtspur—though of quick and recent growth— was as deeply rooted, as if it had existed for years. To be defeated in the eyes of a multitude—struck down from his horse—compelled to cry "quarter"—he, Richard Scarthe, captain of the king's cuir-assiers—a *preux chevalier*—a noted champion of the duello—this circumstance was of itself sufficient to inspire him with an implac-able hostility towards his successful antagonist. Put to suffer this humiliation in the presence of high-born women—under the eye of one whom he now loved with a fierce, lustful passion—worse still; one whom he had reason to believe was lovingly inclined towards his adversary—all this had embittered his heart with more than a common hatred; and filled his bosom with a wild yearning for more than a common vengeance.

It was in planning this, that he passed the interval upon his couch; and his actions, at the end of the time along with his muttered words, proved that he had succeeded in devising a sure scheme of retaliation.

"By heavens!" he exclaimed aloud, springing to his feet, and measuring the floor of his chamber with quick, nervous strides; "it will be a sweet revenge! She shall look upon him in his hour of humiliation. Stripped of his fine feathers, shall he appear under her window, under her aristocratic eyes—a prisoner—helpless, bayed and browbeaten. Ha! ha! ha!"

The exulting laugh told how pleasant was his anticipation of the spectacle his fancy had conjured up.

"Shall he wear the *white gauntlet* in his beaver?" he continued, pondering over new modes of humiliating his adversary. "There would be something sweet in such a sublime mockery? No; better not—he will appear more ridiculous with his head bare—bound like a felon! Ha! ha! ha!"

Again he gave way, unchecked, to his exultant laugh, till the room rang with his fierce cachinnations.

"Zounds!" exclaimed he, after an interval, during which the shadow of some doubt had stolen over his face. "If she should smile upon him in that hour, then my triumph would be changed to chagrin! Oh! under her smile he would be happier than I."

"Aha!" he ejaculated, after another pause, in which he appeared to have conceived a thought that chased away the shadow. "Aha! I have it now. She shall *not* smile. I shall take precautions against it. Phœbus! what a splendid conception! He shall appear before her, *not* bare-headed, but with beaver on—bedecked with a bunch of flowers!"

"Let me see! What sort were those the girl gave him! Red, if I remember aright—ragged robin corn, poppies; or something of the kind. No matter about that, so long as the color be in correspondence. In the distance, Marion could scarcely have distinguished the species. A little faded, too, they must be: as if kept since the day of the fête. *She* will never suspect the *ruse.* If she smile, after beholding the flowers, then shall I know that there is nothing between them. A world to see her smile! To see her do the very thing, which but an instant ago, I fancied would have filled me with chagrin!"

"Ho!" he again ejaculated, in a tone of increasing triumph. Another splendid conception! My brain, so damnably dull all through the night, brightens with the coming day. As our French queen is accustomed to exclaim, '*une pensee magnifique !*' 'Twill be a homethrust for Holtspur. If *he* loves *her*—and who can doubt it —then shall his heart be wrung, as he has wrung mine. Ha, ha! *The right hand glove shall triumph over the left !*"

As Scarthe said this, he strode towards the table on which lay his helmet; and, taking from the breast of his doublet the gauntlet of Marion Wade—the one she had really lost—he tied it with a piece of ribbon to the crest—just under the *panache* of plumes.

"Something for him to speculate upon, while inside the walls of his prison! Something to kill time, when he is awake; and dream of when asleep! Ha! ha! A sweet revenge 'twill be—one worthy the craft of an inquisitor!"

A footstep coming along the corridor put a stop to his changing soliloquy.

It was the footstep of Stubbs; and in the next instant, the flat face of the cornet presented itself in the half-opened door.

"Thirty in armor, captain, ready for the road," was the announcement of the subaltern.

"And I am ready to head them," answered his superior officer setting his helmet firmly on his head, and striding towards the door; "thirty will be more than we need. After all, 'tis best to make sure. We don't want the fox to steal away from his cover; and he might do so, if the earths be not properly stopped. We're pretty sure to find him in his swaddling clothes at this hour. Ha! ha! ha! What a ludicrous figure our fine cavalier will cut in his nightcap! Won't he, Stubbs!"

"Ought to, by Ged!"

And with this gleeful anticipation, Scarthe, followed by his subaltern, stepped lightly along the passage leading towards the courtyard, where thirty troopers, armed *cap-à-pied*, each standing on the near side of his steed awaited the order to spring into their saddles.

In two second's time the "Mount and forward!" was given; not by signal-call of the bugle, but by word of command, somewhat quietly pronounced. Then, with captain and cornet at its head, the troop, by twos, filed out through the arched entrance, directing their march towards the gateway that opened upon the Oxford road, treading in the direction of Beaconsfield.

It was by this same entrance the two officers had come in only a short while before. They saw the hoof-prints of their horses in the dust, still saturated with the rain that had fallen. They saw also the track of a third steed, that had been traveling the same direction, towards the house.

They found the gate closed. They had left it open. Some less negligent person had entered the park after them.

" Our host has got safe home! " whispered Scarthe to his subaltern.

" So much the better," he added, with a significant smile, " I don't want to capture *him*, at least, not now; and if I can make a *captive* of his daughter, not at all. If I succeed not in that, why then—then —I fear Sir Marmaduke will have to accept the hospitality of his majesty; and abide some time under the roof of that royal mansion that lies eastward of Cheap, erst honored by the residence of so many distinguished gentlemen. Ha! ha; ha! "

Having delivered himself of this jocular allusion to the Tower, he passed through the park gate; and at the head of his troopers continued briskly, but silently, along the king's highway.

On went the glittering phalanx—winding up the road like some destroying serpent on its way to wickedness—the pattering of their horses' feet, and the occasional clink of steel scabbards, striking against stirrups and *cuisses*, were the only sounds that broke upon the still air of the morning—to proclaim the passage of armed and mounted men.

CHAPTER XXXVII

ORIOLE SUSPICIOUS.

Shortly after the spies had taken their departure from Stone Dean, the conspirators might have been seen, emerging from the house, mounting their horses, and riding off. They went, much after the fashion in which they had come—in silence, alone, or in small groups; and, after clearing the gate entrance, along different roads. Some half-dozen stayed later than the rest; but before daylight could have disclosed their identity, these had also bidden adieu to Stone Dean; and were journeying far beyond the precincts of its secluded park.

When the last guests had gone, two of Holtspur's improvised grooms, for whose services there was no further occasion, also took their departure from the place. There remained only three individuals in the old mansion, its owner, his Indian attendant, and Gregory Garth.

Of these, the last mentioned, and only he, had yielded his spirit to the embrace of the drowsy god.

On perceiving that his services as stable-helper were no longer in requisition, the ex-footpad, having no other lodging to which he might betake himself, had stretched his tired limbs along the beechwood bench; which, as on a former occasion, he had drawn up close to the kitchen fire. In five minutes after, not only the ample kitchen itself, but the contiguous apartments of pantry and washhouse, with the various passages between, were resonant of his snores.

Holtspur was still in the apartment in which the meeting had been held—the library it was—where, seated in front of a writing table, with pen in hand, he appeared to busy himself in the composition of some document of more than ordinary importance.

Oriole was the only one of the household who seemed to have no occupation; since he was neither sleeping nor acting.

He was not inside the house, nor yet outside, but part of both; since he stood in the doorway, on the top step of the front entrance —the door being still open.

He was in the habitual attitude of perfect repose—silent and *statuesque*. This he had maintained for some length of time, having lingered, vaguely gazing after the last guest who had gone away—or rather, the two woodmen, Walford and Dancey, for they had been the latest to take their departure.

It is difficult to say what may have been occupying the thoughts of the young savage. Perhaps they were dwelling upon scenes of the past—memories of his forest home, thousands of miles away—memories of his early years—of his tawny companions, and their sports—memories, perhaps, more tender of sister or mother? Whether or no, they stirred him not from his silent attitude; and for a long half hour, he remained motionless, wrapped in speechless reverie.

It was only on seeing the first streaks of the dawn, stealing over the beech-clad crests of the hills, that he began to arouse himself; and then only in his eyes were exhibited signs of activity.

These, instead of being directed towards the sky, were turned towards the ground—scrutinizing a space in front of the doorstep, where the close crowding of hoof-prints told of the many horsemen who had late made their departure from the place.

For some time the Indian kept his eyes upon the ground, without exhibiting any apparent interest in the tracks. And yet he appeared to be tracing them; perhaps only in obedience to habit learnt, and indulged in, from earliest childhood.

After a while his glance wandered to a wider range; and something, observed at a few paces' distance, appeared more seriously to engage his attention.

His statuesque attitude became at once disarranged; and, gliding down from the steps, he walked rapidly along the graveled walk leading to the left side of the house.

On arriving at the angle of the wall, he stepped downward, as if to examine some object at his feet.

After remaining motionless for a few seconds, he continued on, still with body bent, towards the back part of the dwelling.

He proceeded slowly, but without making a stop, till he had arrived near the rear of the mansion. There a narrow doorway, opening into the eastern wing, was before his eyes; and into this he stood gazing, evidently in some surprise. It could not be at seeing the door, for he knew of it already. It was its being opened that elicited that look of astonishment.

During his stay at Stone Dean he had never known that side d?? to be otherwise than shut; and locked too. As there was only himself, and his master, who had the right to unlock it, he was naturally surprised at finding it ajar.

He might not have heeded the circumstance but for another, that seemed to connect itself with the open door. He had observed the footprints of two men, plainly impressed in the damp dust. They ran all along the wall, parallel to, and a few paces from it. Near the angle of the building, they were joined by a third set of footmarks; and from that point the three proceeded together till lost among the horse-tracks around the entrance in front.

It was these footmarks that had first attracted the Indian from his stand upon the steps; and, in tracing them, he had been conducted to the side doorway.

To examine the tracks, either of man or animal, and wherever seen, is a habit—indeed almost an instinct—with an Indian; and ruled by this peculiarity of his people, Oriole had hastened to scrutinize the "sign."

The act was not altogether unaccompanied by a process of ratiocination. Slightly as he understood the bearings of those political schemes, in which his master was engaged, the faithful follower knew that there was reason for secrecy, as well as suspicion in regard to the men, with whom he was brought in contact. It was some vague thought of this kind that had caused him to take notice of the tracks.

He remembered having conducted all the gentlemen outward by the front door, on their departure, as he had conducted them inward on their arrival. He remembered that all had ridden directly away. Which of them, then, had gone round to the rear of the building, without his having observed them?

There were three distinct sets of footprints, not going towards the back, but returning towards the front. One set had been made by hob-nailed shoes. These might be the tracks of the three helpers; but the other two were those of gentlemen.

Almost intuitively had the Indian arrived at this conclusion, when his analysis was interrupted by seeing the side-door standing open—a circumstance which strengthened his incipient suspicion that there was something in the "sign."

Without waiting to examine the tracks any further, he glided forward to the doorway; and, stepping inside, traversed the narrow passage which conducted to the antechamber—where Scarthe and his cornet had so silently assisted at the ceremony of the nocturnal assemblage.

The keen eye of the American aboriginal—even under the sombre light of the unused apartment—at once detected evidences of its late occupancy. The unshut doors afforded this: but the deep dust, that for years had been accumulating on the floors, showed traces of having been recently stirred by shuffling feet—leaving no doubt in the mind of Oriole, that men had been in that room; and had gone out of it, only an hour ar two before.

The disturbed spider webs upon the glazed partition did not escape his observation: nor the little spot upon the pane of glass that had been rubbed clean.

Oriole placed his eye to it. He could see the whole of the apartment, late occupied by his master's guests. He could see that master, now alone—seated before his writing table—utterly unconscious of being observed.

The Indian was about to tap upon the glass, and communicate the discovery he had made; but, remembering his own misfortune, and that he could only speak by signs, he glided back through the passage, with the intention of reaching the library by the front entrance.

Daylight had come down—sufficiently clear to enable him to make a scrutiny of the tracks with more exactness; and he lingered awhile retracing them—in the hope of finding some solution of the mystery of their existence. The sun had not yet risen; but the red rays of the aurora already encrimsoned the crests of the surrounding ridges, tinting also the tops of the tall trees that overhung the old dwelling of Stone Dean. The light, falling upon the roosts of the rooks, had set the birds astart, and caused them to commence the utterance of their cheerful cawing.

Whether it was the clamor of the crows, or the rustling of the riotous rats—as they chased one another along the empty shelves, and behind the decayed wainscoting of the old kitchen—or whether the circumstance was due to some other, and less explicable cause, certain it is that the slumbers of Gregory Garth were at this crisis interrupted.

His snoring suddenly came to a termination: and he awoke with a start.

It was a start, moreover, that led to a more serious disturbance: for, having destroyed his equilibrium on the beech-wood bench—

which chanced to be of somewhat slender dimensions—his body came
down upon the hard stone flags of the floor, with a concussion, that
for several seconds completely deprived him of breath.

On recovering his wind, and along with it his senses, which had for a
while remained in a state of obfuscation, the ex-footpad soon comprehended the nature of the mishap that had befallen him.

But the unpleasant tumble upon the flagged floor had cured him of
all inclination to return to his treacherous couch; and, instead, he
strolled out into the open air to consult the sun, his unfailing monitor,
as to the time of day.

Only the morning before, Gregory had been the proprietor of a
watch, whether honestly so need not be said; but this time-piece
was now ticking within the pigeon-hole depository of an Uxbridge
pawnbroker; and the duplicate which the ex-footpad carried in his
fob could give him no information about the hour.

In reality he had not been asleep more than twenty minutes; but
his dreams, drawn from a wide range of actual experiences, led him
to believe that he had been slumbering for a much longer time.

He was rather surprised, though not too well pleased, when, on
reaching the door, and "squinting" outside, he perceived by the sky
that it was still only the earliest hour of the day; and that, after all
his dreaming, he had not had the advantage of over half an hour's
sleep.

He was contemplating a return to his bench-bedstead; when, on
casting a stray glance outwards, his eye fell on the figure of a man
moving slowly around one of the angles of the mansion. He saw it
was Oriole.

As Gregory knew that Oriole was the proper butler of the establishment, or at all events carried the key of the wine cellar, it occured
to him that, through the intervention of the Indian, he might obtain
a morning dram, to refresh him after his uneasy slumber.

He was proceeding outside, intending to make known his wish,
when he perceived that Oriole was engaged in a peculiar occupation
With his body half bent, and his eyes keenly scrutinizing the ground,
the Indian was moving slowly along the side of the house, parallel to
the direction of the wall.

Seeing this strange action, Garth did not attempt to interrupt it;
but, taking his stand by the angle of the building, watched the movement.

Somewhat to the surprise of the footpad, he saw the redskin crouch
cautiously forward to a door, which stood open; and, with all the

silent stealth, that might have been observed .y the most accom
plished cracksman, Garth saw him creep inside—as if afraid of being
detected in the act!

"Humph!" muttered Gregory, with a portentous shake of his
shaggy occiput: "I shouldn't wonder if Master Henry ha' got a
treetor in his own camp. What he be about, I shud like to know—
a goodish bit I shud like it. Can't be wittles, or drink, the dummy's
arter? No—can't a be neyther: seein' he ha got charge o' the keys,
an' may cram his gut, whensomever he pleezes. It be somethin' o'
more concarn than eatin' or drinkin'. That be it, surish. But what
the Ole Scratch kin it be?"

As Gregory put this last interrogatory, he inserted his thick,
knotty digits into the mazes of his matted mop, and commenced
pulling the hair over his forehead, as if by that means to elicit an
answer.

After tossing his coarse curly locks into a state of woolly frowsi-
ness, he seemed to have arrived no nearer to an elucidation of the
Indian's mysterious conduct, as was evinced by another string of
muttered interrogatories that proceeded from his lips.

"Be the red-skin a playin' spy? They be ticklish times for Master Henry, I knows that. But surely a tongueless Indyen lad, as
ha' followed him from tother side o' the world, an' been faithful to
him most the whole o' his life—he ha' told me so—surely sich a
thing as that an't goin' to turn treetor to him now? Beside, what
can a Indyen know o' our polyticks? A spy,—pish! It can't be
that! It may be a bit o' stealin'. That's more likelyish, but what
somdever it do be, hecar go to find out."

Garth was about moving towards the side door, into which
Oriole had made his stealthy entrance, when he saw the latter
coming out again.

As the Indian was seen to return towards the front in the same
cautious manner in which he had gone from it, that is, with the body
stooped and eyes eagerly scrutinizing the path, Garth also turned his
glance towards the ground.

Though no match for the American in reading the "sign"—either
of the heavens or the earth—the ex-footpad was not altogether un-
practiced in the translating of tracks.

It had been long—alas! too long—a branch of his peculiar calling,
and the footpad's experience now enabled him to perceive that such
was the occupation in which Oriole was engaged.

He saw the footprints which the Indian was following up,—not now as before in a backward direction, but in that by which they who had made them must have gone. All at once a new light flashed into the brain of the retired robber. He no longer suspected the Indian of being a spy, but on the contrary perceived that he was in the act of tracking some individual or individuals more amenable to this suspicion. He remembered certain circumstances that had transpired during the night; odd expressions and actions that had signalized the behavior of his fellow helper, Walford. He had re-marked the absence of the latter at a particular time; and also on the occasion of Walford's taking two horses from the stable—the first led out—that he had used some arguments to dissuade both Dancey and himself from giving him assistance.

Garth supposed at the time that Walford had been actuated simply by a desire to secure the perquisites, but now that he looked upon the tracks—which Oriole was in the act of scrutinizing—a new thought rushed into his mind; a suspicion that during that eventful night, treason had been stalking around the dwelling of Stone Dean.

Excited by this thought, the ex-footpad threw himself alongside the Indian, and endeavored by signs to convey the intelligence he had obtained by conjecture—as well as to possess himself of that which the red-skin might have arrived at by some more trustworthy process of reasoning.

Unfortunately, Gregory Garth was but a poor pantomimist. His grimaces and gestures were rather ludicrous, than explanatory of his thoughts; so much so, that the Indian, after vainly endeavoring to comprehend them, answered with an ambiguous shake of the head.

Then gliding silently past, he ascended the steps and hurried on towards the apartment—in which he proposed to hold more intelligible communion with his master.

CHAPTER XXXVIII.

On the departure of his fellow conspirators—patriots we should rather call them—Holtspur, as we have already said, had passed the remainder of night engaged at his writing-table.

The time was spent in the performance of a duty entrusted to him by his friends, Pym and Hampden, with whom and a few others he had held secret conference beyond the hours allotted to the more public business of the meeting. It was a duty no less important than the drawing up of a charge of attainder against Thomas Wentworth, Earl of Strafford.

It was one which Holtspur could perform with all the ardor of a zealous enthusiasm—springing from his natural indignation against this gigantic wrong-doer.

A true hater of kings, he felt triumphant. His republican sentiments, uttered in the assembly just separated—so loudly applauded by those who listened to them—could not fail to find echo in every honest English heart; and the patriot felt that the time was nigh when such sentiments need be no longer spoken in the conclave of a secret conference, but boldly and openly in the tribune of a nation.

The king had been once more compelled to call his "Commons" together. In a few days the Parliament was to meet—that splendid Parliament afterwards known as the "Long"—and from the election returns already received, Holtspur knew the character of most of the statesmen who were to compose it. With such men as Pym and Hampden at its head—with Holles, Hazlerig, Vane, Martin, Cromwell and a host of other popular patriots taking part in its councils—it would be strange if something should not be effected to stem the tide of tyranny, so long flowing over the land—submerging under its infamous waves every landmark of English liberty.

Swayed by thoughts like these did Henry Holtspur enter upon the task assigned him.

For over an hour had he been occupied with its performance—with scarce a moment's intermission; and then only when the soft dream of love, stealing over his spirit, chased from it the sterner thoughts of statecraft and war, which had been the habitual themes of his later life.

He had well nigh finished his work when interrupted by the entrance of the Indian.

"Eh, Oriole?" demanded he in some surprise, as, glancing up from his papers, he remarked the agitated mien of his attendant. "Anything the matter? You look as if something was amiss. I hope that you and Garth have not been quarreling over your perquisites?"

The Indian made a sign of a negative to this imputation—which he knew was only spoken in jest.

"Nothing about him, then? What is it, my brave?"

This question was answered by Oriole raising one of his feet—with the sole turned upwards—at the same time glancing to the ground with an angry ejaculation.

"Ha!" said Holtspur, who read those signs as easily as if they had been a written language—"an enemy upon the trail?"

Oriole held up three of his fingers, pointing perpendicularly towards the ceiling of the room.

"Three instead of one! and three *men*! Well, perhaps they will be easier to deal with than if it was a *trio* of *women*."

The cavalier, as he made this half-jesting remark, seemed to give way for a moment to some reflection altogether unconnected with the intelligence conveyed by his attendant.

"What is it, Oriole? What have you seen?" asked he, returning to the subject of the Indian's communication.

Oriole's answer to this was a sign for his master to follow him. At the same time, turning on his heel, he led the way out of the apartment; out of the front door, and round by the left wing of the house. Thither he was followed by Holtspur and Gregory Garth, when all three commenced re-examining the tracks.

These were again traced in a backward direction to the side doorway.

It could not be doubted that two of the men who made them had issued thence. The third—he who wore the hob-nailed shoes—had met these on their coming out, and afterwards walked along with them to the front—where the foot-marks were lost among the hoof prints of the horses.

There were no tracks leading towards the side entrance; but as there was no other way by which the room could have been entered except by the glass door, and that had certainly no. been unclosed, it was evident that the two men who had come out by the side passage must have gone in by it.

The absence of any foot-marks leading inward had a signification of another kind. It proved that they who had so intruded must have passed inside before the coming on of the rain-storm, and gone out after it had ceased. In other words, two men must have tenanted that chamber during most, if not all of the time that the conference continued.

Other signs pointed out by the Indian—the disturbance of the dust upon the floor, and the removal of the cerements from the glass—left no doubt as to the object of their presence in the unused apartmen Spies, to a certainty!

Holtspur's countenance became clouded as this conviction forced itself upon him.

The hobnails told who was the traitor that had guided them thither. There were plenty of like tracks on the other side of the house, leading to the stable-yard. Oriole easily identified the foot-marks as made by Will Walford.

"It but crowns my suspicions of the knave," said Holtspur, as with gloom upon his brow he walked back into the house.

"Dang seize the white-livered loon!" cried the ex-footpad. "He shall answer for this night's dirty doin's. That shall be sureish sartain, or my name arn't Gregory Garth."

On re-entering the library, Holtspur did not resume his seat, but commenced pacing the floor with quick excited steps.

What had arisen was matter to make him serious. Spies had been present—he could not doubt it—and the fact was full of significance. It concerned not only his own safety, but that of many others—gentlemen of rank and position in the county, with several members of Parliament from other counties; among them Pym, Hollis, Hazlerig, Henry Martin, and the younger Sir Harry Vane.

Sir Marmaduke Wade, too, must have been seen by the spies.

In regard to the latter, Holtspur felt a special apprehension. It was by invitation—his own—that Sir Marmaduke had been present at the meeting; and Holtspur knew that the knight would now be compromised beyond redemption—even to the danger of losing his life.

Whoever had occupied that antechamber must have overheard not only all that had been spoken, but have seen each speaker in turn;

m short, every individual present, and under a light clear enough to have rendered sure their identification.

It needed very little reflection to point out who had been the chief spy. The dispatch taken by Garth from the king's messenger rendered it easy to tell; Richard Scarthe had been in that chamber—either in person or by deputy.

All this knowledge flashed upon the mind of the patriot conspirator with a distinctness painfully vivid.

Unfortunately, the course proper for him to pursue was far from being so clear, and for some minutes he remained in a state of indecision as to how he should act.

With such evidence as Scarthe possessed against him, he felt keenly conscious of danger—a danger threatening not only his liberty, but his life.

If taken before the Star Chamber, after what he had that night said and done, he could not expect any other verdict than a conviction; and his would not be the first head, during that weak tyrant's reign, that had tumbled untimely from the block.

It was of no use upbraiding himself with the negligence that had led to the unfortunate situation. Nor was there any time to indulge in self-reproach; for the longer he reflected the more proximate would be the danger he had to dread.

Henry Holtspur was a man of ready determination. A life partly spent amidst dangers of flood and field; under the shadow of primeval American forests—on the war-path of the hostile Mohawk—had habituated him to the forming of quick resolves, and as quickly carrying them into execution.

But no man is gifted with omniscience; and there are occasions when the wisest in thought and quickest in action may be overtaken.

It was so in Holtspur's case at this particular crisis; he felt that he had been outwitted. In the fair field of fight he had defeated an adversary, who, in the dark diplomacy of intrigue, was likely to triumph over him.

There was not much time to be lost. Was there any? They who had made that stealthy visit to Stone Dean would be sure to repeat it, and soon—not secretly as before, but openly and in force.

Why had they not returned already? This was the only question that appeared difficult to answer.

Why the arrest had not been made at once—a wholesale capture at the conspirators—could be more easily answered. The spies might not have been prepared for a *coup* so sudden, so extensive.

But since there had been time——

"By heavens!" exclaimed the cavalier, suddenly interrupting the train of his conjectures, "there's no time to be lost. I must from here, and at once. Garth?"

"Master Henry?"

"Saddle my horse on the instant! Oriole!"

The Indian stood before him.

"Are my pistols loaded?"

Oriole made signs in the affirmative—pointing to the pistols that lay on the oaken mantel-shelf.

"Enough! I may need them ere long. Place them in the holsters."

"And now, Oriole," continued his master, after a reflective pause, and regarding his attendant with some sadness, "I am going upon a journey. I may be absent for some time. You cannot accompany me. You must stay here—till I either return or send for you."

The Indian listened, his countenance clouding over with an expression of disquietude.

"Don't be down-hearted, my brave!" pursued Holtspur. "We shall not be separated for long—no longer than I can help."

Oriole asked by a gesture why he was to be left behind; adding in a pantomime equally intelligible to Holtspur, that he was ready to follow him to the death—to die for him.

"I know all that, faithful boy!" responded his patron and protector, "right well do I know it: since you've given proof of it once before. But your prowess, that might avail me in the pathless coverts of your native forest, and against enemies of your own color, would be of little service here. The foe I have now to fear is not a naked savage with club and tomahawk, but a king with sword and sceptre Ah! my brave Oriole, your single arm would be idle to shield me where a whole host are to be my adversaries. Come, faithful friend! I lose time—too much have I lost already. Quick with my valise. Pack and strap it to the croup. Put these papers into it. The rest may remain as they are. Quick, good Oriole! Hubert should be saddled by this time. Garth, what is it?"

Garth stood in the doorway—breathless, ghastly pale.

"Ho! what's that? I need not ask Too well do I understand those sounds."

11

"Lor', O lor'! Master Henry! The house be surrounded wi' horsemen. They be the kewresseers from Bulstrode."

"Ha! Scarthe has been quick and cunning. I'm too late, I fear."

Saying this, the cavalier snatched up his pistols—at the same time grasping his sword—as if with the intention of making an attempt to defend himself.

The ex-footpad also armed himself with his terrible pike, which chanced to be standing in the hall; while Oriole's weapon was a tomahawk, habitually worn about his person.

Drawing his blade from its scabbard, Holtspur rushed to the front entrance—close followed by Garth and the Indian.

On reaching the door, which was still standing open, the conspirator saw at a glance that resistance would be worse than idle, since it could only end in the sacrifice of his own life, and perhaps the lives of his faithful followers.

In front of the house was ranged a row of steel-clad cuirassiers—each with his arquebus ready to deliver its fire; while the trampling of hoofs, the clanking of armor, and the voices of men resounding from the rear of the dwelling, told that the circumvallation was complete.

"Who are you? What is your business?" demanded Holtspur of one, who, from his attitude and gestures, appeared to act as the leader; but whose face was hidden behind the closed visor of his helmet.

The demand was mechanical—a mere matter of form. He who made it knew, without the necessity of asking, to whom he was addressing himself; as well as the business that had brought him there.

He had not encountered that cavalier in the field of fight—and conquered him, too—without leaving a *souvenir* by which he could be recognized.

And it needed not the wounded arm—still carried in its sling—to enable Henry Holtspur to recognize Richard Scarthe, his adversary in the equestrian duel.

Without such evidence, both horse and rider might have been identified.

"I came not here to ask idle questions," replied Scarthe, with a laugh that rang ironically through the bars of his umbril. "Your first, I presume, needs no answer; and though I shall be over cour teous in replying to your second, you are welcome to the response you have challenged. My business, then, is to arrest a traitor!"

"A traitor! Who?"

"Henry Holtspur—a traitor to his king.''

"Coward!" cried Holtspur, returning scorn for scorn; "this is the thanks I receive for sparing your paltry life. From your extensive *entourage* of steel-clad hirelings, it is evident you fear a second chastisement at my hands. Why did you not bring a whole regiment with you? Ha! ha! ha!"

"You are pleased to be facetious," said Scarthe, whose triumphant position facilitated the restraining of his temper. "In the end, Master Holtspur, you may find it not such matter for mirth. Let them be merry who win. Laughter comes with but ill grace from the lips of those who are about to lose; *nay, have already lost* ——"

"Already lost?" interrupted Holtspur, driven to the interrogatory by the tone of significant insinuation in which the other had spoken.

"Not your liberty: though that also you have already lost. Not your head: that you may lose by-and-by; but something which, if you are a true cavalier, should be dear to you as either."

"What?" mechanically inquired Holtspur, moved to the interrogatory, less by the ambiguous speech than by the sight of an object which at that moment flashed before his angry eye. "What?"

"Your *mistress!*" was the taunting reply. "Don't fancy, my pretty picker up of stray gloves, that you are the only one who receives such sweet favors. The fair lady of the golden hair and white gauntlets may have taken a fancy to dispose of a pair; and where two are thus delicately dispensed, the last given is the one most prized by me!"

As Scarthe said this, he raised his hand triumphantly towards the peak of his helmet, where a glove of white doe-skin was seen conspicuously set—its tapering fingers turned forward, as if pointing in derision at him who possessed its fellow.

Scarthe's gesture was superfluous. The eye his adversary had been already fixed upon the indicated object and the frown that suddenly overspread his face betrayed a strange commingling of emotions; surprise, incredulity, anger; something more than its share of incipient jealousy.

Rushed into Holtspur's mind at the moment the recollection of the tête-à-tête he had witnessed after parting with Marion Wade—

her promenade up the long avenue side by side with Scarthe—that
short but bitter moment when she had appeared *complaisante?*
If he wronged her in thought he did not do so in speech.
His jealousy kept silence; his anger alone found utterance.
"False trickster!" he cried, "'tis an impudent deception. She
never gave you that glove. Thou hast found it—stolen it more
likely; and by heaven! I shall take it from thee and restore it to its
slandered owner—even here, in spite of your myrmidons! Yield it
up, Richard Scarthe! or on the point of my sword ——"
The threat was left unfinished, or rather unheard; for simultaneous with its utterance came the action—Holtspur raised his naked
blade and rushing upon his adversary.
"Seize him!" cried the latter, reining his horse backward to
escape the thrust. "Seize the rebel! Slay him if he resists!"
At the command half-a-dozen of the cuirassiers spurred their
steeds forward to the spot. Some stretched forth their hands to lay
hold upon Holtspur, while others aimed at striking him down with
the butts of their carabines.
Garth and the Indian had sallied forth to defend their master, who,
had it not been for this, would perhaps have made a more prolonged
resistance.
But the sight of his two faithful followers—thus unnecessarily
risking their lives—caused him suddenly to change his mad design;
and without offering further resistance, he surrendered himself into
the hands of the soldiers who had surrounded him.
"Fast bind the rebel!" cried Scarthe, endeavoring to conceal his
chagrin at having shown fear, by pouring forth a volley of loyal
speeches.
"Relieve him of his worthless weapon! Tie him hand and foot—
neck and crop! He is mad, and therefore dangerous. Ha! ha! ha!
Tight, you knaves! Tight as a hangman's necktie!"
The order was obeyed quickly—if not to the letter; and in a few
seconds Henry Holtspur stood bound in the midst of his jeering
enemies.
"Bring forth his horse!" cried Scarthe, in mocking tones. "The
black horseman! Ha! ha! ha! Let him have one last ride on his
favorite charger. After that he shall ride at the king's expense.
Ha! ha! ha!"
The black steed, already saddled by Garth, was soon brought
round and led towards the captive. There was something significant

in the neigh to which Hubert gave utterance as he approached the spot—something mournful: as if he suspected, or knew, that his master was in a position of peril.

As he was conducted nearer, and at length placed side by side with the prisoner, he bent his neck round till his muzzle touched Holtspur's cheek; while his low, tremulous whimpering proved, as plainly as words could have expressed it, that he comprehended all.

The cuirassier captain had watched the odd and affecting incident. Instead of exciting his sympathy, it only intensified his chagrin.

The presence of that steed reminded him, more forcibly than ever, of his own humiliating defeat—of which the animal had been more than a little the cause.

Scarthe hated the horse almost as much as his master.

"Now, brave sir!" shouted he, endeavoring, in a derisive strain, to drown the unpleasant memories which the sight of Hubert had summoned up. "Such a distinguished individual must not ride bareheaded along the king's highway. Ho, there! Bring out his beaver and set it upon his crown jauntily—jauntily!"

Three or four of the cuirassiers, who had dismounted, were proceeding to obey this last order—and had already mounted the steps leading up to the entrance—when an ejaculation from their commander caused them to turn back.

"Never mind, my lads!" he cried, as if having changed his intention. "Back to your horses! Never mind the hat; I shall go for it myself."

The final words of this injunction were rather muttered, than spoken aloud. It was not intended they should be heard. They appeared to be the involuntary expression of some secret purpose, which had suddenly suggested itself to the mind of the speaker.

After giving utterance to them, the cuirassier captain leaped silently out of the saddle; and mounting the stone steps, entered the door of the dwelling.

He traversed the entrance-hall with searching glances; and continued on along the corridor—until he stood opposite the door of an apartment. It was the library lately occupied by the conspirators. He knew its situation; and surmised that he would there find what he was seeking for.

He was not mistaken. On entering he saw the desired object—the hat of Holtspur, hanging upon the antlers of a stag that were fixed in a conspicuous position against the wall.

He clutched at the hat, ar⌐ rked it down—with as much eagerness, as if he feared that sor .iing might intervene to prevent him.

It needed no close scrutiny discover the white gauntlet, still in
its place beside the *panache*(strich feathers. On the next instant,
the hat, though permitted t etain its plume, was despoiled of the
doe-skin.

With a bitter smile passing over his pale features, did Scarthe scan
the two gloves once more brought together. Finger by finger, and
stitch by stitch did he compare them—holding them side by side, and
up to the window's light. His smile degenerated into a frown, as,
on the completion of the analysis, he became convinced—beyond the
possibility of a doubt—that the glove taken from the hat of Henry
Holtspur, and that now figuring on his own helmet, were *fellows, and
formed a pair*. Right and left were they—the latter being the true
love token! He had entertained a hope, though but a very slight
one, that he might still be mistaken. He could indulge it no longer.
The gauntlet worn in the hat of the black horseman, must have
once graced the fair fingers of Marion Wade.

"*Has* she given it to him? Need I ask the question? She must
have done so, beyond a doubt. May the fiend fire my soul, if I do
not find an opportunity to make her rue the gift!"

Such was the unamiable menace with which Scarthe completed the
comparison of the gloves.

That, just taken from the hat of Holtspur, was now transferred to
the breast of his doublet. Quick and secret was the transfer: as if
he deemed it desirable that the act should not be observed.

"Go!" he commanded, addressing himself to one of the troopers
who attended him; "go into the garden—if there be such a thing
about this wretched place. If not, take to the fields; and procure
me some flowers. Red ones—no matter what sort, so that they be
of a bright red color. Bring them hither, and be quick about 't!"

The soldier—accustomed to obey orders without questioning—hurried out to execute the singular command.

"You," continued Scarthe, speaking to the other trooper, who had
entered with him; "you set about collecting those papers. Secure
that valise. It appears to need no further packing. See that it be
taken to Bulstrode. Search every room in the house; and bring
out any arms or papers you may light upon. You know your work.
Do it briskly!"

With like alacrity the second attendant hastened to perform the part allotted to him; and Scarthe was for the moment left to himself.

"I should be more hungry," muttered he, "after these documents I see scattered about, were I in need of them. No doubt there's many a traitor's name inscribed on their pages: and enough besides to compromise half the squires in the county. More than one, I warrant me, through this silent testimony, would become entitled to a cheap lodging in that grand tenement eastward of Cheap. It's a sort of thing I don't much relish; though now I am into it, I may as well make a wholesale sweep of these conspiring churls. As for Holtspur and Sir Marmy, I need no written evidence of their guilt My own oral testimony, conjoined with that of my worthy sub, will be sufficient to deprive one—or both, if need be—of their heads. So—to the devil with the documents!"

As he said this he turned scornfully away from the table on which the papers were strewed.

"Stay!" he exclaimed—the instant after facing round again, with a look that betokened some sudden change in his views. "Not so fast, Richard Scarthe! Not so fast! Who knows that among this forest of treasonous scribbling, I may not find some flower of epistolary correspondence—a *billet-doux*. Ha! if there should be one from *her*! Strange, I did not think of it before. If—if—if——"

In the earnestness with which he proceeded to toss over the litter of letters and other documents, his hypothetical thought, whatever it was, remained unspoken.

For several minutes he busied himself among the papers—opening scores of epistles—in the expectation of finding one in a feminine hand, and bearing the signature: "Marion Wade."

He was disappointed. No such name was to be found among the correspondents of Henry Holtspur. They were all of the masculine gender—all, or nearly all, politicians and conspirators!

Scarthe was about discontinuing the search—for he had opened everything in the shape of a letter—when a document of imposing aspect attracted his attention It bore the royal signet upon its envelope.

"By the eyes of Argus!" cried he, as his own fell upon the well-known seal; "what see I? A letter from the King! What can his Majesty have to communicate to this faithful subject, I wonder! Zounds! 'tis addressed to myself.

"'*For*
"'*ye Captain Scarthe*
"'*Command*: *H. M. Royal Cuirassiers,*
"'*Bulstrode Park,*
"'*Shire of Buckingham.*'

"The intercepted dispatch! Here's a discovery! Henry Holt-spur a footpad! In league with one, at all events—else how should he have become possessed of this? So—so! Not a traitor's, but a felon's death shall he die! The gibbet instead of the block! Ha! Mistress Marion Wade! you will repent the gift of your pretty glove, when you learn that you have bestowed it on a thief! By St. Sulpice! 'twill be a comical *éclaircissement!*

"Ho, fellow, you've got the flowers?"

"I have, captain. They be the best I can find. There a'nt nothing but weeds about the old place, an' withered at that."

"So much the better: I want them a trifle withered. These will do—color, shape—just the thing. Here! arrange them in a little bunch, and tie it to this hat. Fix them as if the clasp confined them in their place. Be smart, my man; and make a neat thing of it!"

The trooper plied his fingers with all the plastic ingenuity in his power; and, in a few seconds of time, a somewhat ragged bouquet was arranged, and adjusted on the beaver belonging to the black horseman, in the same place late occupied by the white gauntlet.

"Now!" said Scarthe, making a stride in the direction of the door; "take out this hat." Place it on the head of the prisoner; and hark ye, corporal; you needn't let *him* see the transformation that has been made; nor need you show it conspicuously to any one else. You understand me?"

The trooper, having replied to these confidential commands with a nod and a knowing look, hurried off to execute them.

Stubbs, in charge of the guards outside, had already mounted Holtspur on horseback; where, with hands fast bound, and, for additional security, tied to the croup of the saddle, his ancles also lashed to the stirrup-leathers, and a steel-clad cuirassier, with drawn sword, on each side of him, he looked like a captive left without the slightest chance of escape.

Even when thus ignominiously pinioned, no air of the felon had he. His head, though bare, was not bowed; but carried proudly erect, without swagger, and with that air of tranquil indifference which distinguishes the true cavalier, even in captivity. His rough, and somewhat vagabond captors, could not help admiring that heroic courage, of which, but a few days before, they had witnessed such splendid proof.

"What a pity," whispered one: "what a pity he's not on our side! He'd make a noble officer of cavalry!"

"Help Master Holtspur to his hat!" tauntingly commanded Scarthe as he clambered upon his own steed. "The wind must not be permitted to toss those waving locks too rudely. How becoming they will be upon the block. Ha! ha! ha!"

As commanded, his hat was placed upon the prisoner's head.

The "forward," brayed out by the bugle, drowned the satirical laugh of their leader; while the troopers, in files of two, with Scarthe at their head, Stubbs in the rear, and Holtspur near the centre, moved slowly across the lawn; leaving the mansion of Stone Dean without a master!

CHAPTER XXXIX.

DANCEY IN DRINK.

On perceiving that his presence could no longer be of any service to his patron, and might be detrimental to himself, Gregory Garth had betaken his body to a place of concealment—one of the garrets of Stone Dean—where, through a dormer-window, he had been witness to all that transpired outside.

As the last of Scarthe's troopers passed out through the gateway of Stone Dean, the ex-footpad came down from his hiding-place, and re-appeared in front of the house.

Guided by a similar instinct, the Indian had also made himself invisible; and now re-appearing at the same time, the two stood face to face; but without the ability to exchange either word or idea.

Gregory could not understand the pantomimic language of the Indian; while the latter knew not a word of English—the cavalier always conversing with him in his native tongue.

It is true that neither had much to say to the other. Both had witnessed the capture of their common patron and master. Oriole

11*

only knew that he was in the hands of enemies; while Garth more clearly comprehended the character of these enemies, and their motive for making him a prisoner.

Now that he *was* a prisoner, the first and simultaneous thought of both was—whether there was any chance of effecting his escape.

With the American this was an instinct; while perhaps with any other Englishman, than one of Garth's kidney, the idea would scarce have been entertained.

But the ex-footpad, in the course of his professional career, had found his way out of too many prisons, to regard the accomplishment of such a feat as either impossible or improbable; and he at once set about reflecting upon what steps should be taken for the rescue and release of Henry Holtspur.

Garth was sadly in need of a second head to join counsel with his own. That of the Indian, however good it might be, was absolutely of no use to him : since there was no way of getting at the ideas it contained.

"The unfort'nate creatur!" exclaimed he, after several vain attempts as a mutual understanding of signs; "he an't no good to me—not half so much as my own old dummies : for they war o' some sarvice. Well, I maun try an' manage 'ithout him."

Indeed Gregory, whether wishing it or not, was soon reduced to this alternative; for the Indian, convinced that he could not make himself intelligible, desisted from the attempt. Following out another of his natural instincts, he parted from the ex-footpad, and glided off upon the track of the troopers—perhaps with some vague idea of being more serviceable to his master if once to his side again.

"The dummie's faithful to him as a hound;" muttered Gregory, seeing the Indian depart; same as my ole clo' pals war to me. Sir Henry ha did 'im a sarvice some time I dar say—as he does iverybody wheniver he can. Now, what's to be done for *him* ?"

The footpad stood for some moments in a reflecting attitude.

They've ta'en 'im up to Bulstrode, where they're quartered. No doubt 'bout that. They won't keep 'im there a longish time. They mean no common prison to hold *him*. Newgate, or the Tower —one o' the two are sure o' bein' his lodgin' afore the morrow night !

"What chance o' a rescue on the road ? Ne'er a much, I fear. Dang seize it ! my dummies wouldn't do for that sort o' thing

There'll goo a whoole troop o' these kewresseers along wi' 'im? Ne doubt o't.

"I wonder if they'll take 'im up the day? Maybe they woan't, an' if they doan't, theer mout be a chance i' the night. I wish I hed some'n to help me wi' a good think.

"Hang'd if I kinb'live ole Dancey to be a treetur. Tan't possible after what he ha' sayed to me, no later than yesterday mornin'. No, it isn't possible. He ha' know'd nothin' 'bout this bizness; an' it be all the doins o' that devil's get o' a Walford.

"I'll go see Dancey. I'll find out whether he a hed 'a hand in't or no. If no, then he do summat to holp me; an, maybe that daughter o' his 'll do summat? Sartin *she will*. If my eyes don't cheat me, the gurl's mad arter Sir Henry—mad as a she hare in March time.

"I'll goo to Dancey's this very minnit. I've another irrend i' that same d'rection; an' I kin kill two burds wi' the one stooan. Cuss the whey-faced loon Walford! If I doan't larrup 'im as long as I kin find a hard spot inside his ugly skin. Augh!"

And winding up his soliloquy with the aspirated exclamation, he re-entered the house—as if to prepare for his proposed visit to the cottage of Dancey.

Although he had promised himself to start on the instant, it was a good half-hour before he took his departure from Stone Dean. The larder lay temptingly open—as also the wine cellar; and although the captors of Henry Holtspur had foraged freely upon both, the short time allowed them for ransacking had prevented their making a clear sweep of the shelves. The ex-footpad, therefore, found sufficient food left to furnish him with a tolerable breakfast, and wine enough to wash it down.

In addition to time spent in appeasing his appetite, there was an ether affair that occupied some twenty minutes longer. In his master's bedroom—and other apartments that had not been entered by the cuirassiers—there lay a number of valuable articles of a portable kind. These, that may almost be said to be now ownerless, were of course no longer safe—even within the house. Any thief might enter, and carry them away under his cloak.

The man, who made this reflection, was not one to leave such chattels unsecured; and procuring a large bag, he thrust into it silver cups, and candlesticks, with several other costly articles of *luxa*, dress, and armor, one upon top of the other, until the sack was filled to the mouth. Hoisting it on his shoulders, he marched on, of the house; and after carrying the spoil to some distance among the shrubbery, he selected for it a place of concealment.

As this was an act in which the *ci-devant* footpad was an adept, he bestowed the property in such a manner, that the sharpest eye might have passed within six feet without perceiving it.

It is not justice to Gregory to say that he was stealing this treasure. He was merely secreting it, against the return of its owner. But it would be equally untrue to assert, that, while hiding the bag among the bushes, his mind did not give way to some vague speculation, as to the chance of a reversion.

Perhaps it occurred to him that in the event of Holtspur never returning to Stone Dean, or never being again seen by him, Garth, the contents of that sack would be compensation for the loss of his beloved master.

Certainly some such thought flitted vaguely through his brain at the moment; though it could not have taken the shape of a wish: for in the very next instant he took his departure from Stone Dean, eagerly bent on an errand, which, if successful, would annihilate all hope of that vaguely contemplated reversion.

As may be surmised from his soliloquized speeches, his route lay direct to the dwelling of Dick Dancey; and in due time he arrived within sight of his humble abode.

Before coming out into the slight clearing that surrounded it, he observed some one staggering off upon the opposite side. He only caught a glimpse of this person, who in the next instant disappeared among the trees, but in that glimpse Garth identified the individual. It was the woodman Walford, who, from the way he was tracking it, appeared to be in a state of intoxication.

Garth, comprehending the cause, came easily to this conclusion: and making no further pause, except to ascertain that the woodman was continuing his serpentine promenade, passed on towards the cottage.

He had made a correct guess as to Walford's condition: for at that moment the woodman was perhaps as drunk as he had ever been in his life. How he came to get into this state will be made clear, by giving in brief detail some incidents that had transpired since his departure from Stone Dean, in which he and his co-adjutor Dancey had been the chief actors.

It was still only the earliest dawn of morning when the brace of worthies, returning home after their night's stable work, entered under the shadows of Wapsey's Wood; but there was light enough to show that the steps of neither were as steady as they should have been. Both kept repeatedly stumbling against the trees; and once Walford went head foremost into a pool of muddy water, from which he emerged with his foul complexion still fouler in appearance.

The rain, which had rendered the path slippery, might have accounted for this unsteadiness in the steps of the two foresters. But there was also observable in their speech an obliquity, which could not have been caused by the rain; but was clearly the consequence of exposure to a more potent fluid.

Dancey conversed glibly and gleefully, interlarding his speech with an occasional spell of chuckling laughter. He had come away perfectly satisfied with the proceedings of the night; the proceeds of which, a fistful of silver, he repeatedly pulled out of his pocket, and held up to the dim light, tossing it about to assure himself that it was the real coin of the realm that chinked between his fingers.

Walford's palm seemed not to have been so liberally "greased;" but for all that he was also in high spirits Something besides his perquisites had put him in a good humor with himself; though he did not impart the secret of this something to his conpanion. It was not altogether the contents of the stone jar which he had abstracted from the cellars of Stone Dean; though it might have been this that was causing him to talk so thickly, and stumble so frequently upon the path.

There was a stimulant to his joy more exciting than the spirit he had imbibed out of the bottle. It was the prospect of proximate ruin to the man, whose bread he had been just eating, and whose beer he had been drinking.

It was by no means clear to him how this ruin would be brought about. His new patron had not given him so much as a hint of the use he intended making of that night's work. But, dull as was the brain of the brute Walford, he knew that something would follow likely to rid him of his rival; and this, too, without any further risk or exertion, on his part. Both the danger and the trouble of avenging himself—for he felt vengeful towards Holtspur—were not only taken out of his hands, but he was also promised a handsome reward for his easy and willing service. This was the real cause of his secret glee: at the moment heightened by the repeated potations in which he had been indulging.

On arriving at the cottage of his companion, it was not to be expected that Walford, in this state of feeling, would pass by without

looking in. Nor was Dancey in the mind to let him pass; for it so
chanced that the jar of *Hollands*, which the young woodman had abstracted from the cellars of Stone Dean, was carried under the skirt
of his doublet; and Dancey knew that it was not yet empty.

The challenge of the old deer-stealer, to enter his cottage and
finish the gin, was readily responded to by his *confrère*; and both,
staggering inside the hut, flung themselves into a couple of rush-
bottomed chairs. Walford, uncorking the "grey-beare," placed it
upon the table; and, tin cups having been procured, the two woodmen continued the carouse, which their homeward scramble had
interrupted.

It had now got to be daylight; and the beautiful Betsey, who
had been astir long before sunrise, was summoned to attend upon
them.

Neither cared for eating. The larder of Stone Dean had spoiled
the appetites of both; while its cellar had only sharpened their crav-
ing for drink.

At first Walford scarce regarded the chill reception extended to
him by the daughter of his host. He was too much elated at the
prospect—of being soon disembarrassed of his dreaded rival—to pay
attention to the frowns of his mistress. At that moment he believed himself in a way of becoming master of the situation.

By little and little, however, his jealous misgivings began to rise
in the ascendant—mastering even the potent spirit of the juniper.

A movement which Bet had made towards the door—where she
stood looking wistfully out, as if expecting some one—forcibly arres-
ted Walford's attention; and, notwithstanding the presumed restraint of her father's presence, he broke out in a strain of resentful
recrimination.

"Da-ang thee!" he exclaimed, angrily blurting out the phrase,
"thee be a stannin' in that door for no good. I wonder thee allows
it, Dick Dancey?"

"Eh! lad—hic-hic-ough!—what is't, Wull? Say Bets'! what
ha' ye—hic-hic-ough—eh?"

"She be danged! An' thee be a old fool, Dick, to let her go on so
wi' that fellow."

"Eh, Wull? Wha' fella—who you meean, lad—hic-cuff?"

"*She* know who I meean   She know well enough, wi' all her
innocent looks, Ha! He'll make a —— o' her, if he han't did it
a' ready."

"Father! will you listen to this language?" cried Bet, turning in from the door, and appealing to her natural protector against the vile term which her drunken suitor had applied to her. "It isn't the first time he has called me by that name. Oh, father! don't let him say it again!"

"Ye fayther 'll find out some day that it be only the truth," muttered Walford, doggedly.

"Troos!" repeated Dancey, with a maudlin stare, "troos—what is't, lad?—what is't, Betsey, gurl?"

"He called me a ——," answered the girl, reluctantly repeating the opprobrious epithet.

"He did! called you a ——, Betsey? If he called ye th'-th'-that, I'll sm-a-a-ash him into fagots!"

As the woodman uttered this characteristic threat, he attempted to raise himself into an upright attitude, apparently with the intention of carrying it into execution.

The attempt proved a failure; for, after half regaining his legs, the intoxicated deer-stealer sank back into his chair, the "rungs" of which bent and cracked under his ponderous weight, as if about to part company with each other.

"Ee-s!" tauntingly continued the accuser, gaining confidence by the helplessness of Old Dick, otherwise dreaded by him. "Thee deserves to be called it! Thee be all I say—a ——"

"You hear him, father? He has said it again!"

"Said what—what, Bets', gurl?"

"That I'm a ——"

And Betsey once more repeated the offensive word; this time pronouncing it with fuller emphasis.

The second appeal called forth a more energetic response. This time Dancey's attempt to get upon his feet was more successful.

Balancing himself against the back of his great armchair, he cried out—

"Wull Walford! Thee be a villain! How dar' thee call my laughter—a—a—hic-cock? Goo out o' my house this minute; or if thee doan't—hic-coo—if thee doan't, I'll split thy skull like a withy! Get thee goo-o-one!"

"I'll do jest that!" answered Walford, sulkily rising from his chair, and scowling resentfully both on father and daughter. "I ha' got a house o' me own to go to; an' dang me, if I doan't take along wi' me what be my own!"

Saying this, he whipped the stone jar from the table, stuck the cork into it; and, placing it once more under his skirt, strode out of the deer-stealer's dwelling.

"Da-ang thee, Dick Dancey!" he shouted back, after stepping over the threshold. "Thee be-est a old fool, that's what thee be! An' as for thee," he added, turning fiercely towards Bet; "maybe thee hast seen thy fine fancy—for the last time. Hoora! *I've did that this night, 'll put iron bars atween thee an' him.* Dang thee, thou ——"

And once more repeating the insulting epithet, the vile brute broke through the flimsy fence, and went reeling away into the woods.

It was at this moment that his receding figure came under the eyes of Gregory Garth, just then approaching the cottage from the opposite direction.

"What be that he say 'bout iron bars?" inquired Dancey, slightly sobered by the unpleasant incident. "Who be he threatenin', gurl?"

"I can't say, father," replied Bet, telling a white lie. "I think he don't know himself what he says. He is the worse for drink."

"That he be, ha! ha! ha! E-es—hic-coo—he must be full o't—that hol-hol-lands he hed up there at the old house—hic-coo! that ha' done 'im up. The lad han't got much o' a head for drink. He be easy to get overc-come. Ha! ha! ha! I b'lieve, Betsy, gurl, I've been a drinkin' m'self? Never mind! Be all right arter I ha' a wink i' the old arm-ch-ch-air. So here goo-go-es!"

With this wind up, the deer-stealer let himself down into the great beechwood chair, as easily as his unmanageable limbs would allow him, and, in less than ten seconds' time, his snoring proved that he was asleep.

CHAPTER XL.

A PUNISHMENT POSTPONED.

The parting speech of her resentful lover had not fal en upon the ears of Bet Dancey, without producing an effect.

It was not the opprobrious epithet concluding it, that had caused the red to forsake her cheeks—leaving them, with her lips blanched and bloodless.

It was not the villifying phrase; but the hint that preceded it, which caused her to start to her feet, and stand for some time gasping with suspended breath.

"*Maybe thee hast seen thy fine fancy for the last time. Ha. I've did that this night 'll put iron bars atween thee and him.*"

Such were Walford's exact words.

Between her and whom? Holtspur? Who else? Who but Holtspur was in *her* mind? And who but he could be in the mind of Walford?

She knew that Walford was fiercely jealous of the black horseman Glad would she have been for the latter to have given him cause Alas! she alone had exhibited the signs that had conducted Walford to this jealousy.

Iron bars—a prison—for him—the man who in her own wild way she almost adored!

What did it mean? Was it in prospect, this threatened prison for Holtspur? Or might it mean that he was already incarcerated?

The latter could scarce be—else something relating to it would have escaped from the lips either of her father or his guest, during their babble over the bottle of Hollands.

They had been at Stone Dean throughout the whole night.

The girl knew it, and knew how they had been employed; knew also something of the character of the company convened there— enough to convince her that it was some sort of a secret assemblage dangerous to be held under the light of day.

The unlettered, but intelligent maiden, knew, moreover, that the cavalier was a man of peculiar inclinings—that is, one who was suspected of not being loyal to the king.

She had heard all this in whispers, and from the lips of her father—who was accustomed to make no secret of his own disloyalty.

Bet regarded not the republican leanings of the man she admired. Perhaps on this account she admired him all the more? Not because they were in consonance with the professions of her own father; but from the courage required to avow such sentiments in such times; and courage was just the virtue to challenge the admiration of this bold-hearted beauty.

If there was aught to interfere with her approval of Holtspur's political proclivities, it was a vague sense of his being in danger from holding them. This, from time to time, had rendered her uneasy on his account.

The words of Walford had changed this uneasiness into a positive anxiety.

True, he appeared to have uttered them in spite; but not the less likely was his conditional threat to have a foundation in some fact about transpiring, or that had already transpired.

"There *is* danger," muttered the maiden, as Walford went off. "Master Holtspur must be warned of it—if I have to go myself. I *shall* go," she added, as she saw her father sink helplessly into his chair, "and this very instant."

She whipped her hooded cloak from its peg, flung it loosely over her shoulders; and, casting another glance towards the sleeper in the chair, was about to set forth, on her half-spoken errand; when, just at that moment, the lurcher gave out his note of alarm.

The intoxicated deer-stealer heard the bark; stirred slightly on his seat; muttered some incoherent syllables; and wandered off into a fresh maze of drunken dreaming.

"If it should be Will coming back?" said Bet, moving on tiptoe towards the door; "I wouldn't be a bit surprised.

"Thank the stars, it's not! Some one from the direction of Stone Dean! Oh! if it should be ——"

An exclamation of disappointment interrupted the speech, as a tall motley-clad figure, a dark-skinned face, and black bushy whiskers, presented themselves a short distance off, under the branches of the trees.

"It's that new friend of father's— *his* friend, too," muttered the girl. "I heard them say he was at the Dean last night. Perhaps *he* can tell? Maybe he comes——"

"Morrow, my gurl!" saluted Gregory Garth, interrupting Bet's speculations as to the object of his visit.

"Niceish weather. Old bird back to his roost yet?"

"My father, you mean!" rejoined Bet, not showing any displeasure at the bizarre style, either of the salute, or the interrogatory.

"Why, sartin, I means him. Theer an't no other old bird as belongs to this nest, be there? At home, eh?"

"He is. He's asleep in his chair. You see him there?"

"Well, he do appear to be somethin' o' that sort sureish enough. Asleep, eh? He snorts like a good un! An't he a leettleish bit more than sleepin'?" continued the interrogator, seeing that Bet hesitated to make reply to the last interrogatory. "Eh, gurl?

"Well! I won't ask ye to answer the question—seein' he be thy fayther. But theer sartainly be a strongish smell here. Ah! it be coomin' from this cups, I s'pose."

Garth, as he said this, lifted one of the drinking vessels from the table; and held it up the nose.

"That's been Hollands i' that 'ere. Same i' t'other," he added, smelling the second cup. "Got the 'sact *bokay*—as the French say 'bout their wines—o' some o' them spirits over at the Dean. But surely the old un don't need both cups to drink out o'? There's been another un at it? It warn't thyself?"

"No!" replied Bet, pronouncing the denial whith a slightly indignant emphasis.

"Doant be 'fended gurl! I war only a jokin' thee. But who war the other jovial?"

"A friend of father's. You know him, master. Will Walford it was."

"A friend o' yer fayther's, eh? A great friend o' yer fayther's, ain't he?"

"Father thinks a deal of him—more than he ought to, maybe."

"Then it's not true, Mistress Betsey, that ye be so sweet upon this Wull Walford?"

"Sweet upon *him!* Who said I was?"

"Well, nobody as I knows on; but everybody say he be that way about ye."

"I can't help that; nor people's tongues neither I wish people would only mind their own bizness——"

"Ah! if they would, what a happy, comfortable world we'd ha' o't! But they woan't—dang seize 'em! they woan't!"

After giving utterance to this somewhat old-fashioned reflection, Gregory remained for a time in a state of moody silence as if laboring under some regret which the thought had called up.

"You have some biziness with father?" said Bet, interrogatively

"Well—that," replied Garth, appearing to hesitate about what he was going to say—"that depends. Sartin the old un don't look much like doin' bizness jest now—do he?"

"I fear not," was Bet's simple reply.

"Maybe, Mistress Betsey," continued Garth, giving a glance of scrutiny into the face of the girl—"maybe ye might do for the bizness I heve on hand—better, maybe, than thy fayther? I want——"

"What is it you want?" inquired Betsey, too impatient to wait for the words, that were spoken by Garth with some deliberation.

"A friend. Not for meself; but for one that be in danger."

"Who—Who's in danger?" asked the girl, whith an eagerness of manner, that did not escape the quick eyes of him to whom the interrogatory was addressed.

"A Gentleman—a real gentleman. Ye ought to known who I mean."

"I ought to know! How, sir?"

"Ye han't heerd, then, what hae happened at Stone Dean, this mornin'?

Bet made no answer. Her look, while proclaiming a negative, told the presentiment with which the question had inspired her.

"Ye han't heerd as how Master Holtspur ha' been tuk a prisoner, and carried away by the kewersseers o' Captain Scarthe? Ye han't heerd that, eh?"

"Oh," cried Bet, adding a somewhat more emphatic form of ejaculation. "Then that is what he meant. I might have known it. Oh God, it was that!"

"Who meant? What?

"Walford, Will Walford, oh!—the villain!"

"Thee callest him a villain. Do thy fayther think 'im one?"

"When he hears this, he will. Oh, Master Holtspur a prisorer, and to that man who is his deadly enemy! 'Tis Will Walford's doings, I am sure it is."

"What makes thee think that, gurl?"

"He said he had done something, this very hour something to bring it about."

"Did he say so to thy fayther?"

"No; only out of spite to me, just as he was goin' off. My father heard him, but he was too—too sleepy to understand him. If he had——"

"He would ha' been angry w' 'm, as thou art?"

"I am sure he would."

"All right. I tho'ght as much."

"A prisoner! Oh, sir! where have they taken him to? What will they do to him? Tell me, tell me."

"I'll tell thee, when I know myself; an' that, gurl, be jest the irrend ha' bro'ght me over here. I see it be no use wakin' up the old un jest now. Them Hollands 'll keep 'im a prisoner till well nigh sundown. I' the meanwhile, somethin' must be done 'ithout 'im. Maybe ye ken sarve my purpose, as well, or better'n 'im, if thee be that way disposed."

"What purpose? If it be anything I can do for—for—Master Holtspur! Oh, I shall only be too glad."

"That be jest what I want. Thee must know I'm a friend o' Master Holtspur—an old retainer o' his family; an' I'll lay down my life, or a'most that, to get 'im out o' the clutches o' these kewresseers. I know theer captain 'll try to get 'im beheaded. Ah, an' he'll get it done too, if we can't find some way o' escape for him. It's to find that, I want thy holp Mistress Betsey."

"Tell me how I can help thee—I am ready for anything?" responded the girl.

As she said this, both her air and attitude betokened the truthfulness of her words.

"There be no time to lose, then; else I mout ha' waited for yer fayther to goo snacks wi' us. No matter. We ken take the first steps 'ithout 'im. It will be for ye to goo up to Bulstrode—that's where they've taken Master Henry jest now; an' get inside the house. Ye be known there, bean't ye?"

"Oh, yes; I can go in or out when I like. They won't suspect anything in that."

"If be more than I ked do, wi' tnat an' a good many other houses," said Garth, smiling significantly; "else I mout ha' gone meself. But ye'll do better than anybody, mayhap. Find out, if ye ken, first—whether the prisoner be goin' to be taken up to London; then, what time they're goin' to take 'im; then, what part o' the house they've put 'im in: for he's sure to be shut up somewhere.

Find out that; an' as much more as ye ken; an' fetch the whole story back here to me. Maybe by the time ye gets back, the old un 'll be awake, an' ha' his noddle clear enough to holp us think o somethin'."

"I shall go at once," said Bet, moving in the direction of the door.

"Ay, start right off. The minutes be precious for Master Henry. Stay, I'll goo wi' thee a bit. I've got another irrend out this d'rection, that'll jest about take up my time till ye get back. We may as well goo thegither—so far as your roads agree. Good-bye, Dick Dancey! Snore on, old un; an' sleep it off as quick's ye ken: we may want ye badly bye-an'-bye."

And with this jocular leave-taking, the retired footpad stepped out of the house, and followed the girl—who, eager upon the errand that had summoned her forth, had already advanced some distance along the path.

Their routes did not correspond for any great length. At a distance of two or three hundred yards from the cottage, the path parted into two : one, the plainer one, running towards the rearward of Bulstrode Park; the other—which appeared as if used by only a few individuals —tending in the direction of Will Walford's domicile.

The daughter of Dick Dancey faced into the former and stepping out nimbly, soon disappeared behind the hanging boughs of the beeches.

The ex-footpad, lingering a little to look after her, as soon as she was out of sight, turned into the other path, which would conduct him to the hut of the woodman.

Before going far in this new direction, he once more came to a stop, alongside a big bush of holly, that grew near the path. Drawing a clasp-knife from his pocket, he proceeded to cut off one of its largest branches.

Having severed the sapling from its parent stem, he continued to ply his blade upon it, until it had assumed the form and dimensions of a stout cudgel. The purpose for which this weapon was designed may already have been guessed at. If not, the mutterings which escaped from the lips of Gregory Garth will make clear his intent.

"I don't want," said he, paring off some of the more prominent knots with his knife. "I don't want to kill the brute outright— though he desarves that much, an' more too. I'll gie 'im a dose, howsomiver, as 'll keep 'im in-doors, an' out o' further mischief—as long as I'm likely to stay i' this sogerin' neighborhood He han't got much o' a picter to spoil nohow or I'd make his ugly mug so that his own mother, if he ha' one, wouldn't like to swear to it. Next time he goo to play spy, or holp others to do't eyther he'll be apt to remember Gregory Garth. Won't he?

"A tidyish bit o' stick," he continued holding up the piece ol trimmed holly, and surveying it with an air of satisfaction, "an' if I'd let them knots stay on, I shudn't like to ha' answered for the skull case o' Mister Wull Walford, thick as that be. I dar say it'll do now, an' I maun keep on to his house. Ha! theer's his paltry style, I s'pose? I hope the pig's in o' it."

Saying this, he advanced stealthily a few paces, and then stopped to listen.

"Good!" he exclaimed, "the brute *be* inside; I hear his gruntin'. Dang seize it, it's a snorl! They be all asleep i' this Wapsey's Wood! Well, I'll wake '*im* out e' that, wi' a heigh an' a ho; an' here goo to begin it!"

On giving utterance to this threat, he started forward at a quick pace. He was soon inside the hut, and standing over the prostrate form of the slumbering wood-chopper.

The latter was lying upon a low bed—the true truckle of the peasant's cottage—a stout structure of beechen timber, with short legs raising it about a foot from the floor.

The occupant of this coarse couch was upon his back, with arms and legs extended to their full length, as if he had been spread out on purpose to dry. But the liquid that had placed him in that attitude was not water. It was a fluid that had been administered internally; as could be told by the stone jar of Hollands that stood upon the floor, within reach of his hand; and which his uninvited visitor upon examination found to be empty.

"He's stolen it from the cellar o' Stone Dean," remarked the latter, after smelling the jar, and otherwise scrutinizing it. "I knew b' the sniff o' the liquor it's that same; an' I ked sweer to them Dutch bottles afore a full quorum o' justices. Poor Master Henry! He's not only been betrayed, but robbed by this ugly rascal. Well, here goo to gie him his reward!"

As Garth uttered the words, he seized his fresh-cut cudgel; and was about to come down with it upon the carcass of the slumbering woodman when some thought suddenly stayed his hand.

"No!" he exclaimed; "I'll wake 'im first, an' gie 'im a bit o' me

mind. If he ha' the feelin' o' a human creetcre, I'll punish 'im ?
the *moral way*—as the Vicar o' Giles' Chuffont 'ud call it.

"Hee up!" he shouted aloud, poking the sleeper with the point
of his stick. "Roust thee, thou sluggart, an' see what's time o' day!
Twelve by the sun, if it's a' hour. Hee up, I say!"

Another poke of the stick, administered still more sharply than
before, like its predecessor, produced no effect—or only the slightest.
The inebriate rustic continued to snore; and only a low grunt declared his consciousness of having been disturbed; though it seemed
more the mechanical action of the cudgel, that had been pushed
rather forcibly into the pit of his stomach.

"Hee up!" cried Garth, once more giving him a taste of the holly
stick. "Rouse thyself, I say! If ye don't, I'll wallop ye in yer
sleep. Roust! roust!"

At each summons the poke was repeated; but with no better success than before. The sleeper gave forth a series of spasmodic grunts;
but still continued to snore on.

"But for his snorin', I'd think he wur gone dead," said Garth,
desisting from his attempts to wake him. "If not dead, howiver, he
be dead drunk. That's clear enough!

"It be no use tryin' to bring 'im to his senses?" continued he,
after appearing to reflect. "An' what's worse, 'twill be no use beat-
in' 'im i' that state. The unfeelin' brute as I may well call 'im,
wouldn't *feel* it nohow. I moat as well strike me stick agin that
theer bundle fagots. It's danged disappointin'! What be the best
thing to do wi' him?"

The puzzled footpad stood for a while reflecting; then continued :—

"Twoan't do to ha' tuk the trouble o' comin' here for nothin'—
beside the cuttin' o' this cudgel. If I lay it into 'im now, he woan't
feel it, till arter he gets sober. That ain't the satisfaction I want.
I want to see 'im feel it."

Again the speaker paused to consider.

After a moment or two his eyes began to wander around the walls
—as if some design had suggested itself, and he was searching for
the means to carry it into execution.

Presently an object came under his gaze that appeared to fix it.

It was a coil of rope, or thick cord—that had been thrown over
one of the couplings of the roof, and was hanging within reach of his
hand.

"That be the best way, I take it," said he, resuming his soliloquy, "an' I dar say this 'll do. It appear a stoutish piece o' string," he continued, dragging the cord from off the coupling; and trying its strength between hand and heel. " Yes; it be strong enough to hold a bull on his back—let alone a pig like 'im; an' just long enough to make four ties o't. It's the very identical."

Once more taking out his knife, he cut the cord into four nearly equal pieces. He then proceeded to carry out the design that had shaped itself in his mind; and which, judging by his satisfied air as he set about it, appeared as if it promised to extricate him from his dilemma.

This was simply to strap the drunken man to his truckle; and leave him there—until his restoration to a state of sobriety should render him sensible of the chastisement which he, Garth, intended to return and administer !

As the wood-chopper lay with arms and limbs stretched out to their full length, his inviting attitude appeared to have suggested to Garth this mode of dealing with him.

Chuckling over his work, with the quickness of an expert in the handling of ropes the footpad now proceeded to the accomplishment of his task.

In a few minutes' time, he had fastened the wrists and ankles of the sleeper to the trestles of his couch. This done, he stepped back to take a survey; and as he stood over the unconscious captive, with arms a-kimbo, he broke forth into a fit of uproarious laughter.

" An't he a beauty, as he lays theer ? " said he, as if interrogating some unseen individual. " A reg'lar babe o' the woods ! Only wants the robin-redbreasts to kiver him wi' a scatterin' o' beech leaves ! Now," added he, apostrophizing the fast-bound sleeper, " ye stay theer till I coom back ! I don't say it'll be inside the twenty-four hours ; but if 'tain't, don't be impatient, an' fret yerself 'bout my absence. I've promised I'll coom ; an' ye may be sure o't. For the present, Master Wull Walford, I'll bid ye a good mornin' ! "

Saying this, and placing his cudgel in a corner—where he might readily lay hands upon it again—Garth stepped forth from the hut; carefully closed the door behind him; and took the back track towards the cottage in which he had left the other inebriate, Dancey. Him he now hoped to find in a more fit state, for acting as his co-partner in a scheme, he had partially conceived for the rescue of his imprisoned patron.

CHAPTER XLI.

TEMPTING A SENTINEL.

It yet wanted some minutes of midnight, on that same day, when three individuals were seen issuing out through the narrow doorway of Dick Dancey's cottage and starting off along the path towards Bulstrode Park.

They were two men and a woman, the last so shrouded in cloak and hood that her age could not be guessed at, except from her little form and agile step, both proclaiming her to be young.

The cloak, of a deep crimson color, was the property of Bet Dancey, and it was her bold figure it enveloped.

Her companions were her own father and Gregory Garth.

As the narrow path prevented them from walking side by side, they proceeded in single file, the ex-footpad in the lead, Dancey close following upon his heels, and Bet bringing up the rear.

This arrangement was not favorable to conversation in a low tone of voice; and, as the errand on which they were going abroad at that late hour of night might be supposed to require secrecy, by a tacit understanding between them, all three preserved silence throughout the whole time they were traveling along the forest path.

Wapsey's Wood was separated from the park by a tract of pasture, interspersed with patches of gorse and heather.

Through this the path ran direct to a rustic stile, which permitted a passage over the palings. Inside the enclosure was a broad belt of heavy timber, oak, elm, and chestnut, through which the track continued on towards the dwelling.

It was the south-western wing of Sir Marmaduke's mansion that was thus approached, and the timber once traversed, a portion of the building might be seen, with the walls enclosing the court-yard at the back. The garden, with its fruit trees and ornamental shrubbery, extended in this direction, with its encircling fence; but this being constructed in the style of a moat, and, of course, sunk below the surface of the level, was not visible from a distance.

After passing silently over the stile, the trio of night promenaders forsook the ordinary path, and kept on towards the house in a circuitous direction.

Having traversed the belt of timber with the same cautious silence as they had hitherto observed, they arrived upon its edge, opposite the rear of the mansion, and at a point some hundred yards distant from the moated wall.

There, as if by mutual agreement, they came to a stop, still keeping under the shadow of the trees.

If this precaution was for the purpose of concealment, it was superfluous; for the night was pitch-dark, like that which had preceded it, and in the sky above there were similar indications of a storm.

It was in effect a repetition of that electric congestion that had disturbed the atmosphere on the previous night, to be in like manner dispersed by a deluge of rain.

Between the timber and the shrubbery that surrounded the dwelling lay a piece of open pasture, with tall trees standing over it, at wide intervals apart.

Had it been daylight, or even moonlight, from the point where they had paused, a view of the dwelling-house—comprising the buildings at the back, and a portion of its western façade—could have been distinctly obtained.

As it was, they could only make out a sombre pile, dimly outlined against the dark leaden canopy of heaven; though at intervals, as the lightning shot across the sky, the walls and windows, glancing under its momentary glare, could be traced as distinctly as by day.

After arriving at their post of observation, the three individuals, who had come from Dancey's cottage, continued for a time to preserve a silence that spoke of some important design.

The eyes of all three were turned towards the dwelling; and as the electric blaze illuminated their faces, it disclosed the features of all set in a serious expression.

No light could be seen in any of the windows looking westward; and at that hour, it might have been supposed that the inmates of the mansion had all retired to rest. But there were also windows in the outbuildings; and a faint gleam flickering from one or two of these told, that, either some of the domestics of the establishment, or the troopers quartered upon it, were still burning the midnight oil.

The great gateway, that gave entrance into the court-yard, was visible from this point. When the lightning flashed, they could distinguish the huge oaken folding doors, and see that they were shut but while darkness was on, a tiny stream of yellowish light projecting through an aperture underneath, told that a lamp was burning behind it, inside the archway.

There was no sound to indicate that any one was stirring within the establishment. Occasionally a horse could be heard neighing in the stables, in answer to one that wandered over the pastures of the park—and a dog or two, taking their cue from the king of the domestic quadrupeds, would for some seconds keep awake the hollow echoes of the court-yard with their resonant baying.

While Garth and his two co-adjutors were still listening, the great clock—from the tower that overtopped the mansion—tolled the hour of twelve.

"Thee be quite sure, gurl," said the former, breaking silence, for the first time since leaving the domicile of Dancey, "thee be quite sure about the hour?"

"Quite sure," replied Bet, repeating the words of her interrogator. "He said twelve. He said he would be on guard all night; but from twelve till two would be his turn as sentry over the prisoner. The room is just yonder, inside the archway—where you see the light coming through."

"The old store-room it be," put in Dancey. "I know it well. Many's the fat buck I hae carried in theer, afore Sir Marmaduke took a notion I stealed his deer, an' gie me the sack from looking arter 'em. Gad! them were better times for Dick Dancey!"

"Did he say ye war to come exact at twelve?" pursued Garth, without heeding the interpolation of the discharged keeper.

"No," replied Bet, "not exact at twelve, but soon after. He told me not to come near, until the guard had been changed awhile; and the men relieved—I think he called it—should go back into the court-yard."

"How war ye to know that?"

"He said he would set the lamp down upon the pavement, close to the big door. When I should see the light shining out at the bottom, I was to tap at the wicket, and he'd open it."

"Well, it be shinin' out at the bottom now, and has been for some time—before the clock struck. Is that the way he ment it?"

"No. There's a hole where the cats go out and in. He's to put the lamp there."

" Then it han't been been sot there yet. We must keep a sharp
look out for't. 'Twon't do to lose a precious minnit. Thee be sure
he sayed, he'd let thee speak wi' Master Henry ? "

" He did; he promised me faithfully—I had to give *him* a promise.'

" What did thee promise him, my gurl ? " demanded Dancey, in a
serious tone.

" Oh, nothing much, father," replied Bet, " nothing much, consid
ering what I did it for."

" Niver mind yer daughter, Dancey. She be old enough to take
care o' herself. The gurl'll do what's right, I warrant her."

" Ay, and that wouldn't have been any good," pursued Bet; " he'd
never have consented to let me in, but that he believes I'm sent by a
great lady. I had to tell him that story, God forgive me ! "

" It be only a white lie, gurl ;" said Garth, in a tone of encouragement. If ivery lie as be told war in as good a cause, they'd all be forgiven up yonder, I dare say."

As Garth said this, he turned his eyes reverently upward. " Ho ! "
cried he, lowering them suddenly ; and directing his glance towards
the gateway, " Yonner it be ! The lamp is i' the cat-hole ! "

Under one of the folds of the great oaken door—conspicuous through
the aperture already spoken of—a disc of dull yellowish light was
now visible ; which on scrutiny could be seen to be burning inside a
lamp of not very translucent glass. It was one of the common stable
lanthorns of the establishment—now doing guard duty in the quarters of the cuirassier troop.

The signal was too marked to be mistaken.

The girl, on perceiving it, only waited for some further instructions
—given in a hurried manner by her two companions; and which were
but the impressive repetition of those already imparted, previous to
sallying forth from the cottage.

As soon as she had received them, she drew her cloak closely round
her ; and, gliding across the stretch of open pasture, arrived in front
of the great gateway—inside of which was imprisoned the man, for
whose sake she was about to risk moral shame ; and perhaps personal punishment

In front of the wicket, she paused for some minutes—partly to
recover her breath, lost in the hurried traverse across the pasture—
and partly to strengthen her resolution of carrying through the task
she had undertaken.

Bold as was the heart of the deer-stealer's daughter, it was not
without misgivings at that moment. Might not the soldier have sum-

moned her thither to betray her? Might he not have contrived some
design to get her within his power? Perhaps accuse her of treason
to the king: or, by the threat of such accusation, endeavor to procure
her compliance with some love proposals he had already half hinted
to her?

On the other hand, these proposals were not exactly of an insulting
nature. There had been a certain degree of soldierly honor in the
intercourse that had passed between herself and Withers—for Withers it was who had invited her to share his hours of guard.

She had slightly known the young man, previous to his enlistment
into the corps of cuirassiers; and, although he had since passed
through a malignant school, she could scarcely believe him so bad as
those with whom he was associating.

At that crisis, however, it mattered little how bad he might be.
She had gone too far to think of withdrawing from the danger. She
was too near the man she loved—with the full fierce ardor of her out-
cast heart—too near to go back, without making an effort to see, and
if possible, save him. As the thought of *his* danger came once more
before her mind, she threw aside all regard for consequences; and,
advancing with fearless step, she knocked gently, but resolutely,
against the door.

Close succeeding this preconcerted signal, the tread of a trooper's
boot was heard on the pavement inside, and with a subdued sound
that denoted caution. Some one was approaching the wicket.

On reaching the door, the footfall ceased to be heard; and the wicket
was opened with a silence that bespoke expectancy, on the part of him
who drew back the bolt.

Very different from the salutation of a sentry—the bold *brusque*
"Who goes there?"—was the soft whisper that fell upon the ears
of the person claiming admission.

"Is it you, sweet Betsey?" asked the soldier; and then, without
waiting for a verbal answer to his interrogatory, he continued: "Come
in, dear girl! I have been so longing for twelve o'clock, I thought
it would never strike up there. I believe the old time-piece be out o'
tune. It an't often I'm so weary for my turn o' the night guard.
Come in!"

The girl having got over the slight shiver of timidity—that had
temporarily possessed her—accepted the invitation; and, stepping
over the threshold of the wicket, stood inside the arched entrance
which formed a covered passage between the gate and the court-yard
beyond.

This passage was only illuminated by the lantern; which, from its position at the bottom of the door, where it had been placed to effect the signal, gave out but a feeble light. As Withers, at that moment, had no wish for a better, the lamp was allowed to remain where he had placed it.

There was enough light proceeding from it to show the side door conducting into the store-room, the improvised prison of Henry Holt-spur, which was the chief point the sentry had been instructed to guard. Upon this door the eyes of his visitor became directed, as soon as she entered under the archway; and to it her glance kept constantly returning—despite the efforts of Withers to fix it upon himself.

He could not help observing the air of abstraction with which his supposed sweetheart listened to his protestations of love. He noticed her glance repeatedly directed towards the door of the store-room, with an eagerness that caused him some chagrin; though he was only annoyed, that so little attention was being paid to his own bland-ishments.

Had he suspected the true cause of Bet Dancey's indifference, the door of Holtspur's prison would not have turned upon its hinges that night—at least not during Withers' *tour* of guard.

"Come, Mistress Betsey!" said he, in his endeavors to secure a greater share of the girls attention. "Don't talk about that affair just yet. You can deliver your message to the gentleman by-and-by 'Twont take long, I suppose?"

"Only a minute," replied Bet, "and that's just why I want to have it over."

"Ah! that," said Withers, beginning to flatter himself that his sweetheart was impatient to get through with the more disagreeable part of her errand, so as to have it off her hands. "Ah! well; of course, Mistress Betsey——"

"You know," interrupted the girl, "one should always do their business first? Business first and pleasure afterwards."

"Bah!" muttered Withers, "*that* an't always the best way; least-wise not to you or me. Let the bizness stand over a bit."

"Oh! no, no!" answered Betsey, with increasing impatience. "If the lady who sent me only knew that I was trifling in this way, there *would* be a trouble. I'd not get the reward she has promised me. You can't believe how impatient *she'll* be, till she hears the answer I'm to take back to her!"

"Oh! bother *her* impatience! Let her wait, charming Betsey!"

"Nay, Master Withers; listen to reason. Suppose it was you who were in prison; and some one wanted to hear from you; myself for instance. Would you say, 'let her wait,' then? I pray you, don't detain me now : you can see me to-morrow. Come to the cottage; and stay as long as you like. Father will be from home; and you may talk as much nonsense as you have a mind to."

"What a seducing Syren!" said her suitor, evidently gratified at the pretty programme thus sketched out for him. "Well! I agree to it. But you must give me a kiss before you go in; and promise me another on your coming out."

"With all my heart!" readily responded the representative of Maid Marian. "You're welcome to a kiss. Take it."

And, without waiting for Withers to fling his arms around her, or even meet her half way, she craned her neck forward, and pressed her protruded lips against the rough cheek of the trooper.

"There now!" was the ejaculation that accompanied the loud smacking noise caused by the contact, "will that satisfy you?"

"No dear Betsey; nor a hundred thousand of the same. With such sweetness a man would never be satisfied; but always awantin' more. Ah! they may talk about them girls in Flanders. Gi' me the kiss o' a English lass. It's got the jiniwine flavor about it."

"All flattery! Come now! keep your promise—if you expect me to keep mine, when I come out again."

"I'll do it, sweet. But hark'ee! Don't make no noise inside. If the guard corporal should come round and find what's goin' on, he'd change me from a sentry to a prisoner—in less time than it 'ud take to tell what's o'clock. Ah! now; one more afore you go in?"

The girl, without hesitation, a second time delivered her cheek to be kissed by the ready lips of her soldier lover; and then, muttering something like a promise—to permit more than one repetition of the dose when she should come out again—the store-room door was opened to her; and, without further interruption, she was admitted within the precinct of Holtspur's prison.

CHAPTER XLII.

MUTUAL DISTRUST.

During all that day had the imprisoned patriot been chafing under his confinement. Since his capture he had been treated like a criminal—housed and fed, as if he were a criminal already convicted.

There was no furniture in the small apartment in which he had been locked up. Only some articles of storage and lumber; but neither chair, table, nor bed. A rough bench was the substitute for all these. On this he sat, sometimes reclined; though he did not often change from one attitude to the other—on account of the difficulty attending the operation; for like a criminal was he also bound. His wrists were crossed behind his back, and there tightly tied; while as additional security against any attempt to escape, his ankles were lashed together by a piece of splicing rope.

He had made no effort to free himself. The thing appeared hopeless. Even could he have got rid of his rope fastenings, there was a locked door, with a sentry all the time standing, or pacing, outside.

Though keenly feeling the indignity thus put upon him—and sensible of the great danger in which his life was now placed—he had other thoughts that were still more bitter to bear.

Marion Wade was the object of these reflections—she, and her white gauntlet. Not that one, he had himself so proudly worn; but its fellow, which he had seen so tauntingly set on the helmet of the cuirassier captain.

All day long—and it had appeared of endless length—as well as during the hours of the night already passed, scarce for a moment had his mind been able to escape from that harrassing thought.

Notwithstanding his efforts to repudiate the suspicion—despite that reckless disavowal of it before Scarthe himself—he could not hinder its recurrence. A hundred times did he ask himself the question: whether Scarthe had come surreptitiously by the glove, or whether it had been given him as a love token, like his own?

Over and over did he review the various circumstances that had transpired between himself and Marion Wade; from the hour when

12*

riding listlessly along the forest road, he had been startled into a quick surprise at the sight of her peerless beauty—a surprise as rapidly changing into admiration Then the after encounters upon the same road—which might have appeared accidental to any other mind than one quickened with love; the dropping of the gauntlet, that might have been deemed a thing of chance, but for the after interview, and confession that it was *design*; and those fervent speeches, that had passed between them—were they not vows, springing from the profoundest depths of her soul? And had she not, on that same occasion, made to him a complete surrender of her heart—as he to her? If words were to be believed, he had won the heart of Marion Wade. How could he doubt it?

He could, and *did* doubt; not that she had spoken love words to him, and listened to his, with apparent complaisance. He could not doubt that—unless under the belief that he had been dreaming. His uncertainty was of a different character—far more unpleasant. It was the suspicion that Marion Wade could give love-looks, speak love-words, and drop love-tokens at pleasure! That which she had done to him, she might do to another. In short he had given way to the belief *that she had been coquetting with him.*

Of all the pangs that passion may inflict upon the heart of man, this is the most poignant. Love, unrequited, stings sharply enough; but when it has been promised requital—caressed to full fervor, and deluded by a pseudo-reciprocation—afterwards to have its dust-bedimmed eyes open to the delusion—then indeed does jealousy become what it has been the fashion to call it—*a monster*.

There is no cruelty to be compared with that of the coquette.

Was Marion Wade one of this class?

A hundred times did Holtspur ask the question. A hundred times did he repudiate the suspicion; but, alas! as often did a voice speaking harshly within his soul give forth the response:—

"It is possible."

Ay, and probable too! So ran his imaginings.

Perhaps its probability was more conceivable to the mind of Henry Holtspur, from a sad experience of woman's deceitfulness, that had clouded the sky of his early life—just at that period when the sun of his fortune was ascending towards its zenith.

"Surely," said he—for the twentieth time indulging in the conjecture, "she must know that I am here? She cannot help knowing it. And yet, no message from her—not one word of inquiry! I could not be more neglected in a dungeon of the Inquisition Is it that they are hindered—forbidden communication with me? I would fain believe it so. They cannot have so suddenly abandoned a friend-ship commencing so cordially, and which, though only of yesterday, promised to be permanent? Why do they, all at once, thus coldly turn from me?

"Ah! what have men not done—what will they not do, to stand clear of the ruin that threatens to fall? It may be that one and all of them have repudiated me, she, too, disclaiming a connection that could but disgrace her?

"Perhaps even now, on the other side of these massive walls, there is a scene of gayety in which all are taking part, both the family and its guests? Perhaps at this moment she may be the gayest and hap-piest of all? Her new fancy seated by her side, or hovering around her, whispering honeyed speeches into her ear, beguiling her with those words of wickedness, whose usage he well understands? And she, all the while, smiling and listening? Oh!"

The final exclamation was uttered in a groan, betraying how pain-ful was the picture which his jealous fancy had conjured up.

And a fancy it was.

Could his eye at that moment have pierced the massive walls, men-tioned in his soliloquy, he might have discovered how unjust, how groundless, were his hypothetical accusations. He would have seen Marion Wade a sufferer like himself, suffering from almost a similar cause.

She was in her sleeping chamber, and alone. She had been there for hours; but still her couch remained unpressed. The silken coverlet lay smoothly over the pillow of down, without any sign of having been upturned. Nor was there in her attitude aught that would indicate an intention of retiring to that luxurious place of re-pose.

On the night before, in the same chamber, had she been equally the victim of unrest, though not to the same degree. Then had she been only apprehensive of danger to her lover; but still undisturbed by a doubt of his fidelity. Now the danger had descended—the doubt had arisen. Then her apprehensions had been relieved; and she had fallen into a slumber—so profound, that the hoof-strokes of a single horse—heard, half an hour afterwards, passing over the same path traversed by Scarthe and his subaltern—did not awake her Neither had the trampling of thirty steeds ridden by the same num ber of steel-clad cuirassiers, with tinkling spurs and clinking sabres —as several hours after they filed under the casement of her chamber, taking their departure from the park.

It was after daybreak on that morning when Marion Wade awoke from a prolonged slumber. Then only on hearing noises without, that might have aroused even the heaviest sleeper; the braying of a bugle—the quick word of command loudly pronounced, the shrill neighing of hórses—in short, all those sounds that indicate the proximity of a cohort of cavalry.

Marion sprang from her couch, her cousin close following her example.

They stood trembling in the middle of the room. Modesty forbade a nearer approach to the window; while curiosity, and, in the mind of Marion, a far stronger sentiment, urged them towards it.

The *presentiment* was upon her, then more impressive than ever. She could not resist it; and, snatching the first garment that came within reach—a scarf it chanced to be—she threw it over her shoulders, already enrobed in her ample chevelure of golden hair, and silently glided into the embayment of the window.

Not long stayed she there. The terrible tableau, that came under her eyes, prevented her from protracting that daring reconnoissance.

A squadron of cuirassiers, formed in line, with the heads of their horses turned towards the window—on the right flank, their captain, Richard Scarthe—on the left, his subaltern, Stubbs—this was the spectacle presented to her view.

In the centre—and there alone had dwelt the glance of Marion Wade—was a man mounted upon a coal-black horse—conspicuous above all the rest for noble mien, and proud bearing—but, alas! conspicuous also as *a prisoner.*

It required no scrutiny to tell who he was—at least on the part of Marion Wade. A single glance had been sufficient for the recognition of Henry Holtspur.

The long look she gave was scarce one of inquiry. Its object was not to identify the prisoner. It was not directed either upon his figure, or his face; but upon a spray of withered red blossoms that hung drooping over the brim of his beaver.

Marion Wade receded from the window with as much suddenness, as when, some hours before, her modesty had taken alarm at the exposing flash of the electric light.

Far different, however, was the fashion of her retreat. She fell fainting upon the floor !

With such a shaft rankling in her bosom, no wonder that Marion Wade had now no inclination for sleep; and showed no signs of an intention to retire to her couch.

On the contrary, she was equipped as for a journey—at all events, as if she intended going forth into the open air. A dark velvet cloak of large dimensions completely shrouded her figure; while her head was enveloped in a hood, which, by means of its drawstring, almost concealed her face—at the same time covering those luxuriant locks, like streams of molten gold, that gave a sort of divine character to her countenance.

Had her face been seen at that moment, it would have appeared pale—that is, paler than its wont: for the cheeks of Marion Wade could never have shown colorless. Even in death one might have fancied they would preserve that luminous roseate hue; which, like a halo, seemed constantly suspended over her countenance.

Her eyes more truthfully told the tale. They were swollen, and scarce dried of recent tears. Only one had seen them fall. Only one —her cousin Lora—knew why Marion Wade had been weeping. She had kept her chamber all the day, with Lora as her companion; but long before midnight, the latter had been desired to withdraw, and leave her alone. Lora had not been made the confidant of all her secrets. There was one she had reserved.

All day had she been thinking over the spectacle of the morning. The man she loved, worshiped with all the warm wild fervor of her maiden heart, that man a prisoner in the power of a cruel and vindictive enemy; paraded before all the world—before herself—as a criminal; rudely dragged along by a guard of ruffianly soldiers; disgraced—no, not disgraced, for such treatment could not bring disgrace upon a noble patriot—but in danger of his life!

And yet it was not this that had drawn from the eyes of Marion Wade those hot scalding tears! It was not this which had caused her to fall fainting upon the floor. Alas! no. Both the tears and the syncope had a different origin than the beholding Henry Holtspur in bonds. They were not tears of sympathy, but of bitterness— springing from the fountain of love, that had become defiled with jealousy. They could be traced to those flowers, worn upon the beaver of the black horseman. The faded blossoms had been seen; and, in Marion's beguiled imagination, had been recognized.

To think he should be wearing them, and at such a time! In the hour of his adversity; as if to sanctify them by a greater regard

It was this thought that had momentarily deprived Marion Wade of her senses.

She had recovered them; but not along with them her tranquillity of spirit.

To her that day had been one of fearful reflections. Every hour had its chapter of stinging thoughts—every minute its miserable emotion.

Love and jealousy—sympathy and spite—had alternated all day long; each in turn holding possession of her tortured soul.

It was now the hour of midnight, and the wicked passions had succumbed: the virtuous emotions had triumphed. Love and sympathy were in the ascendant!

Marion Wade was upon the eve of attempting the accomplishment of a purpose that would prove, not only the depth of her love, but its noble unselfishness.

Could Holtspur have beheld her at this moment—could he have guessed her design—he would have withheld that recrimination, which in the bitterness of spirit he had permitted to pass from his lips.

CHAPTER XLIII.

A PRISON VISITOR.

It has been deemed strange that two individuals should conceive the same thought, at the same instant of time. Those who are skilled in psychology will not be surprised by such coincidence.

Like circumstances produce like results, in the world of mind, as in that of matter; and an instance may be found in the similar idea conceived at the same time by Marion Wade and Elizabeth Dancey—a lady of high rank, and a lass of low degree.

Both were in love with the same man—Henry Holtspur, the prisoner.

Both had bethought them of a plan for delivering him from his prison; and if there was anything singular, it was, that their schemes were in almost exact correspondence.

The velvet-hooded cloak under which was concealed the face and form of Marion Wade had been put on with the same design, as that garment, of somewhat similar make, but coarser material, that shrouded the shape of Dick Dancey's daughter.

Both were bent upon one and the same errand.

There may have been some difference as to the means and hopes directed towards its accomplishment; but none as to the motive—none as to the time intended for its trial.

Both had chosen the hour of midnight.

Neither was this an accidental coincidence.

No more than Bet Dancey, had Marion Wade trusted to chance as to the hour for making the attempt.

During the day she had made her inquiries; and resolved upon her measures.

Through the medium of a confidential maid—also an old acquaintance of the soldier Withers—she had ascertained that the latter would be on post over the prisoner from twelve till two at night.

She had learnt, moreover, some things about the character and disposition of this trustworthy sentinel—leading her to believe that he would not prove an exception to the general rule of mankind; and that gold would overcome his scruples—if administered in sufficient quantity. For this sufficiency had she provided.

Even without regard to these considerations, the hour of midnight was one that might have been chosen on its own account.

All the dwellers within the mansion—as well as its stranger guests—would be then abed; and there would be less chance of her design being frustrated by discovery.

It was a mere accident that caused a difference of some ten minutes of time, between the arrival of his two deliverers at the door of Holtspur's prison; and in this, the lass had gained the advantage over the lady.

At the moment when Bet Dancey was standing before the wicket, Marion Wade was stealing softly from her chamber to make her way through darkness down the great staircase, and along the silent halls and corridors of the paternal mansion.

Inside his silent cell, Holtspur had heard the clock strike the hour of twelve, in solemn lugubrious tones—too consonant with his own thoughts. It was the twelve of midnight.

"I wish it were twelve of to-morrow's nocn," soliloquized he, when the tolling had ceased. "If I have correctly interpreted the conversation I overheard this morning, ere that hour, I shall be far from this place. So—the Tower is my destination. After that—ay, what after that? Perhaps—the block? Why fear I to pronounce the word? I may as well look it boldly in the face; for I know that the vengeance of that vile woman—that has pursued me all through life—since she could not have my heart, will be satisfied with nothing less than my head. It is *her* hand I recognize in this—her hand that penned the postscript to that dispatch; or, at all events, it was she who dictated it.

"I wish it were the hour to depart hence. There can be no dungeon in the Tower so terrible as this—on one side of the wall hell, on the other side paradise. I can think only of paradise when Marion is present. She so dear to me—so near to me—almost breathing the same atmosphere: and yet oblivious of my existence! Perhaps ——

"Ha! footsteps stirring outside? The sentry talking to some one! 'Tis the voice of a woman!

"One of the domestics of the mansion, I suppose, who has stolen forth to exchange the day's gossip with the guard? 'Tis a late hour for the girl to be gadding; but perhaps 'tis the hour of her choice? I can envy this wench and her soldier sweetheart their easy opportunities. Perhaps equally to be envied is the free and easy fashion with which they enter upon a love affair, and escape out of it? With them there is no such terrible contingency as a broken heart. To morrow he may be gone; and the day after she will be as gay as ever!

"How different with a passion like mine! Absence can have no effect upon it. Not even the terrors of the Tower can bring it to a termination. It will end only under the ax of the executioner—if that is to be my fate.

"These gossips are getting nearer the door. Though they are talking in a low tone, I might hear what they say, by placing my ear to the key-hole. I have no inclination to make myself the depository of their coarse love secrets; but perhaps I may hear something of myself, or of *her*! That may make it worth my while to play eavesdropper."

The prisoner rose from his seat; and succeeded in getting himself into an erect attitude. But all at once he sank upon the bench; and only by adroitly balancing his body did he save himself from falling upon the floor.

"By the good St. Vitus!" he exclaimed, rather amused at his misadventure; "I had forgotten that my feet were not free. After all, what I should hear might not be worth the effort. I'll leave them to keep their secrets—whatever they be—to themselves."

So resolving, he resumed his sedentary attitude upon the bench, and remained silent; but as before, listening.

By this, the speakers had approached nearer to the door; and their words could now be distinctly heard inside the store-room.

"So!" resumed Holtspur, after listening for a short while; "lovers, as I suspected. He talks of kissing her! I can hear that word above all the others. Ho! they are pressing against the door! What! Surely the key turns in the lock? Can they be coming in?"

The question was answered by the unlocking of the door: which upon the next instant swung silently upon its hinges, until it stood half open. Against the glimmer of the lamp outside, Holtspur could dimly distinguish two forms—one of them a woman.

The male figure was the nearer one; though the woman was close behind.

On opening the door, the sentry had thrust his head inside the room; but evidently without any design of introducing his body.

"Are you sleepin', master?" interrogated he, speaking in a low tone that did not seem unkindly, and only a little louder than a whisper.

"No," replied the prisoner, answering the man frankly, while imitating his cautious tone.

"All right, then!" said the sentry; "for there be a lady here as wants to have a word with ye; an' as I s'pose ye don't care to do yer talkin' i' the dark, I'll lend ye my lamp for a bit. But don't make yer di'logue a long un; there be danger in what I'm doin'."

So saying, the trooper walked back into the archway, for the purpose of fetching his lamp; while the woman pushing past him, stepped inside the room.

As the phrase "there be a lady," fell from the lips of the sentinel, the heart of Henry Holtspur throbbed quick within his bosom. Sweet thoughts welled up at the words.

Could he have been mistaken in believing his midnight visitor a domestic of the mansion? *Might it not be its mistress?*

In the dim light he saw a female form closely wrapped in hood and cloak. In that guise, she might be either a peasant or a princess The figure was tall, upright, commanding. Such was that of Marion Wade!

Holtspur's fond fancy was destined to a short indulgence. The lamp was passed through the half-opened door, and placed upon a stool that stood near. Its glare fell upon the form of his visitor—lighting up a crimson cloak—lighting up features of a gipsy type, with dark, flashing eyes—beautiful features, it is true, but altogether unlike the angelic countenance he had been conjuring up—the countenance of Marion Wade.

"It was not she—only Maid Marian!"

Holtspur's hopeful glance suddenly changed to one of disappointment, as he identified the daughter of the deerstealer. Perhaps it was well for him—for both—that Betsey did not observe the transformation. The obscure light of the lamp hindered the girl from having a chagrin, equal, if not greater, than his.

"Mistress Betsey!" he exclaimed, on recovering from the first flutter of his surprise. " You here! What has brought you to my prison?"

"Hush!" ejaculated the girl, moving rapidly forward from the door—which the sentry had taken the precaution to shut behind him. "Speak only in whispers! I've come to save you—to get you out of this ugly place."

"But how? 'Tis not possible, I fear? The door is guarded—the sentry is outside? I could not go forth without being seen?"

"You *will* be seen—that's true. But it won't matter a bit. If you'll follow my directions, you'll get out without being hindered. That's sufficient. Father and Master Garth planned it all before we left home. They are waiting for you on the edge of the wood—up the hill, just behind the house."

"Ah! a plan for me to escape? What is it, my brave Betsey?"

" You're to take my cloak. It's a long one; and will reach nigh down to your feet. But, for fear it wouldn't, I brought an extra skirt along with me. Here it is."

Saying this, the girl whipped the cloak from her shoulders—disclosing at the same time a skirt of some kind of coarse stuff, which she had been carrying under her arm.

"Now, sir!" she continued, in a tone of urgency; "on with them as quick as you can; for he may get impatient, and want to come in."

"What?" exclaimed Holtspur, whose surprise at the proposal was only equaled by admiration of her who had made it. "And do you mean that I am to pass out—disguised in your garments—and leave you here?"

"Of course I do. What other way is there? We can't both get out. He'd stop you for a certainty; and me too, maybe, for trying to get you away. You must go out *alone*."

"And leave you behind—to be punished for aiding me to escape! No, generous girl! I had rather die, than do that."

"Oh, sir! don't talk in that foolish way. Pray go as I tell you to. Have no fear for me! They can't do much to a girl that's got nothing to lose. Besides, I don't feel much afeared of getting him to pass me out afterwards. It'll be no good his keeping me in. That won't save him from whatever they may do to him."

The *him* thus pointedly alluded to was the amorous sentry; who was just then heard passing to and fro upon his round, with a step that denoted impatience.

"Oh, sir, go! I beg of you go—or—I—we may never see you again."

There was a tone of sadness in the entreaty, which Holtspur could hardly have failed to notice. But the appeal had shaken his resolution to remain. From what she had said, he saw that in all probability the girl would get clear, or with some slight punishment. Perhaps she might succeed in deceiving the sentry still farther, and escape without difficulty. Holtspur knew she was clever and quick-witted.

"Never fear for me, sir!" said she, as if interpreting his thoughts. "I can manage *him*. He'll do what I want him to; I know he will."

"If I thought that——"

"You *may* think it," responded she, at the same time cutting the cords that bound the prisoner; "you may be sure of it. Leave him to me. Now, sir, the cloak. No, the skirt first. That's the way to fix it. Now the cloak. Here! put your head into the hood—draw it well over your face. That'll do. When you go out, don't stop to speak to him. He'll want to kiss you—I know that. You mustn't let him; but keep quick on to the door. The wicket is on the latch. When you get outside you can run as fast as you like. Make for the trees at the top of the hill. There you will find father along with your own man, Master Garth. It's dark as pitch outside. I'll keep the lamp here till you get through the passage. I defy him to tell it isn't *me*, if you don't let him kiss you. Don't do that; but pass him as rapidly as you can. Now you're ready? Go!"

This long chapter of directions was spoken more quickly than it can be read. Before the final word was uttered, Bet Dancey had succeeded in disguising the prisoner.

She herself retained her complete dress—the only part of her being left uncovered being her head and shoulders.

Holtspur gazed for a moment upon the generous, boldly beautiful girl; and with a glance that told of tenderness. She might have mistaken it for a look of love. Alas!—for her sake,—alas—it was only the gaze of gratitude.

At that moment the sentry struck his halbert against the stoop—as if summoning them to a separation.

"Coming, Master Withers! I'm coming," cried the girl in an undertone, at the same time placing her lips close to the key-hole: "open, and let me out!"

The bolt was turned briskly at the words. Withers was longing for that promised kiss. The door was re-opened; and the cloaked figure glided forth into the darkness.

Withers closed the door behind it—without going inside for his lantern. He did not desire light just then; nor the delay of getting one. He could return for the lamp at any time—after that pleasant occupation in which he anticipated engaging himself.

He only waited to secure the bolt against any chance of the prisoner's attempting to come forth.

This occupied him scarce ten seconds of time; but short as was the delay, it lost him his expected pleasure.

As he turned round after locking the door, he heard the click of the wicket latch and the moment after saw the cloaked form of his supposed sweetheart outlined in the opening. In another instant she had passed through, slamming the wicket behind her!

Thinking there might still be a chance of securing the kiss, Withers ran to the front entrance; and, re-opening the wicket, stepped briskly outside.

"Confound the vixen!" he muttered, as he stood peering into the darkness; "I b'lieve she be clear gone away! Mistress Betsey! Mistress Betsey! where are ye, gurl? Wont ye come back and keep yer promise?"

As he made this appeal, he fancied he saw her figure some score of yards out in front of the gateway; where the next moment it mysteriously disappeared, as if sinking into the earth!

Neither of his interrogatories met with a response. From the low tone in which he spoke, it was scarce likely he had been heard He dared not call aloud—lest his voice might summon the guard from the inner court.

"Confound the vixen!" he once more muttered; "she be gone for certain, and's tricked me out o' that kiss.

"It an't so much matter, arter all," continued he; making a feint at self-consolation. "I can make up for it to-morrow, by taking as mary as I want. She's afeerd to keep the lady waitin'—whoever she be—an' not gettin' the shiners that's been promised her. She's right, maybe. She knows she'll see me agin; so let her go."

And with this consolatory reflection, he turned back into the arched entrance, with the intention of recovering the lamp left in the apartment of the prisoner.

CHAPTER XLIV.

AN UNEXPECTED ENCOUNTER.

While proceeding along the passage, it occurred to Withers that he had left the wicket on the latch. With this unlocked, and the door of the store-room open at the same time, there might be danger of the prisoner making his escape.

He knew that the latter was fast bound, both hand and foot; but, in his soldiering experience, he had known more than one captive get free from such fastenings.

To make safe, therefore, he turned back towards the outer gate, with the intention of securing it.

As he stood holding the wicket in his hand, a thought influenced him to look once more into the darkness.

Perhaps, after all, Betsey might come back?

Her running away might have been only a frolic on her part; meant merely to tease him?

He would take another look out, at any rate.

There could be no harm in that.

With this resolve he remained, holding the door half open; and peering out into the darkness.

He had been thus occupied scarce ten seconds of time, when an object appeared before his eyes that elicited from him a series of joyful ejaculations.

It was the figure of a woman wrapped in hood and cloak, coming round an angle of the wall, and evidently advancing towards the spot were he stood.

Who could it be but Betsey?

"Good!" cried Withers. "She has not gone arter all. That be she coming back round the corner o' the house. 'Tan't the way I thought she went off; but I must ha' been mistaken. Yes, she it be; cloak, hood, an' all! I might ha' knowed she wouldn't go 'ithout gettin' the kiss. I'm glad on't hows'soever. A bird i' the hand's worth two i' the bush."

As the soldier thus congratulated himself on the re-appearance of his sweetheart, and was chuckling over the near prospect of that promised "smack," the cloaked figure arrived in front of the gateway, and stopped within a few paces of him.

"I thought ye were gone, an' hed gi'en me the slip, Mistress Betsey," said he, stepping a pace or two outward to get nearer to her. "It's very kind o' ye to come back. Why, ye look as if ye were frightened? Don't be scared to come near me. Come up, now, an' gie me the kiss ye promised. Come, that be a good lass!"

He was about opening his arms to offer what he supposed would be a welcome embrace, when at that moment the lightning gave forth a vivid flash, disclosing in the figure before him not the crimson-cloaked peasant girl, from whom he had so lately parted, but a lady richly enrobed in silk, satin, and velvet!

On the slender white fingers, that protruding from her cloak held its hood closed over her chin, he had seen, under the electric light, the sheen of sparkling jewels.

There was no mistaking the style of the personage that had thus presented herself.

Without doubt some grand dame—a "lady of the land."

On perceiving his mistake, the surprised sentry gave way to a series of very natural reflections.

"It be the one as sent Betsey. Sure it be! She's growed impatient, an' come herself. I s'pose she'll want to go in an' see h'm, too? Well, for a kiss, I don't mind lettin' her; though I'd rayther a hed that buss from Betsey."

"Good night, sir!" said the lady, speaking in a tone that courted conciliation, though indicative of some surprise at the style of the sentry's first salutation.

"The same to yerself, mistress!" rejoined the soldier, putting on his most courteous air; "may I be so bold as to ask yer irrend? It be a dark night for a fine lady to be abroad, an' late, too!"

"If I mistake not," said she, without heeding the interrogatory "you are Withers?"

On putting this question, she approached a little nearer to the sentry—as she did so, drawing her jeweled hand within the cloak, and letting the hood fall back from her head.

Her beautiful face would have been visible, but for the absence of light; and trusting to this, she had no fear of being recognized.

"Withers, madam! William Withers; that be my name, at your service."

"Thanks, Master Withers, for saying so: since in truth I want you to do me a service."

"Name it, fair lady!" gallantly challenged the young cuirassier.

"You are on guard over a prisoner. I need not say who that prisoner is—since I believe there is but one. I want to see him. 'Tis on very important business."

"Oh! I understand;" said Withers, looking superlatively wise.

"I want only a word with him. You can give me the opportunity?"

"Certain I can;" replied the sentry, "if ye think it be necessary for ye to see him yerself."

"Oh! sir—it is necessary!"

"Well, I didn't know that. I thought the message ye sent by the gurl would be sufficient. She's been, an' seen 'im an' gone agin. Ye han't met her, then, I suppose?"

"Met her! Who?"

"Why, the young gurl ye sent to speak 'ith 'im inside."

"I—I—sent no one."

These monosyllabic words were pronounced with a choking uttarance; that betrayed something more than surprise.

"O-ah!" muttered the sentry; "there's anotner, then, as has private bizness wi' my prisonner. All the fine ladies i' the land appear to be runnin arter 'im. Well; I won't make fish o' one an' flesh a' t'other. This un shall have her chance as well as the one that sent Betsey; an' since she's come herself, i'stead a' doin' the thing b' deputy. she desarves to heve at least as good a opportunity as the t'other. Fair play in love as well as in war—that be Will Withers' way o' thinkin'.

" I say, mistress," continued he, once more addressing himself to the lady. " I heve no objection to yer goin' inside a minute—if ye promise me not to make it long."

"Oh! I promise it, good Withers! You shall not go unrewarded. Take this in return for your generous kindness."

At these words the jeweled hand re-appeared outside the foldings of the velvet—this time with the palm held upwards.

Another gleam just then illuminated the atmosphere, enabling the sentry to perceive the bounteous bribe that was offered to him.

The outspread palm was covered with coins—as many as could lie upon it. Surely it was not the electric light that had given to them their yellow tint? No. Withers could not be mistaken. The coins were gold!

Without saying a word, he stretched out his own large paw till it touched the delicate fingers of the lady; and then, permitting the pieces of gold to slip into his palm, he quickly transferred them to his pocket.

"Yer hand, mistress, for another purpose;" said he holding out his own to take it; and as the trembling fingers were deposited within his, he stepped sideways inside the wicket, leading the lady after him.

In this fashion, they traversed the dark archway—until they had reached the entrance to the store-room.

There stopping, the sentry once more turned the key in the lock; and, as before, pushed the door partially open.

" Ho! master! " said he, again directing his voice into the room, but without going in himself; "here's another feminine come to speak 'ith ye as were before. Now, mistress; go in! Ye'll find the gentleman inside."

So saying, he handed the lady over the threshold; closed and locked the door behind her; and walked back towards the wicket—partly to see whether Bet Dancey might not still be lingering outside; but also with the idea of submitting his treasure to the test of another flash of the lightning: in order to assure himself that the coins were gold!

It is scarce necessary to say, that the second visitor to the cell of the imprisoned patriot was Marion Wade. That will have been guessed already.

Had the lamp remained where the sentry had first set it, the daughter of Sir Marmaduke could not have been two seconds within the store-room, without discovering who was its occupant. As it was, a short interval elapsed before she became aware of the strange transformation that had taken place in the *personnel* of the prison.

On hearing the key grating in the lock, the substitute of Henry Holtspur—believing it to be a visit of inspection on the part of the guard corporal, or some similar intrusion, had suddenly snatched the lamp from off the stool, and placed it in a less conspicuous position, behind some lumber in a corner of the room.

The result was to make that portion occupied by herself, almost as obscure as if no light was in the place; and the girl, who had glided back to the bench, and taken her seat upon it, might without close scrutiny have been taken for a man—for Henry Holtspur.

And for him was she for a time mistaken. It was under this belief, that Marion made that timid and trembling approach: and this it was that caused her voice to quiver, as she faltered forth his name.

The voice that spoke in response, at once dispelled the illusion. It was not that of Henry Holtspur, which would have been known to Marion Wade, despite the obscurity that surrounded her. It was not the voice of any man. It was a woman's.

Before the lady could recover from her surprise, the form of a woman, tall as her own, was seen rising erect from the bench; then stepping forth from the shadowed side of the room until the face was conspicuously displayed under the light of the lamp.

Marion Wade recognized that countenance, as one that had often, too often, disturbed her dreams. It was Bet Dancey who was thus unexpectedly confronting her.

The short, sharp scream that escaped from the lips of the lady expressed an emotion stronger than surprise.

It comprehended that and far more. She who had uttered it comprehended all!

This was the girl who had been sent to speak with the prisoner Who sent her?

No one,

15

She had come on her own errand.

She had come, and *he* was gone?

She had rescued him, by remaining in his place!

These thoughts followed one another so rapidly, as to be almost simultaneous.

They had all passed through the mind of Marion Wade, before a word was exchanged betwen herself and the individual who stood before her.

The latter, with equally quick comprehension, interpreted the presence of the lady in that apartment.

She had come in the same cause as herself though too late for a like success

Not a doubt had Bet Dancey that she in the dark velvet cloak had entered that room with the design of releasing the prisoner—in the same manner as she had herself done scarce five minutes before.

She well knew who was her competitor in this self-sacrificing game

If the black hair and dark flashing orbs of Dick Dancey's daughter had disturbed the dreams of Marion Wade, so too had the golden tresses and blue beaming eyes of Sir Marmaduke's, more than once, rendered uneasy the slumbers of the forest maiden.

The understanding was mutual.

In her own thoughts each found a key to the actions of the other.

The rivals stood face to face—Marion shrinking, chagrined—Betsey unabashed, triumphant.

There was an interval of embarrassing silence.

It was brought to an end by the girl; otherwise it might have remained unbroken, as the lady was turning to leave the room in silence.

"You've named the name of Henry Holtspur? He's not here, Mistress Marion Wade."

"I can perceive that without your assistance," answered the proud daughter of Sir Marmaduke—who, perhaps, would not have deigned a reply, had she not been piqued by the tone of the interrogator.

"You expected to find him, didn't you?"

Marion hesitated to make reply.

"Of course you did; else why should you have come here? You intended to see him free; but you're too late, Mistress Wade. Master Holtspur has friends who think as much of him as you—perhaps more. One of them, you see, has been before you."

"You mean yourself?"

Marion was constrained to put this question, by a thought that had suddenly occurred to her.

She remembered the words of the sentry, who had spoken of "a girl having been *sent* by a lady."

After all, was Bet Dancey only a messenger?

And was there a real rival, one of her own rank, in the background?

Such a belief would to some extent have been consolatory to the heart of the questioner.

But even this slight hope was crushed, by the reply to her interrogatory.

"A strange question that, Mistress Marion Wade? You see *me* here? You see I have risked my life to save *his*? Do you think I would do that for another? No—not for the queen herself—who I ve heard likes him as much, as either you or me?"

"There's not much risk," replied Marion, becoming irritated in spite of herself, at the insolent tone of her rustic rival. "To you, I should think, not much risk of anything."

"Indeed? And to you—had you been in time to set him free? How then?"

Marion had turned her back upon her taunting interrogator; and was moving towards the door, to avoid the unpleasantness of any further parley with one whose words, as well as actions, had already given her so much pain.

"Stay!" cried her tormentor, as if delighted to continue the persecution. "You appear disappointed, at not having an opportunity to show your friendship for Master Holtspur. You may do something yet, if you have a mind. I dare ye to take my place and let *me* go out. If you do, I'll let *him* know of it the first time I see him. I know that would be doing *him* a service. Now?"

"Away, rude girl! I decline your absurd proposition. I shall hold no further speech with you."

As the lady said this, she stretched forth her hand, and rapped against the door—making as much noise as her trembling fingers were capable of; and without any regard to the precautions with which she had been charged by the sentry.

Withers was waiting outside.

The key turned quickly in the lock, and the door was once more held open.

The lady glided silently out; and on through the wicket, without staying to speak a word of thanks.

But she had thanked the sentry in advance; and was thinking no more of his services.

As she looked forth from the wicket, the storm, for some hours threatening, had burst; and the rain was descending like a deluge upon the earth.

She stayed not under the shelter of the arched entrance—she did not think of staying; but stepped fearlessly over the threshold, and out into the open way—reckless of the rain, and daring the darkness.

There was a storm in her own bosom; in violence equaling that of the elements—in blackness eclipsing them.

There was not a gleam of light in the cloudy canopy of the heavens.

So, on the horoscope of her own future, there was not a ray of hope.

To her, Henry Holtspur was no more—at least, no more to make her happy.

She scarce felt gladness at his escape; though it would have been supreme joy, had she herself been the instrument that had secured it.

After all her fond imaginings—after a sacrifice that brought shame, and a confession that made known to him the complete surrender of her heart—to be thus crossed in the full career of her passion—abandoned—slighted, she might almost say—and for a rival who was only rustic!

Oh! it was the very *acme* of bitterness—the fellest shape that jealousy could have assumed!

It was not merely the last incident that was leading her into the depth of despair.

It only overflowed the cup already at its full.

Too many signs had appeared before her eyes—the report of too many circumstances had reached her ears—to leave her in doubt about the relationship that existed between Henry Holtspur and his late deliverer.

How cordial must it be, on the part of the latter, to stimulate her to such an act as that just performed; and how confident must she have been of being rewarded for her self-sacrifice!

A woman would not do such a thing for one likely to treat her with indifference?

So reasoned Marion Wade; though she reasoned wrongly.

It might be a *liaison*, and not an honest love? Considering the relative position of the parties, this was probable enough; but to the mind of Marion it mended not the matter to think so. On the con trary, it only made the ruin appear more complete.

Both men and women are more painfully affected by a jealousy of the former, than of the latter!

Alas! that the statement should be true; but it is so. He who denies it knows not human nature—knows not human love!

It would not be true to say, that Marion Wade reflected after this philosophic fashion; and yet it would be equally untrue, to allege that her mind was altogether free from such a reflection. Though beautiful as an angel, she was but a woman—imbued with all a woman's sensibilities—her sensualities too, though divinely adorned!

With the reckless air of one crossed in love, she strode forth into the darkness, taking no heed of the direction.

She walked with hasty steps; though not to avoid the pelting of the rain, or shun exposure to the storm.

On the contrary, she seemed to court these assaults: for, having arrived at the end of the verandah—whither she had strayed by chance—instead of seeking shelter under its roof, she stayed outside upon the open sward.

Although within a very short distance of the door, by which she might have found easy ingress to the mansion, she refrained from entering. Flinging the hood back upon her shoulders, she turned her face upward to the sky, and seemed as if seeking solace from the cold deluge that poured down from the clouds—the big drops dancing upon her golden tresses, and leaving them as if with reluctance to saturate the silken foldings that draped her majestic form.

"Oh! that I could weep like you, ye skies!" she exclaimed, "and like you, cast the cloud that is over me! Alas! 'tis too dense to be dissolved in tears. To-morrow ye will be bright again, and gay as ever! To-morrow! Ah! 'twill be the same to me, to morrow and forever!"

"Marion!"

The voice pronouncing her name came not from the sky she was apostrophizing; though it was one that sounded in her ears sweet as any music from heaven!

Were her senses deceiving her? Was it the distant thunder that muttered "Marion?"

No thunder could have spoken so pleasantly: it was the voice of a lover uttering the accents of love!

Once more heard she the voice—once more pronouncing "Marion!"

She had listened for its repetition with an earnestness that brooked not ambiguity.

She no longer suspected the thunder of having proclaimed her name. The voice was recognized.

It was that of one not worshiped in Heaven, but upon Earth.

The lightning aided in his identification. A favoring flash discovered a well-known form and face.

Henry Holtspur was standing by her side!

CHAPTER XLV.

STORM AND CALM

Holtspur's presence at this point requires explanation

Why did he linger upon a spot to him fraught with extreme peril—when almost certain death would be the consequence of his recapture.

'Tis said that the fox and hare delight to roam around the precincts of the kennel—as if fascinated with the danger.

The conduct of Scarthe's prisoner, in thus keeping the proximity of his prison, though seeming to resemble the folly of the fox and the frenzy of the hare, admits of an easy explanation.

On getting outside the wicket gate—which he had taken the precaution to shut behind him—Holtspur had gone off in a line at right angles to the western *façade* of the mansion. He had some remembrance of the moated ditch that surrounded the shrubbery. He had observed that it was waterless, and could be easily reached from the glacis. Once in its bottom, he would be safe from observation; and standing erect, he could see over the parapet and ascertain whether he was pursued. If not, he would go at his leisure along its dry hollow, and get round to the rear of the dwelling without setting foot upon the open pasture ground. If pursued at once, the ditch would still be his best place of concealment.

On reaching its edge he had leaped into it.

It was no fancy of the sentinel that a cloaked figure had disappeared in that direction in a somewhat mysterious manner.

After making his descent into the ditch, Holtspur came to a halt to disembarrass himself of the unbecoming garments that impeded the action of his arms and limbs. Both the skirt and cloak were cast off.

His next action was to elevate his eyes above the parapet, and if possible, ascertain whether his escape had become known to the guards. This action took place just as the sentry had stepped outside the wicket and was calling upon his Betsy to come back. It was so dark, Holtspur could not see the man; but he had noted the lifting of the latch, and could hear his mutterings.

Next moment the lightning flashed, revealing to the astonished eyes of the sentry a lady robed in rich velvet.

Holtspur saw the lady by the same light, deriving from the sight a very different impression.

His first feeling was one of surprise, quickly succeeded by a vague sense of pain.

The first arose from seeing Marion Wade abroad at that hour of the night; for despite the cloak and close-drawn hood, he had recognized the daughter of Sir Marmaduke. Her bounding step and tall symmetrical form were not to be mistaken by any one who had ever observed them; and upon the mind of Henry Holtspur they were indelibly impressed.

His second emotion was the result of a series of interrogative conjectures For what purpose was she abroad? Was it to meet some one? An appointment? Scarthe?

For some seconds the lover's heart was on fire, or felt as if it was.

Fortunately, the dread sensation was short-lived.

It was replaced by a feeling of supreme pleasure. The soul of Henry Holtspur trembled with triumphant joy, as he saw the lady moving forward to the court-yard gate, and seeking admission from the sentry He could hear part of the conversation passing between them. The lightning's flash showed him her hand extended, with the yellow gold glittering between her fingers. There was no difficulty in divining her intention. She was bribing the guard. For what? For the privilege of passing inside?

"I've been wronging her!" exclaimed Holtspur, conjecturally, shaping her purpose to his wishes. "If so, I shall make full atonement. The glove worn by Scarthe may have been stolen, must have been. If 'tis for me her visit is intended, then I shall know to a certainty. Such a sacrifice as this could not come from a coquette? Ah! she is risking everything. I shall risk my liberty—my life—to make sure that it is for me. 'Tis bliss to fancy that it is so."

As he said this, he stepped eagerly up to the moated wall, with the intention of scaling it and returning to the gateway.

He did not succeed in the attempt. The parapet was high above his head. He had been able to see over it only by standing back upon the sloping acclivity of the counterscarp. He could not reach it with his hands, though springing several feet upward from the bottom of the fosse.

After several times repeating the attempt, he desisted.

"The footbridge!" muttered he, remembering the latter. "I can go round by it."

He turned along the outside edge of the moat, in his anxious haste no longer taking precaution to keep concealed. The darkness favored him. The night was now further obscured by the thick rain, that had suddenly commenced descending.

This, however, hindered him from making rapid progress; for the sloping sward of the counterscarp had at once become slippery, and it was with difficulty he could keep his footing upon it.

On reaching the bridge, another obstacle presented itself. The gate that crossed it at midway was shut and locked, as was customary at night, and it was somewhat a perilous feat to climb over it.

It was performed, however; and Holtspur stood once more within the enclosed grounds of the shrubbery.

The delay of gaining access to them had been fatal to his original design. As he faced towards the gate entrance, he heard the wicket once more turning upon its hinges, and saw a woman's figure outlined in the opening.

In another instant it had moved around the angle of the building, and was advancing in the direction of the verandah.

Holtspur paused, and for a moment hesitated to present himself.

Could he have been mistaken as to the purpose of that nocturnal visit to the court-yard? What would he not have given for the secret that had been confided to that *trusty* sentinel?

If in error, how awkward would be an interview! Not that he feared betrayal. Such a thought did not enter his mind. But the oddness of such an encounter, its *gaucherie*, would be all upon his side.

His indecision was but for a moment. It might be the last time he should have an opportunity of speaking with Marion Wade.

This thought, along with a fond belief that he had rightly construed the errand on which she had come forth, once more emboldened him; and, gliding on through the shrubbery, he placed himself by her side—at the same time pronouncing her name.

It was his voice, heard above the rushing of the storm, that had fallen so unexpectedly on her ear.

" 'Tis you, Henry!" she said, yielding to her first instinct of pleasure at seeing him free and unfettered.

Then, as if remembering how he had come by that freedom—with the wild words of his deliverer still ringing in her ears—her demeanor suddenly changed to that haughty reserve which the proud daughter of Sir Marmaduke Wade had a right to assume.

"Sir!" continued she, with an effort at indifference, "I am surprised to see you here. I presumed that by this time you would have been far from this place."

"I should have been; but ——"

"You need not hesitate to tell the reason. I know it. It is easy to guess that."

"Marion!"

"No doubt your deliverer will soon find the opportunity of rejoining you?"

"You know how I escaped, then?" cried Holtspur, who in the delight of discovering that Marion had been to his prison, paid no heed to her scornful insinuation. "You have been inside? You saw ——"

"Your substitute, sir. It is not singular you should be anxious on account of one who has done you such signal service. I can report that she is in the best of spirits—proud of her achievement—only a little anxious, perhaps, to participate in your flight. Do not be uneasy on her account. She will not keep you long waiting One gifted with so much ingenuity will find but little obstacle in a score of sentries "

13*

"Marion!"

' A pity it is not 'Betsey' to whom you are addressing yourself!
A pity she should keep you waiting—especially in such weather.
For myself, I must get out of it. Good night, sir; or good morning
—which you will it."

"Marion—Marion Wade! do not go! Do not leave me thus!
One word—hear me!"

Holtspur could well afford to place himself in the attitude of a
petitioner. That visit to his prison, with its conjectured design, had
re-assured him of Marion's love, lately doubted.

She paused at the appeal. It was too earnest to be resisted.

"It was not *her*, for whom I was waiting," continued Holtspur,
now more clearly comprehending the conduct that had surprised him.
"It was for you, Marion—for *you*."

"This shallow pretense is unworthy of you, sir; unworthy of a
gentleman. How could you have expected to see *me*? Oh! weak
that I have been to trust my reputation to ohe who ——"

"One who will lay down his life to guard it against being sullied
by the slightest stain. Believe me, Marion Wade, it was to speak
with you I have stayed. I saw you as I was hastening away.
Little had I been hoping for such a heaven-sent chance! I saw you
approach the gate and go in. Need I declare to you the hope that
thrilled through my heart, when I fancied your mission might be to
myself? I cannot—word ill not express what I felt—what I
feel!"

Yieldingly did the proud n en turn towards him—as the flower
turns to its natural deity, t sun, from whom it derives all its
delight.

Just as its petals are unclos y his kissing rays after the long
night of damp and darkness, s vas the bosom of Marion Wade
revivified with fresh life, and hope, and joy, while she stood listening
to those earnest asseverations.

As yet she had not put her threat into execution. The shelter
was near, but she had not availed herself of it; and at the close of
her lover's speech she seemed no longer to care for it.

Her hood was still hanging over her shoulders—her head uncovered
to the storm. The rain-drops sparkled upon her golden hair, losing
themselves amid its profuse masses. They chased one another over
her warm, flushed cheeks, as if in very delight. They streamed
down the furrows of her rich robe, freely entering at its foldings—
and still she regarded them not.

of misery, but the moment before, had rendered her insensible to the storm, happiness was now producing the like effect.

Holtspur's appeal was no more rejected—his approach no longer repelled. He was left free to manifest the lover's care; and gently engaging the hand of his beloved, he conducted her within the verandah.

The storm raged on, but neither regarded it.   They had escaped from a storm—far more to be dreaded than the conflict of the elements—that of the two most powerful passions of the human heart—jealousy and love. The struggle was over. The former had fled from the field—leaving the latter triumphant in the bosoms of both.

CHAPTER XLVL

AWAY—AWAY!

The calm after the tempest—the day after the night—sunshine succeeding shadow—any of these physical transformations may symbolize the change from the passion of jealousy to that of love. At best they are but faint emblems; and we must seek in the soul itself for truer representatives of those its extremest contrasting emotions; or find it in our promised future of eternal torture and eternal bliss

It is in the crisis of transformation—or, rather, in the moment succeeding it—that the true agony is endured; whether it be an agony of pain, or one of pleasure.

The latter was the lot of Henry Holtspur and Marion Wade, as they rested under the sheltering *toile* of the verandah.   To both, it was a moment of unalloyed happiness; such as they had experienced only on one other occasion—when, entwined in each other's arms under the verdant canopy of the chestnut-trees, they had, with lips that lied not, made reciprocal surrender of their hearts.

One listening to those mutual vows—poured forth with the tender and emphatic eloquence which love alone can impart—could scarce have believed that mistrust should ever again spring up between them.

It had done so—perhaps not to be regretted. It had vanished; and the reaction had introduced them to an agony of pleasure—if possible more piquant than even that which had accompanied the first surrender of their souls. Both now experienced the pleasure of surrendering them again. No more might jealousy intrude itself upon their enjoyment; and for a while they even forgot those trifling signs that had led to it: she the faded flowers—he that *sinister* gauntlet.

It was only natural, however, that the causes of their late mistrust should become the subject of conversation; which they did.

Mutual surprise was the result of mutual interrogation; though neither could give to the other the explanation asked for.

The flowers in Holtspur's hat, and the glove in Scarthe's helmet, were enigma's equally inexplicable.

As to the latter, Marion only knew that she had lost it, that she had looked for it, she did not say why, and without success.

Holtspur still wore his beaver. Indeed, he had not till that hour found the chance of taking it off. Only within the last ten minutes had his hands been free to remove it.

He had not the slightest suspicion of the manner in which it was bedecked, not until he learned it from the lips of her upon whom the faded flowers had produced such a painful impression.

Marion could not misinterpret his surprise, mingled with indigna tion, as he lifted the hat from his head, wrenched the flowers from their fastening, and flung them scornfully upon the sward.

Her eyes sparkled with pleasure, as she witnessed the act. It was the kind of homage a woman's heart could comprehend and appreciate; and her's trembled with a triumphant joy.

Only for a short moment could this sweet contentment continue Nature is niggardly of such supreme pleasure. It was succeeded by a sombre thought, some dark presentiment pointing to the distant future. It found expression in speech.

"O Henry!" she said, laying hold of his arm, at the same time fixing her earnest blue eyes upon his, ' sometime—I fear to think it, much more to speak it—sometime might you not do the same with——'

"With what, Marion?"

"Sweet love! you know what I mean! Or shall I tell it you? 'Tis a shame for you not to understand me, you, who are so clever, as I've heard say; ah! as I, myself, have reason to know."

"Dearest! I fear I am not very clever at comprehending the ways of your sex. Perhaps if I had ——"

Holtspur interrupted himself, as if he had arrived on the verge of some disclosure he did not desire to make.

"If you had?" inquired Marion, in a tone that told of an altered interest. "What if you had, Henry?"

"If I had," replied her lover, escaping from his embarrassment by a happy subterfuge, "I should not have been so dilatory in declaring my love to you."

The speech was pretty; but, alas! ambiguous. It gave Marion pleasure to think he had long loved her, and yet it stirred within her a painful emotion, by recalling the bold challenge by which she had lured him to the avowal of it.

He, too, as soon as he had spoken, appeared to perceive the danger of such an interpretation; and in order to avert it, hurriedly had recourse to his former interrogatory.

"Do the same, you said, as I have done with the flowers. And with what?"

"The token I gave you, Henry, the *white gauntlet.*"

"When I fling it to the earth, as I have done those withered blossoms, it will be to defy him who may question my right to wear it. When that time comes, Marion Wade ——"

"Oh! never!" cried she, in the enthusiasm of her admiration fervently pressing his arm, and looking fondly into his face. "None but you, Henry, shall ever have that right. To no other could I concede it. Believe me! believe me!"

Why was it that Holtspur received this earnest declaration with a sigh? Why did he respond to it with a look of sadness?

Upon his arm was hanging the fairest form in the county of Buckinghamshire, perhaps in all England; upon his shoulder rested the loveliest cheek; against his bosom throbbed a heart responsive to his own, a heart that princes would have been proud to possess. Why that sigh, on listening to the earnest speeches that assured him of its possession?

But for the darkness that obscured the expression of his face, but for the beatings of her own heart, that hindered her from hearing the

sigh that escaped his, Marion Wade might have asked this question
with fearful interest in the answer.

She saw not the look, she heard not the sigh; and yet she was
troubled with some vague suspicion.   The reply had something in it
that did not satisfy her, something *reticent*.

"O Henry!" she said, "you are going from me now. I know we
must part. When shall I see you again? It may be long—long?"

"No longer than I can help, love!"

"You will give me a promise, Henry?"

"Yes, Marion; any promise you may dictate to me."

"Thanks! thanks! I know you will keep it. Come nearer,
Henry! look into my eyes! 'Tis a poor light; but I need not much
to see that yours are true. I know they are beautiful, Henry."

Holtspur's frame quivered under the searching scrutiny.

"What am I to promise?" he asked in the hope of hiding his embarrassment.

"Do not be afraid, Henry.   'Tis not much I am going to ask of
you.   Not much to you; but all the world to me.   Listen, and I
will tell you. Since we met, I mean since I knew that you loved me,
I have learned one thing.   It is that I *could not live and be jealous*.
The torture I have endured for the last twelve hours has told me
that. You will laugh at me, Henry; but I cannot help it. No. Let
me be happy, or let me die!"

"Sweet life! why should you think of such a thing as jealousy?
You need not fear that, if it should ever spring up between us, it will
be my misfortune, not yours, all mine."

"You jest, Henry! You know not the heart you have conquered.
Its firstlings were yours.   Though often solicited, pardon me for
being so plain, *it was never before surrendered to living man*.
O Henry! you know not how I love you!   Do not think it is the
fleeting fancy of a romantic girl, that may change under the influence
of a more matured age. I am a woman, with my girlhood gone by
Holtspur! you have won me; you have *won a woman's love!*"

Ecstasy to the soul of him thus addressed.

"Tell me, sweet Marion!" cried he.   "Forgive me the selfish
question; but I cannot help asking it.   Tell me why am I thus beloved? I do not deserve it. I am twice your age. I have lost those
looks that once, perhaps, may have attracted the romantic fancy.
O Marion Wade! I am unworthy of a love like yours. 'Tis my
consciousness of this that constrains me to make the inquiry; *why
do you love me?*"

Marion remained silent, as if she hesitated to give the answer. No wonder. The question is one often asked, but to which it is most difficult to obtain a truthful reply.

There are reasons for this reticence, psychological reasons, which men cannot easily understand. A woman's citadel is her heart; and its strength lies in keeping secret its conceptions. Of all its secrets the most sacred, the last to be divulged, is that constituting an answer to the question,—" Why do you love me?"

No wonder that Henry Holtspur received not an immediate answer. Ardor, more than sincerity, led him to press for it.

"I am a stranger to your circle, if not to your class. The world will tell you that I am an *adventurer*. I accept the appellation, qualified by the clause, that I adventure not for myself, but for my fellow-men, for the poor taxed slaves who surround me. Marion Wade, I weary you. Give answer to my question; why do you love me?"

"Henry! I know not. A thousand thoughts crowd upon me. I could give you a thousand reasons all comprised in one, *I love you, because I love you!*"

"Enough, dear Marion! I believe it. Do you need me to declare again? Can I plight my troth more truly?"

"No—no—Henry! I know that you love me *now*.'

"Now! now and forever!"

"You promise it, Henry?"

"I promise it, Marion."

"O Henry! you will promise me something more. You have said you would."

"What more, Marion?"

"I have told you that I would prefer death to jealousy. I only spoke the truth, Henry. I've heard say that the heart sometimes changes, in spite of itself. I don't believe it. I am sure mine can never change. Could yours, Henry?"

"Never! what do you wish me to promise? What is it you would bind me to?"

"I've now but one thing worth living for," responded the daughter of Sir Marmaduke Wade, "and that is your love, Holtspur. Promise me that when you love me no more, you will tell me you do not, truly and without fear. Promise that, Henry; for then I shall be happier to die."

"Nonsense, Marion! Why should I enter into such an idle condition? You know I shall love you as long as I live."

"Henry! Henry! Do not deny me what I have asked. What is there unreasonable in my request?"

"Nothing, dearest Marion. If you insist upon it, you shall have my promise—more than that, my oath. I swear I shall be candid and declare the truth. If ever my heart cease to love you, I shall tell you of its treason. How easily can I promise what can never come to pass!"

"But you may be far away, Henry? Enemies may be between us? You may not be able to see me? Then ——"

"Then, what would you have me do, dear Marion?"

"Return the token I have given you. Send me back my glove—the *White Gauntlet*. When I see that, 'twill tell me that he to whom I had given it—and along with it my heart—that he who once prized the gift, esteems it no more. That would be a gentler way than words—for *your* words telling me that bitter truth might be the last to which I should ever listen."

"If it please you, dearest, I promise to comply with your conditions—however idle I may deem them. Ah, Marion! you shall never get that glove again—never from *me*. I prize the *white gauntlet* too much ever to part with it; more than aught else in the world—excepting the white hand which it once shielded, and which, God willing, shall yet be mine!"

As Holtspur uttered this impassioned speech, he raised the "white hand" to his lips, and imprinted upon it a fond, fervent kiss.

It was the parting salute—though not intended as such.

The lightning flashed at that moment, displaying two forms in an attitude that proclaimed them lovers who had made mutual surrender of their souls.

A third form might have been seen by the same light, standing outside the verandah, scarce ten paces distant.

It was a female figure, with the face of a young girl—uncoifed, uncloaked, despite the pelting of the pitiless storm.

The lovers, absorbed in their own sweet thoughts, might not have noticed this intruder, but for a slight scream that, escaping from her lips, attracted their attention to her.

When the lightning blazed forth again, she was gone.

"Oh!" cried Marion, "it was like the shadow of some evil thing. Away, Henry! there is danger! Away! away!"

Without resistance Holtspur yielded to the solicitation.

Rapidly recrossing through the shrubbery, he sprang down into the moated ditch, and glided on towards the rear of the dwelling.

CHAPTER XLVII

Bet Dancey it was, whose presence, revealed by that ghastly gleam, moving like an ill-omened shadow among the shrubbery, had caused the lovers to bring their interview to such a sudden ending.

On his second supplicant gliding silently past him, the facile sentry had followed with equal alertness—this time not with any intention to plead for a promised kiss, but simply to show his respect to the lady by gallantly conducting her beyond the bounds of his jurisdiction.

He had already satisfied himself how profuse had been her grati-tude—pre-paid as it was.

On reaching the wicket, he was once more doomed to disappoint-ment. Like the first, his second visitor had also disappeared. He remained some moments gazing after her, but soon feeling discon-solate in the darkness, he determined on returning to the store-room for his lamp.

Amidst the many surprises of the night, he was now to experience the greatest of all.

On entering within the apartment, and raising the lantern to the level of his eyes, in order to assure himself of his prisoner's safety, his astonishment scarce equaled his consternation when, instead of the cavalier lying bound along the bench, Bet Dancey stood boldly before him. He no longer thought of claiming that promised kiss. A sudden perception of his own stupidity had driven all amorous inclinations out of his mind.

His first impulse was to rush out and give the alarm to his com-rades of the guard. In obedience to this impulse he hurried off into the yard, but in the confusion of ideas caused by his surprise, he neglected to close the store-room door; and while he was absent upon his errand the substitute for the patriot prisoner quietly slipped out, and gliding along the dark archway, emerged through the wicket without let or interruption.

She had faced towards the rear of the house, with the intention of taking her departure, when an unlucky idea prompted her to turn in the opposite direction.

She remembered Marion's visit to the prison.   Had her lady rival yet gone to rest?   Might they, by some chance, perhaps by design, might they have come together?

Under the influence of this suspicion, the girl glided along the wall towards the western front of the mansion.

A low murmur of voices guided her to the verandah, a few stealthy steps brought her within sight of two figures in juxtaposition, a flash of lightning revealed who they were, at the same time disclosing a sight that scorched her heart to its very core.

Her first thought was to spring forward and interrupt the interview, to revile, upbraid, anything for the satisfaction of her jealous vengeance.

She was on the eve of thus acting, when a noise heard from behind caused her to stay her intent.   It was the murmur of men's voices, mingled with the clanking of steel scabbards.   It was the cuirassier guard issuing forth in pursuit.

This suggested to Bet Dancey a better mode of redressing her fancied wrong.   She could restore Holtspur to the same prison from which she had set him free.   She cared not for the pain it might cause to herself, so that it should wring the heart of her rival.

It was but to return to the gateway; communicate with the guard and conduct them to the verandah.

All this was done in the shortest space of time; but short as it was, during the interval, the lovers had spoken their parting word, and had hastily separated.

Just as Holtspur leaped down into the ditch, half a dozen cuirassiers, headed by a woman, were seen hurrying around the angle of the building towards its western *façade*.

As they spoke only in low mutterings, and advanced with stealthy steps, it was evident they expected to surprise the lovers on the spot they had so recently quitted.   The woman, keeping in the lead, appeared to direct their movements.

The rain, which had now ceased to fall, had been succeeded by a clearing of the sky; and the interior of the verandah could be viewed from end to end.   There was no one inside it !

The cuirassiers scanned the gallery with looks of disappointment

" He's not here, not a sign of him," said one, whose voice, from its altered and lugubrious tones, could with difficulty be recognized as that of the outwitted sentinel.

"Oh Lord! what'll become of me, if he's got off?"

Turning to the woman, he appeared to make some appeal to her in an under-tone.

"If he's gone from here," answered she, speaking in a voice that betrayed deep emotion, "it isn't a minute ago. Oh, I wish you had found him, and her too—how glad I'd be to have her exposed—the proud—saucy dame!"

"Who are you speaking about? Is it the lady in velvet?"

"No matter who. Go after him. You can't fail to overtake him yet. Oh! bring him back, and then we'll see whether she——"

"We may go twenty ways, and not the right one," said the corporal of the guard, coming up and taking part in the hurried dialogue.

"No, no!" cried the woman, "you can't go the wrong one. Pass out by the back of the park. Take the road for Hedgerley; only don't turn that way. Keep the back path straight on by Wopsey's Wood. That's the way they're to take: it was all arranged. Come! I'll go along with you—come! come!"

In a voice thus earnestly directing the pursuit of the escaped prisoner could be recognized that, which, scarce twenty minutes before, had been so earnestly urging him to escape—the voice of Bet Dancey.

Was it a *ruse* to mislead the guard, or send them on a wrong track? No: it was her design to cause his recapture.

In the short period of ten minutes a change had passed over Betsey's proud spirit—transforming her from a self-sacrificing friend, to an enemy equally devoting herself to Holtspur's destruction.

In her outraged bosom a revulsion had arisen, that stirred her soul to its profoundest depths; and filled her heart with eager longings of revenge. She had seen the man she madly loved—for whom she had risked, if not life, at least liberty and reputation—in the arms of another; a bright and beautiful rival; his own arms fondly entwining that other's form; his lips fervently pressing hers. No wonder the heart of the passionate peasant, distraught by such a spectacle, had yielded to the promptings of revenge!

"Come on!" she cried, gesticulating to the cuirassiers to follow her, "on to the Hedgerley road!"

"Our horses?" suggested the guard corporal.

"No, no!" responded the girl. "By the time you could get them, he will have gone where I don't know how to find him. Come as

309

you are; and I'll answer for overtaking . now. *They* won't have any horses till they get beyond Wopsey's . od. Come then, if you want to retake your prisoner."

The others were disposed to set forth at once, and afoot. Withers, although for special reasons the most eager of any, appeared to hesitate.

"Yer sure ye don't want to mislead us, Betsey? Ye've fooled me once this night; an' hang me if I let ye go, till I've laid hands on 'im!"

"Nonsense!" exclaimed the girl, "haven't I told you why I helped to let him out? The lady that sent *me*, would have given her eyes to see him; but since he's taken to the other, I know she'll be only too glad to hear that he's brought back to his prison. Much as she'd a thanked me for getting him out, when I tell her what I've seen, she'll give double to have him retook. Don't be silly then. You'll suffer if he escapes. Come on with me, and I'll promise he shan't."

The prospect of his prisoner getting clear off and its consequences to himself, thus forcibly brought before the mind of the negligent sentinel, at once put a period to his indecision; and without further opposition he threw himself along with the others; who, yielding to the guidance of the girl, hurried off upon the pursuit.

Instead of going to the point of rendezvous, which she had given to Holtspur himself, Bet conducted the cuirassiers out of the park by a path altogether different. She knew that the fugitive must by that time have found those to whom she had directed him. He would be no longer within the limits of the park; but on his way up the back road to Beaconsfield. To intercept him was her design; and this might still be done, by hastening along a by-path well known to her, which by a shorter route debouched upon the road he would have to take. By this path, therefore, did she conduct his pursuers.

On reaching the road the party moved more slowly. The rain had ceased falling, and the moon had suddenly made its appearance in a cloudless sky. The corporal of the guard, who chanced to be an experienced scout, here commanded a halt.

"We needn't go any further this way," said he, glancing towards the ground . "No one has passed up this road before us. You see, my pretty guide, there's not a track?"

' Then we must be ahead o' them," replied the individual thus addressed. "I know they were to come this way—I am sure of it."

"In that case we had best wait here," muttered the corporal to his men. "It's a capital spot for an ambuscade. These bushes will conceal us from the eyes of any one coming along the road. Hush! surely I heard a voice?"

The guard, hitherto addressing each other only in whispers, obeyed the command of the corporal; and stood silently listening.

Sure enough there was a voice—a human voice. It sounded like the moaning of some one who lay upon a bed of sickness! It was low, and apparently distant.

"It's like as if some poor devil was giving his last kick," muttered one of the cuirassiers.

"It's only the owls hooting among the trees," suggested another.

"Hush!" again exclaimed the corporal. "There are other voices —nearer. Hush!

"Good!" he ejaculated, after listening awhile.

"There are men coming along the road behind us! It must be *them*! Here! three of you on this side; the others across the road. Lie quiet till they come close up. When I give the word, spring out upon them. Quick, comrades! Not a movement till you hear my signal!"

Promptly obedient to these instructions, the soldiers drew themselves into the thicket—some dropping upon their knees among the bushes—others standing erect, but screening their bodies behind the trunks of the beeches.

The corporal disposed of himself in a similar fashion; while the guide, having glided off to a greater distance, stood trembling among the trees—like some guilty denouncer—dreading to look upon the spectacle of that capture she had conducted to the probability of a too certain success.

CHAPTER XLVIII

On arriving at the rear of the garden, Holtspur had emerged out of the moat, and struck across the open pasture in a direct line for the timber. The darkness was still sufficiently obscure to hinder his being seen—at least, from any great distance; though there were those standing within the shadow of the trees who had marked his approach.

A low whistle—peculiarly intoned—told him that he was observed, and by friends: for in that whistle he recognized an old hunting signal of his ancient henchman—Gregory Garth.

There was no need to make reply. In an instant after, Garth was by his side—accompanied by the deer-stealer.

The plan of further proceedings took not much time to concert.

The programme had been already traced out subject to such contingencies as might unexpectedly arise.

Dancey was to hurry back to his cottage, where Oriole had been left in charge of Garth's horse—that steed of the royal statues—which, along with Dancey's nag, was the only mount that could be provided for the occasion. But as Dancey himself was to stay behind —there being no call for his expatriation just at that crisis—and as the Indian could track it afoot almost as fast as on horseback, the two horses had been deemed sufficient for the necessity.

The woodman's dwelling lay near the Oxford highway; and as it would waste some time to bring the horses across to the back road, running past Hedgerley, it had been decided that they should be taken along a private path through Wapsey's-Wood, by Dancey and the Indian—there to be met by Holtspur and Garth going afoot along the parallel, but less frequented road.

This arrangement, cunningly schemed by Garth, had in view the possibility of a pursuit, with the probability, in such case, that the pursuers would naturally keep along the high road.

The rendezvous having been arranged, the deer-stalker took his way back towards his own domicile; while Garth, conducting Holt spur through the tract of timber with which he had already made himself acquainted, climbed out over the palings of the park; and turned along the bridle road running towards Hedgerley.

Half a mile brought them to a point where Wapsey's Wood skirted the road- separated from it by a rude fence.

Garth was going in the advance, and for a time keeping silence— as if busied with some abstruse calculation.

"There be a tidyish bit o' night left yet," he at length remarked, glancing up to the sky, "I shed think I've time enough for that biz- ness."

The remark was made to himself, rather than to his companion, and as if to satisfy his mind, about some doubt he had been indulg- ing in.

"Time enough for what?" asked Holtspur, who had overheard the muttered observation.

"Oh! nothin' muchish, Master Henry—only a little bit o' bizness I've got to attend to over i' the wood there. 'Twon't take ten min- utes; an', as time's precious, I can tell ye 'bout it when I gets back. Ah! theear's the gap I war lookin' for. If ye'll jest keep on at yer leisure, I'll overtake yer afore ye ken get t'other side o' the wood. If I doan't, pleeze wait a bit. I'll be up i' three kicks o' a' old cow."

Saying this, the ex-footpad glided through the gap; and striking off among the trees, soon disappeared behind their close standing trunks.

Holtspur, slackening his pace, moved on along the road—not with- out wondering what could be the motive that had carried his eccentric conductor so suddenly away from him.

Soon, however, his thoughts reverted to her from whom he had so late separated; and, as he walked under the silent shadows of the trees, his spirit gave way to indulgence in a retrospect of that sweet scene, with which his memory was still warmly glowing.

From the rain that had fallen, the flowers, copiously bedewed, were giving out their incense on the soft air of the autumn night. The moon had suddenly made her appearance, amid banks of fleecy clouds, that were fantastically flitting across the face of the azure heaven.

Under her cheering light Holtspur sauntered leisurely along, re- viewing over and over again the immediate and pleasant past; which, notwithstanding the clouds that lowered over his future, had the effect of tinging it with a roseate effulgence.

There were perils before, as well as behind him. His liberty as his life, was still in danger. He knew all this; but in the revel of

that fond retrospect—with the soft voice of Marion Wade yet ringing
n his ears—her kisses still clinging to his lips—how could he be
otherwise than oblivious of danger?

Alas! for his safety he was so—recklessly oblivious of it—forget-
ful of all but the interview just ended, and which seemed rather a
delicious dream than an experience of sober real life.

Thus sweetly absorbed, he had advanced along the road to the distance of some two or three hundred yards from the place where Garth
had left him. He was still continuing to advance, when a sound,
heard far off in the wood, interrupted his reflections—at the same
time causing him to stop and listen.

It was a human voice; and resembled the moaning of a man in
pain; but at intervals it was raised to a higher pitch, as though ut
tered in angry ejaculation.

At that hour of the night, and in such a lonely neighborhood—for
Holtspur knew it was a thinly peopled district—these sounds seemed
all the stranger; and as they appeared to proceed from the exact direction in which Garth had gone, Holtspur could not do otherwise
than connect them with his companion.

Gregory must be making the noises, in some way or other? But
how? What should he be groaning about? Or for what were those
exclamations of anger?

Holtspur had barely time to shape these interrogatories, before the
sound became changed—not so much in tone as intensity. It was
still uttered in moanings and angry ejaculations; but the former, instead of appearing distant and long-drawn as before, were now heard
more distinctly; while the latter, becoming more sharper and of more
angry intonation, were not pronounced as before in monologue, but
in two distinct voices—as if at least two individuals were taking part
in the indignant duetto.

· What it was that was thus waking up the nocturnal echoes of Wapsey's Wood was a puzzle to Henry Holtspur; nor did it assist him
in the elucidation, to hear one of the voices—that which gave out the
melancholy moanings—at intervals interrupted by the other in peals
of loud laughter!

On the contrary, it only rendered the fearful *fracas* more difficult
of explanation.

Holtspur now recognized the laughing voice to be that of Gregory
Garth; though why the ex-footpad was giving utterance to such jovial
cachinnations he could not even conjecture.

Lonely as was the road, on which he had been so unceremoniously forsaken, he was not the only one traversing it at that hour.

His pursuers were also upon it—not *behind* but *before* him—like himself listening with mystified understandings to those strange sounds.

Absorbed in seeking a solution of them, Holtspur failed to perceive the half-dozen figures that, disengaging themselves from the tree-trunks, behind which they had been concealed, were closing stealthily and silently around him.

It was too late when he did perceive them—too late, either for flight or defence.

He sprang to one side; but only to be caught in the grasp of the stalwart corporal of the guard.

The latter might have been shaken off; but the sentry Withers—compromised by the prisoner's escape, and therefore deeply interested in his detention—had closed upon him from the opposite side; and in quick succession, the others of the cuirassier guard had flung themselves around him.

Holtspur was altogether unarmed.

Resistance could only end in his being thrust through by their swords, or impaled upon their halberts; and once more the gallant cavalier, who could not have been vanquished by a single antagonist, was forced to yield to that fate which may befall the bravest.

He had to succumb to the strength of superior numbers.

Marched afoot between a double file of his captors, he was conducted back along the road, towards the prison from which he had so recently escaped.

The mingled groans and laughter still continued to wake up the echoes of Wapsey's Wood.

To Holtspur they were only intelligible, so far as that the laughing part in the duet was being performed by the ex-footpad—Gregory Garth.

The soldiers, intent upon retaining their prisoner, gave no further heed to them, than to remark upon their strangeness.

But for the merry peals at intervals interrupting the more lugubrious utterances, they might have supposed that a foul murder was being committed.

But the laughter forbade this supposition; and Holtspur's guard passed out of hearing of the strange noises, under the impression that they came from a camp of gipsies, who, in their nocturnal orgies, were celebrating some ceremony of their vagrant ritual.

She who had been the instrument of Holtspur's delivery, had also played the chief part in his recapture.

Following his captors under the shadow of the trees, unseen by him and them, she had continued a spectator to all that passed; for a time giving way to the joy of her jealous vengeance.

Soon, however, on seeing the rude treatment to which her victim was subjected—when she witnessed the jostling, and heard the jeers of his triumphant captors, her spirit recoiled from the act she had committed; and when, at length, the court-yard gate was closed upon the betrayed patriot, the daughter of Dick Dancey fell prostrate upon the sward, and bedewed the grass with tears of bitter repentance!

CHAPTER XLIX.

TWO TRAVELERS.

About an hour after the recapture of Henry Holtspur, two men might have been seen descending the long slope of Red Hill, in the direction of Uxbridge.

They were both men of large stature, one of them almost gigantic They were on horseback; the younger of the two bestriding a good steed; while his older, and more colossal companion, was mounted upon as sorry a jade as ever set hoof upon a road.

The first, booted and spurred; with a plumed hat upon his head, and gauntlets upon his wrists; in the obscure light might have been mistaken for a cavalier. When the moon made its appearance from behind the clouds, which happened at intervals, a certain *bizarrerie* about his costume forbade the supposition; and the stalwart form and swarth visage of Gregory Garth were then too conspicuous to escape recognition, by any acquaintance he might have encountered upon the road.

The more rustic garb of his traveling companion, as well as the figure it enveloped, could, with equal facility, be identified as belong ing to Dick Dancey, the deer-stealer.

The presence of these two worthies on horseback, and riding towards Uxbridge, was not without a purpose, presently to be explained.

The cuirassiers had been astray in conjecturing that the noises heard in Wapsey's Wood proceeded from a gang of gipsies.

It was nothing of the kind.

What they heard was simply Gregory Garth engaged in the performance of that promise he had made in the morning.

Although he did not carry out his threat to the exact letter, he executed it in the spirit; taking his departure from the bedside of Wil Walford, only after every bone in the woodman's body had been made to taste the quality of the cudgel expressly cut for the occasion.

It is possible that Will Walford's punishment might have been still more severe, but that his castigator was pressed for time, so much so, that he left the wretch without releasing him; with a set of suffering bones, and a skin that exhibited all the colors of the rainbow.

After thus settling accounts with the "treetur," as he called him, Garth had thrown away his holly stick; and hastened back to the road.

Under the supposition that Holtspur was by that time advancing some distance towards Beaconsfield, he hurried on to overtake him.

The moon was shining full upon the track; and in the dust, which the rain had recently converted into mud, the ex-footpad did not fail to perceive a number of footprints.

In the exercise of his peculiar calling, he had been accustomed to note such signs; and had acquired a skill in their interpretation equal to that of a backwoods hunter.

Instantly he stopped, and commenced scrutinizing the signs.

He was upon the spot where the capture had been accomplished.

The footmarks of six or seven men, who had been springing violently from side to side, had left long slides and scratches in the damp dust.

The tracks of the troopers were easily distinguished; and, in their midst, the more elegant imprint of a cavalier's boot.

Garth needed no further evidence of the misfortune that had befallen.

Beyond doubt his master had been once more made a prisoner; and cursing himself for being the cause, he mechanically traced the backward tracks, his despondent air proclaiming that he had but little hope of being able to effect a rescue.

Returning upon the traces of the cuirassier guards, he re-entered the park, and advanced towards the mansion, which the darkness enabled him to do with safety.

There he had discovered Bet Dancey, a sorrowing penitent, prostrate upon the ground, where, in her distraction, she had thrown herself.

From the girl he had obtained confirmation of the re-capture, though not the true cause either of that, or her own grief.

Her statement was simple. The guards had followed Master Holtspur; they had overtaken, overpowered, and brought him back: he was once more locked up within the store-room.

The hope of again delivering him out of the hands of his enemies, might have appeared too slender to be entertained by any one; and for a time it did so—even to the unflinching spirit of his old retainer.

But the ex-footpad, when contemplating the chances of getting out of a prison, was not the man to remain the slave of despair—at least for any length of time; and no sooner had he satisfied himself that his master was once more encaged, than he set his wits freshly to work, to contrive some new scheme for his deliverance.

From the store-room, in which Holtspur was again confined, it would be no longer possible to extricate him. The trick, already tried, could not succeed a second time. Withers was the only one of the guards who might have been tempted; but after his affright, it was not likely that either the promise of kisses, or the proffer of gold pieces, would again seduce the sentry from the strict line of duty.

But Garth did not contemplate any such repetition. An idea that promised a better chance of success had offered itself to his mind. To set free his master by *strategy* was henceforth plainly impracticable. Perhaps it might be done by *strength*?

Not in Bulstrode mansion—where the prisoner was surrounded by fourscore cuirassiers? No—clearly not.

There could be no possibility of accomplishing a rescue there; nor did Gregory Garth give it a moment's thought. His ideas became directed to the road that lay between the two prisons—the store-room and the Tower. He already knew that Holtspur was to be transfer

red from one to the other; and on the following day, during the tran-
sit, might there not be some chance of effecting a rescue?

Garth knew the London Road—every inch of it—and, in one way
or other, was acquainted with most of the people who dwelt near it.

Although upon an odd individual, here and there, he had practiced
his peculiar vocation, there were few with whom he was upon hostile terms. With many he held relations of friendship; and with a
goodly number certain other relations, that should entitle him to an
act of service at their hands.

With a plan—but still only half developed—he had once more hurried back along the Hedgerly road, towards the rendezvous, where
Dancey and the Indian had already arrived with their horses.

He found them waiting, and apprehensive;—almost expecting the
sad tidings he had to communicate—the failure of their enterprise.

As Garth, during the backward tramp, had more definitively arranged his programme of action, there was no time wasted in con-
sultation. Dancey readily consented to the proposal, to become his
confederate in the scheme he had so promptly conceived.

Oriole having been directed to return to Stone Dean, the ex-footpad
sprang upon his stolen steed; and, followed by the deer-stealer on his
scraggy cob, at once started off along a bridle path, which winding
around the southern boundary of Bulstrode Park, would bring them
to the king's highway, where the latter crossed over the elevated
plain of Jarret's Heath.

It is in pursuance of the scheme conceived by Garth, that he and
his companion were descending Red Hill at that early hour in the
morning.

Whithersoever bent, they were evidently in haste to reach their
destination—more especially Garth, who was constantly urging his
companion to keep up with him. The quadruped bestridden by the
deer-stealer was the chief obstruction to their speed; and, despite
the frequent application of a stout stick, which his rider carried in
hand, and the pricking of a rusty spur fastened upon his heel, the
sorry hack could not be urged beyond a slow shuffling trot—discontinued the instant the stimulus of stick and spur were suspended.

"The devil burn yer beest, Dancey!" cried the ex-footpad, losing
all impatience at the slow pace of the animal. "We'll not ha' nigh
time enough to see them all. From what yer daughter larnt yesterd'y
the sogers 'il bring their prisoner down the road, the fust thing i' the
mornin'. They'll do that, so's to make the journey to Lonnon afore

night. No doubt about their gettin' to Uxbridge b' ten o' the clock; an' jest see what we've got to do afore then. Stick the spur into 'im —up to the shank, Dancey! The lazy brute! I'd make 'im goo, if I war astride o' him."

" The poor creetur!" compassionately rejoined Dancey, by way of an apology for his nag; " he han't had' a bit o' anythin' to eat for a week, 'ceptin' what he ha' grubbed off o' the roadside. Ne wonder he bean't much for a fast journey."

" Lucky it isn't a longish one. If we had Lonnon afore us we'd niver get there! As it is—ha! now I think on't, I've got a idea as 'll save time. There be no use for us to keep thegither. Ye go round Denham way, an' warn yer friends there. Ye can cross the Colne higher up, an' scud on to the Harefield fellows. I'll take Uxbridge an' Hillindon, an' along i' the Drayton d'rection. That'll be our best plan. We ken meet at the Rose an' Crown, as soon as we've got through. I'll go there fust, so as te gi'e ole Browney a hint 'bout gettin' his tap ready. Lucky I ha' been able to borrow some money 'pon a watch I chanced 'on—a tydish bit—else we mightn't find these patriots so free to lend us a hand. I shall spend it all—every stiver o't—for the rescue o' Master Henry."

" I han't got nothin' to spend, or I'd do the same for 'im," returned the deer-stealer. " He be the best an' liberallest gentleman ever coom about these parts—that be he."

" Ye're not far wrong about that. Master Dancey. Too good a gentleman to heve his head chopped off for speakin' no more than's the truth; an' we must do our best to holp 'im keep it on his shou'-ders. There's yer road to Denham. Stick the spur into yer blessed beest, an' make 'im do his d—t. Be sure ye meet me at the bridge —afore ten."

And with these injunctions the ex-footpad separated from the deer-stealer—the latter turning off upon the lane which led to the village of Denham; while the former continued along the direct road towards the town of Uxbridge.

CHAPTER L

THE ESCORT.

At that early hour all the world appeared to be asleep—silence and slumber having been seemingly restored to the lately disturbed inmates of Bulstrode mansion; though not all of these had been disturbed by the incidents we have described.

Happy at the thought of having humiliated his rival, and the hope of eventually crushing him altogether, Captain Scarthe had slept soundly throughout the whole night—little suspecting the series of incidents that were transpiring, some scarce a score of yards from his couch, and all, within a mile's circuit of the mansion.

Even after awakening, he was not informed of the various love interviews, hairbreadth 'scapes, and captures, that, during the after-hours of that eventful night, had been following each other in such quick succession.

The whole affair had been managed so silently that beyond the six men comprising the guard, with the corporal himself, not another cuirassier knew what had happened.

Withers had taken care that the tongues of his comrades should be tied—a purpose he might not have succeeded in effecting, but for those golden pieces which the lady had so profusedly poured into his palm, and of which he was now compelled to make a generous, though somewhat reluctant disbursement.

The result was that, at the changing of the guard, the prisoner was handed over to the *relief*, bound as before; and no one in the troop was made acquainted with the facts, either of his escape or recapture. The new guard entered upon its *tour*, under the full belief that their charge had spent the whole of the night within the precincts of his prison.

Of the several individuals who had been privy to his escape, there was only one who by daybreak still remained ignorant that he had been re-taken. Marion slumbered till the morning, unconscious of the re-arrest of her lover, as Scarthe of his temporary deliverance.

On parting with him, she had gone to her couch, though not directly.

The noises heard without had made her uneasy; and, standing by a window on the stairway she had listened.

She had heard voices of men, a woman's as well, but soon after they had ceased.

She knew it must be some of the guard, and the woman's voice she could guess at; but, as so little disturbance had been made, she did not suspect that it was an alarm, or that they had discovered the absence of the prisoner from his place of confinement.

She listened for a long time.

She even returned to the verandah door, opened it, looked out, and listened again.

But all was quiet, outside as within; and supposing that the soldiers had returned into the court-yard, she at length re-entered her chamber, and sought repose on her couch.

Her prolonged vigil, and its happy termination, favored sleep; and at that moment, when Henry Holtspur was struggling in the grasp of the cuirassier guards, Marion Wade was dreaming a delightful dream of his delivery—in which she fancied herself enjoying over and over again that ecstatic interview that had succeeded it !

Her slumber, with its concomitant dream, was protracted far into the hours of daylight.

Long as they had continued, both were destined to a rude interruption.

She was awakened by sounds without betokening the presence of men under the window of her chamber.

Horses, too—as could be told by the stamping of hoofs upon the graveled esplanade.

Several distinct voices reached her ear—one louder than the rest —which was occasionally raised in abrupt accents of command; and once or twice in a tone altogether different—in laughter !

Whichever way uttered, it sounded harsh in the hearing of Marion Wade: she knew it was Scarthe's.

For what was the cuirassier captain abroad at so early an hour ? Was it so early ?

Her arm was extended from under the coverlet, white as the counterpane itself.

Her jeweled watch was taken up from the tripod table on which it lay.

Its dial was consulted: ten of the clock !

At the same instant, the hour was proclaimed in sonorous cadence from the tower overtopping the mansion.

It was not to assist her in conjecturing the purpose of that matutinal commotion, that Marion had so eagerly glanced to the dial of her watch.

After the events of the night, she could have had but one surmise: that Holtspur's escape had been discovered; and the noises outside were made by those preparing to go off in pursuit of him.

She had looked at her watch, to ascertain the time that had elapsed since Holtspur's departure.

She was gratified at perceiving the lateness of the hour.

But why did Scarthe appear to be so happy?

Those peals of laughter were inappropriate to the occasion—proceeding from one who should have been suffering chagrin?

At the thought, Marion sprang from her couch, and glided towards the window.

From that window, but the morning before, she had witnessed the most painful spectacle of her life.

Very similar, and scarce less painful, was that which now greeted her glance: Henry Holtspur, bound upon the back of a horse, and encompassed by a troop of cuirassiers; who, in full armor, were keeping close guard upon him!

They were all mounted, with accoutrements and valises strapped to their saddles—as if ready for a journey.

Scarthe himself was pacing back and forth upon the graveled walk; but in a costume that showed he had no intention to accompany the party, on whatever expedition it was bent.

Cornet Stubbs was to be its leader.

Mounted upon Holtspur's steed, he was at that moment placing himself at the head of the troop, preliminary to commencing the march.

Marion had scarce time to take in the details of this tableau—equally unexpected and sad—when a bugle brayed out the signal, " Forward."

Its notes drowned the scream that escaped from her quivering lips, as the form of her beloved was ruthlessly borne away out of sight.

Nearly half an hour had elapsed before the confusion of ideas—consequent on such a painful scene—permitted on the part of Marion Wade a return to anything like calm reflection.

Even then her mind was still wandering amidst a maze of unavailing thoughts, when voices, again heard below, recalled her to the window,

14*

She looked out as before. The tableau was changed from that she had already contemplated. Only two individuals composed it— Scarthe and a stranger.

The latter was a man in civilian costume; but of a certain guise that betokened him to be in the service of .the king.

He was on horseback—his horse frothing, smoking, and panting as if after a long gallop at top speed.

Scarthe was standing by the stirrup, listening to some communication which the rider appeared to impart, in a haste that proclaimed its importance.

Despite his earnestness, the stranger spoke in a low tone; but his voice ascending to the window of Marion's chamber was sufficiently loud for her to catch the significant words—

" Prisoner—rescue—Uxbridge ! "

On hearing them, Scarthe was seen to spring back from the side of the horseman, with as much alertness as if the latter had aimed a blow at him.

Next moment, and without even staying to make reply to the communication which the messenger had made, he rushed on towards the gate of the courtyard, loudly vociferating, " To horse—every man to horse ! "

With that promptitude to which he had trained his troop, the cuirassiers were almost instantly in their saddles ; and, before Marion Wade could recover from the shock of this new surprise—more gratifying than that which preceded it—she beheld Scarthe himself, enveloped in his steel armor, ride forth at the head of his troop; and go off at a gallop along the avenue leading out towards Uxbridge.

" A rescue, Uxbridge ! " were the words that continued to echo in her ears, long after the trampling of the troopers' horses had died away upon the distant road.

" God grant it may be true ! " was her murmured response to that echo.

The excited suppliant did not content herself with this simple formulary of speech.

Nudely kneeling upon the floor, her white arms crossed over her bosom, she breathed forth a prayer, a fervent, passionate prayer invoking the protection of the God she loved for the man she adored !

CHAPTER LI.

THE RESCUE.

It was approaching the hour of ten, and Uxbridge was in the full tide of active life. More than the usual number of people appeared to be parading its streets; though no one seemed to know exactly why. It was not market-day; and the extra passengers sauntering along the footways, and standing by the corners, were not farmers.

They appeared to be mostly common people, of the class of laborers, and artisans. They were not in holiday dresses, but in their ordinary every-day garb: as if they had been at work, and had abruptly " knocked off " to be present at some improvised spectacle, of which they had just received notice.

The shoemaker was in his leathern apron, his hands sticky with wax: the blacksmith begrimed and sweating as if fresh from the furnace; the miller's man under a thick coating of flour-dust; and the butcher with breeches still reeking, as if recently come out of the slaughter house.

A crowd had collected in front of the Rose and Crown, with groups stretching across the adjacent causeway, and to this point all the odd stragglers from the upper part of the town appeared tending.

Those who had already arrived there were exhibiting themselves in a jolly humor. · The tavern tap was flowing freely ; and scores of people were drinking at somebody's expense; though at whose, nobody seemed either to know or care.

A tall, dark-complexioned man, oddly attired, assisted by the potmen of the establishment, was helping the crowd to huge tankards of strong ale, though he seemed more especially attentive to a score of stout fellows of various crafts and callings, several of whom appeared to be acquainted with him, and were familiarly accosting him by his name of " Greg'ry."

Another individual, still taller and more robust—as also older—was assisting " Greg'ry " in distributing the good cheer ; while the host of the inn—equally interested in the quick circulation of the can—was bustling about with a smile of encouragement to all customers who came near him.

It might have been noticed that the eyes of the revelers were, from time to time, turned towards the bridge—by which the road leading westward was carried across the Colne.

There was nothing particular about this structure—a great elevated arch, supporting a narrow causeway, flanked by stone walls, which extended from the water's edge some twenty or thirty yards along both sides of the road.

The walls were still further continued towards the town by a wooden paling, which separated the road from the adjoining meadows.

These, bordering both sides of the river, extended away towards the south west, as far as the eye could reach.

Between the houses, and the nearer end of the bridge, intervened about a hundred yards of the highway, which lay directly under the eyes of the roistering crowd; but on the other side of the river, the road was not visible from the inn—being screened by the mason-work of the parapet, and the arched elevation of the causeway.

Neither on the road, nor the bridge, nor in the meadows below, did there appear aught that should have attracted the attention of the idlest loiterer; though it was evident from the glances occasionally cast westward over the water, that some object worth seeing was expected to show itself in that direction.

The expression upon the countenances of most was that of mere curiosity; but there were eyes among the crowd that betrayed a deeper interest—amounting almost to anxiety.

The tall man in odd apparel, with the bushy black whiskers, though bandying rough jests with those around him, and affecting to look gay, could be seen at intervals casting an eager look towards the bridge, and then communicating in whispers with the individual in the faded velveteens—who was well known to most of the bystanders as "Old Dick Dancey, the deer-stealer."

"What be ye all gathered here about?" inquired a man freshly arrived in front of the inn. "Anything to be seen, masters?"

"That there be," answered one of those thus interrogated "Wait a bit , an' maybe ye'll see something worth seein'."

"What might it be?"

"Dragoniers—royal soldiers of his majesty the king."

"Bah! what's there in that to get up such a row for? One sees them now every day."

"Ay, an' once a day too often," added a third speaker, who did not appear to be amongst the most loyal of his majesty's lieges.

"Ah! but ye don't see them every day as ye will this mornin'—takin' a prisoner to the Tower—a grand gentleman at that!"

"A prisoner! Who?"

A name was pronounced, or rather *sobriquet*: for it was by a phrase that the question was answered.

"*The Black Horseman*," replied the man who had been questioned. "That's the prisoner ye shall see, master."

The announcement might have caused a greater commotion among the spectators, but that most of those present had already learnt the object of the assemblage. The excitement that at that instant succeeded sprang from a different cause.

A man who had climbed up on the parapet of the bridge—and who had been standing with his face turned westward—was seen making a signal, which appeared to be understood by most of those around the inn.

At the same instant, a crowd of boys, who had been sharing his view from the top of the wall, commenced waving their caps and crying out, "The horse sogers—the king's kewresseers!—they're comin', they're comin'!"

The shouting was succeeded by a profound silence—the silence of expectation.

Soon after, plumes waving over steel helmets, then the helmets themselves, then glancing gorgets and breastplates, proclaimed the approach of a troop of cuirassiers.

They came filing between the walls of grey masonwork—their helmets, as they rose up one after another over the arched parapet, blazing under the bright sun, and dazzling the eyes of the spectators.

In the troop there were exactly a dozen horsemen, riding in files of two each; but the cavalcade counted fourteen—its leader making the thirteenth, while a man, not clad in armor, though in line among the rest, completed the number.

This last individual, although robed in rich velvet, and with all the cast of a cavalier, was attached to the troop in a peculiar manner.

The attitude he held upon his horse, with hands bound behind his back, and ancles strapped to the girth of his saddle, told that he was of less authority than the humblest private in the rank.

He was a prisoner.

He was not unknown to the people composing that crowd, into the midst of which his escort was advancing.

The black horseman had ridden too often through the streets of Uxbridge, and held converse with its inhabitants, to pass them in such fashion, without eliciting glances of recognition, and gestures of sympathy.

He was no longer astride his own noble steed, as well known as himself; though the horse was there, with a rider upon his back who but ill became him.

This was the chief of the escort, Cornet Stubbs, who, an admirer of horseflesh, had that day committed an act of quiet confiscation.

Holtspur was between two of the troopers, about three or four files from the rear; while the cornet—somewhat conceited in the exercise of his conspicuous command—rode swaggeringly at the head.

In this fashion, the glittering cavalcade crossed the causeway of the bridge, and advanced among the crowd, until its foremost files had penetrated to a point directly in front of the inn.

Stubbs had been scanning the countenances of the people as he rode in among them.

He fancied he saw faces that frowned upon him; but these were few; and on the whole, the assemblage seemed simply hilarious and cheerful.

It never occurred to him that there could be any intention of interrupting his march.

How could it?

He presumed that, as soon as his charger penetrated into the thick of the crowd, the individuals comprising it would spring quickly aside and make way for him and his followers.

It was with some surprise, therefore, that on getting fairly in front of the inn, he found the passage blocked by human bodies—standing so densely across the street, that in order to avoid riding over them, he was compelled to bring his horse to a halt.

Just at that instant, a shout rose up around him—apparently intended as a cheer of congratulation to the soldiers: while a voice, louder than the rest, vociferated—"The king! the king! Down with disloyal knaves! Death to all traitors!"

There was a touch of irony in the tones; but it was too delicately drawn for the dull perception of Cornet Stubbs; and he interpreted the speeches in their loyal and literal sense.

"My good friends," he graciously replied, while a gratified expression stole over his stolid features, "glad to find you in such good spirits. Am, by Ged!"

"Oh! we're in the right spirit," rejoined one. "Ye'll see by-and-by. Come, master officer! have a drink. Let's toast the king! Ye wont object to that, I'm sure?"

"By no means," replied Stubbs. "By no means. I shou'd be most happy to drink with you; but you see, my friends, we're on duty; and must not be detained—mustn't, by God!"

"We won't detain ye a minnit," urged the first speaker, a stalwart blacksmith, as hard of face as his own hammer. "We won't, by God!" added he, in a tone which, coupled with the peculiar form of expression, led Stubbs to conceive some doubts about the sincerity of his proffered friendship.

"Look alive there, lads!" continued the village Vulcan. "Bring out the stingo, landlord? Some of yer best wine for the officer; and yer strongest homebrew for his brave men. Dang it—the day's hot an' dusty. Ye have a long ride atween this an' Lunnun. Ye'll feel fresher, arter sluicin' yer throats wi' a can o' our Uxbridge ale. Won't ye, masters?"

The last appeal was made to the troopers; who, without making any verbal reply, signified by nods and other gestures, that they were nothing loath to accept the offer, without calling in question the *brusquerie* of him who made it.

Almost as if by enchantment a number of men, with drinking-vessels in their hands, appeared on both flanks of the mounted escort —each holding a cup or can temptingly before the eyes of a trooper.

These ready waiters were not the regular tapsters of the establishment, but men of other and different crafts; the shoemakers already spoken of, in their wax-smeared aprons—the millers in their snow-white jackets—the blacksmiths in their grimy garments—and the butchers redolent of suet.

Notwithstanding the *sans façon* of the invitation, and the odd apparel of the attendants; the liquor frothing up before their eyes, and within scenting distance of their nostrils, was too much for the troopers to withstand.

A five mile ride along a hot and dusty road had brought them to that condition called "drouthy;" and, under such circumstances, it would not have been human nature to have denied themselves the indulgence of a drink, thus held, as it were. to their very lips.

It would not have been Scarthe's cuirassiers to have done so; and, without waiting the word—either of permission or command—each trooper took hold of the can nearest to his hand; and, raising it to his lips, cried out: "The king!"

The crowd echoed the loyal sentiment; while the improvised pall-bearers—as if still further to testify their respect—took hold of the bridles of the horses, and kept them quiet, in order that their riders might quaff in comfort, and without spilling the precious liquor.

There were two of these attendants, however, who deviated slightly from the fashion of the rest.

They were those who waited upon the two troopers that on each side flanked the prisoner.

Instead of contenting themselves with holding the horses at rest, each of these attendants led the one whose bridle he had grasped a little out of the alignment of the rank.

It was done silently, and as if without design; though the moment after, there was an apparent object—when a tall man, with black whiskers and swarth complexion, passed around the head of one of the horses, and holding up a flagon, invited the prisoner to drink.

" Ye've no objection to 'im havin' a wet, I s'pose ? " said this man, addressing himself in a side speech to the soldiers who guarded him. " Poor gentleman! He looks a bit thirstyish—doan't he ? "

" You may give him a drink, or two of them, for aught I care," said the soldier more immediately interested in making answer. " But you'd better not let the officer see you."

The speaker nodded significantly towards Stubbs.

" I'll take care o' that," said Gregory Garth; for it was he who held up the flagon.

" Here, master," he continued, gliding close up to the prisoner. " take a drap o' this beer. Tan't a quality liquor, I know—such as I s'pose ye've been used to; but it be tidyish stuff for all that, an'll do ye good. Bend downish a bit, an' I'll hold it to yer lips. Don't be afeered o' fallin' out o' yer saddle. I'll put my hand ahind to steady ye. So—now—that's the way."

Gregory's fingers, as he continued to talk, had found their way round to the croup of the saddle, and rested upon the wrists of the prisoner, where they were tied together.

The troopers behind, too much occupied by their potations and the *facetiæ* of the attendants who administered them, saw not the little bit of shining steel, that in the habile hands of the ex-footpad was fast severing the cords that confined Henry Holtspur to his place.

" A goodish sort o' stuff, ain't it, master ? " asked Gregory, aloud, as he held the drinking-vessel to the prisoner's lips. " Then adding. in a quick muttered tone, " Now, Master Henry ! yer hands are free

"Lay hold o' the reins; an' wheel round to the right. Stick this knife into the brute; an' gallop back over the bridge, as if the devil war arter ye."

"It's no use, Gregory," hurriedly answered the cavalier. "The horse is but a poor hack. They'd overtake me before I could make a mile. Ha!" exclaimed he, as if a real hope had suddenly sprung up. "Hubert! I did not think of him. There is a chance. I'll try it."

During all their experience in the Flanders campaign, the cuirassiers of Captain Scarthe had never been more taken by surprise, than when their prisoner was seen clutching the reins of the steed he bestrode—with a quick wrench drawing the animal out of the rank —and, as if a spur had been applied to every square inch of his skin, they saw the old troop horse spring past them, apparently transformed into a fleet courser!

Their surprise was so great, that the drinking-cups instantly dropped from their grasp; though for a good while, not one of them was able to recover his reins—which the lubberly attendants had in the most stupid manner hauled over the heads of their horses!

It did not diminish their astonishment to see the escaping prisoner pull up as he approached the bridge; raise his fingers to his lips; and give utterance to a shrill whistle, that came pealing back upon the ears of the crowd.

It did not diminish their astonishment to hear a horse neighing, as if in reply to that strange signal.

On the contrary, it increased it.

Their surprise reached its climax when they saw that, of all their number, Cornet Stubbs was the only one who had the presence of mind—the courage and command of himself and his horse—to start immediately in pursuit!

That he had done so there could be no mistake.

The black charger went sweeping past them like a bolt fired from a culverin—close following upon the heels of the fugitive, with Cornet Stubbs seated in the saddle, apparently urging the pursuit.

Alas! for Cornet Stubbs! He was not long allowed to enjoy an honor, as unexpected as unsought; no longer than while his fiery steed was galloping over the ground towards the spot where the troop horse had been hauled up.

As the two steeds came into contiguity, Stubbs became sensible of a strong hand clutching him by the gorget, and jerking him out of his stirrups.

The next moment he felt a shock, as if he had been hurled heavily to the earth.

He did, by Ged!

Although all this passed confusedly before his mind, the spectators saw every movement with perfect distinctness.

They saw the cornet lifted out of his saddle, and pitched into the middle of the road.

They saw the cavalier, who had accomplished this feat, change horses with him whom he had unhorsed—without setting foot to the ground; and amidst the wild huzzas that greeted the achievement, they saw the black horseman once more firmly seated astride his own steed, and galloping triumphantly away.

The cheer was an utterance of the most enthusiastic joy, in which every individual in the crowd appeared to have had a voice, the discomfited cuirassiers excepted.

It was the true English "hurrah," springing from the heart of a people ever ready to applaud an exploit of bold and dangerous daring.

Why was it not protracted, for it was not?

It subsided almost on the instant that it had arisen, ere its echoes had ceased reverberating from the walls of the adjacent houses!

It was succeeded by a silence solemn and profound; and then, by a murmuring indicative of some surprise, sudden as that which had called forth the shout, but of a less pleasant nature.

No one asked the cause of that silence; though all were inquiring *the cause of what had caused it.*

The astonishment of the spectators had sprung from the behavior of the black horseman, which at the crisis appeared singular.

Having reached the central point of the bridge, instead of continuing his course, he was seen suddenly to rein up, and with such violence, as to bring his horse back upon his haunches, till his sweeping tail lay scattered over the causeway.

The movement was instantly followed by another. The horse, having gained an erect attitude, was seen to head, first in one direction, then into another—as if his rider was still undecided which course he should take.

The spectators at first thought it was some fault of the animal, that he had baulked at some obstacle and become restive.

In a few seconds they were undeceived; and the true cause to this interruption to the flight of the fugitive became apparent to all—

In the waving plumes and glittering helmets that appeared beyond rising above the cope-stones of the parapet.

Another troop of cuirassiers, larger than the first, was coming along the road in the direction of the bridge. It was Scarthe and his squadron!

Already had the foremost files reached the termination of the parapet walls; and were advancing at a trot towards the centre of the arch. In that direction Holtspur's retreat was cut off—as completely as if he had entered within a *cul de sac*.

He saw it, and turned to ride back; but by this time the troopers who accompanied Stubbs, stirred to energetic action by the trick played upon them, had recovered their reins, and were making all haste to pursue the prisoner. The corporal who commanded them —for the cornet still lay senseless upon the road—had succeeded in getting them into some sort of a forward movement; and they were now advancing in all haste towards the bridge.

For a moment the black horseman appeared undecided how to act. To gallop in either direction was to rush upon certain death, or certain capture. On each side was a troop of cuirassiers with drawn sabres, and carbines ready to be discharged: while the space between the two squadrons was shut in—partly by the parapet wall of the bridge, and partly by the palings that continued them.

For a man unarmed, however well mounted, to *run the gauntlet*, in either direction, was plainly an impossibility; and would only have been attempted by one reckless of life and determined to throw it away.

I have said that for a moment Holtspur appeared irresolute. The spectators beheld his irresolution with hearts throbbing apprehensively.

It was but for a moment; and then, the black steed was seen suddenly to turn head towards the town, and come trotting back over the bridge!

Some believed that his rider had repented of his rashness and was about to deliver himself up to the guard from whom he had escaped. Others were under the impression that he intended to run the gauntlet; and was choosing the weaker party through which to make the attempt.

Neither conjecture was the correct one: as was proved the instant after—when Holtspur suddenly setting his horse transverse to the direction of the causeway, and giving the noble animal a simul taneous signal by voice, hand, and heel, sprang him over the palings into the meadow below!

The taunting cry shouted back, as he galloped off over the green sward—a cry that more than once had tortured the ears of pursuing Indians—was heard above the vociferous huzza that greeted his escape from Scarthe and his discomfited followers.

The shots fired after him had no effect. In those days a marksman was a character almost unknown; and the bullet of a carbine was scarce more dreaded than the shaft of the clumsy cross-bow.

The pursuit, continued by the cuirassiers along the verdant banks of the Colne, was more for the purpose of saving appearances, than from any hope of overtaking the fugitive. Before his pursuers could clear the obstacle that separated them from the mead, and place themselves upon his track, the "black horseman" appeared like a dark speck—rapidly diminishing in size as he glided onward towards the wild heaths of Iver

CHAPTER LII.

AFTER THE ARREST.

In the days of Charles (the Martyr!) a State prisoner was not such a *rara avis* as at present. Laud had his list, and Strafford also —that noble but truculent tool of a tyrant—who ended his life by becoming himself a State prisoner—the most distinguished of all.

A gentleman denounced, and taken to the Tower, was anything but a rare event; and created scarce more sensation than would at the present day the capture of a swell-mobsman.

The arrest of Henry Holtspur passed over as a common occurrence

His rescue and escape were of a less common character; though even these served only for a nine days' wonder in the mind of the general public.

There were few who understood exactly how the rescue had been bought about; or how that crowd of "disloyal knaves"—as they were termed by the king's partisans—had come to be so opportunely assembled in front of the "Rose and Crown."

No one seemed to know whither the fugitive had betaken himself —not even rumor.

It was only conjectured that he had sought concealment—and found it—in that grand hiding place safe as the dese self: London.

For those attainted with "treasonable proclivi " towards the tyrant king, the great city was, at that time, a r asylum than any other part of his kingdom.

The cuirassier captain had done all in his po to hinder the event from obtaining general publicity.

He had not reported at head-quarters, either arrest or what followed; and he had been equally remiss of dut permitting the circumstances of Holtspur's rescue to pass with investigation.

He still clung to the hope of being able to effect his recapture; and to that end he employed, though in a clandestine manner, all the influence he could bring to his aid.

He dispatched secret agents into different parts of the country; and no communication, not even a letter, could enter the mansion of Sir Marmaduke Wade, without Captain Scarthe knowing the nature of its contents.

During this period, his position in the quarters he occupied, may be regarded as somewhat anomalous.

A certain intimacy had become established between him and the family of his host. How far it was friendly, on either side, was a question.

A stranger or superficial observer, might have fancied it so—on the part of Scarthe even cordial. Ever since the first day of his residence under the roof of Sir Marmaduke, he had held is troopers in strict subordination; so strict as to have given these orthies no slight offense.

But Captain Scarthe was a commander not to be trifl rith; and his followers knew it.

For every little incident of trouble or annoyance, occu g to the inmates of the mansion, ample apologies were rendered; 'it might have been imagined, that the king's cuirassiers had been s to Bul strode as a guard of honor to attend upon its owner, ratl than a "billet" to live at his expense!

These delicate attentions to Sir Marmaduke sprang not from any motive of chivalry or kindness; they were simply designed for the securing of his daughter. Scarthe wanted her heart as well as her hand. The former, because he loved her, with all the fierce passion of a soul highly gifted, though ill-guided; the latter, because he coveted her fortune: for Marion Wade, in addition to her transcendant charms, was heiress to a noble domain.

She was endowed second to none in the shire; for a separate property was hers independent of the estate of Bulstrode.

Scarthe knew it; and for this reason desired to have her hand along with her heart.

Failing to win the latter, he might still hope to obtain the former; which, with the fortune that accompanied it, would go far towards consoling his disappointed vanity.

Whether loving him or not, he was determined Marion Wade should be his wife; and if fair means should not serve for the execution of his project, he would not scruple to make use of the contrary.

He was ready to avail himself of that terrible secret of which he had become surreptitiously possessed.

The life of Sir Marmaduke Wade lay upon his lips. The knight was, at that moment, as much in his power as if standing in the presence of the Star Chamber, with a score of witnesses to swear to his treason.

It needed but a word from Scarthe to place him in that dread presence; and the latter knew it. A sign to his followers, and his host might have been transformed into his prisoner!

He had not much fear that he would ever be called upon to carry matters to such an ill-starred extreme. He had too grand a reliance upon his own irresistibility with the sex. The man, whom he had originally believed to be his rival, now out of Marion's sight, appeared to be also out of her mind; and, during his absence, Scarthe had been every day becoming more convinced—his wish being father to the thought—that the relationship between Marion and Holtspur had not been of an amatory character.

The bestowal of the glove might have been a mere complimentary favor, for some service rendered? Such gifts were not uncommon: and tokens worn in hats or helmets were not always emblematic of the tender passion. The short acquaintanceship that had existed between them—for Scarthe had taken pains to inform himself on this head—gave some color to his conjecture; at least, it was pleasant for him to think so.

Women, in those days, were the most potent politicians. It was a woman who had brought on the war with Spain—another who had caused the interference in Flanders—a woman who had led to our artificial alliance with France—a woman who, then as now, ruled England!

Marion Wade was a woman—just such a one as might be supposed to wield the destinies of a nation. Her political sentiments were no secret to the royalist officer. His own creed, and its partisans, were often the victims of her satirical sallies; and he could not doubt of her republican inclinings.

It might be only that sort of sympathy that existed between her and Holtspur?

Had he been an eye-witness to her behavior—throughout that eventful day on which the conspirator had made his escape, he might have found it more difficult to reconcile himself to this pleasant belief.

Her sad countenance, as, looking from the lattice, she once more beheld her lover in the power of his enemies—once more in vile bonds—might have proved, to the most uninterested observer, the existence of a care which love alone could create.

Could he have seen her during the interval which transpired—between the time when the prisoner was borne off towards his perilous prison, and the return of the mounted messenger who told of his escape—he might have been convinced of an anxiety, which love alone can feel

With what unspeakable joy had Marion listened to this last announcement! Perhaps it repaid her for the moments of misery she had been silently enduring.

Deep as had been the chagrin, consequent on that event, Scarthe had found some consolation in the thought, that, henceforth, he should have the field to himself.

He would take care that his rival should not again cross the threshold of Sir Marmaduke's mansion; nor in any way obtain access to his daughter's presence till he had settled the question of his own acceptance or rejection.

During all this while, Sir Marmaduke and his people, in their behavior towards their uninvited guests, appeared civil enough.

Though one closely acquainted with the relationship—or narrowly scrutinizing the intercourse between them—could not have failed to perceive that this civility was less free than forced.

That it was so—or rather that a friendship existed even in appear-ance—needs but little explanation.

Sir Marmaduke's conduct was ruled by something more than a vague apprehension of danger. The arrest of his fellow-conspirator was significant; and it was not difficult to draw from that circum-stance a host of uncomfortable conclusions.

The course he was pursuing towards Scarthe, was not only opposed to his inclination, but exceedingly irksome to him.

There were times when he was almost tempted to throw off the mask; and brave the worst that might come of it.

But prudence suggested endurance—backed by the belief that, ere long, things might take a more favorable turn.

The king had been compelled to issue a writ—not for the election of a new parliament, but for the re-assembling of the old one.

In that centred the hopes and expectations of the party, of which Sir Marmaduke was now a declared member.

Marion's politeness to Scarthe was equally dashed with distrust. It had no other foundation than her affection for her father.

She loved the latter, with even more than filial fondness: for she was old enough, and possessed of sufficient intelligence, to under-stand the intrinsic nobility of his character.

She was not without apprehension that some danger overshadowed him; though she knew not exactly what.

Sir Marmaduke had not made known to her the secret that would have explained it.

He had forborne doing so, under the plea of causing her unneces-sary anxiety; and had simply requested her to treat the unwelcome intruders with a fair show of respect.

The hint had been enough; and Marion, subduing her haughty spirit, yielded faithful obedience to it.

Scarthe had no reason to complain of any slights received from the daughter of his host.

On the contrary, her behavior towards him appeared so friendly, that there were times when he drew deductions from it, sufficiently flattering to himself.

Thus tranquilly did affairs progress during the first few weeks of Scarthe's sojourn at Bulstrode—when an event was announced, that was destined to cause an exciting change in the situation.

It was a *fête champêtre*, to be given by Sir Frederick Dayrell, Lord of the manor of Fulmere—at which a grand flight of falcons was to form part of the entertainment.

The *elite* of the county was to be present, including Sir Marmaduke Wade and his family, and along with them his military guests
---Captain Scarthe and Cornet Stubbs.

CHAPTER LIII.

GOING A HAWKING.

The beautiful park of Bulstrode was radiant with the earliest rays
of the sun.

The dew still glittered upon the grass; and the massive chestnuts
threw elongated shadows far down the sloping declivities.

The stag, that had been slumbering undisturbed during the night,
springing from his soft couch of moss, strode forth to make his
morning meal upon the tempting sward.

The birds had already chanted their orison to the opening day;
and, forsaking their several perches, were fluttering merrily from
tree to tree.

All nature was awake.

Though the hour was an early one, the inmates of the mansion
seemed not to be asleep.

Half a dozen saddled horses, under the conduct of as many grooms,
had been led forth from the court-yard; and were standing in front
of the house, held in hand, as if awaiting their riders.

Two were caparisoned differently from the rest.

By the peculiar configuration of their saddles, it was evident they
were intended to be mounted by ladies.

In addition to the grooms in charge of the horses there were other
attendants standing or moving about.

There were falconers, with blinded hawks borne upon their wrists
and shoulders; and finders, with dogs held in leash—each clad in
the costume of his craft.

15

In the boudoir of Marion Wade were two beautiful women. Marion herself was one; Lora Lovelace the other.

The high-crowned beaver hats; the close-fitting habits of green velvet; the gauntlets upon their hands; and the whips in them, proclaimed the two ladies to be those for whom the side-saddle horses had been caparisoned.

Both had given the finishing touch to their toilettes, before forsaking their separate chambers.

They had met in Marion's sitting-room—there to hold a moment's converse, and be ready when summoned to the saddle.

"Walter promises we'll have fine sport," said the little Lora, tripping across the chamber, light as a fawn, and gay as a lark. "He says the mere has not been disturbed for long—ever so long—and there have been several broods of herons this season—besides sedge-hens, snipe, and woodcock. We shall find game for gos-hawks, kestrels, jer-falcons, merlins, and every sort. Won't it be delightful?"

"Pleasant enough, I dare say—for those who can enjoy it."

"What, Marion! and will not you—you, so fond of falconry, as often to go hawking alone?"

"Ah, Lora, this sport, like many others, may be pleasanter alone, than in company—that is, company one don't care for."

"Dear me, cousin, you'd make believe that there isn't one among the grand people we're going to meet to-day worth caring for?"

"Not one, of my knowing."

"What, not our very gallant guest, who is to be our escort—not Captain Scarthe?"

"I should have expected you to say Cornet Stubbs, instead."

"Ha, ha, ha! No, no! He's too stupid to be a pleasant companion for me."

"And Captain Scarthe is just the opposite to be a pleasant companion for me. In truth, of the two I like Stubbs best, spite of his vulgar patronymic."

"You are jesting, Marion? Stubbs, Stubbs, Cornet Stubbs! How would it sound as Colonel Stubbs? Not a whit better. No: not if he were General Stubbs. Mistress Stubbs? I would not be called so for the world! Lady Stubbs? No, not for a coronet!"

"Between Stubbs, and Scarthe, I see not much to choose."

"Marion, you mistake. There's a warlike sound about Scarthe. I could imagine a man of that name to be a hero."

"And I could imagine a man of that name to be a poltroon—
I do."

"What, not our Captain Scarthe? Why, everybody calls him a
most accomplished cavalier. Certes, he appears so. A little rude
at first, I acknowledge; but since then, who could have acted more
cavalierly? And to you, cousin, surely he has been sufficiently
attentive, to have won your profound esteem?"

"Say rather my profound detestation. Then you would come
nearer speaking the truth: he has won that."

"You don't show it, I'm sure. I've seen you and Captain Scarthe
very happy together, very happy indeed, if one may judge from appearances."

"Wheels within wheels, coz. A smiling cheek don't always prove
a contented heart; nor is a smooth tongue the truest indication of
courtesy. You have seen me polite to Captain Scarthe, nothing
more; and for that I have my reasons."

"Reasons!"

"Yes, good reasons, dear Lora. But for them I shouldn't go
hawking to-day, least of all, with him as my companion. Captain
Scarthe may be a hero in your eyes, my gay cousin; but he is not
the one that's enthroned within my heart; and you know that."

"I do, I do, dear Marion. I was only jesting. I know Captain
Scarthe is not your hero; and can tell who is. His name begins
with Henry, and ends with Holtspur."

"Ah, there you have named a true hero! But hark you, my little
parrot! Don't be prattling these confidences. If you do, I'll
tell Walter how much you admire Captain Scarthe, or Cornet Stubbs.
Of which do you wish him to be jealous?"

"Oh, Marion, not a word to Walter about Stubbs. Do you
know, I believe that he's a little jealous of him already. He don't
like his attentions to me, not a bit, Walter don't. I'm sure neither
do I; but I can't help them, you know, so long as we must meet
three or four times a day. I think the refusal I gave might have
been sufficient. It was flat enough. But it hasn't; and would you
believe it, he still continues his attentions, as if nothing had happened between us? Pray don't make Walter worse; else there might
be a fight between them; and then——"

"The valiant cornet might crack Walter's crown?"

"No, that he couldn't; though he is bigger than Walter He's
not braver, I'm sure. That he isn't, the ugly impertinent."

"What! has he been impertinent to you?"

"Not exactly that; but he don't seem to know much about polite ness. How different with Captain Scarthe. He is polite."

"I suppose—after a fashion."

"Dorothy Dayrell thinks him perfection. I'm sure that girl's in love with him. Why is she always riding up to Bulstrode, if it isn't to have an opportunity of seeing him? I'm sure, it's neither of us she comes to visit."

"She's quite welcome to come—if it be for the purpose you suppose."

"Ay! and it's for nothing else than to get into his company, that she gives the hawking party to-day. She is a dangerous, designing creature—that's what she is."

"If her design be to catch Captain Scarthe, I hope she may succeed in it. I'm sure I shan't be the one to stand in her way."

"Well!" rejoined Lora, "I'm determined to keep my eyes on her this very day; and see how she behaves. Oh! you don't know how I detest that girl; and why, do you think!"

"Really, I cannot tell."

"Well! it is because I know that she is your enemy!"

"I never gave her cause!"

"I know that."

"Perhaps you know why it is so?"

"I do!"

"Tell me."

"Because you are beautiful."

"If that be her reason, she should be your enemy as much as mine?"

"Oh, no! I have not the vanity to think so. My beauty is only prettiness; while yours—ah! cousin Marion, you are beautiful in my eyes, a woman! What must you be in the eyes of a man?"

"You're a simpleton, little Lora. You are much prettier than I; and as for Dorothy Dayrell—don't every one call her the belle of the county? I've heard it a score of times."

"And so have I. But what signifies that? Though you're my senior, Marion, I think I have as much wisdom as you in matters of this kind. Besides I'm only a spectator, and can judge between you. I believe that the belle of the county, and the belle of the ball-room, are never the most beautiful of those with whom they are compared. Very often such reputation is obtained, not from beauty, but behavior; and from behavior not always the best.

"Go on in that way, Lora, and we shall esteem you as the Solon of our sex."

"Nay, nay; I speak only sentiments such as any one may conceive. You and Dorothy Dayrell are just the two to illustrate them. While everybody calls her the belle of the county, everybody thinks you to be so. Indeed cousin! you are truly beautiful! So beautiful that even the peasant children of the parish gaze upon you with wonder and delight!"

"Fulsome flatterer!"

"In troth 'tis true. And that's why Dorothy Dayrell dislikes you. She wants to be everything, and knows that you take her laurels from her. On the day of the fête, she did everything in her power to captivate the man, whom she pretended to disparage!"

"Holtspur?"

"Yes; I saw her. She used all her arts to attract his attention Ah, Marion! He had only eyes for you. And now that he is gone, she's set herself to attract Captain Scarthe. My word! won't she try to-day? Sweet coz! I don't want you to act the hypocrite; but can't you—yes, you can—flirt a little with Scarthe, just to give her a chagrin? Oh! I should so like to see that girl suffer what she deserves—a chapter of humiliation!"

"Foolish child! you know I cannot do that! It is not according to my inclination; and just now less than ever in my life."

"Only for an hour, to punish her!"

"How should you like to be so punished yourself? Suppose some one, to-day, were to flirt with Walter; or he with some one?"

"Then I'd flirt with Stubbs!"

"Incorrigible coquette! I think you like Walter, but only that. Ah, Lora! you know not what it is to love!"

"Don't I, though——"

"Mistress Marion!" cried a groom, showing his face at the door of the chamber, "Sir Marm'duke be mounted. They're only waiting for you and Miss Lora!"

The man, after delivering his message, retired.

"Lora," whispered Marion, as they issued forth from the room not a word of what you know; not to any one! Promise me that; and I may give you the satisfaction you have asked for."

* * * * * * * * * *

During the conversation between the cousins, the two men, who were .he chief subjects of it, were engaged in a dialogue of a somewhat kindred character.

Scarthe's sitting apartment was the scene; though neither of the speakers was seated.

Both were on their feet; and in costume for the saddle—not military —but merely booted and spurred, with certain equipments covering their dresses, that betokened an intention of going forth upon the sport of falconry.

A splendid jer-falcon—perched upon the back of a chair, and wear · ing his hood—gave further evidence of this intention; while their gloves drawn on, and their beavers held in hand, told that, like the two ladies, they were only awaiting a summons to sally forth.

Scarthe, following a favorite habit, was pacing the floor; while the cornet stood watching him with attention: as if he had asked counsel from his superior, and was waiting to receive it.

"And so, my gay cornet," said Scarthe, addressing the subaltern in his usual bantering way, "you're determined to try her again?"

"Yes, by Ged! that is, if you approve of it."

"Oh! as to my approval, it don't need that. It's not a military matter. You may propose to every woman in the county for aught I care; twenty times to each, if you think fit."

"But I want your advice, captain. Suppose she should refuse me a second time!"

"Why, that would be awkward—especially as you're sleeping under the same roof, and eating at the same table with her. The more awkward, since you say you've had a refusal already."

"It wasn't a regular offer. Besides, I was too quick with it. There's been a good deal since that gives me hope. She'll think better of it now—if I don't mistake her."

"You are not quite sure of her, then?"

"Well, not exactly."

"Don't you think you had better postpone your proposal, till you're more certain of its being favorably received?"

"But there's a way to make certain. It's about that, I want you to advise me."

"Let me hear your 'way'?"

Well, you see, captain, though the girl's only the niece of Sir Marmaduke, she loves him quite as much his own daughter does. I don't think she cares about that stripling—farther than as cousin

What's between them is just like sister and brother: since she's got no brother of her own. They've been brought up together—that's all."

"I can't help admiring your perspicuity, Cornet Stubbs."

Perspicuity was just that quality with which the cornet was not gifted; else he could hardly have failed to notice the tone of irony, in which the compliment was uttered.

"Oh! I ain't afraid of *him*, at all events!"

"What, then, are you afraid of? Is there any other rival, you think, she's likely to prefer to you? Maybe young Dayrell, or that rather good-looking son of Sir Roger Hammersley? Either of them, eh?"

"No, nor any one else."

"In this case, why are you in doubt? You think the girl likes you?"

"Sometimes I do, and sometimes I don't. She appears to change every day. But I've reason to believe she likes me now, or did yesterday."

"How do you know that? Has she told you so?"

"No—not in words; but I think so from her way. I hinted to her, that I intended to have a private talk with her upon an important matter, when we should be out on this hawking party. She appeared delighted at the idea—did, by Ged! Besides; she was in tiptop spirits all the evening after; and several times spoke of the pleasure she expected from to-morrow's sport—that is to-day. Now, what could that mean, unless——"

"Unless the pleasure she anticipated from your proposing to her. But if her liking be only on alternate days—as you say—and she was so fond of you yesterday, she might be in the contrary mood to-day? For that reason, I'd advise you to suspend proceedings till to-morrow."

"But, captain, you forget that I've got a way that will insure her consent, whether it be to-day or to-morrow."

"Disclose it, my sagacious cornet."

"If I should only give her a hint——"

"Of what?"

"You know how Sir Marmaduke is in your power?"

"I do."

"Well; if I only were to slip in a word about her uncle being in danger; not only of his liberty, but his life——"

"Stubbs!" cried the cuirassier captain, springing forward fiercely, and shaking his clenched fist before the face of his subaltern; "if you slip in a word about that—or dare to whisper the slightest hint of such a thing—your own life will be in greater danger than that of Sir Marmaduke Wade. I've commanded you already to keep your tongue to yourself on that theme; and now, more emphatically, do I repeat the command."

"Oh, captain!" stammered out the terrified Stubbs, in an apologetic whine; "if you don't approve, of course I won't say a word about it. I won't, by Ged!"

"No; you had better not. Win the consent of your sweetheart after your own way; but don't try to take advantage of a power that does not appertain to you. A contingency may arise, for disclosing that secret; but it is for me, not you, to judge of the crisis."

The further protestations of the scared cornet were cut short by the entrance of a messenger; who came to announce that the party about to proceed on the hawking excursion, was ready to start, and only waited the company of Captain Scarthe and Cornet Stubbs.

Five minutes later, a cavalcade of splendid appearance might have been seen passing through Bulstrode Park, towards one of the side gates that opened out to the eastward.

It consisted of Sir Marmaduke Wade, his son, daughter, and niece —the two officers, his guests—with a large following of grooms, falconers, and other attendants; a number of them on horseback, with hawks perched upon their shoulders; a still larger number afoot —conducting the retrievers; others *chiens de chasse*, employed in the *venerie* of the time.

On clearing the enclosure of the park, the gay procession turned in a southerly direction towards the beautiful lake of Fulmere; which, fed by the Alder "burn," lay embosomed between two parallel spurs of the beech-embowered Chilterns.

CHAPTER LIV

The lake "Fulmere" is no longer in existence, though a village so picturesque, as to appear the creation of a painter's fancy—still retains the name. The "mere" itself—yielding to the all-absorbing spirit of utilitarianism—has disappeared from the landscape, drained off by the brook "Alderburne," and the rivers Colne and Thames, to mingle its waters with the ocean. Its bed has become a meadow, the residue of its waters being retained in sundry stagnant pools which serve to supply the neighboring markets with cress; and the pharmacopœia of the village apothecaries with "calamus root."

Once a broad sheet of crystal water covered the cress-beds of Fulmere, a sheet with sedgy shores, in which sheltered the bittern and blue heron; the bald coot, the water-hen, and the gold-crested widgeon.

It was so on that day, when Dorothy Dayrell, the daughter of Sir Frederick, Lord of the Manor of Fulmere, invited her friends to be present at a grand entertainment—including falconry—the spectacle to be exhibited upon the shores of the lake.

Dorothy Dayrell was something more than pretty. She was what might be termed a "dashing creature," a little devilish, it is true, but this, in the eyes of her male acquaintances, only rendered her prettiness more *piquant*. Following the fashion of her father, she was of the true Tory type, devotedly attached to king and state, and blindly believing in that theory—worthy the conception of a community of apes—the "right divine."

Silly as is the belief, it was then entertained, as now. At that time, human bipeds of both sexes were just as parasitical, as they are at the present hour; and as loudly proclaimed their ignoble longings for King Stork, or King Log. Not, however, quite so unanimously.

The word "republic" was beginning to be heard, issuing from the lips of great statesmen, and true patriots.

It was beginning to find an echo in remote villages, and cottage homes, throughout all England.

15*

Not that such sentiments had ever been spoken in the village of
Fulmere.

To have pronounced them there, would have been deemed rank
treason; and the rustic given utterance to them, would have found
himself in the pillory, almost before the speech could have passed
from his lips.

Dorothy hated the idea of a republic; as small-souled people do
now, and have done in all ages.

We regret having to place the fair Dayrell in this category·
but we must succumb to the requirements of truth; and this com-
pels us to say that Mistress Dorothy, physically *petite*, was morally
little-minded.

Her pretty face, however, concealed the defects of her selfish soul;
and aided by many wiles and winning ways, rendered her sufficiently
popular in that large social circle, of which she was, or wished to be,
both the star and the centre.

Some proof of her popularity was the crowd that responded to her
call, and was present at her hawking party.

Scores of people of "first quality"—dames of high degree, and
cavaliers appropriate to such companionship—collected upon the
shores of Fulmere Lake; cast resplendent shadows upon its smooth
surface; and caused its enclosing hills to resound with the echoes of
their merry voices.

It is not our purpose to detail the various incidents of the day's
sport: how the party, having met at an appointed place, proceeded
around the shores of the lake; how the herons rose screaming from
the sedge, and the hawks shot like winged arrows after them; how
the owners of the predatory birds bantered one another, and wagers
were laid and lost by betters of both sexes; and how—when the circuit of the lake had been accomplished, and the adjacent reedy
marshes quartered by the spaniels, until cleared of their feathered
game—the gay company wended their way to the summit of the
adjoining hill; and there, under the shadows of the greenwood tree,
partook of an *al fresco* banquet, which their knightly entertainer
had provided for them.

Nor need we describe the conversation, varied of course, always
lively under such circumstances; often witty after the wine has
flowed freely.

One topic alone claims our attention, as it did that of the com
pany.

It was introduced by Mistress Dorothy herself, to whom of course every one obsequiously listened.

"I regret," said this charming creature, addressing herself to her splendid surrounding, "that I've not been able to provide you with a more spirited entertainment. After that we witnessed the other day in Bulstrode Park, our fête will appear tame, I know. Ah! if we only had the *black horseman* here. How cruel of you, Captain Scarthe, to have deprived us of that pleasure!"

"Mistress Dayrell," replied the officer, on whom the speech had made anything but a pleasing impression, "I regret exceedingly that in the performance of my duty, in dealing with a rebel, I should——"

"No apologies, Captain Scarthe," interposed Sir Frederick, coming to the rescue of the embarassed cuirassier. "We all know that you acted as becomes a loyal servant of his majesty. It would be well if others, in these doubtful times, would display a like energy." Here Sir Frederick glanced sarcastically towards his neighbor knight —between whom and himself there was not the most cordial friendship. "The only regret is that the fellow, whoever he may be, was permitted to escape; but, I dare say, he will be soon retaken, and meet with his deserts."

"And what would you deem his deserts, Dayrell?" quietly asked Sir Marmaduke Wade.

"The block!" replied the fiery Sir Frederick, who had been partaking rather freely of his own wine. "What else for an adventurer like him, who conspires against his king? I'd chop off his head like a cabbage."

"By so doing," rejoined Sir Marmaduke, in a tone of satirical significancy, "you would only cause a score of like heads to sprout up in its place."

"Let them sprout up. We'll serve them the same way. We shall still have the power to do so—in spite of this parliament of traitors, which the king has been so foolish as to think of recalling around him."

"Oh, dear father," interrupted the pretty Dorothy, in a tone of pseudo-sentimentality, "don't talk of chopping off heads. What a pity it would be if Captain Scarthe's late prisoner were to lose his! I'm so glad he escaped from you, Captain."

"Why is this, girl?" asked Sir Frederick, turning rather sharply upon his daughter. "Why would it be a pity? I've heard you this very morning express the opposite opinion!"

"But I did not know then—that—that——"

"Know what?" interrogated several of the party, who encompassed the fair speaker.

"That there were others interested in the fate of the unfortunate man. Ah, deeply so!"

A malicious glance towards Marion Wade did not escape the attention of the latter; and it was also noticed by Scarthe.

"Others interested in his fate. Who, pray?" demanded Sir Frederick, looking inquiringly towards his daughter.

"His wife, for one," replied Dorothy, laying a peculiar emphasis on the words.

"His wife!" simultaneously echoed a score of voices. "The black horseman a Benedict! Holtspur married! We never knew that."

"Nor I," continued the pretty imparter of the startling intelligence—"not till an hour ago. I've just heard it from cousin Wayland here; who came this morning from court—where it seems Master Holtspur is well known; though not by the name he has chosen to make celebrated among us rustics in Buckinghamshire.'

"'Tis quite true," said a youth in courtier costume, who stood close to her who had thus appealed to him. "The gentleman my cousin speaks of is married. I thought it was known to everybody."

"How could it, dear Wayland?" asked Dorothy, with an air of charming simplicity. "Master Holtspur was not known to any one here—except, I believe, to Sir Marmaduke Wade and his family; and if I mistake not, only very slightly to them."

A significant curling of the speaker's pretty nostril accompanied this final remark—which was intended as an interrogative.

"That is true," answered Sir Marmaduke. "My acquaintance with the gentleman you speak of is but slight. I was not aware o his being a married man; but what has that to do——"

"Oh, ladies and gentlemen!" interrupted the freshly arrived courtier, "perhaps you are not aware of the real name of this cavalier who has been calling himself Holtspur. He has been of some notoriety at court; though that was before my time; and I've only heard of it from others. There was a scandal, I believe——"

"Come, come, Wayland!" cried his fair cousin, interrupting him. "No scandals here. Keep it, whatever it be, to yourself."

"His name, his name!" shouted a score of voices; while twice that number of ears, piqued by the word "scandal"—were eagerly bent to listen to the threatened disclosure.

The courtier gave utterance to a name, known to most of the company; and which ten years before had been oftener pronounced in connection with that of England's queen.

Only in whispers; it is true, and less discreditable to Henry —— than Henrietta.

The announcement produced an effect upon the auditory of a very peculiar character.

It was certainly not so damaging to him who was the subject of their criticisms; for in the minds of many there present, the man of *bonnes fortunes* was a character to be envied rather than despised; and the favorite page—whose mysterious disappearance from court, some ten years before, had given rise to a "royal scandal"—could not be otherwise than interesting.

The knowledge that Henry Holtspur—the black horseman—the mysterious—the unkown—was identical with Henry ——, once a queen's page—the recipient of royal smiles—perhaps, in that assemblage gained him more friends than enemies.

Such as were still disposed to be hostile to him, could no longer avail themselves of that mode of reviling—still so customary among the "*élite*"—by calling him an "adventurer."

This had he been in the true sense of the term, an adventurer, but one to be envied by his enemies.

Even the heart of the dashing Dorothy became suddenly softened towards him, on hearing the new revelation made by her cousin Wayland.

That expression of sympathy for him, supposed by her auditory to have been ironical, was a more sincere sentiment than usually fell from her lips.

The scandal was not discussed among Sir Frederick's guests, at least not in open assembly.

The whisperings of side groups may have referred to it; but it was too old to be interesting, even to the most industrious dealers in *crim. con.* gossip.

The general conversation became changed to a theme more appropriate to the occasion; though a small congenial group, who had gathered around the young Wayland, were treated to some further details, relating to the matrimonial affairs of the patriot conspirator.

Of these not much knew the courtier; nor indeed any one else upon the ground.

He could only inform his auditory, what some of them already

knew; that Henry —— had been secretly married to one of the noble
ladies of Queen Henrietta's court, that the marriage ceremony had
been followed by an affair in which the queen herself had taken an
unusual interest, in short, by a separation between man and wife, by
the loss of the greater part of the young husband's fortune, and
finally by his disappearance, both from the court and the country.

Among other adventurous spirits of the time, he had emigrated to
the colonies of Virginia.

To do Master Wayland justice, he evinced no particular hostility
towards the man, whose history he was narrating; though, on the
other hand, he said nothing in his defense.

It was not his province to make known the nature of that conju-
gal quarrel; or say who was in fault.

In truth, the stripling but ill understood it.

He did not know that royal jealousy had been the cause of that
sudden separation between Henry —— and his bride-wife; and that it
was an act of royal revenge, that had transformed the courtier into
a colonist.

The subject, after a time, losing interest, was permitted to drop,
the conversation changing to other themes.

There was one whose thoughts could not be distracted from
it.

Need I say it was Marion Wade?

Amidst the gay company, her gaiety was gone.

The roses upon which the mid-day sun was but the moment before
brightly beaming, had forsaken her cheeks, on that instant when
the word "wife" fell from the lips of Dorothy Dayrell.

To her the hawking party was no longer a party of pleasure.

The sociality that surrounded her was only irksome and afflict-
ing.

To withdraw from it had been her first thought.

To escape observation as well; for she knew that the dire cloud,
that had settled over her heart, could not fail to be reflected in
her face.

On recovering from the shock caused by the unexpected announcement, she had turned her back upon the company, and stolen silently away.

The trees standing closely around the spot, with the underwood
still in foliage, favored her withdrawal, as also the peculiar topic of
conversation which at the moment was absorbing the attention of
all.

She had not stayed to listen to the further revelations made by the courtier Wayland—the one word spoken by his cousin had been the cue for her silent exit from the circle of conversation.

She needed no confirmation of what she had heard.

A vague suspicion already conceived, springing out of the ambiguity of some stray speeches let fall by Holtspur himself—not only at their first interview, but while arranging terms of that parting promise—had laid the foundation for an easy faith in the statement of Dorothy Dayrell.

Painful as was the conviction, Marion could not resist it.

She thought not of calling it in question.

Once among the trees she glided rapidly on—knowing not whither; nor caring; so long as her steps carried her far from the companionship of her own kind.

After wandering awhile, she came to a stop; and now, for the first time, did her countenance betray, in all its palpable reality, the bitterness that was burning within her.

Her heart felt as if parting in twain. A sigh—a half-suppressed scream—escaped from her bosom; and, but that she had seized upon a sapling to support herself, she would have fallen to the earth.

No pen could paint her emotions at that moment. They were too painful to permit of speech. Only one word fell from her lips—low-murmured and in accents of extreme sadness—the black word "Betrayed."

Though silent in speech, her thoughts flowed fast and freely.

"This, then, is the barrier that might come between us! *Might* come! Oh! the falsehood! And such a promise as I have given! Despite every obstacle, to love him! I thought not of this—how could I? No promise can bridge over such a chasm. I may not—I dare not keep it. 'Tis no sin to break it now. Mother of God! give me the strength!

"Ah! 'tis easy to talk of breaking it. Merciful Heaven! the power has passed from me!

"'Tis sinful on either side. Perjury the one, a worse crime the other. I feel powerless to choose between them. Alas!—Alas! Despite his betrayal—I love him, I love him!

"Am I not wronging him? Was not I the wooer—I, Marion? Was it not I who gave the first sign—the challenge—everything?

"What meant he to have said at that moment, when our last interview was interrupted? What was it, he was about to declare—

and yet hesitated? Perhaps he intended to have made this very disclosure—to tell me all? Oh, I could have forgiven him; but now I may not—I dare not——"

She paused as if conscious how idle it was, to give thought to a resolve she had not the power to keep.

"Married! Holtspur married! Alas! my love dream is ended 'Tis only changed from sweet to sad; and this will never change til. my unhappy heart be stilled in the sleep of death!"

The despairing maiden stood with her white fingers still clasped around the stem of the sapling—her eyes bent upon the ground in vacant gaze, as if all thought had forsaken her.

For some minutes she remained in this attitude—motionless as the tree that supported her.

The sound of an approaching footstep failed to startle her.

She heard, without heeding it.

Her sorrow had rendered her insensible even to shame. She cared little now, who might behold her emotion.

The footstep was too light to be mistaken for that of a man.

Marion had no time for conjecture; for almost on the instant, she heard the voice of her cousin Lora calling her by name.

"Marion! where are you! I want you, cousin."

"Here, Lora!" replied the latter, in a feeble voice, at the same time making an effort to appear calm.

"Oh!" exclaimed the pretty blonde, hurriedly making her way through the underwood, and stopping before her cousin with blushing cheeks and palpitating bosom.

"Lord a merci, coz!—I've got such a story to tell you. What do you think it is? Guess!"

"You know I'm not good at guessing, Lora. I hope you haven't lost your favorite merlin?"

"No—not so bad as that; though I've lost something."

"What pray?"

"A lover!"

"Ah!" exclaimed Marion, with a sad emphasis. Then, making an effort to conceal her emotion, she added in another strain, "I hope Walter hasn't been flirting with Dorothy Dayrell?"

"Bother Dorothy Dayrell!"

"Well—perhaps with one you might have more reason to be afraid of—Miss Winnifred Wayland?"

"Not so bad as that neither. It's another lover I've lost!"

"Oh! you confess to having had another. Have you told Walter so?"

"Bother about Walter! Who do you think I'm speaking of?"

"Captain Scarthe, perhaps—whom you admire so much. Is he the lover you have lost?"

"Not so bad as that neither. Guess again?"

"A third there is, or has been! You wicked coquette!"

"Not I. I never gave him the slightest encouragement. I am sure, never. Did you ever see me, coz?"

"When you tell me who this lost lover is, I shall be the better able to tell you."

"Who he is! Cornet Stubbs, of course."

"Oh! he. And how have you come to lose him? Has he made away with himself? He hasn't drowned himself in the mere, I hope?"

"I don't know; I shouldn't like to swear he hasn't. When I last looked upon his ugly face, I fancied there was drowning in it. Ha! ha! ha!"

"Well, my light-hearted coz; your loss seems to sit easily upon you. Pray explain yourself."

"Marion!" said Lora, catching hold of her cousin's arm, and speaking in a tone of greater solemnity. "Would you believe it—that impertinent has again proposed to me?"

"What! a second declaration! That looks more like finding a lover, than losing one."

"Ay, a second declaration; and this time far more determined than before. Why, he would take no denial!"

"And what answer did you make him?"

"Well, the first time, as I told you, I gave him a flat refusal. This time it wasn't so very flat. It was both pointed and indignant. I talked to him sharp enough: no mincing of words, I assure you. And yet, for all that, the pig persisted in his proposal, as if he had the power to force me to say, yes! I couldn't get rid of him, until I threatened him with a box on the ear. Ay, and I'd have given it him, if some of the company hadn't come up at the time, and relieved me of his importunities. I shouldn't have cared if I had ever given him cause—the impudent pleb! I wonder that keeping the company of his more accomplished captain don't have the effect of refining him a little—the impertinent upstart!"

"Have you told Walter?"

"No—that I haven t; and don't you, dear Marion. You know Walter has been jealous of Stubbs—without the slightest cause—and might want to challenge him. I shouldn't wish that, for the world; though I'd like some one—not Walter—to teach him a lesson such as your brave Henry Holtspur taught——"

"Ah!" exclaimed the speaker suddenly interrupting herself, as she saw the painful impression which the mention of that name had produced. "Pardon me, cousin! I had quite forgotten. This scene with Stubbs has driven everything out of my mind. Oh, dear Marion! Maybe it is not true? There may be some mistake? Dorothy Dayrell is wicked enough to invent anything; and for that foppish brother of Miss Winnifred Wayland, he is as full of conceit as his own sister; and as full of falsehood as his cousin. Dear Marion! don't take it for truth! It may be all a misconception. Holtspur may not be married after all; and if he be, then the base villain——"

"Lora!" interrupted Marion, in a firm tone of voice, "I command—I entreat you—to say nothing of what you know—not even to Walter—and above all, speak not of *him*, as you have done just now. Even if he be what you have said, it would not be pleasant for me to hear it repeated."

"But, surely, if it be true, you would not continue to love him?"

"I could not help it. I am lost. I must love him."

"Dear, dear Marion!" cried Lora, as she felt the arms of her cousin entwined around her neck, and saw the tears streaming down her cheek. "I pity you—poor Marion, from my heart I pity you Do not weep, dearest. It will pass. In time you will cease to think of him."

There was but one word of reply to these affectionate efforts at consolation.

It came amid tears and choking sobs, but with an emphasis and an accent that admitted of no rejoinder.

"Never!" was that word, pronounced in a firm unfaltering tone.

Then, tossing her head backward, and by a vigorous effort of her proud spirit assuming an air of indifference, the speaker clasped the hand of her cousin and walked resolutely back towards the assemblage from which she had so furtively separated

CHAPTER LV

THE RETURN OF THE GAUNTLET.

Of all who enjoyed the sports of the hawking party, no one left it with a heavier heart than Marion Wade.

The shadows of night, descending over the lake as the company took their departure from its shores, might well symbolize the shadow that had fallen upon her heart.

Throughout the afternoon, it had been a hard struggle with her to conceal her chagrin from curious eyes; to appear joyous, amid so many happy faces; to wear pretended smiles, while those around were laughing gayly.

All this, however, her strength of character had enabled her to accomplish; though it was like removing a load from off her breast, when the falling shades of twilight summoned the party to a separation.

That night no sleep for Marion Wade. Not enough to give her a moment's relief from the thoughts that tortured her.

Her pillow was pressed, but with a pale and sleepless cheek.

And often during the night had she risen from her couch, and paced the floor of her apartment, like one under the influence of a delirious dream.

The bosom that has been betrayed can alone understand the nature of her sufferings.

Perhaps only a woman's heart can fully appreciate the pain she was enduring!

Hers had received into its most inmost recesses—into the very citadel itself—the image of the heroic Holtspur.

It was still there; but all around it was rankling as with poison. The arrow had entered.

Its distilled venom permeated the bosom it had pierced.

There was no balsam to subdue the pain; no hope, to afford the slightest solace; only regret for the past, and despair for the future.

Until that day, Marion Wade had never known what it was to be truly unhappy.

Her pangs of jealousy hitherto experienced had been slight, compared with those which were now wringing her breast.

Even her apprehensions for the fate of her lover had been endur-
able; since hope for his safety had never wholly forsaken her.   During the interval that had elapsed since his escape, she had not been
altogether unhappy.

Her heart had been fortified by hope; and still further supported
by the remembrance of that last sweet interview.

So long as Holtspur lived and loved her, she felt that she could be
happy—even under those circumstances hypothetically foreshadowed
in his parting speeches.

There were times when she pondered on their mysterious import;
when she wondered what they could have meant—and not without a
sense of dissatisfaction.

But she had not allowed this to intrude itself either often or long.

Her love was too loyal, too trusting, to be shaken by suspicions.
She remembered how unjust had been those formerly indulged in;
and, influenced by this memory, she had resolved never again to give
way to doubt, without some certain sign—such as the return of the
love-token, as arranged between them.

She might have had cause to wonder, why she had not heard from
him—if only a word to ensure her of his safety.   But she was not
chagrined by his silence.

The risk of communicating with her might account for it.

Under an hypocritical pretense of duty—of obedience to orders
he dared not depart from—the cuirassier captain permitted nothing,
not even an epistle, to enter the mansion of Sir Marmaduke Wade,
without being first submitted to his own scrutiny.

Since the hour of his escape, the only intimation she had had of
her lost lover, almost the first time she had heard his name pronounced—was when coupled with those two words, that were now filling
her with woe—"his wife!"

Marion had heard no more.

She had stayed for no farther torture from those scandal-loving
lips.

She had heard that her lover—the man to whom she had surrendered the reins of her heart—was the husband of another!

That was knowledge enough for one hour of wretchedness—ay,
for a whole lifetime of sadness and chagrin.

Though in the midst of that gay assemblage, she had not essayed
to seek an explanation; she was now desirous of having it.

So long as the slightest remnant of either hope or doubt remains within the mind of one who suspects an unrequited passion, that mind cannot feel any satisfaction.

It will seek the truth—although the search may conduct to eternal ruin.

So determined the daughter of Sir Marmaduke Wade, during the mid-hours of that sleepless night ; and, long before the great bell of Bulstrode summoned its retainers to their daily toil, the young mistress of this lordly mansion might have been seen—closely wrapped in cloak and hood—issuing forth from one of its portals ; and, under the gray light of dawn, with quick but stealthy step, making her way over the dew-bespangled pastures of its park.

The gate through which she had often passed outward into the high road—often, of late, with a heart trembling in sweet anticipation —was the one towards which she directed her steps.

How different was now her prospect—how dissimilar her purpose!

She went not forth to meet one, whom, though still undeclared, she instinctively believed to be her lover—loyal and true.

Her errand was no more of this joyous nature, but the sad reverse. It was to make inquiries as to that lover's loyalty, or seek confirmation of his falsehood.

Who could give the wished-for information? From whom were the inquiries to be made?

She could think of no one save Holtspur himself; and the white paper—clutched in a hand almost as white, concealed under her cloak, gave a clue to her design.

It was an epistle that had been penned by the light of the midnight lamp, and sealed under a flood of scorching tears.

There was no direction upon it—only the name Henry Holtspur. She knew not his address.

She was taking it to a place where she had hopes of seeing some one who might be able to forward it to its destination.

The path she was following pointed to this place.

It was the road leading to Stone Dean.

It was not the first time she had thought of thus communicating with her absent lover.

She had forborne, partly through fear of being betrayed by those to whom her letter might be entrusted—partly by the feminine reflection that he, not she, should be the first to write—and partly by the hope, deferred from day to day, that he would write.

These hindrances she regarded no longer.

An epistle was now addressed to him—far different from that hitherto intended.

It was no longer a letter of love, but one filled with reproaches and regrets.

* * * * * * * *

Marion Wade was not the only one under her father's roof who at that same hour had been employing the pen.

Another had been similarly occupied.

As a soldier, Scarthe was accustomed to keep early hours.

It was a rare circumstance for him to be a-bed after six o'clock in the morning.

In those times of political agitation, the military man often took part in State intrigues; and in this craft the cuirassier captain, under the guidance of his royal patroness, had inextricably engaged himself.

This double duty entailed upon him an extensive correspondence, to which his morning hours were chiefly devoted.

Although essentially a man of pleasure, he did not surrender himself to idleness.

He was too ambitious to be inactive; and both his military and political duties were attended to with system and energy.

On the day of the hawking party his correspondence had fallen behind; and, to clear off the arrears, he was astir at a very early hour next morning and busy before his writing table.

His military and political dispatches were not the only matters that called for the use of his pen on this particular morning.

Upon the table before him lay a sealed packet, that might have contained a letter, but evidently something more, something of a different character, as indicated by its shape and size.

But there was no letter inside; and the object within the envelope might be guessed at, by the soliloquy that fell from the lips of Captain Scarthe, as he sat regarding it.

It was a glove—the white gauntlet, once worn upon the hand of Marion Wade—once worn upon the hat of Henry Holtspur, and thence surreptitiously abstracted.

It was once more to be restored to its original owner, in a secret and mysterious manner; and to that end had it been enclosed in a wrapping of spotless paper, and sealed with a blank seal stamp.

As yet there was no superscription upon the parcel; and he who had made it up sat contemplating it, pen in hand, as if uncertain as to how he should address it.

It was not this, however, about which he was pausing.

He knew the address well enough.

It was the mode of writing it—the chirography—that was occupying his thoughts.

"Ha!" he exclaimed at length, "an exellent idea. It must be like his handwriting; which in all probability she is acquainted with. I can easily imitate it. Thank fortune I've got copies enough—in this traitorous correspondence."

As he said this, he drew towards him a number of papers, consisting of letters and other documents.

They were those he had taken from Stone Dean, on the morning of Holtspur's arrest.

After regarding them for some seconds, with the attention of an expert in the act of deciphering some difficult manuscript, he took his pen and wrote upon the parcel the words—

"*Mistress Marion Wade.*"

"That will be enough," reflected he. "The address is superfluous. It would never do for it to be delivered at the house. It must be put into her hands secretly, as if sent by a trusty messenger. There's no reason why she should mistrust the woodman Walford. She may know him to have been in Holtspur's service, and can scarce have heard of his defection. He'll do. He must watch for an opportunity, when she goes out. I wonder what delays the knave. He should have been here by this time. I told him to come before daylight. Ah, speak of the fiend. That must be his shadow passing the window."

As Scarthe said this, he hastily rose to his feet; scattered some drying sand over the wet superscription; and taking the packet from the table, walked towards the door to meet his messenger.

It was the traitor Walford, whose shadow had been seen passing the window.

His patron found him standing on the step.

He was not admitted inside the house.

The business, for the execution of which he was required, had been already arranged; and a few words of instruction, spoken in a low tone, sufficed to impart to him a full comprehension of its nature.

He was told that the packet then placed in his hands was for Mistress Marion Wade; that he was to watch for an opportunity when she would be out of doors ; and deliver it to her, if possible, unseen by any third party.

He was instructed to assume an air of secresy; to announce himself as a messenger of Henry-Holtspur; and after delivering a verbal message, supposed to proceed from the cavalier, but carefully concocted by Scarthe, he was to hasten out of the lady's presence, and avoid the danger of a cross-questioning.

"Now, begone ! " commanded his employer, when he had completed his chapter of instructions. " Get away from the house, if you can, without being observed. It won't do for you to be seen here at this early hour, least of all on a visit to me. Let me know when you have succeeded; and if you do the business adroitly, I shall double this *douceur*."

As Scarthe said this, he slipped a gold coin into the hand of the pseudo messenger ; and turning upon his heel, walked back towards his apartment.

The woodman, after grinning gleefully at the gold that lay glistening in his palm, thrust the piece into his pocket ; and gliding down from the steps, commenced making a stealthy departure through the shrubbery.

He little thought how near he was to the opportunity he desired, of earning the duplicate of that *douceur*.

But fate, or the fiend, was propitious to him.

On clearing the moated enclosure, he saw before him the form of a woman, closely wrapped in cloak and hood.

She, too, seemed hastening onward with stealthy step ; but the tall, symmetrical figure, and the rich robes that enveloped it, left no doubt upon the mind of Walford as to the person who was preceding him down the sloping avenue of Bulstrode Park.

It was the young mistress of the mansion—she for whom his message was intended—she who would be made wretched by its delivery.

The emissary of Scarthe neither knew, nor would have cared for this.

His only thought was to earn the promised perquisite ; and with this object in view he followed the female figure fast flitting towards the gate of the park.

Quickly and silently did Marion glide upon her errand.

Absorbed by its painful nature, she fancied herself unobserved.

She saw not the dark form skulking but a short distance behind her, like an evil shadow, ill-defined, under the dim light of the dawn, and keeping pace with her steps as she advanced.

Unconscious of the proximity of her suspicious follower, she passed out through the park gates, and on along the forest road, a path well known to her.

Never before had she trodden it with a heavier heart.

Never before had she stood under the shadow of the trysting tree, to her now sadly sacred, influenced by such painful emotion.

She paused beneath its out-spreading branches.

She could not resist the mystic spell which the place seemed to cast around her.

There was something even in the sadness of its souvenirs that had a very soothing effect upon her spirits, that could scarce have been more embittered.

Whether soothing or saddening, she was permitted to indulge only a short time in silent reflection.

A heavy footfall—evidently that of a man—was heard approaching along the path, and shuffling among the crisp leaves with which it was bestrewed.

The sounds grew louder and drew nearer, until he who was causing them came in sight—a rustic making his way through the wood.

Marion knew the man—the woodman Walford.

She knew him only by sight, and but slightly.

She had no words for such as he, especially in an hour like that.

She moved not.

Her eyes were averted.

The intruder might have passed on, without receiving from her even a nod of recognition, had such been his wish.

It was only on hearing her own name pronounced, and seeing the man advance towards her, that the young lady took note of his presence.

"Mistress Wade!" muttered he, awkwardly uncovering his head, and making a bow of doubtful politeness.

"What want you with me, sir?" asked Marion, in a tone that betrayed both annoyance and astonishment.

"I've been follerin' thee, mistress, all the way frae the big house. I want to see thee alone."

"Alone! And for what purpose, sirrah?"

The interrogatory was uttered in a voice that betokened indignation, not unmingled with alarm.

16

No wonder.

He to whom it was addressed was not the man with whom a timid woman would elect to hold an interview alone and in the heart of a wood

Was the rustic intruding himself with an evil intention?

The apprehensions, thus quickly conceived, were as speedily dis· sipated by the woodman declaring himself to have come in the capacity of a messenger.

"I ha' bro'ght thee a package, Mistress Wade," said he, drawing something from under the skirt of his doublet. "It be a small 'un, I trow; but for all that I darn't gie it ye afore company, for I had orders not to b' 'im as sent me."

"Who sent you?" hastily inquired the lady, at the same time taking the packet from the hand of the cautious carrier.

"Master Holtspur," bluntly replied the man.

"I darn't stay here aside ye," continued he. "Some o' them may come this way, an' see us togither. I've only to tell ye that Master Holtspur be safe, an' that it be all right *atween 'im an' 'is wife*. They be reconciled agin. But I needn't be tellin' ye that: I suppose it's all wrote inside the package. Now, mistress, I must away, an' get back to 'im as sent me. Good mornin'."

With another grotesque attempt at polite salutation, the deliverer of the message walked hurriedly away, and was very soon lost to the sight of its trembling recipient.

Marion had listened to his words without knowing their wicked design, without even suspecting that they were false. But false or true, she did not imagine there could be a new pang conveyed in their meaning. She had already felt the sting, as she supposed, in all its black bitterness. She did not believe that in the same quiver there was another arrow, bearing upon its point a still more potent poison.

She felt it, as with trembling fingers she broke the seal, and tore open the envelope of that tiny parcel. To her heart's core she felt it, as her eyes rested upon the contents.

Her token returned to her—that fatal gift—*the White Gauntlet!*

The glove dropped to the ground; and with a suppressed scream, that sounded like the knell of a shattered heart, Marion Wade sank beside it!

For some moments she lay along the grass, like some beautiful statue struck down from its pedestal

She was not unconscious, only unnerved and rendered powerless by a strong, quick spasm of despair.

Beyond the stifled scream, that escaped her as she fell, no sound escaped from her lips.

Hers was a despair that speech was incapable of relieving. There was nothing on which hope could hinge itself.

The restored token told the tale in all its sad reality.

A letter—a volume—could not have conveyed the information nore fully.

Holtspur no longer loved her!

There was even a more fell reflection. *He had never loved her:* else how could he have changed so soon?

The paroxysm at length passed, and the prostrate form once moro stood erect. Erect, but not triumphant. Sad and subdued was tho spirit that animated it—almost shivered by that fearful shock.

In silent agony she turned to go homeward. She no more remembered the errand that had summoned her forth. It was no longer of any importance. The information she would have sought had met her on the way—had been communicated with a fullness and surety that left nothing to be added.

Holtspur loved her no more.

With that thought in her mind, what mattered it whether he were married or no? But the words of the messenger had equally ended all doubt of this.

If there might be any lingering uncertainty as to what she heard, there could be none as to what she saw.

There lay the White Gauntlet under her eyes—down among the weeds. It lay neglected as if without an owner—no more to bo regarded by Marion Wade; or only as the cause of a life-long anguish.

Slowly and sadly she retraced the forest path; slowly and sadly she re-entered the gateway of the park; slowly and sadly she walked back along that avenue, once trodden by her with a bosom filled with supremest joy

CHAPTER LVI.

SCARTHE REJECTED

The course which Scarthe was pursuing may seem strange.

He now knew that for the hand of Marion Wade, Holtspur could not be his rival.

What, then, could be his motive for sending back the glove: for motive there must have been?

There was one; though to say the truth it was not very definite.

He was still uncertain as to the state of Marion's heart—still in doubt whether the white gauntlet had or had not been a *gage d'amour*.

If the former, then the restoring of it, as designed by him, might produce a revulsion of feeling in his own favor; if not, no evil could result to him from the act.

On his side the sending back of the glove was a mere conjectural experiment—made under a vague fancy that it might, to some little extent, further his interests.

If in the mind of Marion Wade there existed a partiality for the patriot conspirator, a sight such as that should crush out every vestige of the feeling, and create a reaction in favor of the first fresh lover who might present himself—Richard Scarthe more likely than any other.

Little did he anticipate the terrible· effect which that returned token, with the message that accompanied it, would have upon her who was to receive it.

He knew nothing of the strange conditions which the lovers had arranged at their last parting.

He had too much experience in the heart of woman to have reasoned thus—had he not been purblind with his own passion.

In this condition, however, he gave way to a fancy that, under other circumstances, he would have instantly rejected.

He was also influenced by considerations of a very different kind.

The hand of Marion Wade was almost as desirable as her heart—or rather the fortune that should accompany it.

The cuirassier captain possessed but his pay—along with proud patronage it is true—but neither was anything to make him what he should become as the son-in-law of Sir Marmaduke Wade.

The crisis had arrived to attempt bringing about this desired relationship.

It must not be delayed.

The power he possessed for its accomplishment might at any moment pass out of his hands.

The times were uncertain; and procrastination might imperil his chances of success.

The sending of the glove was the first move in the matrimonial scheme he had concocted.

It was to be followed by an offer of his hand.

If the offer should be accepted, well; if not, then stronger measures were to be adopted.

Such was the programme that had passed through the mind of Richard Scarthe; and was still before it, as he paced the floor of his apartment, an hour after having dismissed the messenger Walford.

"I wonder," said he, as he reflected upon the importance of time, "when the fellow Walford will succeed in delivering his false message? He's but a dull-brained dolt; though knave enough for that, or anything else. I hope he won't be so stupid as to bring it back to the house; or give it her in the presence of any one. Surely he will have understood my instructions about that? I told him to watch for her till she walked abroad, and alone. But when may that be? Perhaps not to-day; nor to-morrow; nor for many days? I'm burning with impatience to bring the business to a conclusion. What, after all my well-conceived strategy, if—— Ho! who comes yonder? By Heaven! 'tis Walford! What brings the brute back? From the grin upon that hideous countenance of his—intended no doubt for a smile—one might fancy he had already accomplished his errand. I must go forth and meet him—before he shows himself in front of the windows. It's early yet, and I see no one abroad; still some of them may be astir inside? He must not be seen coming here."

With this reflection, Scarthe seized his beaver; and flinging it upon his head, sallied forth from the house.

In the thick of the shrubbery he encountered the returning envoy.

"Well, Walford," said he, "what has brought you back so soon! Has anything miscarried?"

"Not as I knows on, Master Capten. Only as .ein' a' early burd this mornin' I ha' picked up the early wurum."

"Ah! what mean you by that?"

"I gin it to her."

"Gin it to her? What, and to whom?"

"The packidge—to the young lady."

"What, you don't say that you have seen——"

"Mistress Marion? Sartinly I do, Master Capten. Seen her; gied her the packidge; an' sayed, what ye told me to say."

"When? Where?"

"For the fust—it han't been gone a half-hour since the words passed out o' me mouth; an' as to the where, that war 'bout a mile frae heear—on the wood-road as runs froom the Park to Stone Dean."

"She there at this hour? You must be mistaken, my man?"

"No mistake 'bout it, Master Capten; I seed her, an' spoke to her, as ye bid me. I've seed her a many a time along that road. It be a favorite ride wi' her; but she bean't a horseback this mornin'. She be afut."

"And alone, you say?"

"Sartinly, Master: else how could I ha' gied her the packidge? Ye told me to let no one see me handin' it to her."

"This is strange," muttered Scarthe to himself. "You are sure there was no one near her?"

"I seed ne'er a creetur."

"What was she doing?"

"Nothin' capten; only standin' under a tree—the big beech as grows in the middle o' the road. I went up to her pretty quick, lest she might gi' me the slip. Arter I put the packidge i' her hand, an' sayed what ye told me, I coomed directly away."

"You left her there?"

"Left her, just as I found her—under the big beech."

"And you met no one as you returned along the road?"

"Neither met, nor passed, a sinner."

"You think she may be there still? You say you came direct?"

"Straight as the road 'ud let me, capten. I won't say she be theear still—that are, under the tree; but she ain't got home as yet: for I coomed as fast as me legs 'ud carry me. I knew ye didn't want me seen 'bout here, an' I tho'ght I would be safest to coom up afore the sarvints were stirrin'. She beean't got home yet, nor half o' the way—even supposin' she set off right arter me."

"The road to Stone Dean, you say?"

"That as goes thro'gh Stampwell's Wood, an' over the hills. It strikes off from the king's highway, a leetle beyond the gates o' the park."

"I know—I know. There, my man! Something to get you your morning dram. Away at once; and don't let yourself be seen in my company. Go where you like now; but be in your own nest at night; I may want you."

The messenger took the money; and along with it his instant departure.

"What the deuce can she be doing out at this hour?" inquired Scarthe of himself, as he strode nervously across the parterre.

"Ah! the place—the forest road leading to Stone Dean! Can it be possible that he ——. The fiends! If it be so, I may yet be in time to take him. Ho, there!" he cried to the guard corporal, who had just appeared outside the court-yard gate. "A dozen men to horse. Quick, corporal! Let them not lose a moment. I shall be out before they have time to strap on their saddles."

And, having delivered these orders, he turned back into his room; and commenced encasing his body in the steel armor that lay in pieces around the apartment.

In less than ten minutes' time he was armed *cap-à-pied*. Staying only to quaff off a cup of wine—which he hurriedly filled from a decanter that stood upon the side table—he passed out of his apartment; and strode clanking along the stane-flagged corridor that communicated with the rear of the dwelling.

Emerging into the court-yard, he mounted his horse—already comparisoned to receive him; and, giving the word of command to the cuirassiers, who had climbed to their saddles, he galloped out of the court—on towards the entrance of the park that opened in the direction of Stone Dean.

It was a short gallop—ending almost as soon as it had begun. It came to a termination, at the head of the hill—down which trended the long avenue skirted with chestnuts trees.

There Scarthe suddenly checked his steed—at the same time giving his followers the order to halt.

Naturally enough, the troopers were a little surprised at this sudden interruption of their ride; but they were altogether astonished at a second order—following quick upon the first—which enjoined upon them to wheel round, and return to their stables!

They obeyed, though not without a show of reluctance.

They would 𝑚𝑢𝑐𝑕 rather have continued their excursion—supposing it to have been intended for some foraging expedition that promised pleasure and plunder.

They were not entirely ignorant of what had caused the countermand.

As they were wheeling upon the path, they had caught sight of an object at the other end of the avenue, whose motions betrayed it to be animate.

Though but dimly seen through the dawn, and under the shadow of the chestnuts, they could tell what it was—the figure of a woman.

"A sail in sight!" muttered one, who had seen salt-water service. "The captain's going to hail the craft; and don't want us Jack-tars on the quarter-deck."

"'Tis she!" muttered Scarthe to himself, as his followers retired. "Even if he has been with her, 'twould be of little use going after him now. He would scarce be such a fool as to remain upon the ground. 'Tis impossible she can have seen any one, since Walford left her. There has not been time for an interview, such as that. She may have been with him before. If so, the sham message will result in my own discomfiture. Or she may have been expecting him, and he has not come. If so, the parcel will be just in time. I can scarce look for such a lucky combination of circumstances.

"What shall I do?" he continued, after a pause. "If she has not met him, it is a splendid opportunity for my proposal! The events are ominous of success. Shall I make it now—this moment?

"There is danger in delay," he muttered, as the old adage came into his mind. "She may have some means of communicating with him; and the glove trick may be discovered? I shall trust no longer to chance. This uncertainty is insufferable. Within the hour I shall put an end to it, and find out my fate, one way or the other. If accepted, then shall Richard Scarthe play traitor to his king, and the good knight Sir Marmaduke may conspire to his heart's content. If rejected, then—in that contingency—ah—then—the old rebel will risk the losing of his head.

"Now, Mistress Marion Wade," apostrophized he, as he watched the advancing figure. "On thine answer there is much depending, your father's head and my happiness. I hope you will be gracious, and give security to both. If you refuse me, then must I make use of that power, with which a lucky chance has provided me. Surely thy father's danger will undo your objections? If you resist, let the ruin fall—let him suffer his doom !

"I must dismount and meet her," he continued, as he saw Marion coming on with slow steps. "A declaration in the saddle would never do. It must be made on foot—or still more humbly on bended knee; and so shall it, if that be necessary to secure success. Ha, ha! what would they say at court? The invincible Scarthe, who has made conquest of a queen, kneeling in humble suit at the feet of a country maiden—the daughter of a rank rebel—begging for her heart, and worse still, bargaining for her hand! Ha, ha, ha!"

While uttering this laugh, he flung himself from his horse; and, tossing the rein of his bridle over the branch of a tree, commenced descending the hill.

Although advancing towards the interview, with all the *noncha-lance* he was capable of assuming, he was at the same time trembling with apprehension as to the result.

He met the maiden at the bottom of the hill, under the sombre shadow of the chestnuts.

He encountered a look of cold surprise, accompanied by a simple nod of recognition.

Such a reception might have turned him from his purpose; but it did not.

He had made up his mind to propose; and without much circumlocution, he proceeded to carry out the intention.

"Mistress Marion Wade," said he, approaching her with an air of profound respect, and bowing low as he drew near, "if you be not offended by my intruding upon you at this early hour, I shall thank the fate that has favored me."

"Captain Scarthe, this interview is unexpected."

"By me it has been *sought.* I have been for some time desirous of an opportunity to speak with you alone."

"To speak with me alone? I am at a loss to knew, sir, what you can have to say that requires such a condition."

"You *shall* know, Mistress Wade; if, indeed, you have not divined my purpose already. Need I tell you that I am in love? "

"And why, sir, have you chosen me for this confidence? I should think that was a secret to be communicated only to her whom it concerns."

"And to her alone has it been communicated Surely I need not name the object of my love. You cannot have been blind to emotions

16*

—to sufferings— I have been unable to conceal. I can be silent no longer. O, Marion Wade! I love you with all the fondness of a true affection—all the fervor of an admiration that knows no limits.

Do not be angry with me for thus declaring myself. Do not frown upon my suit. O, beautiful Marion! Say that I may hope?"

Scarthe had dashed his helmet to the ground, and flung himself on his knees in the attitude of an humble suppliant.

With eyes upturned to her face, he tremblingly awaited the reply. She was silent.

Her features betrayed no sign of gladness as she listened to that earnest declaration.

Scarce even did they show surprise.

Whatever of this she may have felt was concealed under the cloud of chagrin, that, springing from a very different cause, still overspread her countenance.

The kneeling suitor waited some moments for a response; but none was given.

She to whom he was making suit remained proudly silent.

Becoming sensible of a certain ludicrousness in the situation, Scarthe impatiently continued :—

" Oh, do not deny me! at least vouchsafe an answer. If it be favorable, I promise—I swear—that my heart—my hand—my soul—my sword—my life—all will be yours—yours for any sacrifice you may summon me to make. O Marion! beautiful Marion Wade! I know I am not worthy of you now. Think not of me as I am; but rather what I shall be. I may one day be more deserving of your esteem—perhaps your love. I have hopes of preferment—high hopes.

I may be excused for saying they are founded on the patronage of a queen. With one like you for my bride—my wife—highborn, gifted, lovelier than all others, these hopes would soon be realized. To be worthy of loving you—to have the pleasure of illustrating you —of making you happy by the highest fame—I could accomplish anything. Fear not, Marion Wade. He who sues to you, if now humble, may hope for higher rank. Ere long shall I obtain the much-coveted title of lord. It matters little to me. Only for your sake should I prize it. But on! hapless lord should I be, if not the lord of your heart! A word, Marion Wade! one word! Tell me I may hope?"

Marion turned her eyes upon the eloquent suppliant.

His attitude, the expression of his countenance, and the fervent tone in which he had declared himself were evidence that he was in earnest.

She could not fail to perceive that he loved her.

Whatever may have been the deceit of his nature in other respects, there could be no doubt that he was honest in his admiration for herself.

Perhaps it was this thought that restrained her from making an indignant reply.

Why should she be offended at one thus humbly sueing, one who was willing to become her slave?

The expression of her eye, called up by the attitude of the suitor, seemed to speak of pity rather than indignation.

It soon passed away: and was succeeded by the same calm look of indifference, with which she had hitherto regarded him.

Misinterpreting that momentary glance of kindness, Scarthe for an instant fancied himself successful.

Only for an instant.

His heart fell as he noted the change of countenance that succeeded; and it needed not for Marion to signify her refusal in speech.

Words could not have more plainly told him that his suit was rejected.

In words, however, he was told it; and with a laconism that left him no alternative, but to rise from his kneeling attitude, place his helmet once more upon his head, and bid Marion Wade good morning.

*   *   *   *   *   *

Alone the lady pursued her homeward way—Scarthe standing silent and statue-like, till she had passed out of sight. Then his features suddenly changed expression; his true temper, for the time restrained, escaped from the control in which he had been keeping it; and both voice and gesture testified to the terrible conflict of emotions that convulsed his soul.

"I shall seek no more to sue her," muttered he, as he detached his bridle from the branch. "'Tis not the mode to deal with this proud damsel. Force, not favor, is the way to win her—at least her hand—ah! and maybe her heart? I've known such as she before. Are there not hundreds in history? Did the Sabine women continue to despise their bold abductors? No; they became loving wives loving them for the very act, that, in the fancy of fools, should have excited their hatred! By Heaven! I shall imitate those Roman ravishers —if driven to the *dernier ressort*. Thank fortune! there's another arrow in my quiver. And now to place it to the string. By this time Sir Marmaduke should be stirring; though it seems he keeps not so early hours as his charming child! Curses! what can have carried her abroad? No doubt, I shall discover in time; and if it be that ——"

He interrupted himself, as if some conception, painful beyond common, had caused a sudden suspension of his breath.

"If it be that—a mistress, instead of a wife—shall I make of 'Marion Wade! "

With this vile threat, he sprang nervously to th · back of his horse, and, deeply driving the spurs, forced the animal into a rapid gallop, homeward against the hill.

CHAPTER LVII.

SIR MARMADUKE IN TROUBLE.

Sir Marmaduke was in his library—not busied with b's l a k a, b r' his thoughts.

It is unnecessary to say that these were of serious nature. They were more than serious—they were melancholly. The cause has been already, or may be easily, guessed.

In the circumstances that surrounded him, the noble knight had more than one source of anxiety. But there was one now paramount—an apprehension for his own personal safety—which, o. course, included the welfare of those dear to him.

He had reason to be thus apprehensive. He knew that he had committed himself—not only by his presence among the conspirators of Stone Dean, but by various other acts that would not bear the scrutiny of the Star Chamber.

Conjectures, referring to the midnight meeting at Holtspur's house, were at that moment more particularly before his mind.

The arrest of Holtspur himself upon the following morning- so close upon the breaking up of the assemblage—had an ominous sig nificance.

It suggested—in fact, almost proclaimed—the presence of a spy.

If such had been among them—and Sir Marmaduke could come to no other conclusion—then would his life be worth no more than that of a man already attainted, tried, condemned, and standing by the side of the block !

If there had been a spy, it must either have been Scarthe himself, or one who had communicated with him : else why the arrest of Holtspur ?

Sir Marmaduke believed the captain of the king's cuirrassiers quite capable of the infamous act.

His apparent friendship and courtesy—his professions of regret for the part he was compelled to play—had not deceived his host.

Sir Marmaduke had no difficulty in detecting the spurious preten ses of his guest.

As yet Scarthe had given him no hint of the knowledge he pos sessed.

For his own reasons, he had carefully abstained from this.

Nevertheless, Sir Marmaduke had his suspicions.

Unfortunately, he had no means of satisfying them, one way or the other.

Scarthe had carefully scrutinized his correspondence—under the pretense that he did so by orders from the king—and such of the members of that meeting as Sir Marmaduke had been able to see personally were, like himself, only suspicious.

No one in the neighborhood knew of the doings of that night, ex cept Dancey, Walford, and Gregory Garth.

Dancey and his daughter had both been absent for weeks—it was not known where; Walford had no dealings with Sir Marmaduke Wade; and Garth was utterly unknown to him

The knight knew that his liberty—his life—were in the scales.

A feather—a breath—and the beam might be kicked against him.

No wonder he was apprehensive—even to wretchedness.

There was but one clear spot in the sky—one beacon on which to fix his hopes—the *Parliament.*

This parliament—afterwards distinguished as the "Long," per haps the most patriotic assembly that ever met amongst men—was about to commence its sittings, as well as its struggles with the hoary hydra of *royal prerogative*.

To the oppressed it promised relief—to the condemned a respite—to the imprisoned a restoration of their liberty.

But the royal reptile, though cowering and partially crushed, had not yet been deprived of his fangs.

There were places throughout the realm where his power was rampant as ever—where he could still seize, confiscate and behead.

With reason, therefore, might Sir Marmaduke feel dread of his vengeance.

And no wonder: with Sir John Elliot pining away his life in a prison; with the wrongs of Lenthall, and Lilburne, and Prynne unavenged; with men walking the streets deprived of their ears, and outraged by other mutilations; with Holtspur himself, whom Sir Marmaduke now knew to be the noble patriot Henry ———, an outlawed fugitive, hiding himself from the sleuth-hounds of a spited queen !

The good knight resembled the mariner in the midst of a tempest.

The re-summoned Parliament was the life-boat struggling across the surge—surrounded by angry breakers.

Would it live to reach and relieve him ?

Or was he destined to see it strike upon a rock, and its gallant crew washed away amidst the waste of waters ?

In truth, a gallant crew as ever carried ship of State through the storm—as ever landed one in a haven of safety.

Hark to their names—every one of them a household word !

Pym, Hampden, Hollis and Hazlerig; the Lords Kimbolton, Essex, and Fairfax; and last and greatest, the immortal Oliver Cromwell !

It was a glorious galaxy of names—enough to inspire even the timid with confidence; and by such were the timid sustained.

In the retrospect of two hundred years, alongside such names, how sounds the paltry title of "Carolus Rex ? "

Even then, it was day by day losing its authoritative significance.

A crisis was coming, as when men awake from a drunken dream—when the word "loyalty" only reminds them of liberties surrentitiously stolen, and rights toc slackly surrendered; when "king" sounds synonymous with "tyrant," and "patriot" assumes its proper meaning.

Not as the so-called "statesmen" of the present day—statesmen, forsooth!

Palterers with the people's rights, snug trimmers of parliamentary majorities, bottle-holders, the very chicanes of statescraft—the "smush" of England's manhood, with reputations destined to damnation, almost as soon as their puny breath becomes choked within their inglorious coffins!

Oh! the contrast between that day and this—the difference of its deeds and its men!—distinct as glory from shame!

That was the grandest throe ever felt by England's heart in its aspirations after Liberty.

Let us hope it will not be the last.

Let us hope that the boasted spirit of Great Britain—at this hour lower than it has ever been—will have a speedy resuscitation; and strike to the dust the demon of thraldom, in whatever form he may make himself manifest—in the old-fashioned shape of *serfdom*, or its modern substitute, the *tax*; for, though differing in title, *both are essentially the same*.

    *   *   *   *   *   *   *   *

Sir Marmaduke sat in his library, as we have said, a prey to uneasy thoughts.

They were not tranquilized by the announcement, just then made by one of the domestics, that Captain Scarthe desired an interview with him.

"What business has he *now?*" was the mental interrogatory of the knight, when the request was conveyed to him.

"Something of more than ordinary import," thought he on glancing at the countenance of Scarthe, as the latter presented himself within the apartment.

Well might Sir Marmaduke give thought to the conjecture; for, in truth, was there upon the mind of his visitor something that might well merit the name of extraordinary; which, despite his habitual *sang froid*, did not fail to show itself upon his features.

Upon them a guilty intention was plainly expressed, as if the lines had been letters on the page of a printed book.

The knight knew not this intention by any overture hitherto made to him

He had his suspicions, nevertheless, too truly pointing to the pretentions which Scarthe was about to put forward to the hand of his daughter.

These had been sufficiently painful to him; now more so, when coupled with that other suspicion, already harassing him, as to the power possessed by his soldier guest.

They might have been even more painful, had he known the extent of that power—real and assumed—with which the latter was endowed.

At that moment Scarthe carried in his pocket, signed "Carolus Rex," an order for the knight's arrest and commitment to the Tower of London!

It signified little that both the order and its signature were counterfeits. They would be equally efficacious for the purpose intended.

Sir Marmaduke had not the means, nor would he be allowed the opportunity to test their genuineness.

They were forgeries both.

It was in concocting them that Captain Scarthe had spent the half hour between the time of his parting with Marion Wade and betaking himself into the presence of her father.

Before Sir Marmaduke he now stood, prepared for an emergency he had already contemplated—ready for its extremest measures.

"Pardon me, Sir Marmaduke Wade!" began he, bowing with ceremonious respect. "Pardon me for intruding upon you at this early hour; but my business is of importance. When you have heard it, you will no doubt excuse this deviation from the rules of etiquette."

"Captain Scarthe is, I presume, on the performance of some duty, and that will be his excuse."

"In truth, Sir Marmaduke, I have a double errand. One is on duty—and I grieve to say, a painful duty to me. The other I might designate an errand of *affection*; and could I flatter myself that it would prove a welcome one to you, I should deem it as pleasant as that of my duty is painful."

"You speak in enigmas, sir. I cannot comprehend them. May I ask you to tell me, in plain speech, what are your two errands? One, you say, is painful to yourself—the other, on certain conditions, may prove pleasant. Choose which you please to communicate first."

"Sir Marmaduke Wade," rejoined the cuirassier captain, ' you accuse me of circumlocution. It is an accusation I will not give you cause to repeat. My first errand—and that to me of most importance—is to tell you I love your daughter, and that I wish to make her my wife."

"I admire your candor, Captain Scarthe; but permit me to say in reply that the information you have thus volunteered concerns my daughter more than myself. You are free to impart it to her; as is she to answer you according to her inclination."

"I *have* imparted it. I have already proposed to her."

"And her answer ? "

"A refusal."

"And you come to me ! For what purpose, Captain Scarthe ? "

"Need I declare it, Sir Marmaduke? I love your daughter with all the love of my heart. I would wed her—make her happy—in time, perhaps, high and noble as any in the land. I know that I offer myself under unfavorable circumstances. But with your assistance, Sir Marmaduke—your authority exerted over her ——"

"You need not go on, sir," said Sir Marmaduke, interrupting the petitioner in a calm, firm tone. "Whatever answer my daughter has given you shall be mine. You speak of my authority. I have none in such a matter as this. The father has no right to restrain, or thwart, the inclinations of his child. I have never assumed such a power; nor shall I now—either in your favor or against you. If you have won the heart of Marion Wade, you are welcome to wear it—welcome both to her heart and hand. If not, you need not look to me. So far as I am concerned, my daughter is free to accept whomsoever she may please, or reject whom she may dislike. Now, sir ! " added the knight, in a tone that told of stern determination, "that matter is ended between us—I hope to your satisfaction."

"Enough ! " ejaculated Scarthe, his voice betraying indignant chagrin. "'Tis just as I expected," he muttered to himself. "It will be idle to urge the matter any more—at least until I've got my lever on its fulcrum; then, perhaps ——"

"May I beg of you to make known your other errand, sir," said Sir Marmaduke, impatient to bring the unpleasant interview to a termination, "that which you say is of a painful nature ? "

"I say it with truth," rejoined Scarthe, still keeping up a show of sympathy for his victim. "Perhaps you will not give me credit for the declaration, though I pledge my honor—as a gentleman holding the commission of the king—that a more unpleasant duty, than that which is now before me, I 'have never been called upon to perform.

"When you condescend to make it known, sir, perhaps I shall be the better able to judge. Can I assist you in any way?"

"Oh, Sir Marmaduke—noble Sir Marmaduke Wade—I wish it were in my power to assist you."

"Ha!"

' Alas! But a short month and I could with indifference have enacted the part I am now called upon to play. Then I knew you not. I knew not your daughter. Oh! that I had never known one or the other—neither the noble father, nor the ——"

"Sir!" interrupted Sir Marmaduke, sternly, "I beg you will come to the point. What is this disagreeable communication you would make? You surprise and puzzle me."

"I cannot declare it with my own lips. Noble knight! excuse me from giving speech to it. Here are my orders—too plain—too peremptory. Read them for yourself!"

Sir Marmaduke took hold of the paper, extended to him apparently with a trembling hand.

The hand trembled that received it.

He read:—

" *To ye Captain Scarthe, commanding ye cuirassiers at Bulstrode Park.*

" *It hath come to ye knowledge of his Majestie that Sir Marmaduke Wade, Knight, hath been guilty of treasonable practices and designs against his Majestie and ye government. Therefore Captain Scarthe is hereby commanded to arrest ye said Sir Marmaduke, and convey him to ye Tower prison, there to await trial by Star Chamber, or such other Court as may be deemed sufficient for ye crime charged.*

" *And Captain Scarthe is moreover enjoined and commanded by his Majestie to lose no time in carrying out ye said command of his Majestie, but that he proceed to its execution on ye receipt of these presents*

" Given at our palace, Whitehall.
"CAROLUS REX."

"I am your prisoner, then," said Sir Marmaduke, folding up the paper and returning it to the cuirassier captain.

"Not mine, Sir Marmaduke. Alas! not mine, but the king's."

"And where am I to be taken? But I forget. I need not have asked."

"The place is mentioned in the dispatch."

"The time, too!"

"I regret it is so," rejoined Scarthe, with a pretense of being pained in the performance of his duty. "By this document, you will perceive that my orders are peremptory."

"I presume I shall be permitted to take leave of my family."

"It grieves me to the heart, Sir Marmaduke, to inform you that my instructions are painfully stringent. Even that has been made a part of them."

"Then I am not to bid farewell to my children, before parting with them—perhaps forever?"

"Do not talk thus, sir," said Scarthe, with a show of profound sympathy. "There must be a misunderstanding. Some enemy has been abusing you to the ear of the king. Let us hope it will be nothing serious in the end. I wish it were otherwise; but I am instructed in a confidential dispatch—that, after making known the order for your arrest, I am not to permit any communication between you and your friends—even the members of your family—*except in my presence.*"

"In your presence be our parting, then. Can I summon my children hither?"

"Certainly, Sir Marmaduke. Alas! alas! that I am compelled to be the witness of such a sad spectacle."

* * * * * * * *

Scarthe truly characterized the scene that followed by calling it a sad spectacle. Such it was—too sad to be described: the cuirassier captain appearing as much affected as any of those who assisted at it.

In an hour after, Sir Marmaduke Wade—in the custody of a cuirassier guard—might have been seen passing out of Bulstrode Park, on his way to that famous, or rather infamous, receptacle of political prisoners—the Tower of London.

CHAPTER LVIII.

THE TRIAL.

In less than a week from this time, Sir Marmaduke Wade stood in the presence of the Star Chamber—that Court which for long years had been the dread—less of criminals, than of innocent men.

When accuser and judge are one and the same person, condemnation is sure to follow. In Sir Marmaduke's case the accuser was the king himself. The Star Chamber was a mere mask, a means of carrying out his arbitrary acts while screening him from their responsibility.

The trial was as much a farce as if it had been held before a conclave of the Holy Inquisition. Indeed, both Star Chamber and High Commission Court bore a close resemblance to that terrible tribunal; and like the latter, however farcical might be the form of the trials, they had too often a tragical ending.

Sir Marmaduke's trial, like many others of the time, was a mockery of justice—a mere formality to satisfy the slight remnants of liberty that still lingered in the constitution.

The court had already doomed him.

It needed only for the Star Chamber to indorse the foregone decree; which was done by its truculent judges without any delay, and with as little noise or ceremony.

The knight was accused of treason towards the crown—of conspiring against the king.

The charge was proven; and the criminal was condemned to death by the mode in use against political offenders of the time. His sentence was—to be beheaded upon the block.

He was not even confronted with his accusers; and knew not who they were who bore witness against him. But the most specific charge brought up—that of his presence and speech at the night meeting at Stone Dean left him no reason to doubt that Richard Scarthe was one of those who bore witness against him.

During the investigation, the accused was kept in complete

ignorance, both of the witnesses and the testimony preferred against him.

None was allowed in his favor—no advocate was permitted to plead for him; and, indeed, long before his trial came to a termination, he had made up his mind as to the result.

It was scarce a shock to him when the president of that iniquitous conclave pronounced in mock solemnity the sentence of *death*.

But it was a terrible shock to two tender hearts when his son Walter, hurrying home after the trial, carried the melancholy tidings to the mansion of Bulstrode, soon to be deprived of its master.

Never was the hypocrisy of Richard Scarthe more successfully exerted than in that sad hour.

The children of his victim were almost deceived into a belief in his friendship.

So sincere did his expressions of sympathy appear, and so often repeated, that Walter and Lora became almost disarmed as to his treason; and even Marion wavered in her suspicions of the honesty of this accomplished impostor.

Could Sir Marmaduke have communicated with them, there would have been no danger of such a deception.

But this he was not allowed to do.

From the hour of his arrest, his enemy had adopted every possible precaution to prevent it.

The parting with his children had taken place in Scarthe's presence—where no word could be spoken unheard.

Afterwards, from his prison in the Tower, he had not been allowed to hold the slightest intercourse with the outside world—neither before his trial nor after it.

Only a few minutes had his son Walter been permitted to stay in his company; and then only with spies and jailors standing near and listening to every speech that passed between them.

Sir Marmaduke had not even found opportunity to communicate to his son the suspicions he entertained: that the man who was making such loud protestations of sympathy and friendship was not only his enemy, but the very individual who had denounced him.

To Walter, and Lora, and Marion, all this remained unknown. It had never occurred to them to speculate on the cause of Scarthe's absence from the mansion—during the two days of the trial.

Little did they suspect that the double-tongued villain—so profuse in expressions of sympathy and condolence—during that interval had been himself in the presence of the Star Chamber—secretly testifying against the accused—freely supplying the testimony that had sealed his condemnation.

*　　*　　*　　*　　*　　*　　*　　*

On the morning after the sad intelligence had been conveyed to the inmates of Bulstrode mansion, Marion Wade was in her chamber, the victim of a double sorrow.

The Spaniards have a proverb, "One nail drives out another" (un clavo saca otro clavo), intending to convey by this homely figure that the heart cannot contain two sorrows at the same time, but that one must give place to the other.

To some extent is this proverb true; but, like most others, yielding to certain conditions.

For a while recent sorrow, overweighing that of anterior date, may tend to its alleviation. If it be greater, it may conduct to its cure; but if less, the old grief will in time return, and again resume dominion over the throne of the heart.

Either one of the sorrows from which Marion suffered was enough to have occupied her heart, to the exclusion of the other; and yet her experience confirmed the proverb only in part.

Long after listening to the sad tale told by her brother, she had brooded over the misfortunes of her much-loved father, and the fearful fate that awaited him.

But love is stronger than filial affection; and there were intervals, during which her anguish for a parent she was about to lose was, perhaps, less intense than that for a lover she had already lost!

Judge her not harshly, if, in the midst of her convulsive grief, there were moments when her mind dwelt upon the other and older sorrow.

Judge her not harshly, but as you would yourself be judged!

She was not alone. Her affectionate cousin was by her side; and near by, her fond brother.

They had passed the night together—in vain endeavors to impart mutual consolation.

Their cheeks and eyes told of a night spent in sleeplessness and tears.

Spent in mutual counsel, too, which they seemed to have exhausted as was testified by the words now spoken by Walter.

Marion had suggested an appeal to the queen, had proposed making a journey to London for this purpose.

"I fear it will be of no use," rejoined the ex-courtier. "I fell upon my knees before her, I protested our father's innocence, I entreated her with tears in my eyes; but she gave me no hope. On the contrary, she was angry with me. I never saw her so before. She even insulted me with vile words: called me the cub of a conspirator; while Jermyn, and Holland, and others of the young lords in her company, made merry at my expense. The king I dared not see. Ah, sister; I fear even you would meet no favor among that court crew. There is but one who can help us; and that because he is of their kind. You know who I mean, Marion?"

"You speak of Captain Scarthe?"

"I do."

"Indeed, it is true," interposed Lora. "You know he has more than once thrown out hints as to what he could do to obtain dear uncle's freedom. I would go upon my knees to him if it were of any use; but you know, Marion, one word from you would be worth all the entreaties that Walter and I could make. Oh, cousin, let us not speak in riddles at such a time as this. You know the reason?"

"Marion," said Walter, half divining Lora's implied meaning, "if this man speak sincerely, if it be true that he has the influence he boasts of, and I have heard as much at court, then there may be a hope. I know not to what Lora refers. She says that a word from you may accomplish much. Dear sister, is it a sacrifice?"

"You have styled it truly, Walter, in calling it a sacrifice. Without that, my entreaties would be vain as yours. I am sure of it."

"Say, sister! What sacrifice?"

"My hand, my hand!"

"Dear, dear Marion! If it be not with your heart you cannot promise it, you could not give it."

. "Without such promise, I know he would deny me."

"The wretch! Oh, heavens! And yet it is our father's life, ay, his very life!"

"Would it were mine!" exclaimed Marion, with a look of abandoned anguish, "only mine. The thought of death would be easier to endure than the sorrows I have already."

Walter comprehended not the meaning of her wild words.

Lora better understood their import.

Neither had time to reflect upon them; for, on the instant of their utterance, Marion rose to her feet and walked with a determined air towards the door of the apartment,

"Where are you going, dear cousin?" asked Lora, slightly frayed at Marion's resolute mien.

"To Captain Scarthe," was the firm rejoinder. "To fling myself at his feet, prostrate, if he please it; to ask him the price of my father's life."

Before either cousin or brother could interfere, to oppose or strengthen her resolution, the self-appointed suppliant had passed out of the room.

CHAPTER LIX.

THE FAIR SUPPLIANT.

The sentence passed upon Sir Marmaduke had given Scarthe a new string to his bow; and the crisis had now arrived for testing its strength.

He had easily obtained the knight's condemnation.

From the peculiar interest which he possessed at court, he knew or believed, that with equal facility he could procure his pardon.

In his own mind he had resolved upon doing this.

On certain conditions Marion Wade might expect a prompt answer to the inquiry she was about to make.

It was already determined upon: the price of Sir Marmaduke's life would be the hand of his daughter.

Scarthe did not design addressing his re-iterated proposal to the condemned knight, but to Marion herself.

His former appeal to the father had been met with a refusal so firm, that from him he might readily apprehend a similar response.

True, at that time the knight was only threatened with danger. Now, death stared him in the face—death inglorious, even ignominious.

The prospect could not fail to cause fear and faltering; and an ordinary man should be only too fain by any means to save himself from such a fate.

But Sir Marmaduke Wade was not one of this stamp. On the contrary, he was just the type of those antique heroic parents, who prefer death to the sacrifice of a daughter's happiness.

Scarthe knew it; and believed it quite possible that the conditions he meant to offer might still provoke a noble and negative rejoinder.

Although he had not determined to forego the chances of a last appeal to the condemned prisoner, this was only to be made in case of Marion's rejection of his terms.

Filial affection was first to be put upon its trial. After that it would be time to test the parental.

This design had been conceived before the trial of Sir Marmaduke —even previous to his imprisonment; for it was but a sequence of his scheme; and he who concocted it had only been waiting for the knight's condemnation, to bring matters to a climax.

Of the sentence he had been already advised, in fact knew it before leaving London.

Twenty-four hours sooner he could have communicated the intelligence to those whom it most concerned; but for reasons of his own, he had preferred leaving it to reach them through the natural channel —by the return of Walter from that short, sad interview with his unfortunate father.

It was late in the evening when Walter arrived to tell the melancholy tale. Perhaps had the hour been earlier, Scarthe would have intruded upon the scene of sorrow—to speak his sham sympathy, and mingle his hypocritical tears with those that were real.

As it was, he only expressed himself thus by deputy—sending one of the domestics with a message of condolence and reserving his interview with Marion for the morrow.

It was his design to see her, just at that hour when it might be supposed the first fresh throes of her sorrow had subsided, and his proffer of assistance might stand a better chance of being appreciated.

Ever since the departure of the prisoner he had been cunningly preparing his plans. He had lost no opportunity of letting it be understood, or at all events surmised, that he possessed the *power to save.*

He had hinted at great sacrifices that would accrue to himself in

17

the exertion of this power, at the same time making certain innuendoes, that left the conditions to be guessed at.

His scheme had become matured. To-morrow would see it carried into effect, either for failure or success, and that morrow had now arrived.

On the eve of action he was far from being either confident or tranquil.

As he paced the large drawing-room of the mansion, previous to asking an interview with its young mistress, his steps betrayed agitation. His glance told of mingled emotions—hope, fear, and shame: for, hardened as he was, he could not contemplate his sinister intent without some slight sense of abasement.

Several times had he laid his hand upon the bell, to summon some one, as the bearer of his request; but as often had his resolution failed him.

"By Phœbus! I'm a fool," he exclaimed at length, as if to fortify his courage by the self-accusation: "and a coward, too! What have I to fear? She cannot refuse me—with her father's life as the forfeit? She would be false to filial duty—affection—nature—everything. Bah? I'll dally with doubt no longer. I'll bring it to a crisis at once! Now is the time or never!"

He strode back to the table on which stood the bell. He took it up, with the intention of ringing it.

The sound of an opening door, accompanied by the rustling o silken robes, caused him to turn round. She from whom he was about to ask an interview, stood before him.

Scarthe was surprised—disconcerted—as one detected in a guilty action.

He fancied his visitor had divined his intent. On glancing at her countenance, his momentary abashment became suddenly changed to a feeling of triumph. He fancied that he divined *hers*.

She must have known he was in the room; else why did she not pause, or retire?

On the contray, she was approaching him, she who had never done so before, evidently with a purpose!

There could be but one, *to ask his intercession*.

This forestalling was in his favor.

It gave him strength and confidence.

It gave him a cue, for the disclosure he meditated making.

"Mistress Marion!" said he, bowing low, "you have saved me the chagrin of intruding upon your grief: for, in truth, I had intended soliciting an interview, to offer my poor mite of consolation."

"By your own showing sir," rejoined she, placing herself in a firm yet humble attitude, "you can do more. If I mistake not, you have spoken of your influence with the king?"

"Perhaps it is greater with the king's wife," replied the soldier, with a smile, evidently intended to make a peculiar impression on his petitioner. "True, fair Marion; I own to some little influence in that quarter. 'Tis not much; but, such as it be, 'tis at your service."

"Oh, sir! thank you for these words. Say you will exert it, to save the life of my father! Say that; and you shall win the gratitude of—of —— "

"Marion Wade?"

"More than mine—my father—my brother—our kindred—perhaps our country—will all be grateful; will bless you for the act."

"And of these gratitudes, the only one I should in the least esteem is your own, beautiful Marion. That will be sufficient recompense for me."

"Sir, you shall have it—to the very depth of my soul."

"Say rather to the depth of your *heart*."

"I have said it. You shall have my heart's gratitude now and forever."

"Ah! gratitude is but a cold word. Exchange it for another."

"Another! What mean you, sir?"

"Say your *love*. Give me but that, and I promise—I swear, by my hopes of happiness here and hereafter, that I shall not rest, till your father's pardon be obtained; or till I, by my unwelcome interference in his behalf, be sentenced to partake of his prison and punishment! Oh, Marion Wade, have mercy upon me! I, not you, am the suppliant in this cause. Give me what I have asked; and command me as your slave?"

For some seconds Marion stood without making reply.

From the fervor of his appeal, and the silence with which it had been received, Scarthe was beginning to conceive a hope; and kept his eyes keenly bent upon the countenance of his suitor.

He could read nothing there.

Not a thought was betrayed by those beautiful features—immovable as though chiseled out of stone.

When she at length spoke, her answer told him that he had misinterpreted her silence.

"Captain Scarthe," said she, " you are a man of the world--one as I have heard, skilled in the thoughts of our sex ——"

"You flatter me," interrupted he, making an effort to recover his customary coolness. " May I know why I am thus complimented ? "

"I did not mean it in that sense. Only to say, that, knowing our nature as you do, you must be aware that what you ask is impossible. Oh, sir, woman cannot *give* her heart. *That must be taken from her.*"

" And yours, Marion Wade ? "

" Is not in my power to give. It has been surrendered already."

"Surrendered ! " cried Scarthe, with an angry emphasis on the word ; for this was his first assurance of a fact that had long formed the theme of his conjectures.

"Surrendered you say ? "

"'Tis too true. Stolen, if you will, but still surrendered ! 'Tis broken now, and cannot be restored. O sir ! you would not value it, if offered to you. Do not make that a condition. Accept instead what is still in my power to give—a gratitude that shall know no end ! "

For some seconds the discomfited wooer neither spoke nor moved. What he had heard appeared to have paralyzed him.

His lips were white, and drawn tightly over his teeth, with an expression of half indignation—half chagrin.

Skilled as he certainly was in woman's heart, he had heard enough to convince him that he could never win that of Marion Wade.

Her declaration had been made in a tone too serious, too sober in its style, to leave him the vestige of a hope.

Her heart had been surely surrendered.

Strange she should say stolen !

Stranger still she should declare it to be broken !

Both were points that might have suggested curious speculations ; but at that moment Scarthe was not in the vein for indulging in idle hypotheses.

He had formed the resolution to possess the hand, and the fortune of Marion Wade.

If she could not give her heart, she could give these as compensation for the saving of her father's life.

"Your gratitude," said he, no longer speaking in a strain of fervor, but with an air of piqued formality, "your gratitude, beautiful Marion, would go far with me. I would make much sacrifice to obtain it; but there is something you can bestow, which I should prize more.''

Marion looked—'' What is it ? ''

'' Your hand.''

'' That then is the price of my father's life ? ''

'' It is.''

'' Captain Scarthe! what can my hand be worth to you, without ——''

'' Your heart, you would say? I must live in hopes to win that. Fair Marion, reflect! A woman's heart may be won more than once.''

'' Only once can it be lost.''

'' Be it so. I must bear the chagrin. I shall bear it all the better, by having your hand. Marion Wade! I scorn further circumlocution. Give me what I have asked, and your father lives. Refuse it, and he must forfeit his head.''

'' Oh, sir, have pity! Have you a father? Ah! could you but feel the anguish of one about to be made fatherless. Mercy, Captain Scarthe! On my knees I ask it. O sir! you can save him—you will ? ''

While speaking, the proud, beautiful woman had dropped down upon her knees.

Her rich golden hair, escaping from its silken coif, swept the floor at her feet.

Her tear-drops sparkled, like pearls, among its profusion of tresses.

For a second Scarthe remained silent, gazing upon the lovely suppliant, a Venus dissolved in tears.

He gazed not coldly; though his cruel thoughts glowed only with exultation.

Marion Wade was at his feet!

'' I can save him—I will ! '' he answered emphatically, echoing her last words.

Marion looked up—hope beaming in her tear-bedewed eyes.

The sweet thought was stifled on the instant.

The cynical glance, meeting hers, told her that Scarthe had not finished his speech.

'' Yes,'' he triumphantly continued, '' I have said that I can, and will. It needs but one word from you. Promise that you will be mine ? ''

'' O God! has this man no mercy ? '' muttered the maiden, as she rose despairingly to her feet.

The speech was not intended to be heard; but it was. Involuntarily had it been uttered aloud.

It elicited an instant reply.

"There is no mercy in love—when scorned, as you have scorned mine."

"I have not scorned it. You ask what is impossible."

"No," suddenly rejoined Scarthe, conceiving a hope from the gentle character of the reply. 'Tis not impossible. I expect not the firstlings of your heart. Alas! for me, they are gone. I can scarce hope for even a second love; though I should do everything within the power of man to deserve it. All I ask for is the opportunity to win you, by making you my wife. O, Marion Wade!" he continued, adopting a more fervent form of speech, "you have met a man—never before gainsayed—one who has never wooed woman in vain—even when wearing a crown upon her brow. One, too, who will not be thwarted. Heaven and earth shall not turn me from my intent. Say you will be mine, and all will be well. Reflect upon the fearful issue that must follow your refusal. I await your answer. Is it yes, or no?"

Having thus delivered himself, the impetuous lover commenced pacing to and fro—as if to allow time for the reply.

Marion, on rising from her suppliant attitude, had withdrawn to the window.

She stood within its embayment—her back turned towards that dark type of humanity—her eyes upon the blue heaven; as if there seeking inspiration.

Was she hesitating as to her answer?

Was she wavering between her father's life and her own happiness —or rather, might it be said, her life-long misery?

Did the thought cross her mind, that her unhappiness, springing from the defection, the deception of her lost lover, could scarce be increased either in amount or intensity; and that the sacrifice she was now called upon to make could add but little to a misery already at its maximum.

Whether or not may never be revealed.

Marion Wade can alone disclose the thoughts that struggled within her soul at that critical moment.

Scarthe continued to pace the floor, impatiently awaiting her decision.

Not that he wished it to be given on the instant; for he believed that delay would favor him.

A sudden answer might be a negative, springing from passion, while fear for her father's fate, strengthened by reflection, might influence her to agree to his proposal.

At length came the answer, or what Scarthe was compelled to accept as one.

It came not in words; but in a cry, at once joyous and trium-phant.

Simultaneous with its utterance, Marion Wade extended her arms; and, flinging open the casement, rushed out into the verandah.

CHAPTER LX

A CHANGE OF QUARTERS.

Scarthe stood for a moment astounded—stupified.

Had Marion Wade gone mad ?

Her singular behavior seemed to say so.

But no.

There appeared to be method in the movement she had made.

As she glided through the open casement, he had observed that her eye was fixed upon something outside—something that must have influ-enced her to the making of that unexpected exit.

On recovering from his surprise, the cuirassier captain hastened towards the window; but, before reaching it he heard sounds with-out, conducting him to alarming conjectures.

They might have been unintelligible, but for the sight that came under his eyes as he looked forth.

A crowd was coming up the main avenue of the park—a crowd of men.

They were not marching in order, and might have been called "a mob;" although it consisted of right merry fellows—neither disorderly nor dangerous.

The individuals who composed it appeared to be of every condition in life, and equally varied as to their costumes.

But the greater number of them could be identified as men of the farmer and mechanic class—the "bone and sinew" of the country

The miller under his hoary hat; the butcher in his blood-stained boots; the blacksmith in grimy sheep-skin; the small shop-keeper and pale-faced artisan; the grazier and agriculturist of ruddy hue— alongside the tavern-keeper and tapster of equally florid complexion —could be distinguished in that crowd coming on towards the walls of Bulstrode mansion.

The cuirassier captain had seen such an assemblage before.

It might have been the same, that saluted him with jeers—as he crossed the Coln bridge, returning from his unsuccessful pursuit of the black horseman.

With slight exceptions, it was the same.

One of these exceptions was an individual, who, mounted on horseback, was riding conspicuously in front; and who appeared to occupy a large share of the attention of those who followed him.

He was a man of mature age, dressed in dark velvet tunic, and with trunk-hose of a corresponding color.

A man with an aspect to inspire regard—even from a crowd to which he might have been a stranger.

But he was evidently no stranger to the men who surrounded him; for at every step of their progress, they could be heard vociferating, in hearty hurrah, "Long live Sir Marmaduke Wade!"

It was the Knight of Bulstrode who headed that cheerful procession.

Though much loved, Sir Marmaduke did not monopolize the enthusiasm of the assemblage.

Mounted upon a magnificent horse—black as a coal fresh hoisted upon the windlass—rode by his side a cavalier of more youthful, but equally noble, aspect.

It did not need the cry, "Hurrah for the black horseman!" at intervals reaching his ears, to apprise Captain Scarthe, who was the second cavalier at the head of the approaching cort ge.

The images of both horse and rider were engraven upon his memory—in lines too deep ever to be effaced.

What the devil did it mean?

This was the thought in Scarthe's mind—the identical express'on that rose to his lips—as he looked forth from the open casement.

17*

Sir Marmaduke Wade, on horseback—unguarded—followed by a host of sympathizing friends!

The rebel Henry Holtspur riding by his side!

Marion, with her yellow tresses afloat behind her—like a snow-white avalanche under the full flood of a golden sunlight—gliding forward to meet them!

" What the devil can it mean?" was the interrogatory of Captain Scarthe, repeatedly put to himself, as the procession drew near.

He was not allowed much time to speculate on a reply to his self-asked question.

Before he had quite recovered from the surprise caused by the un-expected sight, the crowd had closed in to the walls; where they once more raised their voices in shouts of congratulation.

"Three cheers for John Hampden!"   "Three more for Pym!" were proposed, and unanimously responded to.

With equal unanimity were accepted two cries, of far more sig-nificance in the ear of the royalist officer: "Long live the Parlia-ment!"   "Death to the traitor Strafford!"

Though still unable to account for what appeared to him some strange travestie, Scarthe could endure it no longer.

Strafford was his peculiar patron, and, on hearing him thus denoun-ced, he sprang forth from the casement; and ran with all speed in the direction of the crowd.

The cuirassier captain was followed by a score of his troopers, who chanced to be standing near—like himself at a loss to make out the meaning of that unlooked for invasion.

"Disloyal knaves!" shouted he, confronting the crowd, with his sword raised in a threatening manner.   "Who is he that has dared to insult the noble Strafford?   Let me hear that traitorous phrase once more; and I shall split the tongue that repeats it!"

"Not so fastish, master!" cried a stalwart individual, stepping to the front, and whose black bushy whiskers, and fantastic fashion of dress, proclaimed him to be the ex-footpad, Gregory Garth—"doan't a be so fastish wi' yer threets; ye mayen't be able to carry 'em out so easyish as ye suppose.   Ye can hove a try, though.   I'm one o' them as cried: "Death to the treetur Strafford!"

As he pronounced the challenging speech, Garth drew from its scabbard a huge broadsword—at the same time placing himself in an attitude of defense.

"Goo it, Gregory!" cried another colossal individual, recognizble as Dick Dancey, the deer-stealer. "Goo it like bleezes! I'll stan' to yer back."

"And we!" simultaneously shouted a score of butchers, bakers, and blacksmiths, ranging themselves by the side of Garth, and severally confronting the cuirassiers—who had formed a phalanx in rear of their chief.

Scarthe hesitated in the execution of his threat. He saw that his adversaries, one and all of them, wielded ugly weapons; while his own men had only their light side-arms—some even without arms of any kind. The attitude of the opposing party—their looks, words, and gestures—told that they were in earnest in their resolution to resist. Moreover, it was stronger than his own; and constantly gaining accessions from the crowd in the rear.

With the quick perception of a skilled strategist, Scarthe saw that in a hand-to-hand fight with such redoubtable antagonists, his men would have the worst of it. This influenced him to pause in his purpose.

The unexpected opposition caused him to change his design.

He suddenly resolved to retire from the contest; arm and mount his whole troop; sally forth again; and rout the rabble who had so flagrantly defied him.

Such was the project that had presented itself to his brain; but before he could make any movement, Sir Marmaduke had dismounted from his horse, and placed himself between the opposing parties.

"Captain Scarthe!" said he, addressing himself to the officer, and speaking in a calm voice, in which a touch of irony was perceptible: "in this matter, it appears to me, you overstep the limits of your duty. Men may differ in opinion about the merits of the 'noble Strafford,' as you have designated Thomas Wentworth. He is now in the hands of his judges; who will no doubt deal with him according to his deserts."

"Judges!" exclaimed Scarthe, turning pale as he spoke; "Earl Strafford in the hands of judges?"

"It is as I have said. Thomas Wentworth at this moment occupies the same domicile which has been my dwelling for some days past; and from which I am not sorry to have been ejected. I know, Captain Scarthe, you could not have been aware of this change in the fortunes of your friend: since it was only yesterday he made his entrance into the Tower!"

"Strafford in the Tower!" gasped out the cuirassier captain, utterly astounded at the intelligence.

"**Yes**," continued the knight; "and soon to stand, not befoie the Star Chamber—which was yesterday abolished—but a court that will deal more honestly with his derelictions—the High Court of Parliament. Thomas Wentworth appears in its presence—an attainted traitor to his country."

"Long live the Parliament! Death to the traitor Strafford!" were the cries that responded to the speech of Sir Marmaduke—though from none to whom the announcement was new.

The men, who accompanied the knight to his home, had already learnt the news of Strafford's attainder; which, like a blaze of cheerful light, was fast spreading over the land.

For some seconds Scarthe seemed like a man bereft of reason.

He was about to retire from the spot, when Sir Marmaduke again addressed him—speaking in the same calm voice, but with a more perceptible irony of tone—

"Captain Scarthe," pursued he, "some time ago, you were good enough to bring me a dispatch from the king. It is my fortune to be able to reciprocate the compliment—and in kind. I am the bearer of one to you—also from his majesty, as you may see by the seal."

Sir Marmaduke, as he spoke, exhibited a parchment bearing the stamp of the royal signet.

"On that occasion," continued he, "you were good enough to have it read aloud—so that the bystanders should have the benefit of its contents. In this, also, shall I follow your example."

On saying this the knightly bearer of the dispatch broke open the seal, and read:—

"*To ye Captain Scarthe, commanding ye king's cuirassiers at Bulstrode Park.*

"*His Majestie doth hereby command ye Captain Scarthe to withdraw his troops from ye mansion of Sir Marmaduke Wade, and transfer ye same to quarters in our royal palace at Windsor; and his Majesty doth further enjoin on his faithful officer, ye said Captain Scarthe, to obey this order on ye instant of receipt thereof.*

"*CAROLUS REX.*

"*Whitehall.*"

The dispatch of his "majestie" was received with a vociferous cheer; though there was not a voice in the crowd to cry "Long live the king!"

They knew that the *amende*, thus made to Sir Marmaduke
Wade, was not a voluntary act on the part of the royal cuckold, but
had been wrung from his fears.

It was the Parliament who had obtained that measure of justice;
and once more rang out the cry—

"Long live the Parliament!"

Scarthe's chagrin had culminated to its climax.

He was black in the face as he strode off to make preparations for
his departure; and the words "coward" and "poltroon" muttered
hissingly through his closed teeth, were not intended for the citizens
who were jeering, but the sovereign who had exposed him to such
overwhelming humiliation.

In less than ten minutes after, he was seen at the head of his
troop galloping outward through the gates of Bulstrode Park, having
left a few stragglers to look after the *impedimenta*.

He was not likely ever to forget the loud huzza, that rose ironically
from the crowd, as his discomfited cuirassiers swept past on their
departure.

    ●   ●   ●   ●   ●   ●   ●   ●   ●   ●

At the moment of his dismounting, Marion had rushed into the
arms of Sir Marmaduke.

"Father!" exclaimed she, joyfully, trembling in his embrace.
"Saved! you are safe."

"Safe, my child! Sure, with such a brave following, I may feel
safe enough!"

"And I am spared. Oh, to come at such a crisis. Just as I was
on the eve of consenting to a sacrifice—painful as death itself."

"What sacrifice, my daughter?"

"Myself—to him yonder. He promised to obtain your pardon
but only on condition, I should become——"

Marion hesitated to pronounce the terms that Scarthe had proposed
to her.

"I know them," interposed Sir Marmaduke. "And you would
have accepted them, noble girl! I know that too. Thank heaven,
my pardon has been obtained, not through the favor of an enemy,
but my friends—foremost among whom is this gallant gentleman by
my side. But for him, the king's grace might have come too late."

Marion looked up.

Holtspur, still seated in his saddle, was tenderly gazing upon her

It was at this moment, that Sir Marmaduke was called upon to

Interfere between the cuirassiers of Scarthe, and his cwn enthusiastic escort.

For an instant Marion and Hollspur were left alone.

"I thank you, sir," said she, her voice trembling from a conflict of emotions—"I thank you for my father's life. The happiness arising from that is some recompense—for—for the misery you have caused me."

"Misery, Marion? I—I——"

"Oh, sir, let it pass. 'Tis better without explanation. You know what is meant—too well you know it. Oh, Henry, Henry! I could not have believed you capable of such deception—such cruelty."

"Cruelty?"

"No more—go—go! Leave me to my sorrow—leave me to a life-long repentance!"

"I obey your commands," said Holtspur, taking up his bridle-reins, as if with the intention of riding away. "Alas," he added, in an accent of bitterness, "whither am I to go? For me there is no life—no happiness—where thou art not. Oh God! whither am I to go?"

"To your wife," muttered Marion, in a low reproachful tone, and with faltering accent.

"Ha, 'tis that! You have heard, then?"

"All—all."

"No—not all—I have no wife."

"Oh, sir! Henry! Why try to deceive me any longer! You have a wife. I have been told it, by those who know. It is true?"

"I have deceived you. That is true, that only. I had a wife. She is dead!"

"Dead?"

"Ay dead."

"I acknowledge my crime," continued he, after a solemn pause. "I should have told you all. For my justification I can plead only my own wrongs, and your beauty. I loved you while she was still living."

"Oh, mercy, what is this? She is dead; and you love me no more?"

"No more? What mean you, Marion? Heart and hand, soul and body, I am yours. I swore it at our last interview It costs ne sacrifice to keep the oath: I could not break it if I would."

"Oh, Henry! This is cruel. 'Tis insulting! Have you not kept that promise? How, then, can you be true to your troth?"

"What promise?"

"Cruel, cruel! You are trifling with my misery, but you cannot make it more. Ah, the white gauntlet. When it was brought back, with your message that accompanied it, my dream of happiness came to an end. My heart was broken!"

"Brought back, the white gauntlet, message!"

"Marion," cried Sir Marmaduke, who had by this time disposed of the petty quarrel between Scarthe and his own following; "indoors, my daughter! and see that your father's house does not forfeit its character for hospitality. There's dust upon the king's highway; which somehow or other has got into the throats of our worthy friends from Uxbridge, Denham, and Iver. Surely there's an antidote in the cellars of Bulstrode? Go, find it, my girl!"

Promptly did Marion obey the orders of her father; the more promptly, from having been admonished, by the surprise exhibited in Holtspur's countenance, that the return of her token would admit of a different interpretation, from that she had hitherto put upon it.

*　　*　　*　　*　　*　　*

Time permitting, it would be a pleasant task to depict the many joyous scenes that took place in the precincts of Bulstrode Park, subsequent to the departure of Scarthe and his cuirassiers.

Lora, no longer subject to the tiresome importunities of Stubbs, found little else to do than listen to Walter's pretty love prattlings, excepting to respond to them.

Near at hand were two hearts equally *en rapport* with one another, equally brimful of beatitude, trembling under a passion still more intense, the one paramount passion of a life, destined to endure to its ending.

It was no young love's dream, no fickle fondness, that filled the bosoms of Henry Holtspur and Marion Wade; but a love that burned with a bold, blazing flame, like a torch that no time could extinguish, such a love as may exist between the eagle and his majestic mate.

With all its boldness, it sought not notoriety.

The scenes in which it was displayed lay not inside the walls of the proud mansion; nor yet within the enclosure of its park.

A spot to Marion Wade reminiscent of the keenest pang she had ever experienced, was now the oft-repeated scene of earth's purest pleasure; at least its supremest.

Oft might the lovers have been seen in that solitary spot, under the spreading beech tree, not recumbent as Tityrus, but seated in the saddles, their horses in close approximation, the noble black steed curving his neck, not in proud disdain, but bent caressingly downward, till his velvet muzzle met in friendly contact with that of the white palfrey.

And yet there was scarce necessity for the clandestine meetings.

The presence of Scarthe and his cuirassiers no longer interdicted the entrance of Henry Holtspur into the mansion of Sir Marmaduke Wade, who was ever but too happy to make his preserver welcome.

Why, then, did the lovers prefer the forest shade, for interviews, that no one had the right to interrupt?

Perhaps it was caprice?

Perhaps the mystic influence of past emotions, in which, to Marion at least, there was a commingling of pain with pleasure?

Perhaps, and more probably, their choice was determined by that desire, or instinct, felt by all true lovers, to keep their secret unrevealed, to indulge in the sweetness of the stolen?

Whatever may have been their motive, they were successful in their measures.

Oft, almost daily, did they meet under the spreading tree whose sombre shadow could not dim the bright color of Marion's golden hair, nor make pallid the roseate hue of her cheeks, always more radiant at parting.

CHAPTER LXI.

MARSTON MOOR.

To bring our drama to a *dénouement*, only two more scenes require to be described.

Two scenes were they, antagonistic in character,—though oft coupled together, like their emblematical deities in the pagan Pantheon.

Over the first, presided Mars. The god called cruel, and not always just, on this occasion gave the victory to the side that deserved it.

For three years had the trumpet of war been braying loudly over the land: and England's best blood, marshaled into the field, was arrayed on both sides of the fraternal strife.

The combatants had become known as royalist and republican: for the latter phrase, first breathed by Holtspur in the secret conference at Stone Dean, was no longer a title to be concealed. On the contrary, it had become openly avowed, proclaimed as a thing to be proud of, as it ever will and must among enlightened and noble men.

There were heard also the words "Cavalier" and "Round-head;" but these were only terms of boasting and reproach—proceeding principally from the lips of ribald royalists, humiliated by defeat, and giving way to the ferocious instincts that have distinguished "Tory-ism" in all times; alas! still rife at the present day, both in the tax-paying shires of England, and the slave-holding territories outre the Atlantic.

The "Cavalier" of Charles' time—so specifically styled—was a true sham; in every respect shabby as his modern representative, the swell—distinguished only by his vanity and his vices! with scarce a virtue: for, even in the ordinary endowment of courage, he was not equal to his "Round-head" antagonist.

His title of "cavalier," and his "chivalry," like that of the South-ern slave-driver, were simply pseudonyms—a ludicrous mis-applica-tion of terms, self-appropriated by a prurient conceit.

It had come to the meeting on Marston Moor—that field ever to be remembered with pride by the lovers of liberty. The rash swaggerer Rupert, disregarding the counsels of a wiser head, had sallied forth from York, at the head of one of the largest armies ever mustered on the side of the king. He had already raised the siege, so gallantly protracted by the Marquis of Newcastle; and, flushed with success, he was in haste to crush the *ci-devant* besiegers; who, it must be confessed, with some spirit were retiring—though slowly, and with the sulky reluctance of wounded lions.

Rupert overtook them upon Marston Moor; where, to his misfor-tune, they had determined on making a stand.

It is not our purpose to describe that famous fight—which for a time settled the question between Throne and Tribune.

Of the many thrilling episodes witnessed on Marston Moor, only one can be of interest in this narrative; and it alone is given.

Among the followers of the impetuous prince was one Richard Scarthe—late promoted to be a colonel, and commanding a "color" of cuirassier horse. On the opposite side, among the foll)wers of Fairfax, was an officer of like rank—a colonel of cavalry—by name Henry Holtspur.

Was it destiny, or mutual design, that brought these two men together, face to face, in the middle of the fight? It may have been chance—a simple coincidence—but whether or no, of a certain they so met upon Marston Moor.

Scarthe rode at the head of his glittering troop. Holtspur, astride his sable charger, gallantly conducted into the field the brave yeomen of Bucks, clad in cloth doublets of forest green—each bestriding a horse he had led from his own stable, to figure in this glorious fight for freedom.

While still a hundred yards separated the opposing parties, their leaders recognized one another. There was also a mutual recognition among their men: for many of those commanded by Scarthe were the cuirassiers who had been billeted at Bulstrode mansion; while many of the " green-coats " in the following of the "black horseman " had figured conspicuously in that crowd who had jeered the soldiers on their departure from its park.

On identifying each other as old antagonists, there was a general desire on both sides to be led forward. This impulse, however, was stronger in the breasts of the two leaders; who, without waiting to give the word to their men, put spurs to their horses, and galloped across the intervening space.

In a second's time both had separated from the general line of battle, and were fast closing upon each other.

Their followers, taken by surprise at this unexpected action, for a moment remained without imitating their rapid advance. Two young officers only—one from each side—had ridden after their respective chiefs; not as if stirred by their example, but to all appearance activated by an analogous hostility.

The action of these youths—known to their comrades as the cornets Stubbs and Wade—did not attract any particular attention. The eyes of all were upon the two chiefs—Scarthe and Holtspur— each exhibiting that mien that proclaimed him determined upon the death of his adversary.

In the breast of Scarthe raged the fires of a long-enduring rancor— fed by the remembrance of former defeats—stimulated to a fiendish fierceness by never-dying jealousy.

In the bosom of Holtspur burned a nobler flame—an impulse alto-

gether unselfish—though not less impelling him towards the destruc
tion of his antagonist.

The proud republican saw before him a true type of the Janizary—
one of those minions who form the protecting *entourage* of tyrants—
ready to ride over and oppress the peoples of the earth—ready even
to die in their infamous harness—on the battle-field breathing with
their last breath that senseless, as contradictory declaration: that
they die for king and country!

Holtspur had no personal antipathy to Scarthe—at least none like
that by which he was himself regarded.

Notwithstanding the wrongs which the latter had attempted to inflict upon him, his antagonism to the royalist officer was chiefly of a
political character—chiefly the sublime contempt which a republican
must needs feel for a partizan of monarchy—whether simpleton or
villain: since one of the two he must be.

It was sufficient, however, to stimulate him to a keen desire to kill
Scarthe—such as the shepherd may feel for destroying the wolf that
has been preying upon his innocent fold, or the game-keeper the
"vermin" that has been spoiling his master's preserves.

Nerved by noble thoughts—confident in a holy cause—sure of the
thanks of millions yet to be—did the soldier of liberty charge forward
upon his adversary.

The action was instantaneous; the event quick as the killing of a
stoat, crushed beneath the heel of the irate keeper.   In less than a
score of seconds—after the commencement of the encounter—Scarthe
lay motionless upon the turf of Marston Moor—doubled up in his
steel equipments, like a pile of mediæval armor!

By this time the two cornets were crossing swords; but before
either could give the other a death wound, the royalist bugles brayed
the "Retreat;" and the gallant "green coats," sweeping over the
field, put the discomfited cuirassiers to flight; who from that moment,
with the rest of Rupert's army, made more use of their spurs, than
their sabres.

    *   *   *   *   *   *

One more act, and the curtain must close upon our drama.

The *mise en scène* of this act has been already presented; and, as
often on the stage, it is again repeated; with but little change in the
dramatis personæ.

Bulstrode Park is once more enlivened by a *fête champêtre*—as before, the old Saxon camp being its arena.

An occasion, even more joyful than then, has called together the friends of Sir Marmaduke Wade; in which category might be comprised every honest man in the shire of Bucks.

The camp enclosure is capable of containing many thousands. It is full: so full, that there is hardly room for the sports of wrestling and single stick, bowls, and baloon—which are, nevertheless, carried on with zealous earnestness, by their respective devotees.

What is the occasion? Another son come of age? It cannot be that; since there is but one heir to Sir Marmaduke's estate; and his majority has been already commemorated.

It is not that. An event of still greater interest has called together the concourse in question.

A double event it might be designated: since upon this day the knight of Bulstrode has given away two brides; one to his own son, the other to an "adventurer," formerly known as Henry Holtspur the "black horseman," but of late recognized as Sir Henry ——, a colonel in the Parliamentary army, and a member of the Parliament itself.

I have told you who are the bridegrooms. I need not name the brides: you have already guessed them.

Behold the two couples, as they stand upon the green-tufted bank—overlooking the sports—pleased spectators of the people's enjoyment.

For a short while your eyes will rest upon the more youthful pair—the pretty Lora Lovelace, and her cousin-husband, Walter.

'Tis well you have first looked upon them: for your eye will scarce care to return to them.

Once bent upon Marion Wade, it will not wish to wander away

There you will behold all those hues most distinguished in nature—the blue of the sky—the gold scattered by the sun—the radiance of the rose.

Shapes, too, of divine ideal corresponding to such fair colors: the oval of the forehead; the arched outline of the nose; the spiral curving of the nostrils; the hemisphere expressed in two contiguous bosoms; and the limitless parabola passing downward from her lithesome waist—are all conspicuous proofs that, in the construction of Marion Wade, Nature has employed the most skillful of architects.

The crowd has eyes for no one else.

She is alike the cynosure of gentle and simple.

It is only when these reflect on their late acquired privileges, that they gaze with grateful pride upon the man who stands by her side —recognized by all present as one of the patriot heroes who has helped them to their liberty.

On this day of the double marriage, as on that of Walter's majority, there are morris-dancers; and as before, are personated the "merry men" of Sherwood Forest.

But, with some unnoticeable exceptions, the individuals who now figure as the representatives of the outlawed fraternity are not the same.

The huge bearded man, who in grotesque attire personifies Little John, can be recognized as the ex-footpad Gregory Garth.

No wonder he plays the part to perfection!

The representative of Robin Hood is different; and so also she who performs the *métier* of Maid Marian.

The latter is a girl with golden hair; and the outlaw chief is the ex-cuirassier Withers—long since transformed into a staunch supporter of the Parliament.

Why is Bet Dancey not there as of yore?

And where is the woodman Walford?

There are few upon the ground who could not answer these questions; for the sad tragedy that will account for the absence of both is still fresh in the minds of the multitude.

A middle-aged man of herculean frame, leaning against a tree, looks sadly upon the sports.

All know him to be old Dick Dancey, the deer-stealer.

His colossal form is bowed more than when last seen, for he has not been abroad for months.

He has come forth to the marriage *fête* for the first time—from his lone forest hut, where for months he has been mourning the loss of his only child—daughter.

There is sadness in his glance and sorrow in his attitude.

Even the ludicrous sallies of his friend and confederate, Garth, cannot win from him a smile; and as he looks upon the timid fair-haired representative of Maid Marian, and remembers his own brave, and brown, and beautiful Betsey, a tear, telling of a strong heart's despair, can be seen trickling down his rudely furrowed cheek.

Ah! the brave and beautiful Betsey—for she was both—well may her father sorrow for her fate, for it was one of the saddest.

Her love—her wild passion—for Henry Holtspur, however unholy in its aim, was hallowed by truth and ennobled by generous unselfishness.

It should be regarded with the the tear of pity—not the smile of contempt. It led to her untimely end. She died by the hand of the lurking ruffian who had laid presumptuous claims to her love—by the weapon he had threatened to wield—but dared not—against the man he foolishly believed to be his rival.

His own end was more just and appropriate.

That with which, during all his life, he had been warring, was called into requisition to expedite his exit from the world. He terminated his existence upon a tree!

* * * * * * * *

The *fête* celebrating the double marriage—unlike its predecessor, came to a conclusion without being interrupted by any unpleasant incident. Everybody on the ground seemed happy, excepting, perhaps, the bereaved father, Dick Dancey, and one other who was present—almost without a purpose—Dorothy Dayrell.

If she had come with a purpose, it must have been to criticise.

But her piquant satire had now lost its point; and no one seemed to sympathize with her when, in allusion to the love-token that appeared conspicuously in the hat of Marion's husband, she made these somewhat fast observations:—

"A white glove! In truth, a true symbol of a woman just become wife! now spotless as snow—soon to be soiled—perchance cast away in contempt. *Nous verrons!*"

The hypothetical prophecy found no supporters among those to whom it was addressed.

Perhaps no one—save the spiteful prophetess—either believed or wished that such should be the fate of the White Gauntlet.

THE END.